SAVING
Soul

ALSO BY ANN PENNY

Capturing Love

Finding Beauty

Saving Soul

SAVING
Soul

ANN PENNY

Arndell

Arndell

This edition is published by Arndell, an imprint of Keeperton in 2026
Dharawal Country, 1 / 18 Manning Street, Kiama, NSW, Australia, 2533
SAVING SOUL

10 9 8 7 6 5 4 3 2 1

ISBN 978-1-923232-13-6 (paperback)

Formatted Edited by Jenn Lockwood Editing
Formatted by Kirby Jones
Cover design by Christa Moffitt, Christabella Designs

Printed and bound by CPI Group (UK) Ltd, Croydon, CR0 4YY

Sydney | Washington D.C. | London
www.keeperton.com/arndell

AUTHOR'S NOTE

Thank you for choosing to read **Saving Soul**. For maximum enjoyment, I strongly advise reading **Capturing Love** and **Finding Beauty** before delving into this novel.

This full-length, contemporary romance contains strong language, sex scenes and sensitive subject matter.

Chapter 1

He saw the ring.

I knew he did.

The lingering gaze on my hand was his irrefutable admission. So, why was he still approaching me?

My wedding ring was my shield against every man who took a second glance. Only, this guy's eyes didn't waver. If anything, his pupils dilated. From the moment he walked into that Midtown Manhattan bar, his piercing gaze caught mine and refused to budge.

Sitting at the far side of the bar, I tilted my head enough to let my golden beach waves tumble over my face to hide the heat in my cheeks. I wasn't used to attention. Marrying my first love at eighteen meant I never had to venture into the wilderness to find a mate. While all my friends were off clubbing and having epic one-night stands, I'd had other priorities.

Shifting uncomfortably on the barstool, I peeked through my hair, praying his gaze had moved to his next option, but alas, there he was. Staring…pondering…smirking. *Dang.*

The mere upward tilt of his lips shot straight to my core. *Hello there, stranger.* It had been years since my body reacted in such a way—and never so instantaneously. This man was a magician… and incredibly sexy, standing well over six feet tall with alluring broad shoulders that belonged in a swimming pool. His striking stubbled jawline and scruffy blond hair were a total contradiction to his immaculately tailored business suit, making me wonder if, perhaps, his day had been as shitty as mine.

My heart lurched as he lifted his drink from the counter and sauntered through the bar in my direction. He oozed confidence, unlike myself with beads of sweat winding down my neck to where I toyed with the crystal dangling between my breasts. This was the sort of guy who knew what he wanted and took it, and the sheer thought had my heart pounding and my core pulsing below.

While my friends were only now settling down and having kids, me? I was a seasoned pro. But this? *Fuck.* I was in over my head. This wasn't me. I wasn't this girl. What would Dominic think? *Fuck.* Why did that even matter anymore? It had been four years.

Maybe this was a good thing. No one but my sister knew me in Manhattan, so there was no harm in pretending to be someone else for one night. With sleep off the cards, a man like him would make the perfect distraction while I waited for the outcome of my interview.

After the day I'd had, I didn't fancy returning to Amy's miniscule apartment, so this made for a tempting solution. If I didn't get that damn job, the almost windowless abode would directly reflect the claustrophobic situation I was in, and it was sure to break me.

I glanced down at my embarrassingly old cell phone resting on the bar and blew out an irritated sigh before pouring the remains of my bank balance down my throat. I needed that job. It was our ticket home and they had assured me they would make a decision by the end of the day.

With only minutes remaining, the weight of my reality crashed down with my empty glass. While my interviewers tucked themselves into their thousand-thread-count sheets, completely oblivious to the impact of their indecision, I had to endure another sleepless night scheming up plan B, or C, or whatever fucking letter was up next.

It wasn't that I didn't like living in upstate New York; it was that I *loved* living in Los Angeles. I craved the sun, and the beach, and holding the memories of my grandmother close. After my mother died, my sister and I were sent to live with Grams in Venice Beach while our father struggled to come to terms with the death of his wife. She provided us with a safe space to grieve, then nurtured us through our child and teen years, when our father couldn't.

Grams taught Amy and me to embrace the gifts, that would've otherwise been ignored. While Amy was gifted at capturing glimpses of the future, I was an empath. Not only did I know what other people were feeling, I could feel it too. It was a gift and a curse at the same time.

Swirling his neat whiskey, the sexiest man alive parted the crowd like fucking Moses and dropped onto the barstool beside me. "Hey," he uttered with an arrogant nod before taking a sip.

My eyebrows lifted, more out of amusement than interest. "Hey…" With the first glimpse of his eyes up close, my breath caught. No human could have eyes that blue.

"A beautiful woman like you really shouldn't be drinking alone." His voice was as smooth as his expensive silk tie.

"I'm not alone…"—the apples of my cheeks lifted with my smile— "…anymore." *Damn girl, who are you?*

His eyebrows lifted, seemingly surprised. Perhaps I had him fooled.

I purposely used my ring-bearing left hand to raise my empty glass, waiting for the penny to drop, but still no reaction. If anything, my subtle attempt to deter him only made the corner of his mouth rise. *Fuck, that's hot.*

"Looks like you need a refill," he said, lifting his finger to the barman before peeking back at my glass. "Gin and tonic?" With my nod, he signaled another round before leaning closer. "Celebrating or commiserating?"

My smile grew tight. "Commiserating…I think."

His eyes narrowed. "You think?"

"I had a job interview today." I tapped my cell. "They said they'd let me know by tonight, and well, it's almost tomorrow."

The gorgeous man leaned back in his chair, watching me. "How do you think it went?"

"Terribly. The interviewer was a complete bitch."

"And you still want the job?"

My stomach roiled. "I *need* the job."

With a slow nod, he took another sip of his drink.

"What about you?" I asked as another gin materialized in front of me. "Celebrating or commiserating?"

A small smile played on his lips. "Celebrating."

"That's great. Are you meeting with friends?" I panned my gaze through the bar, searching for others like him, but I doubted there were.

His panty-dropping grin faulted. "No."

"Oh." My brow furrowed, sensing something I had no business sensing.

"My brother just had a baby," he added quickly. "I thought I'd have a quick celebratory drink before I head to bed." His gaze penetrated mine. "My apartment is across the street."

"Well, congratulations," I said, ignoring the seduction in his mesmerising eyes. "First-time uncle?"

"Yep." He gulped down another mouthful.

A surge of happiness rolled through me, clearly his, but he didn't show it. "Niece or nephew?"

"Nephew."

My heart lit up, but I refrained from elaborating about how great kids were, especially of the boy variety. My son, for instance, was an absolute legend and he'd only been in existence ten years. I could talk about him all day, but much to my heart's utter discontent, today I had to pretend like he didn't exist.

The three-month live-in position I interviewed for left no room for family. My sister told me they were looking for someone without external commitments, so my son would've been a massive barrier. So, in desperation, I manipulated my application just enough to hopefully get the job that was going to resurrect our old lives.

My phone vibrated across the table and I snatched it up, worried something had happened to Finn. I'd become accustomed to bad news, and my heart dropped every time my phone chimed after 10 p.m.

Unknown: **Apologies for the delay. Please call my assistant tomorrow to make arrangements. I'll see you at Harlow Manor in four weeks.**

"Holy shit." I covered my mouth as hope and dread churned through my body.

"What's wrong?"

I stared at the screen. Numb. "I got it."

"But that's a good thing, right?"

"Yeah…" My heart screamed no. "Yes…of course…it's a great opportunity."

The blue-eyed stranger's brow furrowed, but he didn't press. He didn't care. Why would he? He hadn't even asked my name.

"Now we're both celebrating tonight," he said, shifting closer.

I pushed past the guilt already gnawing at my heart. "I guess we are."

He lifted his hand to the perky brunette behind the bar. "A bottle of your most expensive champagne."

Her cheeks burst with color as her eyes bulged. She appeared starstruck, but how could you not be spellbound by this man? Men like this didn't exist in my world. They featured in magazines and movies, or at the very least, some charity ball with a supermodel on their arm. Not here. Not with me. And not staring at me like I was his next meal.

Maybe my luck was changing. First the job, now this. Perhaps the universe was throwing me a bone (quite literally). I needed this. A night off. No worries. No stress. Just me and some handsome stranger clearly craving the same anonymous release. We didn't need to know each other's names. We knew what this was, and damn straight I was going to enjoy every second of it.

———

"Are you trying to get me drunk?" I asked my new friend as he summoned over another bottle of champagne.

"Why would I want you drunk?"

"To loosen me up." I giggled openly, embracing the buzz. I hadn't felt this free in years.

His fingers brushed against my thigh. "Do you need loosening?"

My chest constricted as a surge of electricity rushed straight to my core. *Wow.* I glanced around the bar for prying eyes, but it was far too dark and crowded for anyone to notice his hand's deviant adventures.

He rotated his stool until my side was encased by his large frame. "Because I can help with that," he whispered into my ear as he rested his right arm across the back of my chair.

"I—" my voice caught as his left hand slid over my bare leg.

He grasped my thigh as his gaze locked on mine. "You can stop me anytime. Just say the word."

Not daring to say any word that may hinder his movements, I tipped more champagne into my mouth.

His eyes trailed after my tongue, as it glided across my lips, before falling to my chest. "You've got *spectacular* tits."

I hiccupped at his abrupt remark. "Thank you…I guess."

"Are they real?"

Laughter burst from my mouth. "Of course they are!"

His gaze narrowed as if analyzing the situation. "Bullshit."

"If I had the money, I'd get them reduced, not enhanced."

"Don't you dare," he hissed. "They're fucking perfection."

I shook my head, trying to hide my smile. His forwardness was refreshing.

"I still don't believe you." He rubbed his stubbled jawline. "You're going to have to prove it."

"How could I possibly prov—oooh." I walked right into that one. "You want me to show you my boobs."

"I'd have to feel them to *really* know."

Heat swirled through my body. "Then I guess you'll never know." *Lie.*

"Never?" His hand inched up my thigh.

"Yes," was all I could muster as the hem of my dress rose.

"Yes?" His finger grazed my panties. "Or never?"

I sucked in my breath. "Oh, God."

"Easy, Tiger." He curled one of my blonde waves around his finger before grazing his nose across my neck. "I've barely even touched you."

My chest rose up and down, fighting the building tension, while his finger circled my clit.

He smirked as I squirmed. "Jesus, you're sensitive." *He had no idea.*

Not only was I drowning in desire, I was absorbing his lust. It was all-encompassing, and the pull of our bodies was incredible.

"I think you should come back to my apartment before you scream the place down," he said into the shell of my ear as he increased the pressure below.

"Surely the restroom will suffice." There was no going back now. I was clearly a closet slut.

"No fucking way am I taking you in there." His tongue grazed my earlobe before nipping. "But I'll be taking you every fucking way in my bed."

And just like that, I came all over his hand.

Chapter 2

Slamming my back into the wall of the elevator, his hands slid under my skirt and kneaded my ass as he pressed his hardness into my core. He licked and kissed and bit my neck until I was putty in his hands. It had been so long since anyone had touched me, and no one...*no one*...had ever touched me like that.

We stumbled into his apartment in a lust-and-alcohol-fueled haze, knocking over chairs and lamps as we tore off our clothes. Even in the darkness, I could sense his apartment was a thousand times bigger than Amy's, but I was too distracted by the sex god leading me to his bedroom to take in its extravagance.

Once stripped to our underwear, he backed me into his California King and guided me onto the luxurious sheets with his hungry lips.

"Wa...wait!" I panted, holding my hand to his pounding chest. Barely a breath had been taken between us since our embarrassing exit from the bar.

His eyes burned into mine as he ran his thumb over my wedding ring. "Second thoughts."

"No thoughts. That's the problem."

"Good." With a devilish grin, he yanked my body to the end of the bed where he stood, towering above me. "Because I have big plans for you."

"Oh, really? Do tell." I sounded way more confident than I was.

The mattress dipped as he placed his arms on either side of my body, like a knife and fork. "I'm more of a show-not-tell kind of guy," he said, parting my legs with his knees.

I giggled nervously. I was out of my league here.

"What's so funny?"

"Nothing." But I laughed again.

He pressed his hardness against the cotton of my underwear. "Tell me."

My eyes widened. He was big. Too big. "Everything!" I blurted out, squirming under the gloriously unnerving pressure. "This!" My cheeks pooled with heat. "I've never done this before!"

His eyes flashed to mine, and his jaw twitched. Was he contemplating backing out?

"But I want to." I rolled my pelvis into his to assure him of my intentions. I *really* needed this. It had been six years, for Christ's sake.

His smile grew as he dragged himself down my body. "Then I better make it worth your while."

"I think you already have," I gushed, thinking about the orgasm that got us kicked out of the bar.

"Oh, Tiger." He chuckled over my panties. "That was only the beginning."

"The beginning..." I puffed out as his stubble grazed my thighs.

"Mmhmm," he hummed as he clasped one leg in each hand, then pushed them apart. "I plan to fuck you until the sun comes up." And on his promise, he nuzzled into the damp cotton and ran his tongue over my aching mound.

My body arched off the bed. "Oh, God!"

"Don't you fucking come yet," he snapped, glaring up at me.

"Okay, okay!" I wondered if it was possible to hide an orgasm. "I'll try..."

He kissed the insides of my thighs while I relaxed back onto the bed. "Good girl," he uttered, grasping my ass through my panties. He pulled the flimsy material over my legs until there was nothing between us but his hot breath.

"Hold onto the sheets." His searing gaze did not veer from my swollen lips.

Before I could grasp anything, his tongue dove through my seam, sending a shockwave through my body. I couldn't breathe under the intense pleasure, and it took all my strength to contain myself. Over and over, he stroked, and sucked, and swirled, while my legs threatened to close in on him like a vise. It was sensational.

Instead of the sheets, I grabbed his hair, pulling as another orgasm rippled through me.

"Tiger," he growled, running his hands through his tousled hair once my legs released him.

"I'm sorry." I winced. "I couldn't help it."

"You..."—his lips traveled up my legs— "are going to be exhausted..."—his tongue rolled over my stomach—"when I'm done with you." He hovered over my chest before detouring to my mouth, kissing me deeply.

"Still think they're fake?" I asked as his fingers traced the underwire of my bra.

With a smirk, he lowered his eyes to my breasts before settling to one side of my body. "Hmmm..." His finger slid over and under each breast, as if repeatedly drawing an infinity symbol. "I'll have to run some tests before making my final conclusion."

"Tests?" I tittered. "And what will that entail?"

He glanced up to my smile, and something flickered through his energy. "First..." He cleared his throat as he refocused. "Smell."

My breasts bounced up and down with my laughter as he climbed over me, shadowing my tiny frame with his muscular body.

Cupping a boob in each hand, he squeezed them together before nuzzling his nose into my cleavage. "Hmmm..."

"Hmmm...what?"

"Patience...the results aren't in yet."

"Fine," I huffed, pretending to be bothered. "So, what's the second test?"

He slipped his hand under my back, and with one easy flick, my bra loosened over my chest. "Sight."

My brow rose. This guy was experienced.

He tossed the bra aside and muttered, "Fuck me."

"Convinced yet?"

He rested his finger on my lips, shushing me. "Now for the third test...touch."

I drew in a shaky breath as his hand trailed down the side of my breast, then underneath, then in between, before devouring it into his large, talented hand. His mouth parted while he massaged.

"How am I doing?" I asked, happy to re-take the test if required.

His voice grew hoarse. "It appears you're telling the truth... but there's just one more test."

"And that is?"

"The most important one." He moistened his lips. "Taste."

My head fell back in ecstasy as he lowered his mouth to my erect tips. His tongue swirled around my nipple, first left, then right, until my clit was pulsating with jealousy. Dominic never felt comfortable with my breasts after Finn was born, so this was an absolute delight.

A jolt of electricity shuddered through me as he pinched my peak while devouring the other. The mixture of pleasure and pain was unbelievably arousing, and I shocked myself with how much I enjoyed it. Dominic had been a gentle lover. This man was something else entirely.

As he continued to worship my well-endowed chest, he freed one hand to explore my body. It traveled down every curve and crevice until it settled over my freshly manicured mound that, thankfully, my sister had convinced me to sort out once I had arrived in the city.

"Are you going to behave?" he asked, dragging his mouth from my nipple while his hand dipped closer to my throbbing core.

"No promises," I rasped out, raising my pelvis, craving pressure.

His tongue traced my lips before delving inside, mimicking his finger below. His hand slowed with my gasp. "Fuck, you're tight."

"It's um...well...it's been a while."

"That's a fucking crime." He shook his head. "A woman like you should be taken care of." He kissed my lips as his thumb circled my clit. "I'm going to have to loosen you up. Is that what you want?"

I nodded in lieu of my lost voice.

"Pardon?"

A rush of adrenaline shot through me. "Yes."

His eyes tapered as he slid in one finger and abruptly pulled it out.

"Yes!" I said louder, desperate for him to continue. "But please…go slow."

His deep chuckle vibrated through me. "Oh, baby…I don't do slow."

"Oh," I squeaked as he added a second finger, then a third. "My God."

"You're going to thank me later." He continued to pump and expand. "I'd hate to break you."

"How could you possibl—" His hardness pressed into my leg, and I clamped my mouth shut. I understood perfectly.

His eyes softened, as if sensing my fear. "I'll make sure you're ready."

"But I think it will hurt."

"Oh, it's going to hurt." He pushed his fingers in a little deeper. "But in the best way possible."

Fuck me dead. This guy was everything I didn't know I wanted.

Two orgasms later, I thought I was well and truly ready until he slipped off his boxer briefs. *Lord, have mercy.* I'd never seen anything like it, but then again, I only had one other to compare it to. It wasn't like I hadn't seen others, just nothing this close. This real.

My friends had showed me their collections of unwanted dick pics over the years, but none of them looked like this. Smooth, cut, thick, long, and set amongst professionally manicured grounds. Even his dick looked rich.

"Open your legs for me," he ordered, stroking himself as he gazed over my body. He clearly liked to be in charge, and hell, it was doing it for me.

I parted my legs, exposing the embarrassing wet mess he was responsible for, while he rolled on a condom.

"You're fucking magnificent," he said before climbing over me and encasing my body between his arms.

As his length met my entrance, I closed my eyes with a wince, anticipating the burn.

He paused. "Look at me."

I instantly submitted, opening my eyes to his steely blue gaze.

"You need to breathe." He tenderly wiped a hair from my cheek as he pushed inside. His lips covered my gasp, then smiled when I omitted a pining moan. It had been too long.

Little by little, he increased the pressure until I was drowning with want, but when he hit the spot I'd assumed I didn't have, scorching heat consumed my entire body.

"You okay?" he asked after my embarrassing whimper.

"Yes," I puffed out, not wanting him to stop. "So fucking okay."

When he pulled out, I growled, only to gasp when he thrust back in. He was clearly switching gears.

"Oh God!" My eyes rolled backwards as he hit that profound spot over and over.

"Easy, Tiger. I want to come together this time."

An uneasiness fell over me. Never in my life had I experienced an orgasm through sex. Come time, I knew I'd have to fake it, just like I'd done since I was eighteen. It was humiliating, but this man deserved to know he was good in bed. Until then, I'd simply enjoy the ride.

His long shaft, filling my void and eliminating the proverbial cobwebs, was incredible. I was so completely aroused and unfazed about his size that he slid in and out with ease.

He grabbed the headboard for extra leverage. "Now you're in trouble."

I couldn't form a word, let alone a sentence, as he pounded into me, each thrust harder than the last. He suckled my nipples, bit my neck, and devoured my mouth, all while his pelvis slammed against mine, drawing me closer to that impossible dream.

As if he couldn't get close enough, he elevated my leg around his shoulder to form a new angle, and damn, it worked. Our grunts turned animalistic as the headboard smashed against the wall until my thoughts were jumbled and drenched in desire.

Flipping me over, he took me from behind, rocking me to my core. The pleasure was indescribable, and when his thumb pressed against a previously forbidden land, I almost lost it.

"Not yet, baby." He redirected his hand to my shoulder to steady himself. "I want this to last all night."

And it did. For hours. Over and over, I was on the verge of losing control when he'd stop and take me from a new angle. Positions I never knew existed would forever be imprinted into my memory, leaving me in a constant state of ecstasy that was surely illegal. I'd never been fucked like this. Made love to, yes… but never fucked. This was wild and unadulterated, and I was convinced this man had ruined me for all others.

It wasn't until our pace slowed while I was seated in his lap, face to face, with his arms around my waist and mine grasping his shoulders, that I felt it. Through the heat, the lust and the sweat. A connection. Our bodies linked. Physically and spiritually. His eyes bored into mine as I rocked my body over his, taking him deeper than before. Deeper into my body and deeper into my soul.

"Fuck, I'm going to come," he cried out as his blue eyes glazed over. His hand threaded through my tousled hair to press my forehead to his. "Come with me."

On his words, my body shuddered uncontrollably while his stiffened on release. His pulsing length burst into me, shooting a kaleidoscope of energy through my body.

The blinding ecstasy was too much to bear, and a wave of emotion crashed over me. Tears filled my eyes, and I couldn't bear to lift them. A mixture of guilt, pleasure, hope, dread, love, and fear surged through my soul and I was moments from coming undone in front of a complete stranger.

"Hey…" His voice tempered as he brought his hand to my face, attempting to lift my chin. "Are you crying?"

My lower lip trembled. There was no stopping the onslaught. "Excuse me." I climbed off the bed and rushed into the bathroom. As the door slammed shut behind me, I crumpled against it, unable to hold it in any longer. What was wrong with me?

Once my streaming tears faded into a steady weep, a soft knock sounded at the door. "Hey…are you okay in there?"

"Um...yeah..." I wrapped my arms around my bare waist. "I...I just need a minute."

A moment of silence followed. "Did I hurt you?"

"No!" I gasped. "You were perfect. I've just...um...I've never slept with another man." *Or had an orgasm.*

"Well, if it's any consolation, I've never made a girl cry after sex before."

Laughter burst through my sob as I wiped away my tears. "Would you mind if I took a shower?" I asked, peering around the oversized bathroom.

"Not at all. Jump in and I'll get you a fresh towel."

"Thanks." I barely heard him once my eyes set upon the shower. I wandered over and turned on the rain-style head, filling the room with steam before I stepped inside. The hot water singed my skin and massaged my muscles, pulling me out of my emotion-fueled daze. The lingering embarrassment washed away with the water, leaving me with one realization: one-night-stands were not my thing.

Moments later, his hands slid around my body and cupped my soapy breasts. "Feeling better?" he asked while pressing his soft lips to my shoulder.

"Mmhmm." I instinctively leaned into him as the soap suds flowed down my body.

As if riding the wave, his hand followed, soothing the ache below.

"Much better..." The words floated from my mouth in a blissful haze.

He kissed my neck before bringing his mouth to my ear. "Come back to bed."

"I shouldn't..." My knees weakened under the pressure of his fingers.

"Shower sex it is, then," he said, holding his erection to my lower back.

I spun around with a laugh. "How can you possibly be ready to go again?"

He dragged his finger through my seam with a knowing smirk. "And you're not?"

I closed my eyes, trying not to react to his glorious touch. "How do you do that?"

"What?" He dipped his finger in. "This?" He simultaneously rubbed my clit with his thumb. "Or this?"

I buckled over. "Fuuuck."

He lifted my chin to analyze my lips between his thumb and forefinger. "God, I want to fuck that dirty mouth of yours."

Excitement surged through me. "Why don't you?"

"Wow." His brow rose as his mouth fell open. "Where the fuck did that come from?"

"It appears you bring out the worst in me."

"Oh yeah?" His pupils dilated. "Show me your worst."

With a bashful smile, I sunk to my knees, relishing the opportunity to overpower the sexual beast before me. I took his length into my hand, then dragged my tongue up the beads of water streaming down it, making him grasp the surrounding fixtures to keep his balance.

I persistently stroked and licked, but once I took him entirely into my mouth, his knees trembled. "God, you're a little sex piñata." He rocked his pelvis as I took him deeper. "The more I fuck you, the more surprises you dish out."

The boost of sexual confidence only made me work harder, wanting to pleasure him in all the ways he'd been pleasuring me all night.

"Oh, fuck." He pulled me back up to his mouth and kissed me hard as he came. "That was…incredible."

My face heated under his adoring gaze. "The entire night has been."

As we stared at each other through the falling water, the energy shifted between us. There was something more, something deeper, but I wasn't brave enough to pry. This was a one-night-stand. Nothing more.

"Let's get some sleep," he finally said, as if cutting off the same intrusive thoughts.

"Are you sure?" I hesitantly followed him out of the shower. "I can leave…"

"Do you have to?" He peered back with an unexpected spark of sadness.

"Well, no. I'm crashing at my sister's place, so…"

He grabbed a towel and threw it around my body, drawing me close. "Then don't. Stay here tonight. I've already canceled my morning meetings."

I melted into the luxurious fluffy material and smiled. "Okay."

"But no more sex tonight, you deviant. I need my rest."

I erupted with laughter as I tightened the towel around my torso. "I highly doubt *I'll* be the problem."

"Oh, you're the problem." He dried his privates while his eyes took a tour of my curves.

"Me?!" I followed his gorgeous ass back into the bedroom. "You have trouble written all over you."

With a grin, he climbed under the sheets before resting his muscular arms behind his head. "I'd say that makes us pretty compatible in here," he said, patting the bed.

I propped my hands on my hips. "Maybe I'm pretending to be this way."

His eyes grew serious. "Maybe you pretend with everyone else."

I mused. Maybe he was right.

"Get your ass in here," he said, lifting the covers. "But lose the towel."

"And you'll let me sleep?"

His blue eyes sparkled. "I'm not a monster."

My left eyebrow rose.

"Well…"—he peeked under the sheets—"not yet anyway."

"Fine." I yanked off my towel and dropped it to the floor.

His eyes rolled back before he shoved a pillow into his face.

"You need to behave," I said, crawling in beside him.

"I can restrain." He slid his arm around my waist to tuck my body in line with his. "But come sunrise…" He ran his hand down to my buttock and squeezed. "This ass is mine."

My entire body stiffened.

"Relax," he whispered before brushing his lips over my ear. "You have a few hours to recover."

I forced a yawn. "Then I better get some rest," I mumbled before closing my eyes.

"Night, Tiger."

I tucked my hands under the pillow and relished the warmth of a body next to mine. "Goodnight."

Once his head hit the pillow and his breathing grew soft and steady, I stealthily slid out of the bed. I gathered up my sprawled-out clothes and discarded handbag, and tiptoed through the magnificent apartment that overlooked the entire city. I stopped to admire the twinkling lights before gazing back at the bedroom.

However exhilarating another session of uninhabited fucking sounded, I couldn't risk another influx of raw emotion in front of this man. Not only was it humiliating, but the release he gave me brought up too many feelings. There was something about this man that stirred me up. His energy overpowered my common sense and made me feel something I hadn't felt in years. *Free*. Free of responsibilities and free of grief.

It was a fleeting bliss, because my torture endured. This wasn't my life and I was no more than another notch on this guy's Armani belt. So, ignoring the unnerving ache in my heart, I crept out of the handsome stranger's apartment, and threw myself back into my heartbreaking reality.

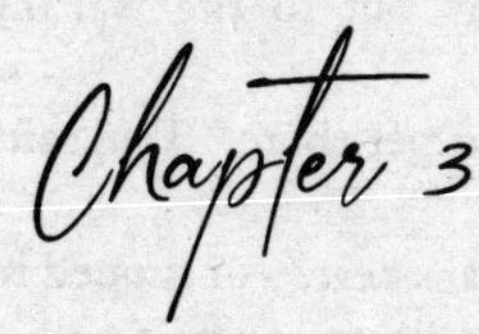

"It'll only be three months, so I'll be back before Christmas."

Finn barely took his eyes off the computer screen. "Okay."

"So, Pa is going to take care of you."

"Cool," he uttered with a shrug.

Dad placed his calloused hand on my shoulder while I watched my son's avatar prepare for battle. "I told you, he'll be fine."

"But he can't be on screens the whole time," I grumbled, disheartened by my son's lack of concern and my father's easy-going nature. "Did you hear that, Finn?"

"Yeah, yeah."

"I'll make sure of it, Cass." My sister's boyfriend's voice boomed through Finn's speaker.

Relief rolled over me. "Thanks for looking out for him, Reed. Tell Amy I'll call her once I'm settled."

"Roger that."

Finn's jade-green eyes peered up at me and softened. "I'll be fine."

I ruffled his hair. "I can't believe I'm going to miss my baby's first day back at school."

"I'm almost eleven, Mom. I got this."

A laugh burst from my mouth followed by a sigh. "I love you, Finn. Can I at least get a hug before I go?"

With an over-the-top eye roll, he pushed out his desk chair and stood. "Love you, too." He wound his lanky arms around me. "You're going to do great."

"Thanks, baby." His ability to read my emotions worried me. While his father's genes conquered his smile, ever-increasing height, and dark hair, his empathetic nature was all mine.

After kissing Finn's head, he launched back into his game while I made my way out to the waiting car in my father's driveway.

"Call me when you get there," Dad said, handing the driver my tattered suitcase.

"Will do." I held back tears as I slipped into the car before my father could attempt any sort of affection.

While he had made more of an effort over the last few years, the strain between us lingered. He wasn't there when I had needed him most, and now, although we had more in common than ever before, it was awkward. Fortunately, he was an amazing grandfather to my son, and that was all that mattered now.

As the car pulled away, I offered my father a quick wave before turning my gaze to the road ahead, pondering what laid in front of me. Three months at Harlow Manor. Three months without my boy. Three months until I finally got my life back on track.

———

"What are we doing here?" I asked, shoving my romance novel back into my handbag when the car turned into an open field.

"This is your transfer."

"But I thought we were driv—" My voice faded as I squinted into the distance. "A helicopter?!"

"Yes."

"How rich are these people?" My sister never went into detail about her boss's family, and I didn't bother asking questions. A job was a job and I needed this one desperately.

The driver chuckled. "Rich doesn't begin to describe this family."

My brow rose, but my shoulders eased. The guilt I felt about accepting such an incredible wage from an elderly man had been gnawing at me. *Not anymore!*

"Enjoy the perks while you can."

Once the car slowed to a stop near the slick black helicopter, I let myself out. I had no intention of *enjoying the perks* of a high-society lifestyle, and that included chauffeur-driven cars. The only man I wanted opening my door was gone.

"Thank you," I said to the driver as he handed my luggage to the pilot.

"Tico will take you from here."

With a parting nod, I tucked my long waves behind my ears and gawked at the blades above. "Wow."

"I'm guessing you've never flown in a helicopter before," Tico said, ushering me through the open door.

My nervous laughter filled the cabin as I climbed into it and swiftly buckled up my seatbelt. "No. This is all very new to me."

"Don't worry." His smile was warm. "You'll be fine. It's just like an elevator that goes up, down, back and forth, and sideways."

My teeth clenched. "Sounds…fun."

"You'll love it. It's much better than a plane."

"I'll have to take your word on that," I murmured as I slipped on huge headphones, much like the ones Reed gifted Finn last Christmas for his gaming.

Little did Tico know I'd never even been on a plane. The only travel experience I had consisted of epic cross-country drives between my dad's place and my grandmother's house on the West Coast.

With a pounding heart, I peeked out the window as we lifted off the ground. I couldn't decipher whether I was scared or excited, but once I caught sight of the beautiful countryside, my lungs filled with air. All I needed to do was distract myself with the picturesque landscape to keep the intrusive thoughts of me plummeting to my death at bay.

At my first glimpse of water, all my fear subsided. I hadn't seen the ocean in months, and it was one of the things I missed most from home. The water may have been cooler out here, but it was just what I needed, and I couldn't wait to immerse myself in its healing properties.

While living with my grandmother in Venice Beach, I spent every morning and afternoon at the beach, recharging. It kept me balanced, and I longed to get back there. But until then, the Hamptons would have to do.

I never wanted to return to New York, but death kept drawing me back. It wasn't my home anymore and hadn't been since I was seven. Thankfully, in the ten years we lived with my grandmother, she taught us everything she knew about spiritual healing. Reiki, crystals, and aromatherapy were only some of the alternative therapies she used to ease the ailments of her friends and neighbors. Some considered her a witch. But to Amy and me, she was our savior.

My father never believed in my grandmother's 'voodoo' and convinced my mother to sever ties with her before I was born. Unfortunately, my mother had a gift, too, but with no guidance, it swallowed her up and tore her apart until she couldn't take the pain any longer. She took her life only days before my seventh birthday.

I grew up that day. I was left to take care of my little sister while my dad drank himself into a stupor almost every night. It wasn't until I found my father on the bathroom floor, surrounded by vomit, that family services sent us to live with my grandmother. To us, she was a complete stranger, but she ended up becoming my best friend, my confidant, and my teacher.

As the helicopter lowered just over a half hour later, my heart mimicked the beat of the blades. *Now I was scared.* I thought I would have a few hours to prepare for my arrival at Harlow Manor, but I didn't even have time to read my book. Reading relaxed me and promised a cool, calm facade upon arrival, but now I was an anxious and fidgety mess.

"Cassidy Ryan, I presume?" an older man in a suit asked once my wobbly feet hit the ground.

I straightened my loose shirt, feeling entirely too casual in jeans. "Yes. Hi."

"My name is Max." He reached out his hand to shake mine. "I'm Liam's butler."

My brow lowered. "Liam?"

"Your client." He smiled warmly. "There are a few William's in this family, so we refer to each with an alternative name to avoid confusion." He cleared his throat. "Except his son. We always address him as Mr. Harlow."

Mr. Harlow was the man who interviewed me alongside his wife, Caroline. He had barely said a word while his wife did the majority of the interrogation. With the sensitive nature of my work, I often expected resistance from family members, so his manner didn't surprise me.

My initial interview with William, *aka Liam*, the elderly man I'd be working for, went beautifully. Although it was over the phone, I could sense his gentle nature through his voice. Now, after meeting his spawn, I was beginning to doubt myself.

"Mr. and Mrs. Harlow are waiting for you in the drawing room. They'll take you to meet Liam." He picked up my luggage. "Please follow me."

"Wait." I gaped up at the building ahead. "This is the house?" I'd assumed it was a fancy hotel.

"This is Harlow Manor. Yes."

My eyes widened. "Wow."

"It's very impressive, indeed."

I quickened my step to match his stride. "How long have you been working here?"

"Almost seventeen years."

"So, you know Liam quite well, then?"

A flicker of sadness crossed Max's eyes. "Very well."

"Is he anything like...his son?"

"Oh no." He laughed. "Quite the opposite."

"Phew."

"I wouldn't worry too much about Mr. and Mrs. Harlow. They're about to embark on a trip through Europe, so you won't be seeing them often."

"Oh, I thought they'd want to be here...for Liam."

"They'll fly back intermittently." Max cleared his throat. "Liam isn't especially close to his son. His grandsons, yes, but not his own."

"Why is that? If you don't mind me asking."

"Much to Liam's disappointment, Mr. Harlow's obsession with wealth and success overrode his father's ideals."

"And his grandsons? Are they just as...ambitious?"

"Yes and no. Grayson has always been the gentler of the two, but Adam…he's yet to be determined."

"Thank you. It helps to know what I'm walking into." As we strode along the pebbled pathway lined with box hedges, I turned my gaze to the vast grounds before me. The gardens were carefully planned, professionally manicured, and absolutely gorgeous.

"The late Elizabeth Harlow designed these gardens herself. Not a cent has been spared in conserving their beauty."

"It's so beautiful here," I gushed. "And that tree…wow." A stunning elm tree, ablaze with red and orange, captivated me instantly. It was one of the largest I'd ever seen.

"Betty planned the entire garden around it."

"I can see why. It's an incredible focal point."

"Liam likes to sit there sometimes. It brings him peace."

"That's good to know."

Instead of the front entrance, Max ushered me through the back and into a mudroom where he left my suitcase. "I'll take this up to your room while you're getting acquainted with the family."

"Thank you, Max," I said, straightening my back in anticipation. I drew in a deep breath before trailing him down the grand hallway toward two French doors.

He rolled them open. "Mr. and Mrs. Harlow. Cassidy Ryan." With a small nod, he moved to the side as I stepped forward.

"Thank you, Max. That will be all." The woman who interviewed me ran her gaze up and down my body. "Cassidy. Take a seat."

I moved to the vacant Chesterfield opposite Caroline, while Mr. Harlow occupied the wingback beside the fireplace. Neither stood to greet me.

"Harlow Manor is very beautiful," I said, attempting to fill the awkward silence as I perched on the edge of the chair.

"It's a little dated for my taste, but yes, it's quite the estate." She placed her interlocked fingers in her lap and exhaled. "Let's get down to business, shall we?"

With my nod, she continued.

"Just so we are clear, Mr. Harlow and I aren't comfortable with this arrangement, however this is Liam's request, so we will tolerate your presence until the time comes."

"I understand this is a diffic—"

"Regardless, it's a perfectly large residence, so I don't foresee any issues with you making yourself scarce while the family is here."

"Of course." *With pleasure.*

"Should you need anything during your stay, please speak to Max."

"What the hell is a *death doula* anyway?" Mr. Harlow's deep voice sliced through our conversation.

"William," Caroline gasped, but he waved her off.

My smile was tight. "That is a perfectly acceptable question." Which I answered on a daily basis. "I offer practical, emotional, and spiritual support for those nearing end of life."

His gaze narrowed. "And what does that entail exactly?"

"It varies, but mostly I provide guidance, support, and companionship to the client and their family during this overwhelming time. I also offer alternative therapies, such as Reiki, to assist with anxiety and pain management."

Mr. Harlow blew out a puff of air.

"I realize this isn't for everyone, but it's really up to the client and their wishes." He wasn't my first skeptic.

He glared at me. *Mr. Harlow doesn't care for strong women. Noted.*

"I'll take you upstairs." Caroline stood. "Liam should be awake by now."

"Fantastic. I'm looking forward to meeting him."

The instructions continued as I followed Caroline up the ornate staircase. "We have a live-in nurse to tend to his medical needs and a doctor who checks in every week. You are expected to work every business day and be on call over the weekend. During this time, you must remain close by but unseen while the family is visiting. My sons will be alternating weekend visits, and we'll return sporadically when our travel plans allow."

She stopped in front of a door and opened it. "This will be your room. I'm sure it will suffice."

Suffice? Holy shitballs! The room was enormous. "Yes, I think it will," I said, completely void of tone.

"I'll take you to see Liam now."

Caroline continued up the hallway and paused, peering through a doorway before entering. "Liam." She sauntered into the room. "This is Cassidy Ryan."

"Hi, Liam," I said to the elderly man holding an empty cup of tea in bed.

"Cassidy." A kind smile radiated across the room. "I knew you would be beautiful."

I laughed. "Pardon?"

"When we spoke over the phone, I just knew. It shines through your voice."

Caroline grumbled. "I think you're being highly inappropriate, Liam."

"Oh, hush, Caroline. At my age, I should be allowed to surround myself with beauty," he said as another lady walked into the room. "Speaking of beauty. This is my nurse, Nora."

Nora shook her head with a chuckle. "Liam, behave. You're going make the poor girl think you're a dirty old man and not the gentleman you really are."

Caroline emitted an inpatient grunt. "Well, I'll leave you all to get acquainted. Cassidy, there's a copy of your employment contract in your room, along with a cell phone you must carry with you at all times."

"Thank you, Caroline."

With a curt nod, Caroline glanced around the room, in clear discomfort before scurrying outside. I'd become accustomed to the sights and sounds of various medical devices but understood how overwhelming it could be to those who weren't.

Once Caroline disappeared, Nora slid a half-empty box of chocolates out from under Liam's pillow. "That was close."

"Just one more?" Liam's hazel eyes pleaded with her. "Come on, I'm a dying man."

"You're going to get me fired," she hissed as she held out the box. "I've got mouths to feed, remember?"

"Oh!" My heart lit up. "You have kids?"

"Two famished teenagers. Our food bill is ridiculous."

Liam chortled. "I remember when my grandsons were like that. Always sneaking into the kitchen to raid the pantry—even in the middle of the night."

"I'm pretty sure they still do," Nora said. "Nancy is always complaining to Max about missing ice cream."

"Does your family live close by?" I asked, envious that her role wasn't impacted by having children.

"In Brooklyn. Liam flies me in and out so I can spend the weekends with my family. You'll meet the weekend nurse on Friday."

"She's a witch," Liam muttered, scrunching up the chocolate wrapper before handing Nora the evidence.

"No, she's not." Nora turned her gaze to me. "She's just very...serious."

Liam grumbled. "My daughter-in-law insisted we hire her."

Nora laid her hand on Liam's. "With your grandsons visiting every weekend, I honestly think you'll be too distracted to care. And let's not forget Master Harry's first visit to Harlow Manor."

Liam's face lit up as he turned to me. "Harrison is my great-grandson. The newest addition to the Harlow family. I'll be meeting him next week."

My heart swelled. "You must be excited."

Nora picked up Liam's chart and wrote something down. "Ever since that baby was born, I've never seen him so happy. Even his health has improved."

"The young ones keep us going." I knew all too well.

"Indeed, they do. Without my grandsons, I think I would've left this earth years ago."

"You sound close to them."

Contentment eased the lines of Liam's forehead. "I'd like to think so."

"They're lucky to have a grandfather like you."

"No, I'm lucky to have them. I just wish I could see them more often." His spark dulled. "Doc says I'm not allowed to fly anymore, and they're always so busy."

"Well, you'll have to make the most out of your weekends, then." There was no point focusing on the negative.

With a hopeful smile, he lifted his gaze to mine. "I must give you the grand tour of Harlow Manor."

"Oh, it's okay." I waved him off. "I'm sure I can figure out where all the important things are."

"Nonsense. It would be rude not to." Liam pressed the buzzer on the side of his bed.

"But shouldn't you be resting?"

Nora checked her watch. "He's not due for his medication for another hour. You've got time."

Within moments, Max appeared in Liam's doorway, pushing a wheelchair.

The head of Liam's bed began to rise. "Nora, will you please show Cassidy down to the elevator? We'll meet you there."

"Of course," she replied, motioning me to follow.

"Are you sure this is okay?" I asked once we'd given Liam some privacy.

"He's allowed one outing a day when he's feeling well enough." She pressed the elevator button. "Should you encounter any problems, Max and I are never far away."

I turned my smile to Liam as Max pushed him toward us. The elevator doors opened, and Max, Liam, and I squeezed inside. It had a four-person limit, however the wheelchair filled most of the space.

"I'll go tidy up." Nora stepped into the hall. "Make sure you're back within the hour."

Once the doors closed, the elevator lowered to the ground floor. "You'll have full use of the property during your stay," Liam said as we stepped out into another lavish corridor. "So, don't be afraid to enjoy yourself while you're here."

"Thank you, Liam. That is very generous, but I doubt I'll need much more than the books I brought with me."

"Oh, you're a reader? Then you'll love the library."

My stomach fluttered in delight. "There's a library?"

"It's upstairs and overlooks the entire estate. I often watch the sunrise from there."

"Oh, I love sunrises."

"Then you should join me in the mornings. They really are something."

"I'd love that, Liam. Thank you."

"I used to enjoy them from the drawing room windows, but with my health deteriorating, it's best I don't stray too far from my room." Sadness radiated through his words before he shook it off. "Nevertheless, it's still beautiful from the library, so I'm not complaining."

"Well, I can't wait to see it."

"And you will, but first, I'll give you a grand tour of the ground floor. It can be a little overwhelming to newcomers."

Max chuckled. "I've been here almost two decades, and I still get lost."

Liam smiled up at his butler. "Those secret passageways can be tricky."

My eyes grew large. "Secret passageways?"

As they both laughed, Liam grabbed my hand. "Come along, dear, Nora will hunt me down if I'm not back within the hour."

Due to the incredible size of the house, I gave up trying to memorize the layout and simply enjoyed the ride. Liam's endearing stories of his childhood captivated me as we ventured through the grand foyer, the drawing room, the dining room, the kitchen, the great hall, the billiard room, the study, the conservatory, and my favorite...the indoor pool.

The long body of water was surrounded by floor-to-ceiling windows overseeing the gardens and my second favorite location...the outdoor pool. Maybe I wouldn't be reading as much as I thought. I loved to swim.

As if sensing my longing, Liam told Max to steer him outside. "This pool is heated all year round and is practically a gigantic hot tub in the winter." He chuckled. "Betty enjoyed swimming but despised cold water."

"Max told me she designed these gardens."

"Yes, she was creative in every way. Most of the artwork inside is hers, too."

"She sounds like an incredible woman."

"She was. I miss her terribly."

Max continued to the old elm tree and parked Liam beneath it before wandering off to speak to the gardeners. I sat on the cast-iron bench beside him.

"This is where I want my ashes scattered," Liam said, relaxing into his chair as he gazed over the gardens. "With my family."

"Your wife is here?" I searched for a memorial plaque on the chair but found none.

"My family thinks she's in an urn on the mantel, but I scattered her years ago. This was our favorite place. I asked her to marry me in this very spot."

I fiddled with my crystal bracelet, fighting the emotion surging through my body—both Liam's and mine. "I think that's a wonderful idea. I'll make sure your wish is fulfilled."

"Thank you." He sighed. "Sometimes, my requests fall on deaf ears around here."

"Well, I'm here to advocate for you now. So, I'll make sure you are heard."

Liam's shoulders eased. "Thank you."

We sat there for some time, getting to know one another, and I found him as warm and charming as he was in my initial phone interview. We connected instantly, and our conversation never wavered. It was hard to believe he had only months left.

"So, tell me, Cassidy. What sort of books do you read?" Liam asked, gazing up at the charming tower overlooking the gardens.

"Oh, this and that." My cheeks reddened. "Mostly love stories, I guess."

"That's nothing to be ashamed of. Betty loved reading romance. Our library is full of them."

I gaped. "Really?"

"I never understood why anyone would shame another for their reading choices. My wife read romance to escape the trauma of losing our youngest son at birth. It gave her a moment's peace, and that is a powerful thing."

The crushing blow to my chest was unexpected. "Oh, I'm so sorry."

"It was a very long time ago." He blinked away tears. "William doesn't like us talking about it, so we don't. My grandsons don't even know they had an uncle."

"What was his name?"

"Adam." Liam gazed at the soil beneath the elm. "He's here, too."

"Isn't Adam your grandson's name?"

Liam's chest expanded. "Yes. William defied our family tradition and named his first-born after his little brother."

"That is very honorable."

"Yes. He surprised us with that one."

"We all have different ways of dealing with these things."

"And that is why I have no time for literary snobs. Feel free to borrow any book you like from Betty's collection. I've been trying to read all of her favorites before...well...before I no longer can, but my eyes tire easily."

"Perhaps I could read to you sometime."

"Oh, I would love that. Adam reads to me, too, but he's only here every other weekend."

"It must be difficult being of sound mind while your body is failing you."

Liam nodded. "Some days I wish for the opposite...but then I'd miss all the good. Like interacting with my first great-grandson."

"How old is he?"

"Five weeks."

"Oh, brand new," I gushed. "Harrison, yes?"

"Harrison William Harlow." His spark returned. "If only my Betty were here."

"She is." I placed a hand on his shoulder. "Just not in the way you envisioned."

His frail fingers found mine. "You've experienced loss before, haven't you?"

I swallowed, forcing back unprofessional emotion. "Much."

"Then you understand how this...*transition* will affect my family. Some will take it harder than others. I need you to be there for them as much as you will be for me."

"Of course."

Liam's bushy eyebrows pulled together as he studied me. "There's something special about you, Cassidy. I think you're going to be a good fit here."

"Well, let's hope the rest of the family thinks so."

"They will...in time" He waved Max over. "Now, let me show you the most underutilized room at Harlow Manor that I'm certain you'll appreciate. The library."

Chapter 4

Although I'd been under the close, watchful eyes of Caroline and William Harlow, my first week had gone well. In our private talks, mostly at sunrise, Liam expressed his end-of-life wishes, and I took detailed notes. With a family like his, Liam foresaw issues and was concerned that when the time came, he wouldn't have the energy to fight for himself.

Not daring to explore the mansion while the family was in residence, I kept to my bedroom and ate my meals in the kitchen with Max and the other staff. Caroline made it extremely clear she didn't want to see me, and I had no intention of rocking the boat. I had no complaints. My bedroom was enormous with a king-sized bed, its own couch, a desk, and an ensuite bathroom with my own fucking clawfoot tub! It was paradise.

While Liam slept, I lay on my bed, reading. It was the only time I could truly switch off and relieve the incessant ache in my heart. I, like Liam's late wife, used the predictable tales of romance to escape the sadness of my past.

A door closed in the hallway, and my ears pricked up. While Caroline and William were staying in the house, they rarely spent time with Liam, so the sound surprised me. Knowing Nora was busy in her room, packing for her trip home, I wondered if the weekend nurse had arrived to take over her station.

I snuck over to the door and held my ear against it.

"He's asleep right now." I recognized Caroline's hushed voice immediately. "Cassidy must have tired him out."

I rolled my eyes.

"Who's Cassidy?" a man's voice floated down the hallway.

"His *death doula*." Her tone expressed her distaste.

The man's obnoxious laugh irritated me instantly. "Is that some sort of witch doctor?"

"It's someone to help prepare him for death."

"How can you possibly prepare for death?"

"Look, it's what your grandfather wants, and I'm not about to argue with a man on his death bed."

"Sounds like a hoax to me."

My temper spiked.

"Well, he's quite taken with her, so please don't make an issue out of it—unless you're planning to live here full-time to keep him company."

He sighed. "If I didn't have so much work, it wouldn't be an issue."

"He knows how busy you are." Her voice grew surprisingly soft. "Harlow Corp. is your priority right now."

There was a moment's silence before the man spoke again. "When are you and Dad leaving for your trip?"

"Monday. We wanted to spend the weekend with you before we left. Your father is itching for a report on the company."

"Itching to tell me how to run it, you mean." His voice grew closer, hovering outside my door.

"Adam…"

"Just get the nurse to tell me when he wakes." The door across the hall slammed shut, and I jumped. His bedroom was opposite mine. *Fan-fucking-tastic.*

An hour later, I crept out of my room to see Nora before she left.

"I bet you can't wait to see your kids," I said, leaning against the doorframe of her bedroom.

"I'm counting the minutes." Nora grinned as she zipped up her suitcase and placed it on the floor. "My eldest has a big game this weekend."

"That's exciting." I smiled through my envy. I was missing my son's swim meet.

"Is there anything you need before I go?"

I forced a grimace. "Advice on how to deal with this family?"

"Is Caroline giving you trouble? Because I can speak to Liam."

"No, no. I can handle her. I heard Liam's grandson arrive earlier. He didn't sound very pleased about someone like me being here."

"Oh, Adam? That boy is all business. I doubt he'll take his nose out of his laptop long enough to notice your existence." She ran her gaze over my body and smirked. "But then again…"

I gaped. "What's that supposed to mean?"

"He's known to be quite the womanizer."

I scoffed. "Well, I'd never go there."

She chuckled. "Have you met him?"

"No, not yet."

"Mmm…" Her crafty smile lingered. "Well, let's just say I wouldn't blame you if you did."

I attempted to object, but an older lady strode past me into the room, stealing my attention.

"That's my cue!" Nora said when the tall, broad-shouldered lady with a tight bun of gray hair, placed her suitcase on the freshly made bed.

"Hi, you must be the weekend nurse," I said when she didn't speak.

With an abrupt nod, she turned her back and unzipped her suitcase.

My brow rose as Nora linked her arm with mine and guided me into the hall. "Mrs. Fredrich is very old school," she whispered once we were out of earshot. "So, best keep your interaction to a minimum."

"Great. Another person to avoid this weekend."

"It's a big house. You'll be fine." Nora poked her head into Liam's room. "Liam's still asleep, so can you tell him to behave while I'm gone? He always stirs her up."

"I will, but I think he likes causing trouble."

"That he does." She shook her head with a chuckle. "His body may be failing him, but his mind is as sharp as a tack."

"I've noticed." Liam and I shared an instant connection the day we met, making me feel like I'd known him my entire life—or perhaps in a different one.

"You try and enjoy yourself this weekend, Missy. You're off the clock, remember?"

I gave her a half smile. "Yeah, we'll see."

"At least go for a swim. You've been eyeing that swimming pool all week."

"I'll definitely try." I was desperate to get into the water again.

"Well, Tico is going to take off without me if I don't leave now," she said, squeezing my arm before dragging her suitcase down the hall. "I'll see you Monday."

After saying goodbye to Nora, I returned to Liam's room. "Oh, you're awake now."

Liam's drawn face brightened. "I must've sensed you coming."

"Would you like me to tell your grandson you're awake? He arrived a short time ago."

"No, no." Liam shook his head with a sleepy smile. "He'll come when he's ready."

"Oh, okay." I moved closer. "Did you have a nice rest? Perhaps our stroll through the gardens was too much for you this morning."

"Nonsense. The fresh air makes me feel more alive."

I adjusted his pillows as he sat up. "I know I don't officially work weekends, but if you ever want to go for a walk or have me read to you, I'd be happy to, anytime."

"You're a sweet girl, Cassidy, but you're young. You should be out enjoying yourself."

"I plan to go to the beach tomorrow," I said, completely aware of how lame I sounded. I had no intention of wasting a single cent shopping or socializing while I was staying in the Hamptons. I was here with the sole purpose of saving enough money to move back to LA and start a new life with Finn.

"Good. Max will arrange for my driver to take you."

"Thank you, Li—" My mouth snapped shut when the weekend nurse trooped into the room and whipped Liam's chart off the end of his bed.

"Good afternoon, Mr. Harlow." She barely glanced my way. "It's time for your medication." She held out his tablets in a tiny paper cup along with a glass of water.

"Lovely to see you, too, Mrs. Fredrich." He unwillingly took them from her hands and did as told.

She watched his mouth until she was convinced he'd swallowed them.

"I'd like you to meet Cassidy Ryan, my end-of-life doula."

She lifted her gaze to mine but didn't smile. "Pleased to meet you, Cassidy," she uttered before dropping her eyes back to the chart. "I'll let your family know you're awake." With the pivot of her foot, she marched out of the room.

I stared at the empty door. "Wow. She really is serious."

"I'll wear her down."

"I'm sure you will." I moved to his bedside and picked up the novel I'd been reading to him all week. "Would you like me to read to you until dinner?"

"I'd love that." He nestled back into his pillows while I lowered myself into the armchair beside him.

Delving into the story we'd left off the day before, I found myself getting lost in the words until approaching footsteps caught my voice.

I was already intimidated before he walked through the door. His purpose-driven steps hastened my heart beat, and the moment he stepped into the room, I dropped my gaze to the book in my hands, endeavoring to remain invisible, as per Caroline's request.

"Hey Gramps." He approached Liam's alternate side.

"Adam. So lovely to see you. It's been some time." The warmth in Liam's voice was immeasurable.

"Yeah, I'm sorry. Work has been…busy."

"I completely understand. Acquiring the Warren Media portfolio has been a tremendous advancement for Harlow Corp. I can only imagine how much extra work you've had to put in."

He let out a deflated laugh but didn't respond.

"You mustn't work yourself too hard, Adam. There is more to life."

"Yeah, yeah. So you keep telling me."

I peeked up to find Adam sitting on Liam's bedside. Faced with his broad-shouldered back, my gaze rolled over his scruffy, dark-blonde hair, then down to his muscular arms. Nora was right. Even without seeing his face, I could tell he was attractive.

Replacing the bookmark, I closed the novel and placed it on the side table. It was time to leave. Adam hadn't acknowledged my existence, nor had I expected him to. The help was ignored in this world and Liam's grandson clearly had a lifetime of experience.

"I'd like you to meet someone." Liam turned his smile my way.

Fuck. That wasn't supposed to happen. I was supposed to remain unseen.

"This is Cassidy. She'll be helping to prepare everyone for my passing."

Begrudgingly, Adam's gaze turned my way, full of disinterest. "Now, Gramps, that's not very optimisti…" His voice trailed off.

I froze as his eyes narrowed. *It couldn't be.*

"Cassidy, this is my grandson, Adam."

Forcing down the growing lump in my throat, I stretched out my hand. "Pleased to meet you." *Surely it wasn't him.*

"Likewise." He hesitated momentarily before wrapping his fingers around mine.

A spark of electricity ricocheted between us, and my eyes snapped to his.

Adam's pupils dilated, confirming my fears. *It was him.*

I whipped my hand out of his and stood. "I'll give you two some space."

"Is everything okay, Cassidy?" Liam asked with a frown. "You look startled."

"No, no." I squeezed his hand to reassure him. "I just remembered something I have to do."

"Well, bless you for reading to me. Enjoy the beach tomorrow."

"I will. Thank you." Not daring another glimpse in Adam's direction, I offered Liam a tight smile before racing out of the room.

"Excuse me, Gramps," I heard Adam say before his footsteps followed. "I'll be back in a sec."

I grasped my bedroom door handle a moment too late.

"This is a pretty elaborate scheme to see me again."

I squeezed my eyes shut. "Trust me. I had no plans of seeing you again." I turned slowly, forcing myself to meet his tapered gaze. "If I'd had any idea, I wouldn't have taken the job."

His ice-blue stare was void of warmth. "Then it will be easy for you to quit."

"What?" My head jerked backward. "I can't. I need this job."

"Then I'll have you fired."

"You're not my boss," I spat back.

He pursed his lips as his tongue rolled around his cheeks.

"Look, just let me do my job and I'll stay out of your way."

"Your job?" Adam stepped closer, entering my personal space and out of Liam's ear shot. "Making money off my grandfather's death is not a job. It's a scam. People like you disgust me."

Fury surged through my body. "How dare you! You know nothing about me."

"Oh...I know you." He drew his arm above my head until my back pressed against the door. "I know you're a liar and a cheater." He ran his knuckle down my arm and over my hand until my wedding ring rested between his fingers. "I bet your husband doesn't know what we did."

My eyelashes fluttered as I tried to regain control. "You're right." I lifted my chin as a tear tracked down my cheek. "He doesn't."

"That's what I thought."

My fingers curled into a tiny fist as I stifled the desire to punch his smug mouth. "Because he's been dead for four years."

As Adam's shoulders fell, I spun around and opened my bedroom door. "Enjoy your visit with you grandfather," I uttered, before slamming it on his arrogant, ignorant, and ridiculously beautiful face.

Chapter 5

It was supposed to be simple. Help an elderly man live his last days on his terms, then head home to live the rest of my days on mine. But my life was never simple, and if the universe had a plan for me, it was a cruel one.

After my grandmother passed away from cancer, my sister and I were sent back to live with my father in upstate New York. Amy adjusted well, but I hated it. The day I turned eighteen, I caught a bus back to LA with no money or plans, only enduring optimism that things would work out. And they did. *Sort of.*

Dominic swept me off my feet the moment he walked into the café I was working at. He was a complete gentleman, handsome, sweet, and treated me right. He had a house in the Valley, a good job, and could offer me the stability I craved. Within a year, I was pregnant and walking down the aisle with my first love. It was a fairy-tale. Only the ending was far from happy.

Finn was only four when Dominic got sick. Five when he could no longer work. And six when he could no longer function. Motor Neurone Disease stole my husband and the father of my child in three heartbreaking years.

After Dominic lost his job, we lost our health insurance, and when I lost my husband, I was left with the astronomical medical bills. I had to sell our home and move back to my father's just to pay off a portion of the debt we owed, and once this job was over, my debt would finally be cleared.

And now this!

Ramming my head into the pillow, I cursed myself for being so careless. Adam must've thought I was a complete slut, letting him consume me for an entire night. The one fucking night I decided to free my inhibitions and have a good time. *What were the fucking chances?!*

I never thought I'd see him again. Sure, I may have dreamt about it, but the fantasy never panned out like this. Adam wasn't supposed to have a name or a backstory. He was simply the hot suit who fucked me senseless after a shitty job interview. That was it. An old-fashioned, no-complication, no-expectation, one-night stand. Now, I was left to endure his presence every other weekend. *The universe can eat a dick.*

———

Although it was easy to avoid Adam in the vast grounds of Harlow Manor, I planned to stay in my room until he left on Monday morning—that was, until my phone chimed.

Wallace (Harlow Manor Driver): **Your ride awaits.**

Fuck. I'd totally spaced on my trip to the beach. It was the only outing I was going to allow myself during my stay, mostly because it cost nothing, but also because it would help me recharge. With the unstable energy I was likely to absorb over the next few months, I was going to need it.

Me: **Thanks. I'll be down in a minute.**

Throwing my cell into my tote, I raced over to my crystal-covered desk and gathered them up, including the hand-woven bracelets intertwined with gemstones. My grandmother had made them for me as she succumbed to cancer.

After checking the hallway for movement, I bolted for the stairs. During my ninja-like decent, William Harlow's voice soared up the staircase from the drawing room, and I froze. Although, he wasn't talking to me.

"I have a right to know what's going on with my company."

"It's my company now, Dad."

"Maybe so, but I'm the one responsible for its success."

Adam growled. "I've made Harlow Corp. more money in the last five years than any of my predecessors. Give me some fucking credit here."

"I'll give credit where credit is due. You got lucky with Warren Media."

"You're unbelievable," he grumbled. "I'm going to spend some time with Gramps."

My heart lurched at his nearing footsteps, so I picked up my pace. The doors flew open and Adam stepped into the hallway, almost colliding with me.

His mouth parted while I emitted a tiny gasp.

"Excuse me," I murmured before lowering my gaze and continuing my journey to the mudroom. As employees of Harlow Manor, we were only permitted to use the back entrance unless we were escorted by a member of the household, and I wasn't about to give Adam a reason to have me fired.

Liam's driver, Wallace, drove me to the closest beach. It wasn't far, but it was too far to walk while I was on call. Wallace remained close by if I needed a quick return, but I wasn't concerned. Liam wasn't going anywhere—not for a couple of months at least.

The beaches in the Hamptons were nothing like LA's, but the ocean was enough to clear my head, my heart, and the assortment of crystals I'd brought with me. My precious collection was filled with negative energy from my first week at Harlow Manor, and I desperately needed to clear them in the salt water.

One by one, I dipped them into the freezing water, cleansing, and recharging, and preparing them for the week ahead. With each dunk, I made certain to cover the bracelets my grandmother had made for me before she died. They were beautiful handwoven strings of crystals, all given to me with a purpose—to help me cope with the gift I inherited from my mother. The gift that was her curse.

I didn't remember too much of my mother, other than the fleeting memories of walking into the bathroom to find her crying in the bathtub. She'd quickly cover her tears with a splash of water and pretend everything was okay. I knew she wasn't, but I didn't know how to help her back then. *If only.*

My father believed she was too sensitive and unstable, and he convinced her to go to the doctor. She was prescribed anti-depressants in an instant, and seemingly, all our problems went away…until the day they came flooding back. The day she left us.

Without my father's knowledge, she'd stopped taking her medication. My mother must have felt every emotion she'd muted in those years, and without knowing how to channel her gift, the pain was too much to bear. My father bore that guilt and, in turn, neglected us.

I returned to Harlow Manor an hour later, feeling much lighter. The house was quiet, so I tiptoed up the stairs and into my bedroom, closing the door softly behind me. Placing my bag onto the desk, I picked out my glistening bracelets and slipped them over my wrist before methodically arranging the other crystals around the room.

Amethyst by my bed to help me sleep, citrine in the far-left corner to attract money, and rose quartz by Finn's picture on my bedside. My love.

As I positioned the lovely pink stone on the nightstand, a light tap on the door had me knocking the crystal to the floor. "Damnit," I muttered, scooping it into my hand as my heart hammered in my chest. I could already sense Adam's presence.

I cautiously approached the door and opened it a fraction to find Adam shuffling his feet while his hands rested in the pockets of his jeans.

"Does Liam need me?" I squeezed the crystal tight in an effort to stop my eyes from wandering down the tight sleeves of his navy t-shirt.

"No." He gazed down the hall. "He's um…taking another nap."

"Can I help *you* with something?" I asked with an edge of impatience. The longer I stood in front of him, the more I wanted *more* from him.

He shook his head. "No."

"Then, why are you knocking on my door?"

"I, um…" His jaw pulsed, clearly struggling with his next words. "I wanted to apologize."

My eyes widened. "Oh."

"For assuming you were a scam artist." He rubbed the back of his neck with a wince. "And the other stuff." He swallowed. "I didn't know...about your husband."

"How could you?" I huffed. "You didn't even know my name until yesterday."

"You didn't know mine either." Adam folded his arms. "So you're hardly the innocent party here."

"You saw my ring and slept with me because of it." I matched his stance. "What does that say about you?"

His deep chuckle made me equally irritated and aroused. "It says, I like to fuck women who won't bother me again."

I bit the inside of my cheek as I stared into his blue eyes, ignoring how much they'd softened since the day before. "Well, you hit the jackpot with me."

His gaze dipped to my lips as molten lava swirled between us. The memory of our night together still burned, but there was something else. Something deeper. Something innate.

"Goodnight, Adam," I muttered, ignoring the pull.

"Yeah." He cleared his throat as he fell back a step. "Goodnight, Cassidy."

I quickly closed the door and planted my head against it as I attempted to catch my breath. He felt it, too. I knew he did. The energy between us was as vibrant as the night we met. This was going to be a problem, albeit an every-other-weekend one, so I'd have to be well prepared. While Adam was around, there'd be no drinking, no losing inhibitions, and no forgetting my purpose here. I had to remain in complete control at all times, or I was screwed.

———

Thankfully, Adam was gone the next morning while his parents left that afternoon for Europe. Once Mrs. Fredrich departed Monday morning, I was finally able to get back into the routine Liam and I had agreed upon the week prior. It was so much easier to do my job without the added stress of his family.

While Liam slept—which was a lot—I visited the library at the end of the hall, not far from his bedroom. It was my favorite room in the entire house, situated within the magical turret of Harlow Manor, and I spent most of my free time there.

Bursting bookshelves lined every wall, only broken apart by a huge window overlooking the gardens below. Each view held a million stories, and I couldn't wait to dive in. I'd finished the book I'd brought from home and was ready to choose another.

Using the ladder on wheels, I rolled myself across the wall, inspecting Liam's late wife's collection of romance novels. She was clearly a sucker for a happy ending as much as I was, so the options were endless. There were all types of romance: historical, contemporary, rom-coms, even a little erotica thrown into the mixed bag of treats for me to enjoy.

Piling a few of interest under one arm, I carefully climbed down and made my way past the two antique wingbacks to the excessively cushioned window seat. Not only was there a spectacular view of the estate, but I could see the ocean in the distance.

While choosing which novel to delve into first, I found myself chewing the side of my thumbnail—a bad habit I'd broken years ago. With Adam at the forefront of my mind, I questioned whether a billionaire romance would be a sensible option. Would it make me more hot and bothered? Or would it scratch the enduring itch I'd had since our night together?

I hadn't been able to erase Adam from my mind since we locked eyes—not just this weekend, but at the bar over a month ago. It was the most intense session I'd ever had, and I wasn't likely to forget it anytime soon, if ever. Every character of every book I'd read since had morphed into him. His face, his body, those hands…argh. I couldn't let myself think about those things now. He was Liam's grandson. My client. A no-go zone.

Frustrated that the mere thought of Adam was disrupting my book choice, I piled the novels onto the windowsill, and left the room, grumbling.

———

"Are you excited about this weekend?" Nora asked Liam while she filled in his chart.

"Bursting," he replied, emitting a glow.

My gaze panned between them as I sat at his bedside. "What's happening this weekend?"

Liam grinned. "My great-grandson is coming to stay."

"Oh, that's wonderful!"

"You'll love Josie, Cassidy." He swallowed the medication Nora handed to him. "I think you two will hit it off immediately."

"Well, I can't wait to meet them." Josie had been my sister's best friend for years, but we'd yet to meet.

"And don't worry." Liam's eyes softened. "Grayson is nothing like Adam."

"Why would you say that?" Had he overheard our argument in the hallway?

Nora lifted her gaze and watched me as I shifted in my chair.

"I'm assuming Adam wasn't very hospitable while he was here."

I forced a nonchalant shrug. "He was fine."

"Cassidy…" Liam's tone grew deeper. "I will not have you treated with disrespect in this house. So, if he, or anyone else in my family, causes you any grief, you let me know."

"Thank you, Liam, but honestly, it's fine." I squeezed his hand. "There are always teething issues when it comes to these situations."

"Maybe so, but I want you to feel comfortable during your stay here."

"You don't need to worry about me, Liam. I can handle your family." *Well, most of them.*

Liam smiled as he closed his eyes. "I believe so, too."

Chapter 6

Grayson, Josie, and baby Harrison arrived late Friday afternoon and I was immediately struck by how similar Grayson was to his brother. They were both textbook attractive with their muscular builds and chiseled jawlines, but Grayson's dark hair was a complete contrast to Adam's blond locks, and his eyes were an undefined hazel-green as opposed to Adam's crystal blues. I imagined their main differences laid within their personalities.

From what my sister had told me, Grayson was a sweetheart, totally smitten with his wife and now a doting dad. He cared about the people in his life and moved away from the family business to follow his heart. She never mentioned his brother.

Josie, Amy's best friend, was just as striking and completely different to what I had envisaged. I expected her to be a snooty rich girl, but she surprised me with her down-to-earth, quirky sense of humor with a refreshing Australian accent. I quickly understood why Liam thought we'd get along. We were outsiders—or at least, Josie used to be.

Although Liam wanted me to stay and chat with his family, I remembered Caroline's instructions and returned to my room to give them privacy.

While they caught up, I lay on my bed and continued reading the steamy romance novel that had been keeping my libido in check all week. But when pacing footsteps and the unforgettable sounds of a grizzly baby sounded from the hall, I slipped in my bookmark and placed the book back on the nightstand.

When the crying increased, I opened my door and peeked out to find Josie rocking her son.

Her tired eyes lifted to mine. "I'm so sorry for disturbing you." She tapped Harrison's back as she swayed. "I don't know what's wrong with him today."

"It's perfectly okay." I offered her a warm smile, remembering those early days. "Would you like me to try and settle him?"

"I'll try anything right now. He really needs to go to sleep."

"He may be picking up on your stress." I reached out as Josie placed the baby into my arms. "This must be a very overwhelming time for you both."

She glanced back toward Liam's room. "Yeah…it is."

"Why don't you go and sit with him, and I'll stay out here with Harrison."

"Are you sure? I don't think babysitting is in your job description."

"But caring for Liam's family is. You go. I'll be here with a sleeping baby when you get back."

Josie's eyes welled. "Thank you so much, Cassidy."

Within minutes of Josie returning to Liam's room, Harrison had fallen asleep in my arms. He was a beautiful baby with dark-brown hair, long lashes, ten tiny fingers and toes, and the cutest little dimple in his cheek. How I longed for those days again, when everything was simple and the biggest decisions I had were working out if Finn needed sleep, food, or a diaper change. Now, I had a whole slew of worries. How quickly things can change.

"You're so natural with him," Josie whispered, breaking me out of my baby daze.

I smiled down at his sweet little face. "What can I say, babies love me."

"If that's the case, I love you, too. Maybe even more than Grayson at this point."

I laughed. "Don't worry. It gets easier…" I cleared my throat. "So I hear…"

Josie's hand grazed my forearm. "Cassidy…it's okay, I know about Finn."

My eyes widened in fear.

"Don't worry, I won't say anything," she quickly added. "Amy has already sworn me to secrecy. Not even Grayson knows."

My stomach knotted. "Do you think I'm a terrible mother?"

"The opposite, actually. You've been dealt a terrible hand, and you're trying your best to move on with your life. I know all about that."

I breathed a shaky sigh. "I miss my boy so much, and it's only been two weeks."

"Of course you do." She rubbed my arm. "He's your world."

I held back tears and smiled. I could feel her empathy. She understood.

"And if you ever need baby cuddles to ease your heartache, I know a guy."

"Well, I'll happily give you a hand with Harrison. He's an angel."

"Not at night he isn't."

"If you ever need some time to yourself…or with Grayson… or you just want a nap, I can mind him for a little while. I'm sure Liam would love to spend any extra time with him."

"Thank you, that is very generous, and I think I'll be taking you up on it. Grayson isn't dealing with this situation with Gramps very well, and the lack of sleep isn't helping."

I offered her a sad smile. "I'm sure it's hard on you, too. Liam told me you've grown close."

Tears glazed her eyes. "He's just so…genuine. Without him, Grayson would've been a very different person—even Adam, to an extent."

I frowned. "How so?"

"Have you met their father? He's obsessed with wealth and power. Grampa has been the only person in their lives keeping them grounded. He reminds them of what life is really about and gives them the love and understanding they deserve. He encouraged both Grayson and Adam to find their own paths, and in completely different ways, they have."

"And how do you think Grayson's brother is coping with this?"

"Adam? Ha. He's not. He just buries himself in more work to avoid facing it. To be honest, we're all a little worried about him."

"Is there someone else in the business who could take over for a while?"

"There are many, but he chooses to be involved in everything. Personally, I think he's avoiding feeling any emotions at all."

My heart dipped. "You're probably right."

———

The next day, I helped Liam down to his garden, where Josie and Grayson waited with Harrison with a surprise picnic under the elm tree. Liam held the baby in his frail arms while Josie took photographs of the two of them and close ups of their hands entwined. The perfect contrast of old and new.

In many ways, a baby helped soothe the transition into end-of-life. I could already feel Liam's love for their little family and the contentment of watching them together. His peace radiated through his hazel-green eyes, and he knew, come time, they'd be okay.

"There you are," a voice called out, drawing our attention.

A good-looking man in his mid-thirties strode toward us with Max by his side. His dark hair and sparkling brown eyes were no match for the stethoscope draped over his neck. Any man who saved lives for a living instantly scored a ten, regardless of looks.

"Hey, Doc," Liam said with a welcoming smile.

"I was in the area and thought I'd check in on you."

"No need. I'm as fit as a fiddle."

The doctor laughed, showing off his perfectly straight teeth. "Alright, then." He caught sight of me and did a double-take. "Is this your new girlfriend?"

Liam chortled in delight. "Don't scare the poor girl, Marc. Cassidy is my death dealer."

"Doula," I corrected.

Grayson sniggered while Josie punched his arm.

"Hi, Cassidy." He reached out to shake my hand. "I'm Liam's doctor, Marc. I'm sure I'll be seeing a lot more of you."

The way he gazed over my body spread the heat in my cheeks

southward. "I hope so—I mean, yes. I'll be here." I closed my eyes with a wince as he diverted his attention to Liam.

"I'll return in a few days for a full check-up." With a nod of acknowledgment to Josie and Grayson, he turned back to me as I endeavored to reclaim composure. "Lovely meeting you, Cassidy."

"Likewise," I rasped out.

While Grayson wheeled his grandfather back into the house, Josie sidled up beside me. "He was cute."

"Was he?"

"As if you didn't notice." She giggled. "And he had his eye on you."

I gushed. "He was cute, wasn't he?"

"Maybe he'll ask you out."

"Oh, I don't think that would be appropriate."

"I can't see why not. You're free on weekends, aren't you?"

"It's not that. It's just…" I twirled the ring on my finger.

Josie gasped. "I'm so sorry. You're not ready. I shouldn't have said anything."

"No, it's okay. You'd think after four years I would be."

"It's hard letting someone in after you've lost someone, but it can be worth it. Grampa reminded me of that when Grayson and I were just starting out, and look at us now." She smiled down at Harrison, babbling in her arms. "When you meet the right person, you'll find there's more room in your heart than you think."

"I hope so, for Finn's sake more than mine. He going to be a teenager before I know it, and he's going to need a man to talk to."

"Perhaps Reed could offer some advice when the time comes."

I cackled. "Finn would be mortified. They're gaming buddies."

"Well, I'm sure you'll find someone. Or just take the bull by the horns, do some research, and give him the run down. He'll probably benefit from a female point of view—or at least, his girlfriends will."

I sniggered. "You're probably right, plus I barely have time to date anyway. I need to focus on getting our lives back on track."

"Amy mentioned you're still paying off your husband's medical costs. I'm really sorry. You shouldn't have to deal with that after such a loss."

"I just have to keep moving forward, little by little."

"You'll get there."

I stopped in my tracks and turned to her. "Hey, thanks for putting my name forward for this job. I'm sure you had a lot of resistance to the idea."

"There aren't many people like you, and Grampa thought you were perfect. I think this family—even if some of them don't realize it yet—is blessed to have you here during this time."

"Hopefully I can make a difference."

"You already are. I've never seen Grampa this happy."

"I think Harrison has something to do with that."

"Maybe...but I think your company has lifted his spirits."

"I hope so."

"May I ask how you do it? This job, I mean? After my parents died, I couldn't bear to be around the grief that followed. It's the reason I moved from Australia to New York."

"I thought the same way after my mother died suddenly. But after watching my grandmother succumb to cancer and a vicious disease take my husband, I realized that losing someone through illness was different. The grieving process starts while the person is still alive, and I'd do anything to help ease that pain for others. That was why I became a death doula. I decided to embrace death instead of wallowing in the misery of it."

"That's actually really beautiful." Josie blinked away tears. "You're a fucking superhero."

I burst out laughing. "Or just a new-age whack job."

She linked her arms through mine. "New-age whack jobs are my favorite people."

Chapter 7

Once Liam and I sorted out the details of his final wishes, I began some alternative therapies to help relieve the pain and anxiety I knew he was feeling. I preferred to get the harder, more emotional stuff out of the way earlier on, because the closer we came to the end, the less coherent the patient got, and the harder they were to understand.

As I sat beside him with my hands hovered over his body, I closed my eyes. My grandmother taught me Reiki before she passed, and I used it daily on my husband in his final years. I'd placed crystals around Liam's room to create a more peaceful space and played soft music all day and night. They were small things, but if I could make him a fraction more comfortable, I would.

"Reiki, I presume," a voice crept up beside me. I was so absorbed I hadn't noticed we had company.

I lowered my hands and stepped back with a nervous smile. "Yes."

Liam's doctor moved closer. "May I feel your hands?"

A shiver of anticipation rolled over me. "O…kay," I stuttered, sliding my hands into his waiting palms.

"I've always been fascinated by how warm your hands get after treatment."

"You're familiar with the practice?"

"I familiarize myself with everything that can make someone feel better."

I cleared my throat. "Well, it's your turn now." I pulled back and rotated to Liam, who was watching curiously. "I'll come back and read to you once the doctor is finished with your check-up."

Marc slipped out his cell phone and handed it over. "Put your number in my phone, and I'll buzz you when I'm done."

"Sure." I hesitantly took it from his hands, entered my new cell number, then handed it back.

Marc slipped it into his back pocket. "We shouldn't be too long."

"Thank you, Cassidy," Liam said on my way out. "I'll see you soon."

My phone chimed half an hour later.

Marc: **All done *smiley face***

Me: **How's he doing?**

Marc: **Apparently, he's in no pain whatsoever.**

Me: **Well, he's a big, fat liar.**

Marc: **LOL I know. I want to run some blood tests, so I'll be back in a few days.**

I grinned. It was nice receiving texts from a man especially a smart, charming, and handsome one. It may have been on professional grounds, but I sensed his curiosity.

I was flirting with the idea of dating him when my thoughts pulled me back to my night with Adam. It took me days to recover after that. Not only physically, but emotionally. I wasn't built for one-night stands. It wasn't in my make-up, and the embarrassing tear fest Adam had induced that night only affirmed it.

After reading to Liam, I returned to my bedroom to video-call Finn before dinner—our nightly routine. Through a terribly slow and unreliable internet connection, we talked about school, his friends, and how he was doing with his swimming. He seemed happy enough, which eased the weight off my shoulders, but I hated not being there to feel his energy.

In person, I could read Finn like a book, but through the screen, I was clueless. Who knew what was whirling through his mind? My father assured me everything was fine, but he was never very good with emotional support, so his opinion meant nothing.

He had shut down after my mom died and shut us out. Amy and I were left to fend for ourselves in our darkest time, and I'd never forgiven him for it. He knew it too. He was trying extra hard with Finn, and in some ways, I was grateful, because as a grandfather, he was pretty great.

My phone buzzed, and I picked it back up, assuming Finn had forgotten to tell me something.

Amy: **How's it going, sis?**

Me: **Great.**

Amy: **Any cute guys?**

Me: **Did Josie tell you about the doc?**

Amy: **What doc?**

Me: **Never mind.**

Amy: **Tell me about the doc?!**

Me: **He's cute.**

Amy: ***face palm***

———

Marc returned to Harlow Manor on Friday afternoon to go over Liam's medication with the nurses. While chatting and laughing with him in the hallway, I spied Adam walking up the hall, rolling his suitcase behind him. His hard gaze met mine, then Marc's, before disappearing into his room with a notable snarl.

"I should get going," Marc announced with a sigh. He clearly didn't want to leave as much as I didn't want him to.

"So, I'll see you next week?"

"Yes. Liam's bloodwork should be ready by Tuesday."

"Great," I said, too enthusiastically.

His dimples deepened with his smile. "Perhaps I could check in with you over the weekend?"

"Of course! I'll be here!" *Oh my God, kill me now.*

"Good." He pressed his lips together, like he was holding back. "Well, I better go. I have to get back to the city. You know how it is."

With equally awkward grins, we returned to Liam's room, where Marc collected his medical bag.

"Enjoy your weekend, Cassidy." His gaze held mine before drifting to Liam. "And Liam. No parties, okay?"

"No promises," he uttered with a coarse chuckle. "Mrs. Fredrich is a wild one."

As Marc snickered on his way out, I moved to Liam's bedside, sensing his pain from across the room. I sat in the chair beside him and took his hand to massage his pressure points, hoping to ease some discomfort.

"Marc's quite taken with you."

"Oh, he's just doing his job."

"He normally just calls the nurse to take my blood, so I suspect he was here to see you."

My mouth slackened but snapped shut when Adam strolled into the room.

"Hey, Gramps." He nodded in my direction but remained expressionless. "Cassidy."

I smiled tightly in acknowledgment but said nothing.

"How was your week, Adam?" Liam asked with genuine interest.

"Busy." His gaze locked onto the crystals on his grandfather's nightstand. "What the hell are those for?"

I stood. "I should go."

"Nonsense." Liam grasped my hand. "Unless you have a date with a certain young doctor you need to get ready for?"

Adam's gaze shot to mine. "That's not very appropriate."

"Oh, they're grown adults, Adam...relax."

My temper spiked, but I diffused it with a deep breath. "Unfortunately for me, my evening entails a good book and a glass of wine."

"Adam, why don't you show Cassidy where we keep the good wine."

He gaped. "But I just got here."

"And we have the whole weekend. Plus, I need a nap in preparation for our game of chess later."

Adam sighed. "Very well."

"You're a good boy, Adam."

I met his gaze and lifted my brow. *Not last I checked.*

He tipped his head toward the door. "Let's go."

Once we were a safe distance from Liam's room, I turned around. "It's okay, Adam. You don't have to."

He marched past my solitary stance and down the hall. "Come on."

I had to jog to catch up with his strides. "Slow down. I'm going to get lost." I trailed his steps down the staircase, through the dining room, and into the kitchen, wishing I'd scattered breadcrumbs in my wake. There was no way I'd find my way back. Harlow Manor was a labyrinth.

We finally reached a spiral staircase that descended into an ominous dark hole in the floor.

"Are you taking me to the dungeons?"

"Something like that." Adam chuckled. "Unfortunately, I left my handcuffs at home."

At the shockingly welcomed visual, Adam flicked on the light switch. "Are you coming?" He peered back as he ran his hand over the handrail. "Don't forget to hold on."

I was momentarily stunned by his innuendo before shaking it off and following him into the void below. I took each step with care until I reached the floor of a long, narrow room lined with hundreds of wine bottles. "Holy shit."

"Wait until you taste one." He ran his fingers along the dusty bottles. "What year were you born?"

"1991."

"That's a good year."

"How do you know?"

With soft chuckle, Adam ignored my question and pulled out a bottle. He showed me the label printed with my birth year, then grabbed a corkscrew. After opening the bottle, he placed it on a wine-barrel table to aerate.

He slid two large wine glasses from the tiny, purpose-built bar off to the side of the room. "So, you and the doc, eh?"

I rubbed my arms, suddenly aware of the cooler temperature in the room. "I don't think so. I barely know him."

He placed the glasses next to the wine bottle, then lifted his gaze to mine. "I didn't think that mattered."

My lips pursed as I looked away. "Well, it does…normally."

Adam grew silent as he poured the wine. "So, how much do you know about wine?"

"Oh, loads. I used to spend my summers working at this little vineyard in the south of France."

He frowned. "Really?"

"No." I snorted. "But I'm guessing you did."

"Well, no…" He cleared his throat. "Not every summer."

I smiled. "My mistake."

"Come on," he grumbled, pulling up two stools. "I'll show you how to pick a good wine."

Before I was allowed to take a sip, Adam divulged into his vast knowledge of the region, the grapes, and the process, all while swirling his glass in circles to examine the residue dripping down the sides. It was long, and I was thirsty, and he was lucky he was so pretty, because anyone else would've lulled me to sleep by now.

He took a sip, swished it around his mouth, and finally swallowed. "And that's how you can tell a good wine."

I held onto a straight face until laughter burst from my lips.

"What?" Adam narrowed his gaze.

"Seriously? You sound like a complete douche."

His mouth fell open.

"You want to know how *I* can tell a good wine?" I lifted the wine to my mouth and tipped it in. I was about to swallow when the glorious flavor hit my tastebuds. "Oh, wow. That's actually pretty fucking amazing."

Adam shook his head with a smile. "Like I said, it's a good year."

I took another sip of the heavenly liquid. "So, what does your year taste like?" I asked before my head caught up with my mouth. My eyes bulged.

His deep chuckle stirred something below. "We'll open that another time."

I cleared my throat and looked away, suddenly fascinated by the walls of wine while I enjoyed the rest of the glass. I occasionally peeked back and found his gaze had migrated south. He was clearly still fascinated by my breasts, and by the two small rises of my top, my nipples were fascinated by him. I needed to distract us both. "I met your brother and sister-in-law last weekend." I grinned. "And your gorgeous nephew."

Adam refilled his glass, then mine. "I haven't seen them since Harrison was born."

"What?" I gasped. "Why?"

"I live in LA, they live in Manhattan, and we both run multi-million-dollar companies—wait." He sniggered. "That's Gray. I run a multi-*billion*-dollar company."

"Surely you can take some time off," I said, ignoring his declaration of wealth. "What's the point of all the money if you can't find time to enjoy it?"

He folded his arms and leaned back on his stool. "I enjoy making money."

"More than spending time with loved ones?"

His eyes narrowed. "Did Grampa ask you to talk to me?"

"No," I said, screwing up my nose.

He lifted a brow. "Josie?"

"No."

He shook his head. "Look...I'm a busy man. I have more responsibility now than ever before, and I don't need anyone in this family making me feel guilty about where my time is spent."

"Do you feel guilty?"

"I didn't say that."

"No, you didn't." *But I felt it.*

He lifted his glass and let the wine slide down his throat. "I'm here now, aren't I?"

"On the alternate weekend to your brother."

"So? I don't want to overcrowd Grampa."

"It's Harlow Manor. I don't think that will be an issue."

I felt his anger before his words surfaced. "Well, maybe I don't want Grayson's perfect fucking life in my face while I'm drowning in all the fucking work I've had to do since he left the company."

My mouth dropped at his abrupt and unexpected honesty.

"And maybe, just maybe...I don't want to watch the greatest man I've ever known whittle to nothing in front of my eyes."

"Adam…"

"I think we're done here," he snapped, snatching the bottle off the barrel as he stood. "I'm taking this back to my room."

"Adam, wait a sec," I said, instinctively following his anguish.

"You're welcome to join me," he said, turning into my personal space. His chest grazed mine as he lowered his mouth. "But you'll be tasting an older vintage."

I sucked in my breath as I fell back a step. "I…I'm fine."

"That's what I thought," he muttered before whirling around and marching back up the staircase, leaving me incredibly aroused and potentially lost within the maze of Harlow Manor.

——

Adam remained surly for the entire weekend, so I steered clear, barely venturing out of my bedroom until Sunday morning. The walls struggled to mute Adam's heated work calls as he unleashed an angry tirade on his staff, so I grabbed my swimwear and slipped out of the house. It was freezing outside, but the pool was heated, and I'd been dying for a dip since the moment I'd set eyes on it.

I changed in the pool house and left a towel on the sun chair before diving in. The rush of the water over my face provided instant relief from the negative energies flowing through the house.

After a few laps, I released all the air from my lungs and sunk to the bottom of the pool. I loved the quiet under the water. Being a Pisces, it was my element, and once surrounded by it, I felt total peace. Opening my eyes, I stared up through the water's surface, watching the sunlight dance through diamond-like prisms, until it suddenly grew dark.

Waves crashed around my body, flipping me in circles as I tried to make sense of the disturbance. Water sucked into my lungs moments before a strong force brought me to the surface. I coughed and spluttered while glaring at the muscular arms wrapped around my body.

"What are you doing?!" I screamed, pushing Adam off before wading to the water's edge. I hung from the side of the pool and coughed some more.

"What the fuck, Cassidy?! I thought you were drowning!" he yelled back, wide eyed. It was only then that I noticed he was fully clothed. "I was heading out for my morning jog, and I saw you at the bottom of the pool. What was I supposed to think?"

I attempted a retort, but nothing came out. "I guess that would've looked kind of weird."

"Weird?" he growled as he swam to the side of the pool. "You're fucking crazy." He climbed out of the pool and stole my towel, flicking the water out of his hair as he patted down his face.

I followed closely behind. "Just because I do things a little differently, doesn't make me crazy."

His gaze ran down my dripping body, and I was now hyperaware of wearing nothing but a bikini. I wrapped my hands around my body with a snarl.

With a huff, he threw the towel at me and stormed into the pool house to grab another. Once through the doors, he tore off his wet running clothes that were now glued to his well-defined body.

I froze at the sight of his naked torso and drew in an unsteady breath. "Look, I'm sorry. I didn't mean to frighten anyone. It's something I do when I'm feeling overwhelmed. The water relaxes me."

"I can think of a million different ways to relax that don't involve drowning yourself."

"I was hardly drowning. I'm an excellent swimmer."

"Sure."

"I am! I probably would've made it all the way if I didn't..."

"Didn't what?" He scoffed. "Enlighten me on your broken dreams."

I glared back as anger tore through me. "Which one?"

Adam pinched the bridge of his nose. "I'm sorry, Cassidy. That was an ignorant thing to say."

"Yeah." I laughed, only to stifle the threat of tears. "It was."

Before he could respond, I bundled up my clothes and stormed back to the house.

———

That afternoon, I sat in the library, half-reading one of Betty's romance novels and half-spying on Adam from the window seat. He was taking his grandfather for a walk around the gardens.

Why did it have to be him that night? I was perfectly happy keeping that memory under lock and key. Of course, I let it slip out for special late-night occasions, but I was only human. He did things to me, to my body, that I didn't think were possible, and now I craved more.

As if sensing my desire, Adam peered up at the window, and my heart somersaulted. My eyes shot back to the pages in front of me, but I couldn't process a single word.

Once they disappeared from sight, I snuggled under the fur blanket that laid across the seat and basked in the warmth of the fire Max had prepared earlier. If it wasn't for the slight hiccup of Liam's irritatingly gorgeous grandson and missing my son like crazy, this would've been the perfect job.

"What are you reading?"

Adam's voice tore me out of another world. "It's nothing." I flustered with the bookmark until my page was secure.

He leaned against the door frame. "You've been up here for hours. It must be a page turner."

"You could say that." I held up the cover of a man and woman in an intimate embrace. I may as well get the ridicule out of the way.

"Rooomance," he dragged out the word, making my face burn hotter. "I'd hate to spoil it for you…but they get together in the end and live happily ever after."

"Ha-ha." I rolled my eyes as he walked into the room.

"I never would've pegged you as a romance reader."

"What about your grandmother? It's from her collection."

Adam's face fell as he glanced up at the shelves. "Really?"

"Plus, it's not about the ending. It's about the journey of how they get there."

His brow furrowed. "But doesn't it get boring? Knowing the outcome?"

"Not at all. I like the certainty."

His mouth twitched. "And the sex?"

I shrugged. "That's pretty good, too."

Adam knelt down and stoked the fire. "Don't you think those books give women unrealistic expectations of men?"

"Are you worried about being compared to a fictional character?"

He dusted off his pants as he stood. "Like anything could compare to this."

"I wasn't talking about appearance," I said, trying not to smile at his cockiness.

His arms crossed over his chest as he watched me. "Well, you tell me. What's better…real sex…or book sex?"

"Book sex," I replied without taking a breath.

Adam's eyes penetrated mine. "You want to think about that answer?"

I shifted uncomfortably under his stare. "No."

"Well…" He closed the distance between us. "I better up my game."

My back straightened as he leaned over me. "Wha—what are you doing?"

With a chuckle, he grabbed my reading pile from the windowsill. "Research," he uttered inches from my mouth before loading the books into his arms.

My mouth parted as he retreated to the fireplace, where he placed the books onto the coffee table and plonked himself onto the wingback chair.

Not bothering to read the blurb or judge the cover, he grabbed the top one and flipped it open. *Oh shit*. If Adam got any more skills in the bedroom, they'd be writing books about him.

Chapter 8

A twinge of loneliness radiated through my body the moment Adam left the mansion Monday morning. The subtle shift in his attitude the night prior left me wondering if we could be friends. While I read, he continually interrupted me with the funny and unrealistic situations from his book, then encouraged me to disclose mine. As much as I pretended to be irritated, I enjoyed his presence.

It wasn't until Max called Adam to dinner that I felt the divide. Adam's conflicted gaze struck mine, and I almost thought he was going to ask me to join him…until he didn't. He simply offered me a tight smile, dropped his head, and silently left the room.

I scolded myself for expecting more. Men like Adam Harlow didn't interact with the help. He was merely using me to pass the time, or to distract himself from his ailing grandfather. Either way, it was nice to have company in this lonely place, if only for an afternoon.

———

"Ladies," Marc greeted us with a nod when he arrived for Liam's check-up a few days later.

"Oh, hi," I said, from the cozy couch in Liam's room while Nora smiled.

I'd been working on the finer details of the funeral while Nora sat on the couch opposite, organizing his medication.

"If I was twenty years younger…" Nora whispered as Marc continued to Liam's beside.

I couldn't help but giggle. He was definitely a catch.

Marc placed his hands on his hips as he stared down at Liam. "I don't know what you're doing, old man, but your bloodwork came back and everything is looking great. Better than expected, actually."

Liam smiled over to where we sat on the other side of his bedroom. "Looks like surrounding myself with beauty is working a treat."

I shook my head with a smile. Adam was definitely Liam's grandson.

"Oh, Liam." Nora's large frame jiggled with her laughter.

"You're a lucky man indeed," Marc said, catching my gaze.

My cheeks warmed, but there were no butterflies. Not the familiar flutter that invaded my stomach every time Adam was near. I smiled tightly and lowered my gaze back to the job at hand while chastising myself. A perfect, charismatic doctor was making eyes, and I was cock-blocking with the memory of a one-night stand. It was ridiculous. I needed to get Adam out of my head. Fast.

———

"Surprise," Adam's voice filled the room from Liam's doorway.

"Adam!" Liam cried out happily.

I dropped my pencil and lost it amongst the funeral papers sprawled out across the coffee table. I'd been working from Liam's sitting area all week and had a few things to finish before I packed up for the weekend.

"This isn't your weekend," Grayson said, walking around his grandfather's bed to greet his brother.

Josie eased Harrison into Liam's arms. "Most unexpected."

I rummaged up the paperwork and closed my laptop, hoping to sneak out before Adam noticed me.

"I thought it'd be nice to spend some time with my family." He rotated his gaze to mine like the freaking Terminator. "Hi Cass."

I barely found my voice. "Hey."

Josie exchanged a look with her husband before turning back to Adam. "Who are you, and what did you do with Grayson's brother?" She held up her hand. "Wait! Forget that. We'll keep this one," she said, cackling as she approached him for a hug.

Adam grumbled but returned her affection. "I thought I'd delegate some of my responsibilities this week and deal with the rest from here. That's what the internet is for, right?"

Week? Surely, he meant week-end.

Grayson stared at his brother, completely dumbstruck, while Liam's smile grew ear to ear.

"Well, I love seeing my grandsons together." Liam squeezed Adam's hand as he shook it. "It reminds me of the summers you spent here as children. Your grandmother lived for those days."

"So did we." Adam chuckled. "It was a vacation from our parents."

Liam's laughter subsided as he gazed down at Harrison. "You both must promise me that you'll bring all my great-grandchildren here after I'm gone."

"Gramps," Adam growled. "Don't talk like th—"

"Of course we will," Grayson interrupted, watching his son wriggle in Liam's arms. "Harry already loves it here."

Josie's eyes glistened. "We'll come back every season. The gardens are too beautiful to miss."

Liam smiled adoringly at his granddaughter-in-law. "Betty would love that. Make sure you take lots of photos. You can never have enough photos."

"Of course."

While they continued to reminisce about their childhood at Harlow Manor, I discreetly peeked over at Adam while he spoke. His energy completely changed when he was with his grandfather. His shoulders eased, his jaw slackened, and his easy laughter was a shocking delight to my ears. I liked this Adam.

Unfortunately, the Adam I got last weekend was a complete mess. Incredibly well put together on the outside, but on the inside, a complete clusterfuck. I tried not to read his energy, but there was something about him that kept seeping through, like he had a secret gateway into my soul, and I had no means of protecting myself. It was disconcerting.

Not wanting to overstay my welcome while the family was there, I placed the funeral documents into a folder and slipped them into Liam's bedside drawer.

Liam peered up from his great-grandson. "Thank you, Cassidy. I'll take a look at those later."

"There's no rush." I smiled down at the sweet baby. "Enjoy your family time."

"And enjoy your weekend off," he added with a wink.

"Oh, it's going to be epic."

"If you don't have any plans, you should have dinner with us tonight," Josie said, sensing I indeed had none.

I panned my gaze over their faces, taking in their warm smiles until I struck Adam. His expression was unreadable. "Thank you, but you should spend time as a family."

"Don't be silly. We'd love for you to join us."

I bit my lower lip, unsure of my next move.

"I think she prefers the company of books," Adam uttered, barely looking my way.

Annoyance overrode my embarrassment. "Says the man who practically lives in his office."

"She's got you there, brother."

I turned back to Josie. "I'd love to join you," I said, wanting to prove I wasn't the boring bookworm he was insinuating. "I just have to make a call first."

"Great! Meet us back here in an hour. We'll order some pizza."

With a nod, I threw Adam a discreet scowl before marching out of the room. How dare he make assumptions about my life.—*even if they were true*.

———

After my phone call to Finn went unanswered, I spent the next sixty minutes pacing my bedroom. What was I doing accepting a dinner invitation from Liam's family? And with Adam there? I had to tell them no. But once I marched back into the room and spied the pizza boxes sprawled over the coffee table, my stomach insisted I stay.

Liam was fast asleep, but he loved having his family close regardless of his consciousness. He'd arranged for an extra bassinet for his room so Harrison had a place to sleep while Josie and Grayson visited, and that was where their baby was now.

While both young and old slept peacefully, Josie and Grayson occupied one couch, while Adam sprawled out over the other.

"Just in time." Josie handed me a plate as I approached. "We didn't know what you liked, so we ordered a few for you to choose from."

Adam shifted his legs off the couch, but I diverted to the single chair beside him. He snickered softly as I sat, while Josie opened all the boxes to reveal an array of cheesy goodness.

"So, we've got pepperoni, cheese, sausage, and…"—she grimaced— "The Adam special." Josie pretended to gag as Adam's smile grew.

"The spiciest pizza in existence," he said, adding a few slices to his plate. "*Plus* anchovies."

"Spiciest, eh?" I scoffed. "I'll give it a go."

"Uh-uh. No way." Adam pulled the box onto his lap while creating a protective shell around it with his arms.

Josie sighed. "Adam's not a sharer. Clearly."

"Come on, bro." Grayson nodded in my direction. "Give the girl a slice."

Adam's eyes tapered to mine before grumbling. "Fine, but you're going to have to get a little closer if you want some," he said, tapping the empty space beside him.

With an inaudible groan, I stood and carefully maneuvered myself onto the couch. His freshly washed scent doused my sinuses, enticing me to lean closer. The pizza was no match for Adam.

"Are you sure you can handle it?" he asked, adding a slice to my plate. He was either underestimating my tolerance for chilis or something else entirely.

I chose the former. "Are you kidding?"

Adam's eyes dilated as I brought the slice to my mouth and took my first bite. He watched my lips as I chewed, waiting. As the heat filled my mouth, I ran my tongue over my bottom lip, spreading the sensation. "Mmm…it's good." My gaze met his with a shrug. "But I've had hotter."

Adam fell back into the couch cushions and ran his hand over his jawline, speechless.

"Wow, Adam." Grayson hooted. "You've finally met your match."

"So it seems." Adam opened the box so I could take another slice.

As I reached in, our eyes collided.

"I'll have to make it hotter next time," he added with a sly wink.

As the heat in my mouth migrated below, I swallowed, wishing I'd chewed more. Thankfully, Josie and Grayson were too preoccupied with their dinner to notice the sexual energy pulsating between us.

"God, I'm starving," Josie mumbled through her full mouth.

Grayson's eyes widened. "Didn't you just eat an entire bag of *Cheetos*?"

Her narrowed gaze rotated to her husband. "And?"

"And…nothing." Grayson held up his hands.

"Breastfeeding can take a lot out of you," I said, watching Josie rummage through the boxes for her next slice.

"See!" Josie nudged her husband's side. "It's what I've been telling you. Harrison is sucking the life out of me."

As if hearing his name, Harrison stirred awake, causing an enduring groan from his parents.

"How does he always know when we're eating?" Grayson grumbled.

Josie threw her food back onto her plate. "Reheated pizza, it is."

"Just leave him to grizzle for a little while. He may fall back to sleep."

"Easy for you to say, Gray. Every time that kid makes a noise, my boobs think there's a fire to put out."

"Oh my God." Adam squeezed his eyes shut. "Remind me to never have children."

Grayson snorted. "As if you're ever going to."

When Harrison's crying picked up a notch, I stood and approached the bassinet. "May I?" I asked, careful not to interfere. I remembered how sensitive I was as a new mom.

"Oh…" Josie blinked rapidly. "Are you sure?"

"Of course. It's probably a little wind."

Adam sniggered under his breath. "Takes after his father."

Josie and I rolled our eyes in unison while Grayson threw an olive at his brother.

"Seriously, eat." I bundled Harrison up into my arms. "You need your calories."

Josie and Grayson proceeded to argue about who was on night duty, while I wandered around the room, tapping Harrison's back. Once a small pocket of wind escaped his mouth, I placed him back into the bassinet and watched his eyelids fall. There was nothing like the face of a sleeping baby. So beautifully innocent.

When I lifted my gaze, I discovered Adam observing me, and my heartbeat accelerated. Had I given myself away? Did I look too maternal? Too experienced with children? Guilt churned within as I returned to my seat, striving for nonchalance as I nibbled the last piece of pizza Adam had left aside for me.

If he found out I had a child, he'd surely tell his parents or, worse, think I was an unfit mother. Why his opinion of me mattered, I had no idea, but I hadn't come this far to lose my job now.

"Do you do nannying as well?" Grayson asked, donning a charming grin.

Josie punched his arm. "There is no need for a nanny. We can do this, Gray."

"Yeah, I know…but it's been two months…"

Adam frowned. "And?"

I pressed my lips together, trying not to laugh.

"Gray, can we not talk about our sex life in front of strangers— or worse, your brother?!"

Adam snorted. "Oh, man…"

"I'd like to see you go eight weeks without it."

Adam's gaze caught mine, and I sucked in my breath. "It's not that difficult." He turned back to his brother. "You just need better reading material."

Pfft. As if he'd gone without sex for that long. A man like Adam couldn't go a day.

"I don't need to succumb to porn."

"I didn't say porn…" The corners of his lips twitched. "There're better things."

"Fuck, man. I don't want to know what you're into these days—or who." He slumped into the chair and pondered his wife adoringly. "But seriously, Jos. When are we going to have any alone time?"

"Why don't you guys go on a date tomorrow night?" I said without hesitation. "I can look after Harrison."

Grayson's eyes lit up. "Yes!"

Josie grimaced, clearly torn between her motherly duties and husband. I understood her guilt.

"I can help," Adam spoke up out of nowhere.

All heads spun to him.

"What?" Josie let out a strained laugh.

Adam shrugged. "I haven't spent much time with the little guy, so why not?"

Grayson gaped. "Then it's a done deal."

"As long as Cassidy is supervising," Josie added quickly.

Adam folded his arms. "What makes her more responsible than me?"

"It's just that…she has more experience with…"

My eyes widened.

"…looking after people," she added quickly. "Like Liam, for instance."

Adam rolled his eyes. "Seriously, how hard could it be?"

———

"Why do people do this to themselves?!" Adam exclaimed, simultaneously pacing and tapping Harrison's back while he bawled.

"You need to relax." I leaned forward in the wingback chair. "He can sense your tension."

Adam's body stiffened as he endured another wail. "Can you take him now?" His eyes pleaded with mine. "Please?"

"Just give it a few more minutes." I tucked the knitted blanket around my legs with no intention of moving. I was entirely too comfortable and maybe enjoying Adam's discomfort a little too much.

When Harrison's cries grew louder, Adam's nervous energy pulled my attention from the novel I was attempting to read. "Just relax…"

"This is torture. Are you not helping on purpose?"

"Why would I do that?" I asked, frustrated to have lost my place for the fifth time.

"I get the impression you don't like me very much."

"It's not that." I sighed. "I just don't know you."

"What do you want to know?"

"I think, given our situation, it's probably best to keep our distance."

"What are you afraid of? Falling for my charm again?"

"Unlikely. It was bad enough the first time."

"Bad?" His jaw dropped. "It got you into my bed in record time."

"Maybe it was my charm that worked on you."

"Are you saying if another guy had walked into that bar that night and sat beside you, you would've gone home with him?"

A small smile played on my lips. "Perhaps."

"Perhaps my ass."

"Look, let's not talk about the past. You're here to bond with your nephew."

"Well, he needs to stop screaming in my ear."

"He has."

Adam cocked his head back. "Oh." Harrison had fallen asleep on his shoulder.

"Give it a few more minutes, then transfer him to the bassinet." I'd moved it from Liam's room into the library after

Josie and Grayson left for their big date in town. Liam needed the rest after a long day with his family.

Defying my suggestion, Adam took Harrison to the other wingback and cautiously lowered himself into it. Harrison lay across his broad chest, and I feared my ovaries would burst on sight.

"Boring book?" he asked, sensing my stare.

I snapped my gaze back to the words before me as he smirked.

"It's fine." I nodded to the pile of his grandmother's romance novels on the coffee table. "How's the research going?"

"There's no point. I already know every trick..."—he grinned—"*In the book.*"

"Wow." I mocked. "If you think so."

"Enlighten me."

I slid a random book from the pile and pushed it across the table. "Enlighten yourself."

Adam's brow rose as he stared down at it. "Have you read this one?"

"Not yet, but I'm sure you could learn something from it. They're full of surprises."

He grew silent for a moment before easing forward. "I guess I could try another," he uttered before snatching up the novel. After adjusting Harrison into the nook of his neck, he opened the book and began reading.

A half hour later, I peeked over my book to find Adam completely engrossed in his. "You can put Harrison in the bassinet now."

"He's fine." Adam turned the page. "He's keeping me warm."

I had loved it when Finn fell asleep on me as a baby. His steady heartbeat and breathing always lulled me into a deep state of relaxation. "Sounds like you have baby paralysis."

"Yeah." Harrison bounced up and down with Adam's chuckle. "I guess I do."

I basked in Adam's aura and found myself at ease for the first time around him. His softer side was intoxicating, and I couldn't help but steal glances while we read.

"What's so funny?" I asked Adam when he snickered for the sixth time.

"This book." He tapped the page. "It's hilarious. I didn't know romance books could be so…comical."

"You've never heard of a rom-com?"

His expression didn't falter. "Am I supposed to know what that means?"

"Rom-com? Romantic comedy? It's a sub-genre."

"A sub-genre?" Adam's forehead crinkled. "Will there still be hot sex?"

"They all have different heat levels."

"Where do I find the kinky shit? That's what I've been waiting for."

I giggled. "That would be erotica."

Adam closed his book and rested it on his lap. "So, what's your favorite *sub-genre*?"

"Well, up until about a month ago, I'd say… contemporary romance."

He narrowed his gaze. "And now?"

Heat devoured my cheeks as I opened my mouth, with every intention to lie, when the library door creaked open.

"How's my baby?" Josie whispered, creeping into the room. Her mouth fell open when she discovered Harrison asleep on Adam's chest. "Oh."

Thankful for the distraction, I rested my book on the coffee table and stood.

Grayson spotted his son moments after Josie and did a double-take. "Never thought I'd say this, but that suits you, bro."

Adam snorted. "Don't be ridiculous." He held Harrison out to Josie like he'd suddenly developed an infectious disease. "Fun uncle will be as far as I go."

"Fun?" Grayson chuckled. "You may need to work on that, then."

Adam crossed his arms. "I know how to have fun."

Josie, Grayson, and I all laughed in unison.

"See, even Cassidy thinks you have a stick up your ass," Grayson said. "And she's only known you five minutes."

My mouth snapped shut. Grayson had thrown me to the wolves.

Adam's tapered gaze diverted to mine. "I seem to remember having quite a lot of fun some weeks back."

"I'm talking about your All Work, No Play policy," Grayson grumbled. "Not the streams of woman in and out of your bed."

My stomach dropped with my eyes. How many women had he slept with since me? "I should head back to my room." I brushed fuzz off my jeans before meeting Grayson's and Josie's smiles. "I'm glad you got to spend some quality time together tonight."

"Thanks so much, Cassidy. You've gone above and beyond, and Grayson and I really appreciate it."

"Anytime." I offered Josie a small smile. "Harrison was no problem at all."

Adam's eyes bulged.

"Goodnight, guys," I uttered on my way out.

"Night," Josie and Grayson said while Adam mumbled something like it.

Once the library door closed behind me, I raced down the hall and into my bedroom, needing to distance myself from Adam. How could he not be a player? He was a gorgeous billionaire, for fuck's sake. He could have anyone he wanted—or all of them, apparently.

After a quick shower, I threw on my pajamas and climbed into bed, hoping sleep would push away the unsettled feeling in my stomach. I was just another woman who had fallen for his charm, then into his bed, and I was ashamed of myself for being so careless. God knew how many women he'd slept with.

As I lay, staring at the ceiling, I was startled by a quiet knock on the door.

"You asleep?" Adam's voice slipped through the crack with the light from the hallway.

I wanted to keep quiet, but the pull of his voice was too powerful. Before I could scorn myself for having no self-restraint, I slid on my silk robe and opened the door. "What's up, Adam?"

"You forgot your book," he said, holding out the novel I'd left behind.

"Oh." I tried to take it, but he moved it out of reach. "Is this what you like?"

I stared at the sensual book cover, then into his intense blue eyes. "You read it?"

"A few pages." The corners of his mouth lifted.

I planted my hands on my hips. "It has a great storyline."

"I bet it does." He flipped the book over to read the blurb. *"No longer sweet and innocent after being ravished by billionaire, Alex Walker, Sophie yearns fo—"*

I snatched the book out of his hand. "Was there anything else?"

Adam rested his arm on the door jamb and leaned closer. "If you ever want to re-enact any of those scenes, I'll happil—"

"Go to bed, Adam," I said, stepping away from the carnal energy pouring off him.

"I'd prefer yours."

"Adam…" I fought the innate urge to give myself to him.

Adam sighed heavily. "Fine," he muttered before stealing the book out of my hands. "But I'm taking this for inspiration."

As my mouth fell open, he marched across the hall and into his room, leaving me breathless and incredibly hot. And he hadn't even touched me.

Chapter 9

"What the hell is this?" Adam yelled as he stormed into my room the next morning.

I launched out of bed to find him pacing in jogging clothes, waving a folder around. I was too surprised to speak.

Adam's eyes traveled down to my silk-covered breasts, and I quickly threw on my robe. At least my breasts were distracting him from my son's beautiful face on my nightstand.

He slammed the folder onto my bed, seething with rage. "He's not even dead yet, and you're planning his funeral?!"

"Adam." I tugged my robe tighter, holding myself together while I endured his outburst. "This is what I do. This is what I'm here for."

"Well, it's fucking morbid!"

I lowered my gaze, reminding myself he was angry at the situation, not me. "He's dying, Adam."

"But he isn't dead!"

"I know." I met his gaze, hoping the connection would calm him. "But he wants to make sure everything is in place when he does."

"Then why hasn't he spoken to me about this, or anyone in the family?"

"Because he doesn't believe you'll do as he wishes."

Adam stilled. "He doesn't trust us?"

"It's not that." I sighed as I edged closer to where he stood. "Grief can make people quite irrational, and it often leads to families fighting over these important decisions. Liam wants this to be a peaceful time, so that's why he hired me. I'm not a part of this family. I'm objective, and I can make sure his final wishes are fulfilled, before and after his death."

"Oh." Adam drew in a deep breath. "I guess that makes sense. I'm…um…"—he cleared his throat—"sorry for waking you."

As he proceeded to walk out of the room, I called out his name, and he paused.

I waited until he turned before speaking. "In the future, you will knock and only come into my room when invited. This may be your house one day, but while I'm an employee of your grandfather, you will respect my privacy."

With a curt nod, he left my room and I scrambled to hide the framed photo that Finn had given me last Mother's Day into the bedside drawer.

———

The next morning, Adam was gone and so was my book. He'd fucking left for LA after his confrontation and took the novel I was halfway through with him.

Yeah, I could read another, but I was loyal. I couldn't start a new book without knowing how the last one ended. I was invested in the characters. Their love story was enthralling, and the sex…phew. The sex was the raunchiest I'd ever read, and thanks to Adam, very much relatable.

Who knew when he'd decide to come back, or if my book would ever return…or worse…if he was reading it. God knew what he'd think of me if he did. He was practically the main character.

Not wanting to dwell on the possibility of Adam enjoying my latest fantasies, on Monday morning, I threw myself back into work, only to discover another fantasy waiting—the hot doc.

"We're going to have to reduce his outdoor exercise," Marc said after Liam's check-up. "His body is slowly shutting down, and he needs more rest."

I followed the doctor farther down the hallway. "How long do you think he has left?" I asked, dreading his answer to the question I hated to ask.

Marc's sincere gaze surprised me. "My guess…he'll be gone before Christmas."

I closed my eyes. As much as I wanted to go home, I'd never wish this upon Liam's family.

"Don't fret." He placed his hand on my shoulder. "I'll inform the family of his progress."

My heart dipped, and my first thought was Adam. He wasn't going to take it well. "Thanks. I'll do what I can to keep him comfortable."

Marc's hand ran down my arm and cradled my elbow. "I know you will. I'll see you in a few days." His eyes lowered to my lips as I smiled, but they shot up when Max appeared in the corridor, carrying Liam's afternoon tea. "Goodbye, Cassidy," he added quickly, letting my arm slip away.

My eyelashes fluttered as I bathed in his undeniable affection. "Bye, Marc."

———

Over the next few days, I moved Liam's favorite paintings from the walls of Harlow Manor into his bedroom. If he couldn't go outside, he wanted to surround himself with the next best thing: his late wife's beautiful artwork. Each painting presented their garden in a different light, different angle, and different season, all featuring the grand elm tree.

Betty loved spring, so naturally Liam wanted this piece at his bedside. The flowers were in full bloom, creating a striking painting full of color and happiness. I could sense how much Liam loved her, simply by the way he stared into her paintings. His eyes glazed over as he lost himself amongst the delicate brush strokes.

"Your wife was an exceptional artist." I twirled the ring on my finger as I examined the stunning work. "It's no wonder you want to surround yourself with her creations."

"It's not just the painting." A hint of a smile touched his lips. "I see Betty in every detail."

"I understand that." Except, Dominic's creation was a ten-year-old boy.

Liam placed his hand over mine. "Nora told me your husband passed some years ago."

My breath hitched. Thankfully, I hadn't told her about Finn. "Yes."

"Was it sudden?"

My shoulders lowered. "No."

Curiosity filled his paling eyes. "You're a brave woman to do what you do."

"After all the tragedy I've had to endure in my lifetime, I've had to change my stance on death. I don't see it as the end anymore, only a transition."

"Well, as long as I'm with my Betty, I wouldn't care if I was sent to the fiery depths of hell."

"Liam…" I shook my head with a laugh. "Betty's not in hell."

"Oh, I know. She's here. Waiting. But don't mention it to my son. He thinks I'm losing my mind."

"You're not."

"I know it's silly, but sometimes when I'm alone, the scent of her favorite flower fills my room, and I swear she's here with me."

I smiled. "Freesias?"

"How did you know?"

"I've smelled it, too," I said, finally understanding its origin. "It was so beautiful I asked Max what oils he was burning, and he looked at me like I was a crazy person."

He chuckled. "Then we can be crazy together."

"The best people are."

———

Halfway through the week, Max warned of an incoming visit from Caroline and William. After speaking with Liam's doctor, they decided to pause their trip and return to Harlow Manor.

Caroline's mouth fell open when she walked into Liam's room. "What on earth is all this?" she asked, frowning at the easels spread throughout the room.

I closed the book I'd been reading to Liam and rested it

on my lap. "Liam asked me to bring up some of his late wife's paintings."

Liam grinned. "Now I have the best view in the house."

A small sound emitted from Caroline's throat, but she didn't utter another word about it. "May I speak with my father-in-law in private?"

"Of course." I placed the book on his nightstand as I stood. "I'll come back later to finish the chapter."

"No." Caroline moved closer. "The doctor says he needs more rest."

My irritation flared. "Reading is hardly strenuous."

"Listening even less so," Liam added with a snicker.

Caroline's eyes burned into mine. "Regardless..." She turned to Liam. "We were hoping to have dinner with you this evening, so you'll need to have a nap."

"Well, in that case..." He turned to me with a grin. "Cassidy can have the afternoon off."

My gaze panned between Caroline's sneer and Liam's cheeky smile. "Thank you, Liam." I rose to my feet. "But I'll check in with you later regardless."

After Liam thanked me, I strode to the door, only to slow when Caroline blocked my path. "Remember your place here," she said, keeping her voice hushed.

"Oh, I remember. Enjoy your dinner." As my fingers curled into tiny balls at my sides, I stormed out and straight into a solid chest in the middle of the hallway.

"Whoa." Large hands grasped my forearms to steady me. "Who pissed you off?"

I gazed up at the handsome mirage and blinked twice. "What are you doing here? It's not Friday."

Adam dropped his hands and shoved them into his pockets. "I'm well aware, but I heard my parents were visiting, so I thought I'd come a few days earlier to spend time with them." He nodded toward Liam's bedroom. "I'm assuming my mother's in there."

"She sure is," I said with mock enthusiasm.

The line between his eyes deepened. "Did she upset you?"

Frustration simmered beneath my skin. "No, it's fine. Enjoy spending time with your family." I brushed past, eager to disappear, but his hand caught mine. Tingles shot up my arm as I looked up at him in question, but he said nothing. His jaw twitched, his Adam's apple bobbed, and his pupils dilated, but no words came out of his mouth.

My heart quickened. "Adam…"

With a sharp intake of air, he released my hand and disappeared into his grandfather's bedroom without another glimpse my way.

———

Once I was back in my room, faced with an afternoon of twiddling my thumbs, I decided to call my sister-in-law back in LA. She had a knack for cheering me up, and I needed something to take my mind off that bizarre encounter with Adam—and his evil mother.

"Is he dead yet?"

My eyes bulged. "Tash!"

"I'm sorry! But you get paid for the three months regardless, right?"

"Don't be awful. He's a really sweet man."

"You know I'm joking. I just want you back here."

"I know…I do, too. I want to see that belly of yours."

"Oh, it's ridiculous. I'm huge already. I was never this big with Tristan."

"Well, the Ryans produce big babies."

"We sure do. I still don't know how you pushed Finn out of that tiny body of yours."

"Oh, there were stitches. Dominic passed out, remember?"

"My brother was never great with blood."

Our laughter faded with the happy memory. Everything was different now.

"How's Finn coping without you?"

"He tells me he's okay, but I think he's holding back. I'm not there to pick up those subtle clues, and I have to rely on him telling me, and well…he's a boy."

"I'm sure he's fine. Tristan and Finn talk every few days, and he hasn't picked up on anything."

My heart filled with warmth. "I love how close they still are."

"Tragedy will either bring you closer or tear you apart. There's no getting rid of us now."

Moisture gathered in the corners of my eyes. "I miss you guys."

"We miss you, too."

After another hour of catching up on all things Tash, I sat on my bed, shuffling through the books I'd already read on my nightstand. I thought about visiting the library to pick another, but my heart was still stuck in the pages of the book Adam stole. I'd have to find another way to pass the time.

Not wanting to monopolize Liam's driver while his family was around, I ruled out the beach and headed to the pool instead. According to Max, Caroline and William never used the facilities at Harlow Manor, so I was free to enjoy myself.

As I stepped outside, a crisp wind whipped around my face, and I scurried back, opting for the indoor pool instead. Even the promise of warm water couldn't get me out there. Winter in the Hamptons was clearly on its way, and I didn't like it.

The impressive fifteen-meter indoor lap pool was wide enough for two people to swim side by side, and it was any promising young swimmer's dream. The pool spanned across the entire room, with a spa and sauna on one end and a change room at the other. The peaked ceilings complemented the Tudor style, but all the fixtures were modern and impeccably maintained, like the pool was used every day.

The tiles were cool under my feet as I slipped off my flip flops, but it was a welcome contrast to the humidity in the room. I dropped my robe onto the bench and revealed the only swimsuit I owned. As I tightened the straps of my bikini, I stared out the floor-to-ceiling windows, admiring the vast gardens. Harlow Manor was a beautiful place, full of wasted luxuries that people like me could only dream of.

A throat cleared behind me, startling me out of my envious daze.

"I'm sorry, I—" my voice faltered. Adam stood before me in nothing but a towel with sweat glistening all over his sculptured body. "I thought I was alone."

"You were." He moved closer. "I was in the sauna."

"It must've been hot," I murmured, hypnotized by the beads of sweat sliding down his chest.

"It was." His eyes rolled to my breasts and grinned. "The way I like it."

His clear innuendo snapped me out of my trance. "I thought you were spending time with your family."

"I was…" Adam picked up another towel from the stack and wiped it over his face. "But then I remembered my father is a jerk, and my mother is a…" He snickered. "What did you call her the night we met?"

I groaned. "I'd rather not say."

"Oh, that's right. I remember. A complete bitc—"

"Well, I'm sure your grandfather appreciates you being here," I cut in, not wanting to rehash the mortifying conversation.

The light in Adam's eyes grew brighter. "Gramps always does."

I dipped my toes into the pool. "He talks about you and Grayson all the time."

"Oh yeah, what does he say?"

"Oh, that's confidential." The corner of my mouth twitched. "Death doula/client privilege."

Adam's deep chuckle ricocheted off the tiles. "That's not a thing."

I placed my hands on my hips. "It's totally a thing."

"Well, you *are* good at keeping secrets."

I froze. "Why would you say that?" Did he know about my son?

"Like our night together?"

Relief flooded my body. "I don't know what you're talking about."

"As if you've forgotten."

I rolled my eyes as I positioned myself at the head of the pool. "I'm going to swim some laps now."

"Yeah…to cool off."

My tapered gaze panned to his. "I'm swimming to relax."

He crossed his arms, pronouncing his well-defined biceps. "I thought reading relaxed you."

"Well, that would've been an option…had you not stolen my book."

"Oh, yeah." He threaded his fingers through his damp blond hair and grinned. "It was good, too."

My jaw slackened. "You read it? All of it? *In three days?*"

"What can I say? It was…engaging." His smile made my core twitch. "And fucking eye-opening."

"I highly doubt anything shocked you."

"Are you kidding?" He massaged his jawline. "In chapter ten, when he used his tongue to—"

"Stop!" I held up my hand, not to stop him from ruining the story, but to stop his words from becoming my next fantasy.

"Oh, my apologies. You haven't finished it yet. I can tell you what happens, if you want." He stepped closer until his breath grazed my shoulder. "Or I could show you."

"Argh," I grunted before moving to the next diving block.

"Maybe I'll underline my favorite passages."

I blew out all the air from my lungs as I stepped onto the elevated platform. "You're driving me crazy, Adam Harlow."

He chuckled softly as I moved into position. "Likewise, *Tiger.*"

As the familiar pet name struck home, I dove into the water with a loud, embarrassing belly whack, never wanting to resurface.

———

After I had dinner with Finn through a video-call, Max knocked on my door to collect the dishes.

"Thank you, Max. That was delicious."

"It's a family favorite. Liam requests it every time the family visits."

"I can see why." I peeked into the hall. "Are they still downstairs?"

"I just took Liam back to his room, but the others are in the drawing room."

"How is he feeling?"

"Extremely fatigued. Nora may need to speak to the doctor about increasing his pain medication again."

I grimaced. "He's not going to like that." Liam wanted to stay coherent for as long as possible, so upping his meds was the last resort. "Perhaps I could do more Reiki. Liam always sleeps well after our sessions."

Max peered up, hopeful. "If that's possible...we've really exhausted every other avenue."

"Of course. I can see him now if that helps."

"Oh, Cassidy, would you? I know Liam gave you the evening off, but he's very uncomfortable...even if he doesn't say so."

"Say no more. I'm here to help in any way I can."

While Max returned downstairs to tend to the family, I made my way up the hall.

"How did you get past the Wicked Witch of the West Coast?" Liam asked as I entered his room.

I sniggered. "I thought I'd see if you wanted some Reiki to relax you."

"Oh yes." His face brightened. "The last time you did that, I dreamed of Betty."

"Then we shall continue every night. What do you think?"

"I think you're an angel, Cassidy."

I couldn't help but smile as I closed my eyes, taking a moment to prepare. Once I'd taken three deep breaths, I lifted my hands over Liam's chest to channel a stream of healing energy into his body.

"I thought I told you not to come back in here." Caroline's nasty tone snapped me out of my trance.

Liam glared at his daughter-in-law. "You are not in charge here, Caroline."

Her eyelashes fluttered. "But this is ridiculous."

"I'll decide what's ridiculous in my house!"

Liam's burst of anger transformed into a coughing fit right as William and Adam walked into the room.

"Gramps?" Adam rushed to his grandfather's side, while his father paused in the doorway.

"I told you this was out of control," Caroline uttered to her husband.

William scowled at the crystals and oil diffuser. "If I knew she was going to turn the place into some hippy convention, I would never have agreed to this."

"How dare you!" Liam wheezed. "I want Cassidy here."

I grasped Liam's hand. "Please calm down." I kept my tone level. "It's okay. This is a hard time for everyone, and my presence can sometimes exacerbate this. There is no need for you to get worked up." I waited until his eyes softened into mine. "I'll see you at sunrise, okay?"

Liam calmed almost instantly. "My favorite time of day."

I smiled at him once more for reassurance before dropping my head and walking out of the room without a glance in his infuriating family's direction.

———

I couldn't sleep after the altercation with Liam's family, so I tiptoed up the hall and into the library. Leaving the lights off, I pulled the faux *(I hoped)* fur blanket off the wingback chair and dragged it to the oversized window seat, lit up by the full moon.

To my surprise, the book Adam had stolen was sitting on the window ledge, clearly awaiting my discovery. My cheeks burned as I flicked through the pages, wondering if he'd really read it or skimmed for the dirty bits. I guessed the latter.

After tucking the blanket around my curled-up legs, I leaned back against the wall and found the last scene I remember. I was eager to escape the cruel world I lived in, if only for a few chapters.

Before I had a chance to delve back into the story, the door creaked open, letting in a stream of light to where I sat.

Adam's eyes met mine before stepping into the darkness. "I thought you went to bed."

I turned my gaze back to the book. "I'm too wired to sleep."

"Do you need some more light? I can turn on the lamp."

"Please don't. The moon is bright enough."

Adam moved closer to where I sat and peered out the window. "I forgot how bright the stars are out here."

"It really is beautiful."

Adam's gaze burned into my side before I turned to him.

He nodded to the paperback nestled in my hands. "You found your book, I see."

"And the pages weren't even stuck together."

Adam's mouth gaped before emitting a laugh. "Lucky I didn't find my grandmother's romance collection in my teens."

I screwed up my nose. "Oh, gross."

After our amusement subsided, the room fell quiet once again.

"Hey, listen…" Adam rubbed the back of his neck. "I'm sorry about earlier…with my parents."

I gazed down at the now meaningless rows of words. "It's fine."

"No…it's not."

"I'm a professional." I shrugged. "I don't take these things personally."

Adam lowered himself onto the seat beside me, forcing me to look at him. The moonlight lit up half his face, accentuating every beautiful feature. "I haven't seen Gramps put my parents in place like that since Josie came into our lives," he said, resting his forearms on his knees as he clasped his hands together.

"I wish he hadn't."

Adam's eyes shot to mine, hooded under his brow. "You'd prefer to be treated like shit?"

"Of course not. But this isn't about me. Your grandfather doesn't need any more stress."

"But he's doing okay." Adam's denial was evident. "The doc says he just needs to rest more."

"He's in pain, Adam. All the time."

"Gramps told you that?"

"He doesn't have to." I sighed. "I can feel it."

"I…I don't understand. How can you possibly feel what he's feeling?"

I bit my lip, preparing myself for Adam's adverse reaction. "For most of my childhood, I struggled to disperse my emotions from others. My mother and grandmother were the same, even my sister to an extent. I feel people's energies. The good, the bad, and the ugly."

"That sounds…tiring."

"It can be, but my Grams taught me how to protect myself. So now, I can embrace the gift and use it to help people like your grandfather. I use Reiki to help ease his pain and emotional stress, but sometimes, no matter how much I try to shield myself, it seeps through." I blinked back tears. "So, that's how I know Liam's in pain…and your mother's venomous tone is the last thing he needs right now."

Adam's eyes lowered as he pondered my words. "So, that hand thing you do…is Reiki?"

I tilted my head, willing him to look up. "Have you been spying on us?"

He shrugged. "Maybe."

"Look, I don't care if you think it's a bunch of new-age bullshit. You wouldn't be the first."

"No." The V between his eyes deepened as he stared at me. "I don't think that at all. I…I've just never experienced it."

His curious energy ignited my passion. "Do you want to?"

"What?" Adam's head recoiled. "Right now?"

"Right now." I shifted my legs under my body and tapped the space beside me. "Lie down and rest your head on my lap."

"Oookay." He shifted his large frame onto the window seat and lay back, settling his head on my thighs. "I like it already," he uttered, staring directly up at my breasts.

"Adam." I knocked his shoulder. "You'd normally be on a bed for this, but this will do for now."

"I could arrange a bed for our next session."

"You're unbelievable." I endeavored to overpower the rising corners of my mouth. "Now, close your eyes and be quiet. I need to concentrate."

"Is it going to hurt?"

"No." I laughed. "But you may feel some heat, tingling, or pulsing through your body."

His grin widened. "I like the sound of that."

With a groan, I nestled my hands under his head and closed my eyes, taking in long deep breaths until a familiar tingle rippled through my body. "I said close your eyes."

"Alright" He chuckled.

After a few minutes, I moved my hands over his shoulders, and his whole body stiffened. Energy flowed through me and into his body, nurturing every molecule of his being until his entire body relaxed under my touch.

As his breathing slowed, a rush of emotion poured into me, and my eyelids lifted in a dreamy haze. Adam's lustful gaze stared back at me, pulling me in, and I mindlessly succumbed. My head tipped over his, crashing a wave of golden hair over his shoulders as I brought my lips to his mouth. It wasn't until his hands wound through my hair to deepen the kiss that the spell broke.

I pulled away with a gasp. "How did you do that?"

Adam sat up while running his tongue over his bottom lip. "Do what? Kiss you?"

"No." My mouth grew dry as I stared at him, full of trepidation. "You break through every shield, every protection. Our energies entangle, and I can't decipher what emotions are yours and what are mine." I shook my head as I stood. "This has never happened before."

His hand grasped mine, pulling me between his legs. "Then let me help you figure it out." He ran his fingers up and down my arm. "All I've been able to think about is kissing those fuckable lips..." He brought my bracelet-covered wrist to his mouth and dragged his tongue over my pulse. "And the rest of you."

I stumbled backward. "No...this can't happen."

The corner of Adam's mouth quirked upward. "But it already did happen."

"Well, that was a mistake."

Adam rose to his feet. "Maybe..." He closed the distance between us until my backside collided with the wingback chair. "But it's one I intend on repeating."—he dipped his head into the crook of my neck and kissed my delicate skin—"again"—then under my earlobe— "and again"—before crashing down on my lips.

My mouth parted as his hands grasped my lower back, making his arousal clear. My mind turned to mush as his tongue encircled mine, wanting...needing... Or were those feelings mine? *Fuck.*

Fear shot through my body, and I shoved him away. "No." I scowled. "This is my workplace, and I'm a professional. You need to stop."

"It's too late for that, Tiger." He penetrated my soul with his stare. "All I can do now is slow down."

As my mouth fell open, Adam flashed me a drop-dead-gorgeous grin before striding out of the room, leaving me panting helplessly in the dark.

Chapter 10

"Good morning, Adam," Liam said while I poured us a cup of tea. We'd just witnessed another beautiful sunrise.

My head shot up, and I spilled hot liquid all over the saucer.

"Morning, Gramps." Adam's smile widened as he spied me mopping up the mess in a fluster.

"I'm assuming by that smile that your parents are leaving?"

Adam chortled. "They are, but Cassidy is responsible for this grin."

My eyes grew large as I glared at him. *What a fucking prick.*

"She did some of that voodoo that she does on you," he continued. "And I slept like a baby last night."

Liam's brow rose. "Well, I'm glad she did. You need it. You're under far too much stress."

Adam's gaze didn't shift from mine. "Did you sleep well, Cassidy? Or did you stay up all night…reading?"

My stomach clenched. "I fell straight to sleep." *Lie.*

The truth was, while reacquainting myself with the book Adam stole, I discovered he'd underlined an incredibly steamy sex scene, and I couldn't move on. The fact that he'd read those words and pictured those erotic scenes was not only embarrassing but an unbelievable turn-on. He didn't even have to touch or look at me to induce pressure below, and now I was on edge.

"Bullshit," Adam muffled with a cough.

"What was that, son?" Liam asked. "My hearing is going."

His grandson barely flinched. "I asked if you'd like to play some chess."

"Oh yes." Liam sat a little straighter in bed. "The board is in the library."

"I'll get it for you," I said, desperate to put some space between Adam and myself. As I raced out of the room, heavy footsteps followed. "I said I'd get it."

Adam sidled up beside me. "You have no idea where it is."

"I'm sure I can find…" my voice trailed off as I entered the library and panned my gaze over the floor-to-ceiling bookshelves and ornate cabinets.

"It's up the ladder to the right."

With a grumble, I grasped the edges of the ladder and climbed. "Which shelf?" When he didn't answer, I glanced down to find him holding the ladder while admiring my ass. "Adam!"

"What? I'm making sure you don't fall."

I stomped back down until my feet connected with the floor and spun around. "It's not even up there, is it?"

His mouth curved into a smile. "Nope."

"Adam…" I growled. "Stop messing with me."

His blue eyes danced with mine, teasing…beckoning. "I'm trying, but you get worked up so easily." His finger hooked over the waist of my jeans. "In more ways than one."

"Adam," I hissed, ignoring the pulsating heat between my legs. I attempted to push past him, but his hands grasped the ladder behind me, trapping me in.

The tip of his nose grazed along my jawline. "Maybe you should finish that book and take a load off. Masturbation can be quite the stress reliever."

I gasped as I shoved him away. "You're disgusting."

"When you're done, we can compare our favorite passages. I underlined a few."

"Is that what that scribble was?" I resumed my search for the chess board. "Didn't your nanny ever teach you not to write in books?"

Adam snickered. "So, you did read them?"

I began opening cabinets one by one, slamming the doors a little harder each time. "No."

"You should."

I turned to him with crossed arms. My patience obliterated. "And why is that?"

His Cheshire grin pulled my eyes away from the chessboard in his hands. "Because I plan to bring every one of those fuck-filled pages to life."

———

From that moment, under absolutely no circumstances would I allow myself to be alone with Adam Harlow. He had no intention of keeping his hands to himself, and I couldn't trust myself to stop him. How I let that kiss happen was beyond me. The intense energy swirling between us was more powerful than I'd ever anticipated. I felt it that night in Manhattan, but I had assumed it was all me. Adam was the first man I'd been with since Dominic, so it made sense for me to be confused emotionally. But now I wasn't sure about anything.

All I had to do was get through the weekend. Without Adam's parents around, I was on full alert, only leaving my bedroom to sporadically check on Liam or head to the beach to cleanse my crystals.

Clearly aware of my avoidance tactics, Adam made his presence known in another way. A way that had me hot and bothered, resulting in multiple cold showers.

Each time I left my room, I'd return to discover a little note slipped under my door.

The first one read:

Page 154

Once my initial confusion subsided, my cheeks filled with heat. Equally mortified and aroused, I scurried over to my nightstand and flicked through the pages of the book until I found it. Another underlined sex scene with an adjoining smiley face. *Damn.*

The following one read:

Page 230

Another sex scene, steamier than the first. *Very* descriptive.

Then:

Page 342

Wow.

Then, the night before he was leaving:

Fuck me dead. It was too much for my libido to handle.

I slammed the book shut, but it wasn't long before I was peeking back at the words and turning the lights down low. It was going to be a long night.

———

"You're still here." I stopped dead in my tracks as I pushed Liam back into his room after another beautiful sunrise.

Adam was relaxed on the couch, holding his laptop. "I thought I'd work from here this week." He smirked up at my wide eyes. "Turns out, I enjoy the quiet."

And torturing me, no doubt.

"Glad to see you taking a break, Adam," Liam said as I positioned him beside the window.

"I don't *take* breaks, Gramps." Adam typed something into his computer before looking up. "Now that I've upgraded your terrible internet, I can yell at people through the screen just as well as I can in person." He grinned. "While spending more time with you, of course."

My heart lit up. *Faster internet?* I'd finally be able to have a proper conversation with Finn.

"Plus," he continued, running his fingers through his hair. "I think all the travel is getting to me."

Or the grief. It was rolling off him, and he had no idea.

Liam smiled softly. "Well, I'm not complaining. Having you around makes me feel young again."

I remained focused on Liam to avoid any eye contact with his grandson. "Shall I tell Max you're ready for breakfast?"

"That would be lovely, Cassidy. Will you be joining me today? Adam, you're welcome also."

"Sounds great!" Adam's tone was peppier than usual, making me suspicious.

"I'll grab a bite later." I placed my hand on Liam's shoulder. "I have some calls to make, but I'll return soon. I promised Nora I'd have you back in bed before Marc arrives."

"Marc?" Adam's eyes panned from mine to Liam. "Don't you mean Doctor Morrison?"

"Oh, Adam, don't be so formal. Marc is a lovely man who happens to be quite taken with our Cassidy here."

I groaned inwardly. "He's just being friendly, Liam."

"Oh, let an old man have his fun." He waved me off. "It's boring up here."

"Well, your grandson is here to entertain you now, so you can stop trying to meddle."

"Very well." Liam smiled as Adam hammered away on his keyboard. "I'll meddle in his life instead."

Adam moaned. "Gramps…"

"You two are no fun. Perhaps the two of you should go out."

Our fearstruck faces collided.

"I'll go find Max." I made a beeline to the door.

"I've got work to do," Adam muttered at the same time.

As Liam's laughter filled the room, dread filled my stomach. If only he knew how compatible we were…but only in bed.

———

"Your boyfriend is coming up the hall," Nora whispered as she strode into Liam's room to where I sat at his bedside.

My gaze snapped to Adam on the couch in time to witness the subtle pulse of his jaw while he continued working on his laptop.

"Very funny." I enlarged my eyes to alert her to the pricked ears. Adam was adamant about sticking around for the doctor's appointment.

Nora's eyebrows rose. "Oh, Adam, I didn't realize you were still in town."

"Yes, I've decided to stay the week."

Her twinkling eyes traveled to mine. "Your grandfather must love that."

"You bet I do." Liam smiled groggily as he stirred awake.

"It's a full house today," Marc said, waltzing into the room.

He acknowledged everyone with a nod, but his gaze lingered on mine a fraction longer.

I squirmed under Adam's judgment. "Perfect timing. Liam's just waking up now."

"Wonderful." His perfect smile widened as he panned his gaze to his patient. "How have you been feeling, Liam?"

"Fine."

"Tell the truth, Liam," I said, taking a sterner tone.

"Alright... The pain's getting worse."

Marc's eyes softened before picking up his chart. "Unfortunately, that's to be expected at this stage. I'm going to increase the medication for your pain."

"Do we have to do that?" Liam's face was riddled with apprehension. "It makes me so sleepy."

"Your body is under a lot of stress. If we don't, you'll increase your risk of heart failure."

Adam materialized at Liam's bedside. "Can't Cassidy just do more of that Reiki stuff?"

"She does enough, Adam." Liam grasped his grandson's hand before turning to the doctor. "Give it to me straight, Doc. How much time do I have?"

With a growl, Adam tore his hand away and marched out of the room.

My heart ached as I stared at the empty doorway. *Why can't I shut him out?*

Liam sighed. "Cassidy, can you please talk to Adam? He seems to respond to you."

"Of course." With a nod, I trailed after the man I'd sworn to avoid.

Adam's bedroom door was open, but I didn't enter. It was his domain, and I wasn't about to enter a lion's den without permission—*or even with.*

I spied him staring aimlessly out the window. "Want to take a walk with me?"

His despondent gaze turned to mine. "Only if you plan to seduce me."

"Very funny." I muted my smile. "Come on."

We walked through the gardens in silence for some time before I spoke. "When my husband got sick, I tried everything to keep him alive. He was only twenty-five, and we'd barely started our life together. The day he told me he wanted to stop treatment, I was crushed. He had so much to live for, and I thought he was giving up. So, I utilized what my Grams had taught me. Who knows if the Reiki gave him a few extra months or years, but the result was always going to be the same. All I could do was make his final moments as comfortable as possible and celebrate the small pockets of time we had left together."

I stopped walking and turned to Adam. "That's all you have now—those precious pockets of time where your grandfather is alert and happy. You need to make the most of it. Liam doesn't want your tears or your anger. He wants your happiness. Just you being here with him is better than any pain relief I can offer."

Adam blew out a shaky breath before sinking onto the chair under the giant elm tree. "He's just always been my person. My sounding board. He gives the best fucking advice, and it's only taken me until now to follow it. Who am I going to…"

I slipped my hand over his forearm as I sat beside him. "You'll be okay."

Adam reached over to touch my bracelets, grazing my skin as he inspected the stones one by one. "What is it with you and crystals?"

My arm hairs rose. "They're *supposed* to help me stay balanced and protected."

"Protected against what? The boogeyman?"

"Sometimes… There are positive and negative energies everywhere. The crystals can act as a barrier or a gateway. My grandmother made these bracelets in her final weeks, and each one serves a purpose."

"Oh yeah?" He threaded his finger around the string of amethyst. "What do these purple ones do?"

"This is amethyst. It's meant to boost my intuition, clear negative energies, and ease stress and anxiety. It's probably the most versatile."

"And this one?"

"The citrine enhances my focus. It keeps me optimistic and energized. It's also meant to attract money, but I've yet to believe that one," I said with a chuckle.

"I like this black one."

"This is my most important one. The black obsidian is used for protection and grounding. It's a great healer, and without it, my heart would've shattered years ago."

He gazed up at his grandfather's window and sighed. "I think I'll be needing one of those."

I instinctively placed my hand over his but snapped it back when his sorrow channeled through. "We should get back." I stood up. "I need to check in with the doctor before he leaves."

Adam's eyes burned into mine, before he sighed heavily. "You go. I'll be up soon."

Chapter 11

When Adam wasn't consumed with work, he spent every minute with his grandfather, leaving me anxious and idle. I preferred to be busy, but now that I was on top of all Liam's paperwork, I was left with more time to myself than anticipated.

Come Friday afternoon, I video-called Finn straight after school. He'd had a swim meet earlier that day, and I was desperate to know how he did. And now that the internet was fixed, I was able to video-call him without the infuriating drop-outs.

"How's my beautiful boy?" I asked as soon as the screen flickered onto Finn's adorable face.

"Hey, Mom!" His smile brightened my existence.

I adjusted my headphones to hear him better. "How did you do today?"

"Yeah, alright." Finn lifted a giant trophy up to the camera with a huge grin.

"Oh, Finny!" I gushed. "Congratulations!"

My father's face popped onto the screen. "And *alright* doesn't even begin to describe how well my grandson swam today."

"Hey, Dad, thanks for being there."

With an uneasy nod, he ruffed up Finn's hair. "I'll let you two talk."

As my father walked away, I shook off the sadness of what our relationship could have been. I would've loved to forgive and forget, like my sister had, but we both knew there was more healing to do. Until then, his redemption was my son. Since moving into my father's home, he'd made every effort to be there for him, attended every important event, and offered Finn the guidance he craved.

While Finn dove into a descriptive play by play of the race, I smiled and laughed at his impeccable storytelling until there was a knock on the door.

"I have to go," I whispered. "I'll speak to you tomorrow, okay?"

"Okay, love you," he said with a wave.

"I love you, too." I blew him a kiss before ending the call, then made my way to the door.

"Who are you talking to?" Adam glanced into my room as I swung open the door.

"Oh." My face burned as I took off my headphones. *How loud had I been talking?* "I was just on a call...with a friend..."

"I thought you had a visitor."

I scoffed. "Like who? I don't know anyone in the Hamptons."

He shoved his hands into his pockets. "Right...well, Gramps would like to speak with you."

"Is everything okay?"

"Yeah, he has some project he wants your help with. He wouldn't tell me any more."

"Sounds mysterious." I stepped into the hallway and closed the door behind me.

"He may be ninety, but his brain doesn't rest."

I met his gaze with a soft smile. "Sounds like that runs in the family."

Adam dipped his head with a chuckle before turning into his bedroom. "On that note, I have work to do. Tell Gramps I'll see him later."

———

Liam's secret project involved searching through old photo albums to create a book of memories to give each family member after his passing. It was a beautiful idea, and I was happy to help.

Once Liam started to tire, I carried the albums back to the library and left them on the coffee table, ready to pick up again on Monday. The trip down memory lane was an emotional roller-coaster for Liam, so we had to take it slow. Grayson, Josie, and Harrison were due to arrive at any moment, and he needed to preserve his energy.

While he rested, I searched the internet for quality do-it-yourself photobooks until Adam strolled into the room, carrying a glass of wine in each hand.

I closed my laptop. "I'm working, Adam."

"It's Friday night. You're off the clock."

I checked the time, then stared at the wine, almost salivating. "Fine," I muttered, delicately removing the glass from his fingers.

Adam grinned. "You'll like this one."

"Oh yeah? What vintage?"

"1987."

I smirked. "So, I'm guessing you're…thirty-three?"

His eyes twinkled as he sat on the chair opposite. "What are you doing with these?" He picked up a photo album from the stack and flipped it open.

"Your grandfather has been feeling a little nostalgic of late, so we took a trip down memory lane this afternoon."

Adam's eyebrows drew closer as he reviewed the photos before him. "I've never seen these before." He held up the page. "Check out my dad's hair!"

"Oh, we didn't get to those." I jumped up from my seat and moved to his, perching on its arm as I peered over. "I got stuck looking at your old baby photos."

"Hey, I was a cute kid."

I shrugged. "Okay."

"I was!"

"If you say so." I enjoyed the provocation too much.

"I'll prove it." Adam flicked over a few more pages, only to find more photos of Liam, his wife, and a very young William. "This must be the wrong album." As he slammed it closed, the rush of air blew out a loose photograph, and it slid across the floor. "Wait, there's one." He reached for the photograph that had *Adam* written in tiny, cursive writing across the back and flipped it over to discover a tattered black-and-white photograph of a newborn baby.

I peered over his shoulder. "Aww, you *were* cute."

Adam's forehead crinkled. "That's not me."

"Then who…" My words faded as realization settled over me. It was a photograph of Adam's deceased uncle who he knew nothing about.

"It must be a mistake."

"Yeah, it has to be." I attempted to hide the shake in my voice with a laugh. "Because that baby is way cuter than you ever were."

With a growl, Adam tore me off the arm of the chair, and I fumbled into his lap with a squeal. "Take that back," he said, tickling my sides.

Laughter burst from my lips. "I take it back! I take it back!"

"Good." His eyes paused on my mouth.

The swirling heat between us shocked me into reality, and I leapt off as he leaned in. "Fuck." I stumbled back to my chair. "You can't do that."

"Can't do what?" Grayson appeared in the doorway, making us both jump. Thankfully, he was reading something on his phone, completely oblivious to the incident.

My mind scrambled for an explanation. "Adam was touching the photos."

Grayson frowned at his brother. "Don't tell Josie. She loses her mind over shit like that."

Adam's gaze zeroed in on mine, ignoring Grayson. "Maybe the *photos* wanted to be touched."

Heat filled my cheeks, but Grayson was too distracted to notice. He'd spotted the photo albums on the coffee table and was already rummaging through them.

"I haven't seen these in years." He picked one up and moved to the spare armchair.

"There are some there I've never seen."

"You've already gone through them?" Grayson looked up at his brother. "How early did you arrive?"

"Adam's been here all week," I said when he grew silent.

"What?" Grayson's jaw slackened. "All week? What about the Ferguson deal?"

Adam sighed. "It's under control."

"Adam…" The warning in Grayson's tone was evident.

"It's none of your concern."

"Alright." Grayson dropped his shoulders. "It's your business, not mine."

I panned my gaze between them but said nothing. It wasn't my business either.

"So, where's Josie?" Adam was clearly trying to deflect.

"In our room, trying to get Harry to sleep. She'll be up soon."

"Did you ask her about Thanksgiving?"

"Yep." Grayson grinned. "We're coming."

"Are you sure?" Adam appeared surprised. "I know it's a hard time for her."

"She's adamant about making new memories for our son."

My heart dipped. This would be my first Thanksgiving without mine.

"And Mom and Dad are coming, too," Grayson murmured like it would go unnoticed.

Adam took a long sip of his wine to hide his grimace. "Wonderful."

A dramatic sigh filled the room, drawing our attention. "He's finally asleep!" Josie placed the baby monitor on the coffee table. "Hi, Cass." She smiled my way before nodding at her brother-in-law. "Adam."

"Hi, Josie." I reflected her warm energy. "How's your gorgeous boy?"

"Five minutes ago, or now?"

I laughed. "They're always angels when they're sleeping."

"It's the weirdest thing. You want them to go to sleep so badly, but once they do, you want to pick them up and squish their little cheeks."

Grayson reached for his wife's hand and pulled her onto his lap.

"You can sit here if you want," I said, realizing there were no chairs left. "I need to check in on Liam anyway."

"Oh, I just did. He's fast asleep. Mrs. Fredrich said he'll be out til morning." Josie nodded to my glass. "Stay and chat." She leaned back into her husband's arms. "I'm happy here."

"Okay, but just for a little while." Envy washed over me as Grayson toyed with Josie's hair. Their connection was undeniable. "I need to go to bed early. Liam loves watching the sun rise."

"So, that's where Harry gets it from," Grayson said as he kissed his wife's cheek.

"Well, I hope he's the replica of your grandfather," she replied. "I've never met a nicer man."

"I concur." I lifted my glass. "There aren't many like him these days."

Josie smiled softly before turning to Adam. "So, are you coming up every weekend now?"

Grayson smirked at his brother. "Apparently, he never left."

Josie's eyes traveled to mine, then back to Adam. "You spent the entire week here?"

Adam scowled. "So what if I did?"

"So, nothing." Josie raised her hands. "We're going to try to get up here more, too. Did Gray tell you the good news?"

"Oh God, you're not pregnant again, are you?"

She screwed up her nose. "No, of course not. I haven't adequately repressed childbirth enough to even think about that."

"If you're talking about Thanksgiving, then yeah, he mentioned it."

Josie shot Grayson a look. "Did you tell him about Christmas, too?"

"What about Christmas?" Adam asked, now curious.

"We want Harry's first Christmas to be at Harlow Manor." Grayson ran his hand up and down Josie's arm.

My heart burst with joy. "Oh, Liam would love that."

Josie's smile grew melancholy. "We know he's not expected to make it, but we can hope, right?"

"Of course." I wished it was guaranteed. "But even if he isn't here, his spirit will be."

Silence fell over the room as Adam stood. "I've got work to catch up on." He abruptly scooped up his wine glass and moved for the door. "Goodnight, all."

"Oh, don't forget! Melanie's wedding is next week," Josie called out. "You're coming, right? She said she invited you, but you haven't responded."

Adam's head fell back with his groan.

"Adam William Harlow!" Josie's eyes flared. "That girl gave you her entire company. You're going to her wedding."

"And suffer the singles table? No, thanks."

"There's nothing wrong with the singles table," Grayson said, tickling Josie's side.

She pushed him away with a giggle. "Then why don't you invite Cassidy as your plus-one?"

My widened gaze snapped to Adam, then back to Josie. "Oh, I can't…"

"But you have the weekends off," Josie continued. "And the wedding isn't too far from here."

"But Liam may nee—"

"Liam will want you to go. Plus, I know Amy would love to see you."

Adam's tapered gaze met mine. "How do you know Amy?"

"She's, um…my little sister."

He pinched the bridge of his nose. "Of course she is. I guess that explains how you got your foot in the door."

"Maybe so," Josie retorted, "but Cassidy is exactly what this family needs right now."

Adam glared at his sister-in-law. "So, being a Harlow for five minutes makes you an expert on that, does it?"

Grayson's back straightened with his growl. "Adam…"

"It's fine, Gray." Josie placed her hand over his curling fingers. "He's just deflecting."

Adam's jaw pulsed. "What's that supposed to mean?"

Grayson sighed. "You refuse to acknowledge Grampa's condition."

"I'm here, aren't I?"

"And that's great," Josie said, taking a softer approach. "But it wouldn't hurt to talk about it. To me, or your brother, even Cassidy. That's what she's here for."

Adam pursed his lips. "In that case…hey, Cass, want to come back to my room…and *talk* it out?"

"Goddammit, Adam!" Grayson scowled at his brother. "Cassidy's a professional. You're not going to treat her like one of your playthings."

"Why can't she be both? I'm sure we're paying her enough."

"Someone has clearly had too much wine." Josie rose to her feet and marched toward Adam. "I'll be back in a sec." She grabbed his arm and yanked him toward the door.

As they disappeared into the hallway, Grayson closed his eyes with a sigh. "I'm so sorry, Cassidy. He didn't mean that."

I gulped down another mouthful of wine. "I know."

"He's not processing our grandfather's prognosis very well."

"I've noticed."

"Our father saw our emotions as a weakness. It was only here, in this house, where Adam and I could be our true selves. With Josie's help, I've learned to follow my heart, but Adam… he has no one to walk his path with. Our parents won't be able to fill the hole Gramps will leave, and I'm concerned Adam will switch off his compassion entirely in an effort to feel closer to them."

"Why *is* your father the way he is?"

"I've been trying to figure him out for years. He had amazing parents, grew up in this incredible home… Perhaps kindness can skip a generation?"

"Maybe," I said, but I suspected something deeper. "The grandparent/grandchild relationship can be vastly different from that of a parent and child."

"I don't even know if my parents want a relationship with Harry at all. They keep taking these trips, yet not one of them has been to visit us since he was born. They dote on him every time they see him, but it's always so fleeting."

"Have you told them how you feel?"

Grayson grimaced. "We haven't exactly been on the best terms since I left the family business."

"Maybe they don't know how they fit into your life anymore."

He pondered my words. "No, I guess not."

"It wouldn't hurt to have the conversation. Who knows? Maybe your gorgeous boy is just what your father needs to soften him up."

"Oh, if anyone has the power to conquer my father, it's Harrison," Grayson said with a chuckle.

"It may even take the heat off your brother. I sense a lot of pressure there."

"Oh, Adam thrives off it. He lives and breathes Harlow Corp."

"Like your father?"

"Yeah, he's struggling to let go since retiring."

"That must be hard on Adam. Seeking his father's approval while wanting independence can create some extremely conflicting emotions. And with your grandfather's prognosis… it's a lot. For anyone."

"You're right. I should cut him some slack." He stared at the doorway. "I don't know if Josie will, though."

"Why don't you do something fun together this weekend?"

"I wouldn't even know what he does for fun." He chortled. "Except supermodels."

The knot in my stomach tightened as I forced a laugh.

"Maybe I need to take him out," Grayson continued. "Get him laid."

I emptied the entire contents of the glass into my mouth. "If you think that will work, go for it." I rose to my feet. "Well, I better get to bed. Enjoy your weekend with your grandfather. He really loves it when you're all here."

Grayson smiled. "Goodnight, Cass, and thanks for putting up with our shit. We appreciate it."

I shrugged. "That's what I'm here for."

If only my heart followed the same job description.

Chapter 12

My heart skipped a beat when I found Liam missing from bed the next morning.

"Where is he?" I asked Mrs. Fredrich, who was noting something in his chart. She didn't care for pleasantries, so I jumped straight to the point.

"He was adamant about seeing the sunrise through the drawing room window this morning, so I authorized his grandson to take him downstairs."

"Oh." My eyebrows drew together as I left the room and headed for the stairs.

Once I reached the French doors, I peeked inside to find Liam gazing out at the soft glow of the sun while Adam stood beside his wheelchair with his hand resting upon his grandfather's shoulder. The intense energy from their bond was as bright as the streams of light cutting through the glass, and I suddenly understood the grief Adam was facing.

As if sensing my presence, Adam turned my way.

"Hey," I whispered, knowing Liam enjoyed the morning silence.

"Sorry for stealing him this morning." Adam squeezed his grandfather's shoulder before stepping toward me. "It's my grandmother's birthday."

"Oh…" I lowered my gaze to Liam. "I didn't know."

Liam's eyes glazed over, clearly reliving a memory we weren't a part of.

"Hey…" Adam grazed my bicep. "I didn't know it either. Max told me late last night."

"I wish he'd told me."

"Well, you're not supposed to be working today."

"I know." My brow furrowed. "But I care about him." More than I should.

His playful smirk returned. "Should I be jealous?"

"Absolutely."

As we both endeavored to hide our smiles, Max walked in with a pot of tea. "Good morning, Cassidy. Shall I bring you another cup?"

"It's okay, Max," Adam answered. "I'll make Cassidy a coffee."

My head recoiled. "You will?" Not that I was complaining.

"Come on." He motioned for me to follow. "I had my favorite blend delivered yesterday."

I trailed Adam down the hall and into the kitchen. "What's wrong with Max's coffee?"

"It does the job, but it never leaves me satisfied."

"Like all the women in your life," Grayson muttered as he strolled in behind us with Harrison fussing in his arms.

"Not all the women," Adam mumbled under his breath as he moved to the coffee machine.

"Is Harry okay?" I asked, trying not to overthink Adam's words.

"He's still hungry, but Josie's exhausted, so I'm going to top off his feed with some formula while she sleeps in."

"I can help with that." I reached for the empty bottle in his hand. "Why don't you take Harry to see Liam in the drawing room while I heat it up?"

"Really?" Grayson's shoulders eased. "Thanks, Cassidy. The formula's sitting by the coffee machine."

Adam grabbed the tin and handed it over before turning to his brother. "Hey, don't forget whose birthday it is today."

Grayson's eyebrows arched. "Oh, fuck, of course. I'm so tired I can barely remember my name let alone what day it is."

Once Grayson left the kitchen, I turned to find Adam drawing in the aroma of the new coffee beans before placing them into the machine.

"Wow...you really like that coffee."

"It's better than sex," he said before peeking my way. "Most sex."

With the roll of my eyes, I diverted my focus to making a bottle of formula for Harrison. Adam and I moved around the kitchen like a synchronized dance routine, close enough for our energies to interweave, but far enough to avoid touching.

Adam studied me as I dripped warm formula onto my wrist. "You look like you've done that before."

I quickly wiped it off. "I…um…used to do a lot of babysitting." *It wasn't a lie.*

"I think once was enough for me."

"Harrison is hardly a bother."

Adam snorted. "Have you seen the bags under my brother's eyes?"

"I'm sure they're worth it," I said on my way out the door. In fact, I knew they were.

"Not convinced," Adam called out.

With a shake of my head, I returned to the drawing room to find Harrison in Liam's arms, with Grayson crouched beside him. "Are you on feeding duty, Liam?" I asked, devouring the beautiful moment.

Liam's face brightened. "May I?" he asked his grandson.

"Of course." Grayson smiled as I passed over the bottle.

Liam's eyes glistened, but his aura exuded happiness. "Betty would have loved this."

"Oh, I'm certain of that." I stepped back to give the three generations some space. At the whisper of my name, I turned to find Adam standing in the doorway, wearing a heavy winter coat and a devilish grin, while holding two steaming cups of coffee.

I wasn't sure if it was the coffee or his eyes beckoning me, but I surrendered to the pull and stepped into the grand hall.

Adam tipped his head to the front door. "Take a walk with me."

"I…don't have my jacket."

"I grabbed you one of mine."

I spied a coat draped over the bannister, and my heartbeat accelerated. "Oh, okay," I said, struggling to lift the heavy material that was tailored for broad shoulders and not my tiny frame.

"Let me." Adam placed the coffees on the hallway table and held up the jacket while I slipped my arms inside.

"Thanks," I rasped when his finger grazed my neck. His touch drew my face toward the collar, and I breathed in. Adam's glorious scent encased my body, and when he spun me around to zip me up, my head grew light.

"You okay?" His body was entirely too close to regain my senses.

I dipped my head as I fell back a step. "I clearly can't function without caffeine."

"Well, I can help with that." Adam picked up both coffees and handed one over. "Shall we?"

With my nod, I followed him outside. Under the watchful eyes of his grandfather and brother, I was confident Adam wouldn't push the boundaries as long as we stayed within view of the drawing room window.

I was merely steps into the garden when I brought the coffee to my lips. "Oh, wow." I paused in surprise.

"It's fucking amazing, isn't it?" Adam watched me relish another sip.

I closed my eyes as the liquid gold swirled around my mouth. "You're right. It *is* better than sex."

"Most sex," he uttered, sternly.

"I don't know about that." I gazed longingly into my mug. "This is incredible."

"Cassidy…"

I peeked up to find a storm brewing behind Adam's eyes. "So, your barista skills have upstaged your bedroom prowess. Don't be offended. Be proud." I grinned, enjoying his temper. "You could run a successful coffee shop one day."

His mouth gaped. "You'll pay for that."

"Oh, okay." I pretended to check my pockets. "How much? Two dollars? You really shouldn't charge more than the going rate, or you'll go out of business."

The corner of his mouth twitched before he pivoted on

the stone pathway to resume our walk. "You're entirely too comfortable with me."

I matched his pace. "Am I supposed to be scared of you?"

"Most people are."

"Well, you know what they say…people are *way* less intimidating once you've seen them in their birthday suit."

His eyes traveled up and down my body. "You think?"

"You've never been so nervous before a presentation that you've had to picture everyone naked to feel less vulnerable?"

"No."

"Well, that confirms it."

"Confirms what?"

"You're not human."

He nudged my side. "Ha-ha."

"I had my suspicions—especially after last night's efforts."

Adam slowed his pace before stopping entirely. "That's actually what I wanted to talk to you about." He lowered his head as he turned to me. "I was a complete dick to you last night, and I'm sorry. I can't seem to control my mouth when I'm angry, and I guess you're an easy target."

"Adam, it's ok—"

"It's not okay." He met my gaze. "And I want to make it up to you."

"You really don't hav—"

"I want to buy you a dress."

I burst out laughing. "A dress?! This isn't Pretty Woman! Although you did, in a roundabout way, call me a prostitute last night."

"Fuck." He winced. "No…I want to buy you a dress so you'll have something to wear to Melanie's wedding."

"Adam, no."

"Come on. Your sister with be there, and Grayson and Josie are going. It'll be fun—if you come, that is."

"And if I don't?"

He crossed his arms. "Then I won't either."

"But Melanie is a family friend. You have to go!"

"I don't *have* to do anything."

My teeth gnashed. A wedding was the perfect occasion to let loose and release some stress. Just what Adam needed. "Fine, I'll go…but on one condition. No working. No phone. Just you."

Adam tipped the last of the coffee into his mouth as he pondered my request. "Fine. But only if the same rules apply to you."

"I have to be on call for your grandfather." *And Finn.*

"Fair enough. He is the only exception."

I stared at him, wondering if he could really go a day without work. "Then I guess I better get shopping."

His blue eyes sparkled back at me. "My favorite color is green. Just saying."

"I look terrible in green."

"Hardly," he scoffed. "You were wearing it the night we met."

"You remember what I was wearing?"

He stepped closer. "I was especially fond of your pink panties."

As heat flooded my face, I pivoted on my heel and marched back to the house.

"I'm joking, Cass," he called out through his laughter. "They were blue!"

———

After helping Liam back to his room, I disappeared into mine to scold myself in the mirror. Accepting Adam's invitation was asking for trouble. We couldn't have a simple conversation without it turning sexual, so a night out together had the potential to escalate things.

Unfortunately, it was the only way I could draw Adam away from his all-consuming work. A celebration with his friends and family offered the perfect opportunity to extract some real emotion from him. With his guard let down—and perhaps a few whiskeys—there was a good chance Adam would open up to me. And if he didn't, well, at least I'd have fun trying—under the necessary supervision of Grayson, Josie, and my little sister, that is.

Before Dominic died, I used to love weddings. The love, the laughter…the dancing. We were the first couple on the dance floor and the last to leave. Now, I watched from the sidelines with my feet firmly planted on the floor. Others had asked, but new partners were tiring. Their energies were unfamiliar and full of expectations, and I could never relax long enough to enjoy myself.

As I scoured the internet for dresses in stores nearby, I became acutely aware of Adam's rising voice across the hall. It was one-sided, meaning the argument must've been taking place over the phone. His menacing tone cut straight through me, and when something crashed against his wall, I gathered up my swimsuit and robe and headed to the pool. I wasn't willing to absorb Adam's temper any longer.

After several laps of the indoor pool, I sank to the bottom, enjoying the peace, until a shadow hovered over the water. I pushed off the pool floor and through the surface. "I'm not drowning!" I yelled before we had another incident.

Adam smiled, but his eyes were dull. "I know."

I waded to the ladder and climbed out. "What's wrong?" I grabbed a towel and wrapped it around my bust before approaching. "Things were getting pretty heated up there."

He rubbed his stubbled jaw. "You heard that?"

"*Australia* heard that."

Adam hung his head. "Someone really fucked up at work, and I've got to go clean up his mess."

I spied his suitcase by the door, and my heart dipped unexpectedly. "Oh. I'm sure everything will be okay."

"Being sued for twenty-five million dollars is not fucking okay," he growled as he tore his fingers through his hair. "This is what I get for slacking off."

My brow furrowed. "Why do you put so much pressure on yourself?"

"Because the success of Harlow Corp. is all on me now."

"So, losing this money is going to ruin you?"

"No, but my father doesn't accept mistakes."

"Your father doesn't run the company anymore, you do. If your company isn't in ruin, just let it go. All this stress isn't good for you."

His laughter was forced and tired. "Yeah, well, unfortunately, I was born this way."

I shook my head. "No, you weren't."

"How the fuck would you know?"

I flinched at his words. "Because I can feel your soul, and it's a total contradiction to this."

"Says you," he spat.

My hands found my towel-covered hips. "What's that supposed to mean?"

"I may not be an empath, or whatever the fuck you want to call it, but I know your actions don't match your feelings." He stepped closer until his designer shoes grazed my wet toes. "You wear a big fucking facade just like the rest of us."

I glared up at him. "I do not."

"Then you won't feel a thing when I do this." His hands grasped my face as his lips crashed down onto mine. They were soft, and warm, and oh so alluring that I hadn't realized I was kissing him back until a moan escaped my lips.

I pushed him back. "Argh. That doesn't prove anything."

"No." He returned to his suitcase with a smug chuckle. "It proves everything."

Chapter 13

"There's something going on between you two, isn't there?" Josie asked while we were dress shopping the next day.

I flicked through the rack while striving to keep my tone neutral. "I don't know what you're talking about."

"I have an eye for these things." She rocked Harrison back and forth in the stroller. "Just ask your sister."

My head shot up. "Please don't mention it to her. Nothing is going on."

"I mean…she would know…" Josie smirked. "If something *were* going on, that is."

"Then I have nothing to worry about." Amy knew better than to tell my future. She stopped the moment she saw my husband die years before it happened. "Adam and I are just friends. That's it."

"Adam doesn't have friends. He has colleagues."

"Then I must fall into the latter category." My fingers paused on a pale-green dress before shooting to the next option.

"I doubt that. I've seen the way he watches you."

"That's creepy."

"No, not in a stalker way!" Josie laughed as she pulled out the dress I'd just passed. "You captivate him. And knowing he can't have you must be eating him up inside."

My chest tightened. Perhaps he just liked the chase. With a sigh, I slipped out a navy dress and held it up to my small frame. "What do you think of this one?"

"It's nice…" Josie tilted her head to inspect. "But I saw you eyeing this one." She thrust the pale-green material into my arms and grinned.

"Oh, I can't. I—"

"Don't be worried about the price tag." Josie shrugged. "Adam isn't."

My mouth parted, but nothing came out. I'd been too busy avoiding every shade of Adam's favorite color to worry about the cost.

"Try it on," she continued, pushing me toward the change room. "That color will make your green eyes pop."

"That's what I'm afraid of," I mumbled while disappearing behind the curtain.

Drawing a deep breath, I slipped the knee-length dress over my body and reluctantly lifted my gaze to the mirror. *Wow.* Not only was the cut comfortable and flattering, the intricate lace was unexpectedly soft. *If only it came in another color.*

"Don't you dare tell me it looks awful," Josie called out. "I can hear you gushing."

With a soft giggle, I pulled the curtain aside. "I think I should try the other one."

"The fuck you will." Josie shoved the navy dress back on the rack. "You're getting that one."

I hung my head back with a groan before yanking the curtain closed. While carefully removing the dress and returning it to its hanger, I couldn't help but steal a glimpse of the price tag. *Four thousand dollars!?! For a dress?!* My car didn't cost that much. I was about to argue my point to Josie when I caught sight of the finer details.

Made in France

Size: 2

Color: Mint.

Mint? Mint wasn't necessarily a shade of green…it could be blue! A light blue!

"So, did you decide on the green one?" the shop assistant asked through the drapes.

My eyes squeezed shut. "It appears so," I muttered, before stepping out and handing over the troublesome dress.

Josie rejoiced before handing over her credit card. "We'll take the matching shawl, too."

After we'd found a clutch and suitable shoes for a beach wedding, Josie took me out for lunch. She wanted Grayson to spend some quality alone time with Liam, so there was no rush to return, and Harrison was still fast asleep.

"Thank you for taking me out today, Josie," I said, twirling the pasta on my fork. "I can't remember the last time I went shopping for something other than groceries."

"It's been fun for me, too." She gazed down at her sleeping son. "I feel like I'm surrounded by boys at the moment."

"You'll have to try for a girl next. Even the playing field."

"Ugh, I can't imagine how tiring *two* kids would be."

I wished I knew. Although I got pregnant young, Dominic and I wanted more kids. We had a beautiful home with a big backyard, perfect for a growing family. But now, it was just me and Finn, and for the past four years, I could barely keep a roof over our heads.

"I think you would manage just fine," I said as she tucked in Harrison's blanket. "You and Grayson are naturals."

Josie grew somber. "It must be hard raising a child on your own."

"You do what you have to." Sorrow filled my heart. "That's why I took this job."

"You must miss him."

I blinked back the tears as they formed. "So much."

Josie reached over and rested her hand upon mine. "Have you told Grampa yet?"

I shook my head. "I can't risk Caroline and William finding out. They never would've hired me if they knew I had a son."

"But that doesn't matter now. You have the job, and you're killing it." Her brown eyes widened. "That's not an appropriate thing to say in your line of work, is it?"

My chuckle morphed into a sigh. "I just don't want anyone thinking I'm a bad mother for leaving him."

"Liam won't. Nor will Grayson, or Max, or Nora, or even Mrs. Fredrich."

"What about Adam?"

"Adam?" Josie scoffed. "Who the fuck cares what he thinks?"

I dropped my eyes as shame poured over me.

"Cassidy…" Josie's tone grew serious. "Adam's a complex person. If something *is* going on between you two, you need to tread carefully. He's not the type to—"

"Like I said." I lifted my head as I cleared my throat. "We're just friends. That's all."

She stared at my face, reading every quiver and twitch. "Well, your *friend* is going to fall to his knees when he sees you in that dress…as will every other single guy at the wedding."

"I'm not going to the wedding to hook up. I'm going to see my sister."

"Oh, that reminds me. Amy told me to tell you to wear the necklace she gave you before your interview."

I rolled my eyes. Of course she did.

"I'm assuming it matches your dress."

I sighed. "Perfectly."

———

The next morning, after Josie, Grayson, and Harrison left, I fell back into my usual routine. Knowing Liam's pain and anxiety was increasing, I performed Reiki on him each morning and night and distracted him with photographs during the day. The adjoining stories filled the room with laughter and pushed away the discomfort of his failing body.

It was only when Liam slept that my mind began to wander. To Finn. To Dominic. *To Adam.*

His parting kiss had me all stirred up. As much as I didn't want him, I did. The pull of his soul, buried deep within his hardened persona, was too much to combat with crystals and mantras, so I was giving in. If Adam liked to chase, then I was going to stop running. Maybe then, he'd see that his infatuation with me was merely a deflection of his grief and nothing more. Liam's end-of-life care had to be my focus, and as much as Adam's eventual rejection was going to hurt, I'd been through much worse.

While sitting up in bed, chatting to Tash on my laptop, my cell phone buzzed on my nightstand.

She narrowed her gaze into the camera. "Who's texting you at this hour?"

"It's probably just one of Amy's late-night rambles," I said, reaching for the phone.

My heart stopped when I glanced down at the screen.

Unknown: **Page 234**

"Holy shit." I covered my mouth with my hand.

"Who is it?"

I placed the phone on my bed face down. "No one."

"Your face is bright red…it's definitely not *no one*. And don't lie to me. I know you."

I groaned. "Remember that guy…you know, the one I slept with after my interview?"

Tash's eyes bulged. "You mean the guy who fucked your brains out? I thought you didn't leave a number."

"Well, I guess he figured out who I am."

"And you've been texting each other?" She clapped her hands. "Are you going to see him again?"

"No…there's no point. He just wants to go another round."

"So! Go another round!"

"I'm in the Hamptons! And he's in LA."

"Then get creative. Phones have cameras these days."

I covered my burning face. "I'm not having phone sex. I wouldn't even know how."

"Argh, come on, Cass. Live a little. You deserve to."

She was never going to let this go until I gave her something. "Fine, I'll think about it."

"Doo iiit."

I held my finger over the *End Call* button. "Good night, Tash!"

She blew me a kiss. "Night, Cass! I love you! So do Bryce and Tristian…and the bump!"

"I love and miss you all, too."

After closing my laptop, I picked up my novel and shuffled further under the covers. The underlined passage on page 234 described a scene so hot it had my core pulsing. With only one way to relieve the tension, my hand slid down my silk gown, like the hero tracing the curves of the heroine, and settled over my mound. As the memory of my night with Adam flashed through my mind, I gave in to desire and buried my face into my pillow as I cried out.

Once my breathing slowed, I scoured the pages for more of Adam's notations, curious to know what turned him on. A man with that much experience would surely have particular tastes. Tastes a girl like me could never satisfy...unless I did my research.

A few chapters later, my eyes locked onto Adam's familiar scrawl, and a tired giggle floated from my lips. The scene was just as steamy but entirely focused on the hero's arousal. I couldn't help but pick up my phone and send a message of my own.

Me: **Page 328**

Almost instantly, three little dots appeared, then disappeared, then appeared, then disappeared, until they were completely gone. Perhaps I wasn't allowed to play his game. Although my heart dipped, it was a good sign. The sooner he thought he had me, the sooner he'd let me go.

———

Liam's company made it easier to pass the time. I hadn't heard from Adam since his text, and now I was anxious for his return. It was Friday afternoon, and he was due to arrive earlier than usual, with Grayson and Josie, to be present for Liam's doctor appointment.

"Hey, Gramps," Grayson greeted as he walked in with Harrison nestled in his arms. "Hey, Cassidy."

Josie scurried in moments later, carrying his bottle. "Did we miss the doc? Harrison had a poonami on the drive here, so we had to pull over and sort it out. Luci's farts smell like roses in comparison."

"How is that beautiful beast of yours?" Liam asked as I adjusted his pillows so he could sit up straighter.

My eyes widened. "Beast?"

"Our Irish Wolfhound." Grayson grinned. "You'll meet him next week."

Liam beamed. "You're bringing him for Thanksgiving?"

"We sure are."

"Wonderful. I'll ask Max to save some big juicy bones for him."

Josie laughed. "You spoil him as much as you do Harrison."

"Speaking of spoiled children…" Liam panned his gaze to the door. "Where is your brother? I thought you were picking him up from the airport."

Josie's eyes flickered my way. "Something came up last night, so he had to cancel his overnight flight."

"Something came up alright." Grayson's snicker stopped short under his wife's glare.

My mouth grew dry. "Will he be here for the wedding tomorrow?"

Josie took Harrison from Grayson's arms and moved to the couch. "It's a six-hour trip, so if he rescheduled to the first flight out this morning, he should be here within a few hours."

Her words did nothing to calm the impending storm of doubt closing in on me.

"Even if he doesn't show, you're still coming to the wedding." She tipped the bottle into Harrison's mouth. "That dress needs to be worn."

Liam's eyes softened as they turned my way. "If my grandson proves to be a fool, perhaps you could ask Marc."

"Ask me what?" The doctor strolled into the room, donning his gorgeous smile.

My cheeks seared instantly. "Oh, nothing," I said, shooting Josie a pleading glare.

"Oh…um…Cassidy…isn't feeling well."

"Oh, that's no good." Marc's brown eyes stayed with mine. "Why don't you wait in your bedroom, and I'll have a look at you after I'm done here?"

"It's okay." I forced a smile through my embarrassment. "I'm fine. Really."

"We can't have Liam catching any bugs…no matter how small."

"Doctor's orders, Cass," Josie sang out from the couch.

My mouth parted, but nothing came out. I didn't want Marc thinking I'd risk Liam's health, so I yielded. "Fine, but I can assure you, it's nothing." With a huff, I marched out of the room, narrowing my gaze at Josie's growing smile before disappearing out the door.

———

An hour later, there was a soft knock at my bedroom door. Thinking I'd heard the helicopter land moments prior, part of me hoped Adam was waiting on the other side.

The thought of going to a strangers wedding on my own had my stomach churning. I was already rummaging up a million excuses as to why I couldn't go and was seriously thinking about convincing Marc I was really sick to get out of it. But then I'd be barred from seeing Liam, and I wouldn't accept that.

Holding my breath, I opened the door to find Marc standing in the hallway, wearing a sheepish grin. My gaze lingered over the stethoscope hanging around his neck, and my heart quickened. He really was the perfect catch. Cleanly shaven, perfectly combed-back hair, caring profession…perhaps I *should* ask him to the wedding.

"May I come in?" he asked when I said nothing.

I cleared my throat. "Of course." I opened the door to let him through. "But I'm feeling fine, honestly."

"Doesn't hurt to be sure." Marc placed his bag at the end of my bed and opened it to retrieve a blood pressure pump and tongue depressor.

"Fine." I plonked myself beside his equipment and peered up at him. "How do you want me?" As the suggestive words registered in my brain, my eyes bulged. "I mean, what do you need me to do?" *Kill me now.*

Unperturbed, he reached for my arm. "I'm just going to check your blood pressure."

"Oh, okay." I blew out a shaky breath as he wrapped up my arm and pumped. "What's the update on Liam?" I asked, desperate to fill the awkward silence between us.

"He's doing great, considering," he said, seemingly happy with my blood pressure reading. "He may even last beyond Christmas at this rate."

I smiled. "The family will be happy to hear that."

With a nod, Marc checked my ears, then told me to open my mouth.

"I'm sorry. I probably have bad breath." I grimaced. "I had tuna for lunch."

His shook his head with a chuckle. "I'm sure it's fine—whoa!"

As his head recoiled from mine, I snapped my mouth shut, mortified.

"I'm joking, Cassidy!" Marc's laughter filled the room. "You smell fine."

I poked his arm with flaring eyes. "Marc!"

"I'm sorry, but I couldn't resist." His features softened as he sunk onto the bed beside me. "I'm not used to my patients being so young...and pretty."

"Well, I'm not used to my doctors looking like...like you."

He dipped his head with a chuckle before shifting the stethoscope into his ears. "Would you mind loosening your shirt a little?"

My eyebrows rose.

"To check your lungs," he added, holding back his amusement.

"Oh...okay." I untucked my shirt.

"This may be a little cold at first." He slipped his hand under my shirt and hovered millimeters over my breast as he listened.

"I told you I was fine," I said, trying to cover the hammering of my heart that was surely deafening him.

His eyes traveled to mine, searching. "That you are."

A throat clearing from the open doorway snapped the building tension.

"Oh...hey, Adam," I stammered as Marc removed his hand.

"Cassidy." His expressionless gaze panned to Marc. "Doctor Morrison."

"Hello, Adam." Marc wound up his stethoscope as he stood. "You appear perfectly fine, Cassidy."

My hands trembled as I fastened the buttons of my shirt. "Marc was just giving me a checku—" My lame excuse was shut down by the door slamming across the hall.

"Adam's not one for small talk, is he?" Marc said as he packed his things away.

I smiled tightly. "No."

"Well, if you ever need more conversation while you're here, I'd love to take you out sometime."

"Oh..." My gaze floated to Adam's door before meeting Marc's hopeful gaze. "We probably shouldn't...I mean, with Liam...and well...I don't think it's a good idea."

He pressed his lips together as he stood. "You're right. I've overstepped."

"No, no..." I followed him to the door. "You didn't. I'm just...not in a position to think about myself right now."

"Well, when you are..." He smiled. "You have my number."

"I do."

He gave my forearm a squeeze before continuing down the hall, leaving me standing there, staring at Adam's door.

As if sensing my presence, or waiting for Marc to leave, Adam threw open his door. "I thought there was nothing going on between you two?"

I turned away from his impenetrable gaze. "There isn't."

"His hand was up your shirt."

"He was checking my lungs!" I cried, entirely too defensive.

Adam's eyes lowered to my chest. "Your nipples say otherwise."

"He grazed them, so what?" Heat rose up my neck as I folded my arms, hiding the evidence. "It's been a while—not like you'd understand."

He stepped into the hall. "You have no fucking idea how much I understand."

I bit the inside of my cheek, but there was no stopping my mouth. "Like you haven't been seeing other women back in LA?"

"*Other women?*" He leaned forward. "That would mean I already have one."

I froze. He was right. "I'm going to bed," I muttered breathlessly before returning to the safety of my threshold. "I'm too tired for your games."

"Good thinking. You'll need to rest if you're going to keep up with me at the wedding tomorrow."

"I think I can handle it."

"Oh, I know you can…" He tilted his head with a chuckle. "But will you?"

With a growl, I seized the door and swung it closed before I melted before him. I was entirely out of my depth with Adam. His words made me blush, his behavior drove me crazy, and his touch made me submit. Adam was a force of nature—and one my grandmother never prepared me for.

Chapter 14

Josie peeked around my head to look at my reflection. "Wow, that necklace really does match perfectly."

I touched the garnierite crystal dangling from the silver chain and smiled. "It's supposed to heal and open my heart chakra."

"I love that. Can we slip it into Adam's pocket?"

"It will take more than a crystal to open him up…but I'm working on it. At least he's agreed to part with his phone for the wedding."

"What? No cell phone? Adam will go into shock."

"We have a deal. Neither of us are allowed to discuss work— unless Liam needs me, of course. So, Adam will have no choice but to talk to me."

"Oh, you're crafty, but I highly doubt Adam will be able to speak once he sees you in that dress."

"I'm sure I pale in comparison to the girls he dates."

"Cassidy, you're way sexier than the girls he's used to…and you're *real*. There is nothing real about them. Now, you need to stop overthinking and enjoy yourself. You deserve a little fun, too."

"Thanks, Josie."

She gathered up her makeup and headed to the door. "Now, I'll go feed Harry, pop on my dress, and meet you and Adam outside in half an hour, okay?"

I smiled. "Sounds like a plan."

Once she left, I twirled around with a giggle. I hadn't dressed up in years. Along with my gorgeous *mint* dress, my usual beach waves were set in a smoother and more classical style, and my makeup, while understated, illuminated my green eyes. I felt like a movie star, and I was savoring the moment. It was easy to look this good with money, and I may never have the opportunity again.

Unable to wait any longer, I gathered up my essentials and made my way to the door, only to discover Adam hovering on the other side.

His eyes lifted as his mouth fell open. "Wow."

My smile widened as my gaze rolled over his tailored suit. "Wow, yourself."

"You look…beautiful." Adam's jaw pulsed, but his hands didn't budge from his pockets.

I closed the door behind me. "I hope you weren't waiting long."

"No…I was just giving myself a stern talking to before knocking."

"About?"

"Not screwing up."

"Work will be there tomorrow, Adam. You need to stop worrying—at least for today."

Adam rubbed his freshly shaven jawline. "Yeah, I know."

"Do I need to frisk you for your phone?"

His eyebrows rose as he held his arms in the air. "You can do anything you want to me in that green dress."

"It's mint!"

"It's green."

With a growl, I grabbed his arm and pulled him down the hall. "Come on. Josie's waiting."

Once we reached the waiting limo, where Josie was settling Harrison into his carseat, Adam's hand grazed my lower back, and a shiver rolled over me. "It's green," he whispered into the shell of my ear. "And it's sexy as fuck."

The hairs on my neck danced under his breath. "Adam…"

"What? I'm just having a little fun."

"Are you guys coming?" Josie poked her head out of the limo door. "Grayson will kill us if we're late."

Melanie and Scott's wedding was at their beach house farther up the coast, so we hired an eight-seater limo so we could all go together. Josie sat with Harrison toward the front, Adam sprawled himself over the side seat, and I enjoyed the back to myself. It was luxurious and spacious, and Adam had no good excuse to be close to me.

Fifteen minutes later, we arrived at Reed's parents' house, and Amy and Reed piled in.

Amy dove onto me with a squeal. "Cassidy!"

"Hey, sis." I giggled at her overenthusiastic affection, before returning it. She was such a free spirit, and I loved that about her.

"Hey, Cassidy. Hey, Jos." Reed settled beside Adam and shook his hand. "And you must be Adam."

"He prefers Mr. Harlow," Amy said with a snigger.

"I'm not your boss anymore, Amy. You can call me Adam."

My eyebrows lifted. "Mr. Harlow? Like your dad?"

Adam pursed his lips. "At work, yes. And we're not talking about that, *remember*?"

"How's baby H, Jos?" Amy launched across the limo to the empty seat beside her. She peered into his baby carseat and cooed. "Remember when Finn was this little, Cass?"

All the blood drained from my face while Josie poked Amy in the ribs.

"Oh." Panic consumed my sister's eyes. "You know, Finn… our…cousin?"

"Yes," I forced out while my heart pounded against my chest. "He was a gorgeous baby, too."

Reed screwed up his nose. "Cousin? I didn't kn—"

"Yes, our cousin!" Amy shot Reed a look. "Who you haven't met yet."

"Oookay," he said, shaking his head in confusion.

Thankfully, Adam was preoccupied with a bottle of champagne and was too busy filling glasses to notice the awkwardness bouncing around the limo.

Josie eagerly reached out for the first poured glass. "One of those better be for me."

Adam looked at me apologetically before passing it to his sister-in-law. "Aren't you breastfeeding?"

"I have a two–bottle window, and I plan to abuse it."

Adam shrugged, clueless to her meaning, and poured another. "Here." He handed me the next glass.

Our hands touched, and our eyes collided, and the usual coolness of his blue eyes was gone. Instead of peering into the depths of the Arctic Ocean, the shade had morphed into the warm turquoise waters of the Maldives, and I could already feel myself drowning.

"Thanks," I uttered, trying to draw a breath.

The corner of his mouth rose as he picked up the next glass and poured.

"Alright, shove over." Amy pushed Adam aside. "You're taking too long…and where's the music? Driver!"

With a chuckle, Adam took the glass he'd filled and rolled onto the seat next to me while Amy filled the cabin with noise. His alluringly sweet cologne, slightly heavier than his usual scent, had me drawing closer.

Adam tipped his glass toward mine. "Cheers."

"Cheers." I clinked my glass against his and brought it to my mouth. Not seeing any movement beside me, I peeked over to find his eyes glued to my mouth.

I licked the sweetness off my bottom lip. "Why aren't you drinking?"

"I'm pacing myself…you should, too."

"Weddings take a lot out of me." I held up my glass. "This helps."

Something flickered through his energy—empathy, perhaps. "Because they remind you of Dominic?"

"I wish it were that simple."

Without elaborating, I listened to the animated conversation between Josie and Amy. They'd been best friends for years, and their constant banter reminded me of my relationship with Tash. I missed her.

"We're here," Adam said, drawing me out of my homesick trance.

Everyone was already piling out, leaving Adam waiting beside me.

"You okay?" He tilted his head to search my face. "Because we can ditch this thing—"

"No!" I pulled him out by the sleeve of his jacket. "We're going to have fun."

Once we caught up to the others, I peered up at Melanie and Scott's house, taking in all its Hamptons glory. It was big and beautiful and, to my delight, on the beach.

Josie took the stroller through the front door while we followed the flaming torches around the side of the house.

Amy flashed me an excited grin. "It's your dream house."

I ripped off my shoes and spread my toes in the sand. "Anything by the ocean is my dream."

She squeezed my hand. "You'll get there."

"Beachside apartments in LA are a little out of my budget, Ames."

Adam's gaze shot to mine. "You're moving to LA?"

"That's the plan—once I have enough saved and find a job, that is." I emitted a nervous laugh. "*If* I find a job."

"Don't *you* live in LA?" Amy asked Adam. "Maybe you could ask around...and be Cassidy's reference?"

"Ames..."

"Of course I will," he said, before his brow lowered. "Although, I don't think I know many people in need of a death doula, which is a good thing...I guess."

"That *is* a good thing. But I'll probably go back to waitressing anyway."

Adam stopped walking. "Waitressing?"

"Jobs like these don't come around often," I said, slowing my steps. "So, I'll need something to pay the bills in the meantime."

Adam's mouth pursed as he continued walking over the sand dunes. "We'll see about that."

"Adam..." His determination scared me.

"No work talk, remember?"

I shook my head with a sigh. "Fine."

"Oh, there's Scott!" Amy hooked her arm into Reed's as she waved to a gorgeous dark-haired man in the distance.

Adam and I followed closely behind, watching Amy and Reed greet the groom.

"Adam!" Scott shook his hand. "Thanks for coming today, man."

"I couldn't miss Smelly's big day."

Scott glanced my way, then did a double-take. "I thought Grayson was joking when he said you were bringing a date."

"Hi, I'm Cassidy." I reached out my hand. "I'm more of a tag along than a date. I'm Amy's sister."

Scott grasped my hand with a smile. "Well, I'm sure you'll keep this guy out of trouble."

"I don't think that is actually possible."

A younger man, with an uncanny resemblance to Scott, called out, "Scott! She's ready."

"Thanks, Rils." Scott's eyes sparkled. "I better get in position."

As Scott jogged up the sandy aisle and stood to the right of the marriage celebrant, Adam placed his hand on the small of my back and ushered me to the opposite side. It didn't seem like a formal wedding, but from what Josie had told me, Adam and Grayson considered Melanie family.

The warmth of Adam's hand remained in place as the music commenced, and I welcomed it. Although the heaters were blasting, they were no match for the cool breeze rolling off the ocean, and I'd only brought a light shawl.

An attractive woman with long brown hair was first to appear over the dunes. Her endearing doe eyes glittered under the fairy lights as she made her way through the crowd. Once she reached the groom and best man, Scott offered her a nervous smile before gazing back toward the house, waiting.

Moments later, as the sun set the horizon on fire, he saw her, the love of his life, walking toward him with Grayson by her side. She was incredibly beautiful, with long blonde hair cascading over her shoulders, sky-blue eyes, and a mesmerizing smile that grew with each step. The soft white silk of her dress fell effortlessly over her protruding belly while her bare feet glided through the sand.

They both blinked back tears as she neared, and I gasped at the overwhelming energy flowing between them. I felt their story. The love, the loss, the devastation…but there was so much more. So much love. So much joy. And it gave me hope that, one day, after the darkness faded away, I could find love again.

I swiped away the tear rolling down my cheek, but it didn't go unnoticed. Adam took my hand and squeezed, grounding me instantly. I should've pulled away, but I couldn't. His touch settled my soul, and without my grandmother's crystals hugging my wrists, it was the only way I could get through the ceremony without breaking down.

Once the formalities ended and the guests surged toward the bride and groom, I slipped my hand out of Adam's and snuck away.

I didn't realize I was being followed until Adam grasped my arm. "Where are you going?"

"I just need a moment."

He turned me around to study my face. "What's happening here?"

"It's a system overload, that's all." I gazed out at the water. "All this love and happiness…it's…"

"It's the worst, I know." The corner of Adam's mouth twitched. He was trying to make me smile.

"No…" I nudged him away with a solemn chuckle. "It's beautiful…but so fucking draining."

He grew silent for a moment before bending down to untie his shoes.

"What are you doing?" I asked when he proceeded to tear off his socks and roll up his pants.

"Well, I read somewhere that saltwater helps empaths recharge, so…" He tugged me toward the shoreline.

"Adam…it's freezing!"

"Come on, just our feet," he said right before the water rushed over his toes. "Fuck!"

With a laugh, I jumped back before it hit me, too. "I told you!"

"Cass, trust me, you're going to need your energy tonight."

My gaze tapered. "Why?"

"Why do you think?" His sexy grin grew closer.

My mouth parted at the unspoken suggestion.

"So you can keep up with me on the dancefloor, of course," he continued with a laugh.

"Oh." My shoulders lowered, equally relieved and disappointed.

"What did you think I meant?"

My eyes turned into slits as I backstepped toward the party. "Enjoy your swim, Adam. I'm heading back to congratulate the happy couple."

As I turned and marched up the sand, Adam picked up his shoes and his pace.

"Looks like I'll have to get you wet another way," he uttered on his way past.

As my jaw dropped and my temper flared, Adam quickened his steps to the bride.

"Adam!" Melanie threw her arms around him.

"Smelly!" He returned her embrace. "Congratulations! You look gorgeous as always."

Melanie spotted me over his shoulder and pushed him aside. "And you must be Cassidy."

I reached out my hand, but she pulled me in for a hug. "Thank you for everything you're doing for Gramps. Gray says he's doing really well."

"Liam's a fighter. He won't give up easily, and neither will I."

She smirked at Adam. "Sounds like the Harlows are in good hands."

Adam narrowed his gaze at her before moving to congratulate Scott a few feet away.

"It really was a beautiful ceremony," I said, smiling as Melanie rubbed her stomach. "And congratulations on the impending arrival."

"Thank you…and thank you." The apples of her cheeks rose as she peered down at her belly. "We're over the moon right now."

"After all you've been through, you deserve every happiness."

She studied me with a bemused expression. "Do you and your sister share the same...*abilities*?"

"Not exactly. I can't see the future, but I can feel energies. Good and bad."

Her eyebrows rose. "And you have to hang out with Adam? I'm so sorry."

Laughter burst from my lips.

Adam returned to my side. "What's so funny?"

"Oh, nothing." I ran my hand over my mouth to smother my smile.

"Well, I better get back to my *husband*," Melanie said before turning to Adam. "You play nice."

"Yeah, yeah." He waved her off. "I'm always nice."

With a hoot, she disappeared into the crowd.

"I like her," I said, panning my gaze around the crowd. "I can see why she's so popular."

"She never used to have this many friends. She was notoriously hard to deal with growing up."

"Happiness doesn't come easily for everyone, but I'm glad she found hers."

"There you guys are!" My sister flung herself between us. "We're up on the deck, where it's warmer." She linked her arms into ours and directed us through the sand dunes and up the rickety timber stairs to a massive deck nestled under a sea of fairy lights.

"This is gorgeous," I said, admiring the space.

Josie grinned. "Melanie is a superstar when it comes to events."

My brow raised as I absorbed the details, including the custom-built dancefloor and bar. "She planned the entire wedding herself?"

"In the space of two months," Grayson said, tucking his arm around Josie's waist. "Which is two months longer than we had."

Josie giggled as he kissed her cheek.

"I'll get us a drink." Adam ran his hand across my back as he left for the bar.

Amy turned my way with arched eyebrows. "Us?"

"Don't read into it, Ames."

"Oh, I'm reading." She giggled.

"Leave your sister alone, babe." Reed passed her an appetizer. "And eat some of these. They're delicious."

"Zach's recipe, no doubt." Josie's eyes darted to the roving waiters. "I'm going in."

As she chased down the food, Adam returned, holding two drinks.

He handed over the lighter liquid. "Gin and tonic."

My eyes met his, and their warmth surprised me. "Thanks."

"Adam…" Amy rolled her head his way. "How do you know what Cassidy drinks?"

A hint of blush touched his cheeks as he swallowed a mouthful of whiskey. "I must be psychic."

"Unlikely." Amy cackled. "You hit on Josie while she was secretly dating your brother."

I almost spat out my drink. "You did?

"To be fair," Grayson said, rocking the stroller by his side, "he hits on every pretty girl he meets."

Adam and I took long sips, equally uncomfortable with the conversation.

Amy grabbed her boyfriend's hand. "Reed, it's time to dance."

His face fell. "But I'm not drunk yet."

"Reed, please," I begged. "She needs to release some energy." Amy had always been like this, bouncing from task to task, saying exactly what she thought. The doctors diagnosed her with ADHD in her early teens, but when she refused to take the medication, my grandmother found natural treatments to help ease her chaotic mind. They didn't always work, but that was okay. It was part of her gift, and I loved it about her. She was a free spirit and entirely happy in her own skin.

Josie reappeared, disheartened. "We'll have to wait until the next round," she said, tugging Grayson's arm. "Let's get in a better position. The food seems to be coming out that door."

"We'll be back," Grayson called out as he let Josie pull him and Harrison away.

And then it was just us.

"So…you and Josie, eh?"

Adam hung his head back with a groan. "It was a work Christmas party. If I'd had any idea she was hooking up with Gray, the short-winded encounter never would've happened."

"At least you're loyal to your brother."

"I'm loyal to everyone I love." He took a sip of his whiskey. "It's just a very short list."

Our eyes met, but we said nothing. There was a ball of energy growing between us that desperately needed dispersing.

The tapping on a microphone drew our attention to Scott walking into the middle of the dancefloor. "Where's my beautiful wife?" he asked, panning his gaze around the crowd.

Melanie appeared, jogging barefoot to be by his side. "Sorry, I had to pee—again."

I laughed with the majority, while Adam shifted closer. "What's so funny about that?"

"It's a pregnancy thing."

"Oh."

"I think," I muttered before taking a sip of my drink.

Adam's shoulder pressed up against mine, and I barely took in a word of the speeches. His jacket was off, so the heat radiating through his rolled-up shirt sleeve was warming my body.

The cool breeze off the ocean tickled my neck as I watched Scott and Melanie's first dance as husband and wife. As the music morphed into a more upbeat number, couples merged onto the dancefloor to join the happy couple.

Adam placed his empty glass on a nearby table and returned to my side, leaning over the handrail to face the ocean, seemingly disinterested in the action.

"For someone so confident with their endurance…on the dancefloor, I mean…I thought you'd be the first one out there."

"Not without you," he said, watching the water disappear into the night. "And you haven't finished your drink yet."

I gazed down at my last mouthful. "Oh."

"Then, you're in trouble."

Exhilaration tore through my body. Adam's words rarely matched the energy surging through him, but when they did, they knocked me off kilter. My heartrate accelerated as I lifted the glass to my mouth and swallowed my last-ditch effort at resistance. Adam had me, if only for the night.

I lowered my glass to find Adam's smile waiting. He took it and placed it beside his. "You ready?" He held out his hand.

Pushing past my reluctance, I drew a shaky breath and placed my hand in his.

Without hesitating, Adam pulled me through the crowd. My sister and his brother were smitten with their current dance partners, so our presence went easily undetected.

True to his word, we danced all night. With twinkling lights overhead, we twirled and dipped and laughed until we lost our breath. Our bodies were intoxicated with the perfect mix of alcohol, elation, and attraction, and I didn't even flinch when Adam drew me close when the music slowed.

"I haven't had this much fun in years," he said as his chest rose up and down.

I smiled. "Me too." I wrapped my arms around his broad shoulders, absorbing his mood. "Your soul feels so much lighter."

His blue eyes sparkled. "I'm starting to feel a little violated."

"Tell me about it." My chuckle evaporated. "No matter what I do, I can't seem to block you out."

His dilated gaze penetrated mine. "I know how you feel."

As our eyes spoke a million unsaid words, a baby's scream tore through the crowd.

"Sounds like your nephew wants to go home." I dropped my arms when I realized how close we were.

Adam reluctantly turned to watch his brother fussing over Harrison, while Josie gathered up their things. "Yep. He's turned into a pumpkin alright."

"We should go with them."

Adam's shoulders lowered as he ran his fingers through his hair. "I'll get our coats."

After I'd bid my farewells to Amy and Reed, I minded the stroller while Josie and Grayson said goodbye to the bride and groom.

The warmth of my shawl settled over my shoulders, and I glanced up to find Adam standing behind me. "Thanks." I tried to wrap every inch of my bare skin before we left the glorious warmth of the industrial heaters.

"You're going to freeze under that measly piece of material."

Little did he know, that measly piece of material had cost him four thousand dollars, but he was right. It wasn't enough.

He held up his coat. "Here."

"And what's going to keep you warm?"

"Whiskey. Come on, put it on."

Caving easily, I slipped my arms into his winter coat and relished the instant warmth.

"Better?"

"Much. Thanks, Adam."

Once Melanie gave Grayson an enduring embrace, she turned to us with Scott by her side. "Thanks for coming, Adam," she said, hugging him. "You actually looked like you had fun tonight."

A blush rose up his neck as he shoved his hands into his pockets. "I did, but you always know how to throw a good party."

Melanie peeked my way. "I think it's more about the company." She smiled before wrapping her arms around me. "Anyone who can get Adam Harlow on the dancefloor must be pretty special."

"Alright, alright..." Adam grasped my elbow and directed me toward the door.

With a quick wave to Scott, I followed the Harlows to the waiting limo.

Grayson moved to the seat behind the driver with Harrison and Josie, while I stayed in the back beside the window. Adam sat on the sideways-facing seat, but directly in front of me, blocking my view of the rest of the cabin. I didn't mind, though. Josie was already curling up with her head on Grayson's lap, while Grayson was concentrating on keeping Harrison's pacifier in place.

Although Adam and I were close enough to have a conversation, we remained quiet until Grayson's head dipped forward.

"Thank you for coming tonight," he said once certain his brother was asleep.

"Thank you for inviting me. Your friends are great."

He leaned back in the chair, spreading his legs wider. "They're Grayson's friends."

"So why were you invited to the wedding?"

His mouth opened, then closed, then opened again.

"You don't give yourself enough credit," I continued, tucking his jacket around my body a little tighter as I rested my head against the window. "You have a good heart, and they clearly see through your bullshit."

"Do you?" His emotionless expression did nothing to hinder the longing energy rolling toward me.

I closed my eyes, forcing him out. "I can't see anything else."

"Cass…" My name left his lips like a prayer, and when I didn't answer, he placed his hand on my exposed knee. "Cass…"

His warmth spread throughout my body, but my heart ached. How was I supposed to let Adam in if I couldn't control the way I felt? This man was going to destroy me. "I'm sleeping," I murmured, refusing to meet his gaze.

His finger drew circles over my skin, leaving goose bumps in its wake. "You're not."

"I am."

Adam's hand curled around the back of my knee. "You're not." He ran his finger back and forth over the crease.

My staggered breath confessed my arousal. "I…I'm…" My eyes flew open as the limo jerked to a stop. "I'm getting out." I launched across the cabin toward the exit. Before the chauffeur had a chance, I opened the door, leapt out, and marched toward the grand doors of Harlow Manor.

Moments later, Adam appeared next to me with his grumbling brother and Josie dragging behind. Throwing me a sideways glance, he slid the key into the lock and pushed open the oversized door.

The hall was dark, but I was used to it now. "Goodnight, guys," I said, jogging up the stairs.

"Night, Cass," Josie called out, cradling Harrison while Grayson placed the stroller by the door.

Adam's footsteps followed.

"Wait," he called out in a whisper as I opened my bedroom door.

I pressed my lips together and pivoted on his approach. "What is it, Adam?"

"You have my coat."

"Oh." I tore it off in a fluster. It was too hot in the mansion anyway. As I passed it over, his gaze held mine. "Thank you for not letting me freeze to death," I said when he said nothing.

As he stepped forward, I withdrew into my room. "Goodnight, Adam," I uttered before closing the door. I rested my head against the ornate timber as I steadied my breath. I wasn't equipped to play this game.

Two creaks led to my door. "Goodnight, Cassidy," he whispered from the other side.

I jumped back from the door, waiting for it to open. A moment passed before his footsteps retreated, leaving me both relieved and disappointed. My plan failed. We were so busy enjoying each other's company that I forgot my purpose. I forgot to protect my heart while I reached for his. It was impossible to get close to him without getting burned. I knew that now. Because Adam was the freaking sun.

Chapter 15

I threw off the blankets, desperate to cool down, but it didn't help. My room was too hot.

Each evening, Max would light the fireplaces in every room, filling them with enough heat to last through the night. Normally, I enjoyed watching the glowing embers die down, but tonight, they weren't going anywhere, and neither was the built-up yearning of my body. I needed to cool down before I did something stupid—*like knock on Adam's door.*

Giving up on sleep entirely, I slipped my silk robe over my matching nightdown and opened my bedroom door. Another enduring wave of desire rushed over me as I stared across the hallway, but I didn't succumb. Instead, I continued down the corridor to find another solution.

I tiptoed down the stairs, avoiding each creaky step, until my feet reached the cool floorboards of the grand hall. Not wanting to alert the staff, I used the light of the moon and dying fires to guide me through the dark mansion.

Another log burned within the original oven of the kitchen, giving me enough light to find what I was looking for. I opened the large freezer and rummaged through the contents, hoping to find a tub of ice cream to satisfy at least one of my cravings.

"You won't find the good stuff in there," a deep voice sounded from the doorway.

I sprung back with wide eyes, too surprised to speak.

Adam leaned against the door frame, in full-length pajama pants, with his arms folded across his naked torso. Add his irritatingly gorgeous smirk, and my temperature morphed into a fever.

"It's kept under lock and key," he continued as he entered the kitchen.

I stepped backward until my butt collided with the stainless-steel island bench.

He chuckled softly at my attempt to keep a safe distance. "Luckily, I know where the key is hidden."

As he approached the shelves full of fruit preserves, my gaze traveled to his ass, then traced up his muscular back and across his broad shoulders.

"Close your eyes," he said as he ran his fingers over the jars.

I'd assumed I'd been busted perving on his godlike body until I realized he simply wanted to keep Max's hiding place a secret. With a roll of my eyes, I closed them. "I'm hardly going to steal your precious ice cream."

"You haven't tasted it yet," he said, clinking jars around. "When Grayson and I were little, we used to sneak downstairs once everyone was asleep and devour every sweet we could find in here." He snickered. "Until our mother caught us, that is. We weren't allowed treats, so she demanded all the good stuff be locked away."

"But you're grown now. Surely you have some self-control."

There was a short silence before his husky voice sounded only a few feet away. "Apparently not."

I opened my eyes to find his gaze glued to my body. My robe had come undone, giving him a full view of every curve. With a growl, I quickly wrapped myself back up. "So, did you find the key?"

His jaw clenched as he dragged his eyes away. "Of course." He moved toward another freezer and unlocked it. "I never told Grayson, though."

"That's mean."

Adam shrugged. "I'm not much of a sharer. Plus..."—his twinkling eyes met mine— "It's nice to have a few secrets... don't you think?"

My mouth parted at his suggestive smile.

He held up two tubs. "Mint chocolate chip or vanilla?"

It took me a moment to respond. "Vanilla," I finally said, a little breathless.

With a chuckle, he returned the vanilla to the freezer. "Mint chocolate chip, it is."

"But I said—"

"I think you're done with vanilla." He rummaged through a drawer for two spoons before turning to me with a raised brow. "Don't you think?"

I gnashed my teeth at his meaning. "Fine." I reached for the ice cream. "Hand it over."

Adam opened the tub and leaned against the opposite bench, grinning as he dug his spoon inside.

"Quit teasing, and give it to me."

He pushed off the bench. "Easy, Tiger," he said, moving to my side to place the tub on the counter between us.

I snatched the spare spoon from his hand and perched myself on the bench to create more space between us.

As Adam filled his mouth, I scooped up a spoonful and joined him. "Oh," I gushed. "Wow."

He rolled his tongue over his smirking lips. "I bet you're not thinking of vanilla now."

"Vanilla who?" I dove in again. His sexual innuendo was lost on me now.

"And *this* is why I didn't show you where the key is."

"Excuse me," I scoffed. "I have self-control."

"You pretend you do."

"I don't *pretend* anything."

"You pretend like you don't like these little games we play." He drew circles over my knee, like he had in the limo.

I squirmed under his touch, fighting the all-encompassing desire he induced. "I don't play games."

"So, remind me again." He ran his fingers across the hem of my nightgown. "What happens on page 328?"

"Oh." I almost choked. "Um…"

"Don't hold out on me now, Tiger." He shifted closer. "You had me up all night." My nipples rose under my silk pajamas, drawing his gaze and amplifying his smile. "It must've been good."

"On the contrary." I surrendered to the ache below. "It was very, *very* bad."

Adam's pupils darkened as he slid his body between my legs and braced each hand on the kitchen counter, caging me in. "You like it bad?"

"I...I don't know." But my body screamed yes.

His lips grazed the sensitive skin under my earlobe. "I think we should find out." As he pressed his hardness against my core, the spoon fell from my fingers and clattered onto the floor. "Whoops," he murmured while his mouth trailed down my neck and across my collarbone.

My chest pushed out as my head hung back, relishing his touch. With his tongue dipping into my cleavage, Adam emitted a low growl before sliding his hands under my robe and up my thighs. Once they found my breasts, his cool fingertips circled my nipples through the silk, inducing a shiver that rattled my entire body.

"You like that?" Adam asked, orbiting the rise again. "The cold against your hot body?"

With my voice depleted, I nodded, desperately wanting him to do it again.

He reached for the tub of ice cream. "I better keep these fingers cold, then." My mouth parted as he poked his finger inside and scooped some out. "And my tongue."

A gasp floated from my lips as he placed the ice cream into his mouth and threw my leg over his shoulder. Before I could comprehend what was happening, his rascally smile lowered to my center and delved into my seam. His ice-cold tongue stroked and circled while my body buckled off the counter.

I cried out, over and over, while he feasted on me, experiencing an orgasm like no other. It was incredibly erotic and like nothing I'd ever read in my books.

"Where did you read how to do that?" I panted as he lapped up the mess he made.

A small smile played on his lips as he lifted his lust-infused gaze. "I'm writing my own book now, Tiger. And it's far from over."

As he lowered my quivering legs, he pulled my body up to meet his and crashed his lips onto mine. The sweet chocolate-mint flavor danced around my mouth along with his tongue while I grasped his stubbled jaw, wanting more. He deepened the kiss with a rumbling growl while pulling down the straps of my nightgown to fondle my breasts. His hands, his mouth, and his body were everywhere, yet I ached for more. I needed him inside me.

"Tell me what you want, Cass," he said between mind-altering kisses.

I could barely think, let alone form a coherent answer.

"Tell me." He pinched my nipple while wrapping his mouth around the other.

"I…" My heart pounded along with my core.

He lifted his lust-filled gaze. "Say it, Cassidy. Tell me what you want."

"I want you to fuck me."

The corner of his swollen lips curved upward. "That's my girl," he said, pressing his erection against my throbbing center.

Ready to reveal the extent of his desire, Adam hooked his thumbs over the elastic of his pants but froze at the sound of creaking floorboards in the adjoining room.

My head snapped to the door, and when I caught sight of the approaching shadow, I scrambled off the counter to hide behind it moments before they entered.

"What the fuck are you still doing awake?" Grayson asked as he walked into the kitchen, carrying Harrison's bottle.

I spied his movements through the pots and pans stored underneath the counter, along with Adam's erection as he leaned over the bench.

"Thought I'd have a midnight snack," Adam said, filling his mouth with another spoonful of ice cream.

"What are you? Twelve?" He paused. "Wait. Is that what I think it is?"

"Yes, and fuck off." He pushed his brother away. "It's mine."

"Whatever." Grayson continued to the bottle warmer. "Hey, I've been meaning to ask you. How was your date with Staci last night?"

My heart stopped as a deafening silence filled the room and plummeted when Adam didn't deny it. How could I have been so naïve?

A deep sigh followed. "It was fine," Adam said, admitting what I already knew. He was a manwhore.

"To be honest, I was surprised you agreed to it."—Grayson sniggered— "Since you told me she was terrible in bed."

Adam slammed his hand down on the lid of the ice cream tub before turning around, his erection now gone. "I don't want to talk about it."

"Since when don't you brag about your conquests?"

"Since now," he snapped, bending over to pick up the spoon I'd dropped moments before.

I turned away, refusing to look at the man who had fooled me into thinking I wasn't one of many.

"What's going on with you, man?" Grayson's voice softened. "You've been acting weird since Harrison was born…maybe longer."

"How would you know? I've barely seen you in the past year."

"And whose fault is that?" When Adam didn't say anything, Grayson continued, "Look, I know you're upset about Gramps—"

"It has nothing to do with Gramps!"

"Fine…" Grayson sighed. "But whatever it is, sort it out quickly. Gramps doesn't have a lot of time left, and he wants to see us *both* happy." His footsteps retreated to the door but paused before leaving. "And don't dick around with Cassidy. She's had enough heartache to last her a lifetime."

Tears burned my eyes because it was true. I'd had more than my fair share.

Once Grayson left, a shiver rolled over me as my blood ran cold.

"Cass…" Adam's voice called through the fog, but I refused to answer. "Let me explain."

"That won't be necessary," I muttered, keeping my eyes lowered. He reached out, but I recoiled from his touch. "Don't."

"Cassidy...please..."

Clenching my jaw to stall the impending tears, I wrapped my robe around my waist, like it was the only thing holding me together, and hurried out of the room.

Chapter 16

Adam's steps slowed at my door, but he didn't knock. I held my breath, praying he'd listened to his brother, and exhaled when his bedroom door closed moments later. It was an epically bad idea to get close to Adam. He wasn't sweet and caring like Dominic. He was hard and callous, yet had the face of an angel. Fallen. No wonder I fell for his tricks. He was the fucking devil.

After washing away his touch and the lingering chocolate-mint aroma, I threw on an old t-shirt and shorts and crawled into bed. Needing to ground myself, I reached into my nightstand drawer and pulled out the photo of my son. My reason. I traced the dark hair he'd inherited from his father and stared into his green eyes, so much like mine, and my heart filled with love. I held on, imagining him with me, until I finally fell asleep.

———

Early the next morning, a light tapping on my bedroom door stirred me awake.

"Cass," Adam whispered through the crack. "Are you awake?"

Ignoring the hammering of my heart, my head sank back onto the pillow while the mortifying memory of the night prior coursed through my brain.

"Cass…"

My fist curled around the edge of the pillow, then threw it across the room. It smacked into the door, giving him my answer.

The door knob jiggled, and I launched out of bed, forgetting I'd locked it the night prior.

My cell vibrated across my nightstand, giving me another start.

Adam: **Open the door.**

When I didn't respond, another message appeared.

Adam: **There's a situation at work, and I have to leave. I need to see you before I go.**

Relief settled over me. This was going to be easier than I thought.

Me: **Have a safe flight.**

There was a thud on my door, presumably his forehead, moments before his bedroom door slammed shut across the hall. He got the message.

————

After Grayson, Josie, and Harrison left that afternoon, I had dinner with Liam before returning to my room to video-call Finn. We chatted until he grew tired of my never-ending questions, then promptly disappeared when his favorite television show came on.

Dad appeared in his place. "He's doing fine."

I offered him a solemn smile. "I know. I just miss him so much."

"He misses you, too, sweetie," he said as a squeal of laughter sounded from the living room behind him.

I rolled my eyes. "Clearly."

"Well, he does. I do, too." After an awkward pause, my father continued, "How's it all going there?"

"Liam's so great, Dad. I think you'd like him."

"And the family?"

"They're…a handful."

"Well, in a month, it will all be over, and you'll never have to see them again."

My heart dipped unexpectedly. "Yeah, I guess."

"Thanksgiving won't be the same without you, squirt."

Emotion surged through my body. "We'll make up for it at Christmas." I held back tears as I blew him a kiss. "I'll speak to you Thursday."

"Bye, Cass."

Once I closed my laptop, my cell phone burst into song.

"Everything okay?" Amy asked the moment the phone hit my ear.

I wiped away my tears. "I'm fine, Ames."

"That's bullshit, and you know it. What's going on?"

"I'm missing Finn, that's all."

"Are you sure that's all of it?"

"Oh, didn't I tell you? My boss is dying."

"Ha-ha. You live in a very morbid world, Cassidy Ryan."

"I wouldn't go pointing fingers, weirdo."

"Well, my Spidey senses told me to check in with my sister, but if everything's okay...I'll get back to my half-naked boyfriend."

"Ames..." I grimaced. "Please tell me you weren't in the middle of having sex when you had to stop and call me?"

"I can't control these things."

I pinched the bridge of my nose. "Poor Reed."

"Oh, he gets plenty. Don't you worry about him."

"Ames!"

My sister giggled. "It was so good to see you last night. Shame you won't be at Dad's for Thanksgiving. The Harlows better give you an amazing recommendation after this."

I exhaled heavily. "Here's hoping."

"You've definitely won over Adam, and that's virtually impossible."

"I don't know about that."

"Are you kidding? I've never seen Adam so...so..."

"It was all an act, Ames." I didn't want to hear it. "Nothing more."

"Cass..."

"Don't read into it."

"Fine," she grumbled before instantly cheering up. "Well, at least you'll be there to keep an eye on Josie over Thanksgiving. It's the anniversary of her parents' accident, and she hasn't dealt with it well in the past."

My heart ached for her. Dominic's anniversary was the worst. "Of course."

"I knew you would understand." A muffled voice stole her attention. "Okay, okay!" she called out. "Look. I better go. Reed's got an hour before his next tournament, and I'm his good luck charm."

"And how do you bring him luc—" My mind caught up with my mouth. "Oh, gross! Forget I asked." As her laughter filled my ear, I groaned and swiftly hung up the phone before texting her.

Me: **Love you, Ames.**

Amy: **Love you too.** 🍒🍀

———

It was the day before Thanksgiving, and Josie, Grayson, and Harrison surprised Liam by arriving earlier than the rest of the family. Their giant dog burst into the house and up the stairs, almost knocking me over as he searched for Liam.

"There he is," Liam announced as Luci lifted his paws onto his bed. He stood taller than me.

Josie bolted in after him. "I'm so sorry! He got away from me."

"That's perfectly okay." Liam tickled his chin. "He's welcome up here anytime."

"I don't think Mrs. Fredrich will like that very much."

Liam waved her off. "I'll handle her."

"Well, Luci does deserve some TLC." Josie stroked his mass of wiry hair. "He's been a little neglected since Harry was born."

"At least he hasn't eaten him," Grayson said, walking into the room with Harrison asleep on his shoulder.

"He would never." Josie scowled before squeezing her dog's chops. "Would you, Lucifer?"

And all of a sudden, the name made sense. Luci-fer. With a soft chuckle, I puffed up the pillows behind Liam to help him sit up.

"Would you like to hold Harrison?" Grayson asked his grandfather. "He's refusing to go into his bed, and I can no longer feel my arm."

"Bring him here." He reached out his rickety arms. "I'd refuse mine, too, if I could."

While Liam was happy and engaged, I took the opportunity to head down to Betty's garden to gather a bouquet of fresh flowers for his room. Although we were on the cusp of winter, there were still many varieties to choose from: daphnes, snowdrops, geraniums…even a few daffodils. If only it was the season for freesias. Liam would love that.

As I returned to the house some time later, I overheard Grayson and Josie talking in the drawing room. After promising Amy I'd keep an eye on Josie, I peeked through the crack of the closed French doors to make sure she was okay.

"I told Dad to get rid of Craig, but he wouldn't listen." Grayson paced the room. "Now Adam has to clean up the mess."

Josie sighed from the armchair where she was feeding Harrison. "How bad is it?"

"The whole Ferguson deal is screwed. Adam's had to sack everyone he hired for the project."

Josie gasped. "Right before Thanksgiving?! That's awful."

"Normally, he'd wait until after the holidays and phase them out over time, but he's so furious right now he can't see reason."

"He must have a lot of emotion bottled up. With work and Gramps' condition…"

"He says it has nothing to do with Gramps, but I don't know." Grayson lowered his head as he scuffed the Persian rug with his foot. "I guess I haven't been in his life too much lately to know what's going on in his head."

"Or who," Josie added with a chuckle.

Grayson's eyes shot up. "What?"

"You haven't noticed the way he looks at Cassidy?" Josie smiled. "How he was with her at the wedding?"

My heart pounded in my chest. I should've left, but my feet were frozen in place.

"Yeah, I noticed," he grumbled before crossing his arms. "But he also slept with Staci the night before."

My stomach roiled at the reminder.

"You don't know that." Josie shook her head. "I think he's changing."

"Yeah, well, I told him to stay away from her anyway."

"You what?"

"She's here to look after Gramps, Jos. She doesn't need my womanizing brother sniffing around."

"Well, I don't think you should be getting involved."

"After what you said she's been through, I don't think it's a good idea."

"Maybe not, but I know what I saw on Saturday night, and I wish I'd captured it on my camera."

Grayson sighed. "Fine, I'll stay out of it." He peered down at his son and smiled. "Has he finished already?"

"Yep! Milk drunk and ready for another round of Grampa cuddles," Josie said, lifting Harrison onto her shoulder.

As she stood, my flight reflex kicked in, and I bolted up the stairs, dipping into my bedroom moments before they ambled up the hallway.

"When's everyone else getting here?" Josie asked as they made their way to Liam's room.

"The helicopter's bringing Adam over now, and Mom and Dad are arriving in the morning."

"Oh, in that case, why don't you take your brother out tonight? Try and get him to open up over a few drinks."

I peeked out as they passed my doorway to see Grayson stop and turn to his wife. "Josie, I'm not leaving you for one second over this holiday."

"It's going to be different this year, I promise." She clutched his bicep while carrying Harrison in her other arm. "I finally have something to be thankful for. My own little family."

Grayson swallowed back emotion as he gazed into his wife's eyes. "And we love you so much."

Josie kissed Harrison's forehead before relishing her husband's lips. "And I love you too."

I grasped my bracelets, endeavoring to block their energy, but it was so beautiful I let a little seep through. The love they had for each other was intoxicating.

Knowing Adam would be arriving soon, and Marc was due for Liam's check-up, I asked Warren to drive me to the beach. I was free to do as I pleased over the holidays, so I took the opportunity to cleanse my crystals. It was going to take all my strength to combat the entire Harlow family over the next four days, so I needed every edge.

I arrived back at Harlow Manor in the early evening, after Warren was summoned back to the estate to take Grayson and Adam out. I was hoping to avoid Adam altogether, but the universe had other plans, and when the car pulled up, it was Adam who opened my door like the chivalrous man he was not.

"Hey, Cass," he said softly as I stepped out.

Pain radiated through my chest when our eyes met—his or mine, I couldn't tell. "Hi, Adam."

"How are you?"

"Fine, thanks. You?"

"I've had better weeks."

My jaw tightened as I tried not to care.

"Sorry, Cass," Grayson called out as he jogged down the entrance steps. "I was happy to book a taxi, but someone was adamant about using our driver."

"It's fine. I was ready to come back anyway."

Adam pressed his lips together and looked off into the distance while Grayson sidled up beside him.

"Josie told me to tell you she has wine and pizza in our room, if you're interested." Worry flickered through his aura. "I know she'd love the company."

I smiled his way. "That sounds nice. I'll head up there now."

"Thanks, Cassidy."

As Grayson jumped into the car, my gaze traveled back to Adam when he didn't move.

"You coming?" Grayson yelled out.

"Yeah." Adam gave me a *'we'll talk later'* glare before climbing in. "Let's go."

Straightening my back as he closed the door, I spun on my heel and marched toward the house, feeling Adam's eyes on me at every step. It looked like I'd be spending the rest of the Thanksgiving holiday locked in my bedroom, which was fine with me. A good book and a direct line of communication with my son was all I needed to feel grateful.

Once I reached the top of the staircase, I turned right, instead of left, to enter the west wing of the house. I rarely ventured to this side, for fear of getting lost, but from the music blaring up ahead, I was heading in the right direction.

I peeked my head around the open door. "Hey, Josie."

"Cassidy! You came!" Josie mumbled excitedly through a mouthful of pizza. She motioned me to their couch as she swallowed her food. "Please sit, eat, and listen to music with me!"

With a laugh, I sank onto the chair opposite and peered around their room. It was even bigger than mine.

"As you can probably tell, I'm a little excited about having a break from my son," she said, turning down the music.

"Where is he?" I asked, glancing around the room with a frown.

"He fell asleep in Gramps' room, so he told me to leave him there until he wakes."

"Oh, Liam would love that."

"I wish Mrs. Fredrich did. Apparently, babies aren't in her job description, so we've set up a monitor." She pointed down at the little screen on the coffee table. "If he cries, I have to be up there within twenty seconds."

"It's a shame Nora went home for the holidays. She would've loved the baby cuddles."

Josie leaned back into the chair and pondered me quietly. "You must feel like a prisoner here." Her eyes were full of remorse. "I'm sorry their rules are so strict."

"Please don't apologize. This is going to help us so much. I can deal with a few missed holidays if it means Finn and I can move back to LA."

"You wouldn't consider staying on the East Coast? I know your sister would love it."

My heart dipped. "I know…but it's not my home anymore."

"I understand," Josie said with a solemn smile. "I loved Australia, but this is where I belong."

A rush of sadness vibrated through her as she filled two glasses with wine and handed one over.

"Amy told me about your parents," I said, hyperaware of her surfacing pain.

She took a sip of her wine. "Please don't say you're sorry."

I chuckled. "You hate that too?"

Josie gazed up at me through glazed eyes. "It must've been so hard losing your husband like that." Her voice grew hoarse. "Sometimes I wonder what's worse: losing someone instantly or from a long illness."

I swallowed back emotion with a mouthful of wine. "They're both awful."

The song switched to Tom Petty's "I Won't Back Down", and Josie grinned at the stereo. "This is one of my dad's favorite songs."

"Dominic loved this one, too. He played it on repeat throughout his treatment."

"We should take it as a sign, then." Josie brought her glass toward mine. "To keep living, no matter how much it hurts."

"And to men with exceptionally good music taste," I added before clinking her glass.

"Speaking of men…" She sheepishly ran her finger around her glass. "Did anything happen between you and Adam after the wedding?"

"No," I uttered too quickly. "I mean…not really."

"Not really?" Her brows raised.

"We didn't sleep together, if that's what you're asking."

"Maybe *that's* why he's been so crabby lately. He's not used to getting turned down."

"I'm not risking my job for…" *The best sex of my life.* "For *that.*"

"I don't think you need to worry about your job here. Liam loves you, and his doctor says you're making all the difference."

I grasped the opportunity to divert the conversation. "So, his check-up went well today?"

"Amazing, actually. Marc said Gramps is well enough to have Thanksgiving dinner with us downstairs, and it's made his week."

I smiled. "That's so great."

"I never knew how powerful Reiki could be."

"Liam's still here because he wants to be. The Reiki only helps manage his pain where medication can no longer."

"It's for physical and emotional pain, right?"

I nodded. "Has Amy tried it on you?"

"A little over the years…" She lowered her eyes as pain simmered under her cheerful façade. "When I've really needed it."

"I can do some for you now, if you'd like?"

Her eyes lit up. "Really? I mean, I'll pay you…"

"Don't be silly. It's really no bother." I stood and walked around the coffee table. "Lie down and close your eyes."

Over the next hour, I held my hands over her body, channeling healing energy as I did for Liam each morning and night.

Josie's features softened through the treatment until a small smile played on her lips. "Wow." She yawned. "You have a gift."

"You'll sleep well tonight," I said, moving back to my chair.

"If only." Josie poured me another wine. "Grayson is out drinking with his brother, so I doubt he'll be fit to be on Harrison duty tonight."

"Boys' night?" I pretended I didn't know.

"Something like that. Adam's having a rough time at work, so Grayson's taking him out to blow off some steam."

And get him laid, no doubt. "His work sounds…intense."

Josie sighed. "Since Grayson left the company, Adam won't let anyone help him, and since he's acquired the Warren Media portfolio, he is swamped. Now, due to someone else's fuck-up, he's on the verge of being sued…and thus reinforcing the fact that he can't trust anyone."

"But surely these things happen all the time."

"Oh, they do, but not to the protégé of William Harlow. Their dad doesn't take lightly to failure, and I think, deep down, Adam is still vying for his approval."

"And now he gets to spend the whole weekend with them." I sipped my wine. "He must be thrilled."

"I'm actually surprised he didn't stay in LA. I thought he would've bailed on Thanksgiving altogether."

"Well, hopefully he'll get the release he needs tonight." *Into some gorgeous woman's vagina, no doubt.*

Josie hung her head back and groaned. "Why do I feel another Harlow storm brewing?"

"Well, they better not get into it around Liam. He deserves a wonderful Thanksgiving, and I won't have anyone ruining that for him."

"You know what, Cassidy?" Josie grinned. "You're exactly what this family needs."

"This family needs to talk," I stated bluntly. "I've never experienced so many bottled-up emotions under one roof."

"The Harlows?! Talk openly? I'd like to see that."

"So would I." I stared into my glass, thinking of Adam as I examined the wine. "Liam's peace may depend on it."

"What do you mean?"

"Liam's in incredible pain, but he refuses to pass over until he knows, deep down, that his family will be okay without him."

"He's worried about Adam, isn't he?"

I lifted my gaze. "Aren't you?"

Josie sank back into her chair. "Grayson's trying to get him to open up, but I don't like his chances. He's never even seen his brother cry—even as kids."

"That's a lot of built-up emotion."

"Sometimes, I wonder if he feels anything at all, but then he'll do the smallest thing, the most unexpected gesture, and it changes everything. My brother-in-law is a fucking conundrum."

I chuckled at her description. "I know what you mean."

"You see it, too?"

"All the time. One minute he's the fucking devil, and the next..." I froze, unable to express my feelings without revealing too much.

"You can't think of anyone else?" Josie tilted her head, trying to see truth in my eyes. "I know how that feels."

"I…" Fear stole my words.

"It's okay, Cass." Josie's understanding filtered through her energy.

"Is it that obvious?"

"Not to the untrained eye."

My shoulders plummeted. "It's so stupid, I know."

"It's not stupid…and it's definitely not one-sided."

"Are you sure about that? He slept with someone else less than a week ago."

Josie withdrew her glass from her mouth. "He told you that?"

"Well, no…but I can safely assume."

"I don't think you can safely assume anything with Adam."

I shook my head. "Regardless, I'm nothing more than a convenient distraction while he's here. If anything, I'm making this entire situation worse. Liam wants me to guide Adam through this grief, and I can't…" I closed my eyes. "I can't be that person for him."

"Then be someone else." Josie moved to my side and took my hand. "Stop resisting your heart, and see where it goes. I'm not promising he won't fuck it all up, but I know it's worth the risk."

"Josie…"

"If it doesn't work out, you'll never have to see him again. You've been through worse things than a broken heart."

"But what about Finn?"

"If he genuinely cares about you, he'll care about him, too."

"Adam doesn't want kids…you said so yourself."

"If that's true, then you'll know to walk away."

As I sculled the last of my wine, a cluster of scenarios crashed through my mind like dodgem cars.

"And I really don't think he slept with Staci. Adam doesn't repeat mistakes."

I groaned inwardly. "So, they have history?"

"Barely," Josie scoffed out. "One drunken night in college, apparently. He only went out with her to appease his mother." Josie welcomed another mouthful of wine. "Caroline and William are relentless when it comes to their sons' love lives."

"Another reason to steer clear."

"I hear ya." Josie tittered. "But don't let them deter you. Adam's not a pushover…and he rarely does anything he doesn't want to."

"Like accepting his grandfather's diagnosis?"

Josie chest deflated. "Exactly."

———

After midnight, the obnoxious sound of drunken laughter announced Grayson and Adam's return. Their singing grew louder with each step of the grand staircase and divided in two as they parted ways.

Adam's humming morphed into a hiss as he knocked something off the hallway table. "Whoops," he mumbled, stumbling closer to our rooms.

I listened for his door to close, but only silence followed. *Where did he go?*

A clumsy tap sounded at my door. "Cassssidy…"

My fingers froze as I turned the page of my novel. *Shit.*

"Come on, Cass…I know you're reading. I can see the light under the door."

With a growl, I reached over to my nightstand and switched off my lamp.

"I'm not leaving until you speak to me."

With a deep sigh, I climbed out of bed, slipped on my robe, and whipped the door open. I raised my brow at his heavily glazed eyes. He'd clearly had more than a few drinks.

"Hey." He stumbled back in surprise.

"It's late, Adam, and I'm not on the clock. If Liam doesn't need me, then you have no reason to be knocking at my door."

He raised his arm on the door frame and leaned forward. "But what if I need you?"

"Goodnight, Adam," I grumbled before grasping the door handle.

Adam pressed his hand against the closing door. "Don't freeze me out, Cass."

"I…" I lowered my voice. "I'm not freezing you out. I'm… reinstating our boundaries".

"Fuck boundaries." He stepped closer. "I want you in my bed."

"And turning up at my door, reeking of whiskey, was your plan to woo me there?" I stared up into his gorgeous blue eyes. "That may work on other girls, but it will never work on me."

Adam's eyes rolled over my silk-covered body. "Romance isn't my style, Cass. You know that."

"And you'd fuck a different girl every night to prove it."

His furrowed gaze lifted to mine. "The only girl I've fucked lately is you."

"And I'm supposed to believe that." My eyebrows raised as I crossed my arms.

He grasped my upper arm as his eyes pierced mine. "Nothing happened with Staci."

"So, you've never fucked her?" I asked, curious to see if he'd deny it.

His gaze faltered. "Well, no…but it was years ago."

I shrugged him off, needing the conversation to end. "Look, who you date…or *fuck*—is none of my business."

"Then why do you sound so fucking jealous?"

My mouth dropped. "Jealous?!"

"Easy, Tiger. You're turning green."

"You're unbelievable," I muttered as I slammed the door in his face.

"You would know…" Adam sang out before a loud thud sounded against the door. "I'm not going to bed without you, Cassidy."

With a wince, I slipped back into bed and stared at the door, pondering my conversation with Josie earlier. Maybe I was wrong about him. Maybe he was worth the risk. Maybe, away from Harlow Manor, we could be more. I knew he had a heart hidden under his ruthless façade, but if it didn't have space for my son, I could never give him mine.

———

An hour before sunrise, I woke to the alarm reminding me to take Liam to the library. After washing my face and changing into a pair of skinny jeans and an oversized wool sweater, I swung open my door to have a grown man tumble to my feet.

Adam winced and groaned as he stirred awake.

With a sigh, I bent over and pulled him up. "Come on," I muttered, steering his large, broad-shouldered body across the hall.

After dumping him onto his bed, he gazed up at me with a lazy grin. "I knew you'd take me to bed eventually."

The corner of my mouth twitched, but I fought off the smile. Drunk or not, I couldn't show any weakness to his charming ways. "Do you need any pain relief?"

"Mmmhmm," he murmured, unzipping his fly. "Please."

"Oh my God, Adam!" I smacked his arm. "That's not what I meant!"

"I know…but it was worth a try."

Shaking my head, I searched his bathroom for the pain killers he'd need within hours—especially with his parents arriving soon—and filled a glass of water. As I placed it on his nightstand, my gaze traveled to the gorgeous man before me.

His chest rose and fell in steady succession, but the deep line between his eyebrows remained. Although he was fast asleep, his face wore tension that stirred my soul. Reaching out, I traced my finger over the line, wanting to draw his pain away, but snatched it back when Adam emitted a heavy sigh.

"Don't go," he whispered, but his eyes remained closed and body still. He was talking in his sleep.

As my racing heart slowed, I backed out of the room, needing to get to Liam before the sun rose on his final Thanksgiving.

Chapter 17

"I want you to have dinner with us," Liam said as the sky lit up before us. "Doc says I'm well enough to join the family in the dining room, and I'd like you to be my date."

"I don't think Caroline and William would be very accepting of that notion."

"I don't care what they think. You have been by my side every day since you arrived, and I'll forever be grateful for the time you've given me. I want you at my table, Cassidy, and I won't take no for an answer."

I sniggered at his persistence. Adam clearly inherited that trait from his grandfather. "Then I better go find something to wear."

"Wonderful. I'll pick you up at seven."

"It's the 21st century, Liam. I'll pick you up."

His laughter filled the library as he grasped my hand. "Oh, Betty would've loved you."

"And I can see why she fell for you." He was as smooth as his grandson. "Now, let's get you back to bed before Caroline and William get here."

———

My entire day was spent on a video-call with my family. I watched my son muck around with Reed in the background, while Amy and I chatted with my father as they prepared dinner. A few family friends came and went, and my dad's latest girlfriend dropped by before Finn pulled the laptop into his bedroom.

"You okay, Mom?" His voice was full of concern.

"Don't worry about me, Finny." I admired his empathic nature. "Are you excited about your birthday on Sunday?"

Finn shrugged. "I guess…"

"I've arranged for Aunty Amy to make your favorite meal."

"It won't be the same."

"I know, but I'm trying." Guilt churned my stomach. "You know how desperately I want to be there with you, don't you?"

Finn sighed heavily. "Yeah, I know."

"We're a team, you and I, and we'll get through this, just like everything else."

"At least you'll be home for Christmas," he said with eyes full of optimism.

The pressure in my chest increased. Although my contract ended mid-December, the fine print stated it may extend if Liam lived beyond his expected time. The thought of Christmas without my son tore at my heart, but so did the notion of this wonderful old man passing away without the peace I could bring him.

I smiled through my angst as Finn's name was called to dinner. "You better go, Finny, before Aunty Amy steals all the mac and cheese."

His eyes tapered. "She wouldn't."

"Remember last year?"

"I gotta go! Love you, Mom."

"Love you, too, Finn."

Once Finn ended the call, my smile faded. While my family was delving into an array of glorious Thanksgiving platters, I felt like I was preparing for war. Although I loved Liam's company, and Grayson and Josie were friendly, the rest of the Harlows were problematic. And if Josie's prediction was correct, I had to be ready to diffuse the ticking time bomb.

———

Just before seven, there was a knock on my door. I hurriedly straightened my sweater dress and tore my hair from my mom-bun, letting the waves cascade over my shoulders.

"Liam, I said I'd come to you." I swung open the door, annoyed that he'd somehow ventured down the hall on his own.

Adam stole my breath as he stood before me in slacks and a shirt with rolled-up sleeves. His blond hair was combed back, still damp from the shower.

"Oh, it's you."

Adam lifted his tired gaze. "Sorry to disappoint you, but Gramps asked me to escort you to dinner."

My brows raised as I closed the door behind me. "I'm more surprised you made it out of bed."

"The pain-killer fairy helped out with that one." He rubbed his cleanly shaven jawline. "Thank you, by the way. The next few hours are going to be brutal."

I grimaced internally as I continued down the hall.

"About last night…" Adam caught up in a few easy steps. "I'm pretty sure I said some inappropriate things."

"You've said worse sober."

"Right. Well, I want to apologize."

My head recoiled. "Oh, really?"

"Not for everything." His grin grew wide and incredibly sexy. "Only for what I can't remember."

Trying not to smile, I made my way down the stairs but slowed when Adam didn't follow. "Are you coming?" I asked, turning back.

"Yeah." He stalled again in the grand hallway when William Harlow's distinct voice sounded beyond the dining room doors.

"You haven't seen them yet, have you?" I understood his apprehension.

Adam's jaw twitched as he shook his head.

"Come on." I tugged his hand. "If I can walk in there, so can you."

Once we reached the double doors, they suddenly flew open, giving us no time to gather our senses. With a gasp, I pulled my hand from Adam's and smiled sheepishly at Max as he stepped aside.

"Mother, Father." Adam strolled into the room, seemingly clear of worry.

His mother wrapped her arms around his stiff body. "Adam, darling. We've missed you."

He kissed his mother's cheek before turning to his father, but William didn't rise from the table, or look at his son.

While Caroline flustered over Adam, my gaze tracked to Josie, who motioned me over to the seat between her and Liam. Eyeing the most festive array of Thanksgiving foods I'd ever seen, I moved around the table to join them.

Caroline's eyes grew large when her gaze caught mine. "What are you doing?"

My entire body tensed under her unrelenting glare.

"Cassidy is my guest, Caroline," Liam snapped, unnervingly stern. "And you will not say another word about it."

Her nose raised as she sank into her chair. "Very well."

"I'd like to start with a toast." Liam lifted a glass in his trembling hand. "I wasn't expecting to make it this far, let alone be sitting here for Thanksgiving dinner, and I have one special person to thank for that." He leaned into my side. "Cassidy, you've given me the most precious gift of all. Time."

My cheeks warmed as everyone's gazes panned my way, some warm, some cold, and the one directly opposite...completely unreadable.

"To Cassidy!" Grayson called out as he held up his drink.

Josie, Liam, and Adam followed, leaving Caroline and William shifting in their chairs with agitation.

Adam and Grayson winced as they swallowed the champagne.

Josie laughed. "I told you two to go out for a few drinks... not all of them."

"Hey, I stopped early," Grayson said defensively. "Adam's the one who doesn't know when to quit."

Adam's eyes traveled to mine and smirked. "I clearly have more reasons to drink."

Grayson followed his gaze but said nothing.

"So, Adam..." their mother interrupted. "I heard your date with Staci went well last week."

Adam pressed his lips together as Max placed his dinner in

front of him. "Thanks, Max," he said as if his mother hadn't spoken. "This looks great."

"You're very well suited," she continued, oblivious to his brush-off.

Adam picked up his fork before placing it back down with a huff. "And why is that exactly?"

Caroline ran her finger over the rim of the champagne flute. "Well, she's attractive…"

Adam winced.

"And she…"

"Has money?" Adam turned to his mother, clearly bored. "Because her personality definitely isn't a selling point."

"Adam…" Caroline sighed. "Staci understands the world we live in. Most women don't."

"She may even look the other way with your…indiscretions," William added.

I almost choked.

Adam's face grew red. "Thanks for the relationship advice, but I don't plan on following in your footsteps."

Caroline gasped. "Your father and I are very happy."

"Clearly," Adam muttered before pouring the entire contents of his glass down his throat.

William wiped the sides of his mouth with his napkin. "Adam, the Warner family is worth almost as much as the Warrens. I think it would be wise to reconsider."

"Don't you think we have enough money?" Adam asked, exasperated.

"Nonsense. You need to keep growing, especially when you're losing money."

Adam's hands turned white as he grasped his cutlery. "I lost one business, Dad," he growled. "One!"

"And it wasn't even his fault," Grayson added.

"Keep out of this," Adam snapped back at his brother.

Grayson raised his hands as he leaned back in his chair, raising his eyebrows at his wife.

"But he's right." Adam turned back to his father. "Your beloved *Craig* screwed up that contract."

Liam cleared his throat. "Alright, boys. That's enough business talk at the table."

William snarled. "And you didn't review it?!"

"Forgive me, but I haven't exactly had time since doubling the size of Harlow Corp in twelve months."

"And you clearly can't handle it," William uttered. "I'll come in next week and—"

"And what?! Save the day? Believe it or not, I have it sorted."

"Tell me how. Because the way I see it, you're in way over your head."

"You can read about it in the papers, like everyone else."

William's eyes flared. "I have a right to know."

"Actually, you don't. It's not your company anymore."

"How dare you speak to me like that. I made you."

Adam dropped his knife and fork as rage tore up his neck while Liam lowered his shaking head.

"Stop!" I slammed my hands onto the table before standing. "Adam. Mr. Harlow. Come with me, please."

"I don't take orders from you," William spat.

Liam glared at his son. "You will today, William."

The entire room grew silent as I stormed out of the double doors and down the hall. Once I was confident we were out of earshot. I spun around to face the grown men who were grumbling like sullen teenagers.

"This is the last Thanksgiving you'll *ever* spend with Liam. Do you think this is what he wants? For the first time *in weeks,* he's able to come downstairs and share a meal with his entire family, and you sit there, throwing heartless words around like it means nothing." Tears stung my eyes as my anger piqued. "I won't have it. You either get along for the duration of this meal, or I'll take Liam back to his room."

Adam ran his fingers through his hair with a grimace. "Cassidy's right, Dad. We shouldn't be arguing about work while we're here."

Without uttering a word, William offered us a curt nod before whirling around on his heel and trudging back into the dining room.

Adam's shoulders slumped once his father was gone. "Cass… I'm sor—"

"God, your dad's a dick," I blurted, interrupting his apology.

His entire face lit up. "Pardon?"

"I'm sorry." I drew in a deep breath in an effort to cool down. "That was completely out of line."

Adam grasped his chest as he laughed. "Are you kidding? *That* was hot."

"It was not."

"I'm literally sporting a boner right now."

"Adam!" I hissed, trying my hardest not to look down. "Your family is in the next room."

"And?"

When I didn't answer, he took my hand to prove it.

My core pounded on impact. "Jesus, Adam." I snatched my hand back from his firm bulge. "You need to sort that out before you go back in there."

"Come upstairs with me."

"We're in the middle of dinner!"

Adam moved closer until his face was merely inches from mine. "Well, I'm ready for dessert."

"Adam," I whispered. "I'm not that kind of girl."

His heated gaze begged to differ.

"Go fuck yourself," I growled, pushing past him and my unrelenting desire. This man was infuriating.

As I marched back to the dining room, Adam's laughter drifted up the stairs. "Like I have another choice."

———

"What happened to you?" Grayson asked when Adam resurfaced ten minutes later.

"Cassidy sent me to my bedroom."

His brother's jaw dropped, along with mine.

"I'm joking." He peeked over at my wild eyes. "There was something I needed to attend to."

Grayson pursed his lips. "Are you done?"

Adam chuckled deeply as he returned to his chair. "For now." He met my gaze as he lifted his wine.

"Good, because we're heading to Melanie and Scott's beach house later."

Adam dragged his gaze to his brother. "So, the annual board game tournament continues. I guess I could make an appearance."

Josie ran her fingers through her husband's dark hair. "Grayson thinks he's got a chance of winning this year because Melanie has baby brain."

I giggled as I scooped another piece of pie onto my plate.

"What's baby brain?" Adam asked, studying my amusement.

Josie jumped in. "When your brain temporarily turns into a pile of mush while pregnant."

"Bullshit," Adam muttered.

"It's true," Caroline chimed in, surprising us all. "I had it with both of you boys."

"As did your grandmother," Liam added. "When she was pregnant with Adam, she forgot her own birthday."

"Don't you mean *William*?" Caroline tittered nervously while her husband grew pale.

"Oh, yes. My mistake." Liam lowered his eyes. "It was so long ago my mind is playing tricks on me. Perhaps baby brain is contagious."

While everyone laughed, I took Liam's hand in mine, trying to absorb his inner turmoil. He remembered all too well.

"I can't even imagine you as a kid." Grayson smiled at his father. "You never talk about growing up here."

"Well, there's not much to say." William turned to his wife. "Caroline, would you pass me another slice of pie?" He switched topics smoothly, and no one persisted.

"So, are you coming?" Grayson asked Adam, but his brother was distracted. Grayson turned to the cause. "Cass, you're welcome to come, too, of course."

My eyelashes fluttered between them. "Oh, no, I can't. I'm um...expecting a call."

"Of course you are." Josie's gaze softened as she smiled "It's Thanksgiving. Tell Amy I said hi."

"Oh, I spoke to her earlier." Anxiety filled my body. "This is…um…Dom's family."

"Who's Dom—" Grayson blurted before Josie punched his arm. "Ow."

Something flickered across Adam's expression, but I refused to face him.

"It's fine, Josie." I smiled in appreciation. "Dominic is my late husband."

Liam's shaky hand found mine. He was returning the comfort.

"Oh shit." Grayson winced. "I'm sorry."

I sniggered when Josie punched him again. "It's fine, really. You don't need to apologize."

"On second thought," Adam interrupted, drawing everyone's attention. "I think I'll stay here and challenge Gramps to a game of chess—if he's up to it, that is."

Liam chuckled. "As long as we finish it this weekend. I don't want to wait until your next visit to beat you."

Adam's eyes narrowed playfully. "You're in trouble, old man."

"I'm shaking in my boots," Liam uttered with a hoot.

After our laughter settled, we returned to our meals, while Max helped feed Liam. He was eating less and less these days but remained in good spirits. Having his family visit every weekend was game changing, more than any alternative medicine I could offer, as I could feel him living for the next moment they walked through his door. If only they knew how much they all meant to him—even William.

"Please tell me who you're working for," Tash pleaded over our video-call.

"You know I can't."

"What if I guess and you just nod or wink or something."

"No!"

"Tom Cruise?"

"What?! No!" I cackled. Tash always made me laugh.

"Ugh, you're so…" Tash narrowed her eyes.

"Unfun?"

"Professional," she muttered, crossing her arms. "Whoever they are, they better give you a great reference."

"I need the money more than I need the reference."

"Well, whatever gets you back here quicker. LA isn't the same without you."

"I'll be back before you know it." I smiled excitedly. "I've already found some apartments within my price range that look promising."

Tash's shoulders dropped. "Apartments? Cass, you need a backyard."

"I'll be lucky to get something near a park, Tash. This job may pay well, but the money will eventually dry up."

"Then live with us."

"No." I grimaced. "I'm sick of imposing on everyone."

"It's just until you get back on your feet." Her eyes were full of worry. "Then work out a game plan from there. Who knows? Maybe things will work out with that man you're sexting."

My eyes bulged. "We're not sexting!"

"You used video?" Her mouth dropped. "You go, girl!"

"No!" My laughter morphed into a wince. "We haven't done anything like that."

"Cassidy! Loosen up a little," Tash said, taking on her stern-teacher persona. "What else are you going to do in your downtime? Surely you've run out of romance novels. Time to get the real thing."

"He's not the real thing." Adam was a dream.

"Does it matter?"

"Yes! I'm not a one-and-done girl. You know that."

"Then I guess you'll have to wait until you get back here. There's a guy from Bryce's office who is dying to meet you."

"Please, no." I cringed inwardly. "I can find my own dates. In fact, my client's doctor asked me out the other day."

"What?!" Her face swamped the screen. "Is he hot?"

I thought about the man due to return on Monday for Liam's check-up. "He's gorgeous, actually."

"So, what's the problem?"

"He's my client's doctor!" I cried. "And before you harp on that, I'm just not sure about him. He seems…too…perfect."

"Well, maybe he has a small dick. There are work-arounds for that."

I burst out laughing. "Oh, Tash. I miss you so much."

"I miss you, too." She shook away her welling eyes. "What are the plans for Finn's birthday this Sunday?"

"I'll video-call in the morning, watch him open the presents I left, then he's going to the movies with his Pa. I've arranged for Amy to make his favorite dinner, so I'll call again that night to sing "Happy Birthday" and watch him blow out the candles on his cake."

"And how are you feeling about this?" She knew me too well.

"To be honest…I'm feeling like a pretty shitty mom right now."

"You're not a shitty mom. You wouldn't be doing this if you were."

The knot in my stomach didn't budge. "He says he understands…but I don't know…"

"So mature…just like my little brother."

"He's looking more like him every day," I said, loving the fact.

"Lucky devil." Tash's smile grew solemn. "Dom would be so proud of you guys."

"I hope so," I whispered, wishing to God he could tell me himself.

"Hey, I have to go." She grimaced into the camera. "The in-laws are here."

"Have a great Thanksgiving, Tash." I blew her a kiss. "Send my love to the fam."

"Happy Thanksgiving, lovely. Call me again soon…after you go out with that doc!"

———

I remained in my room for the rest of the weekend. Liam was inundated with both family and friends visiting, so I kept my distance. If he was happy, I was happy—for him, that is.

"Where's Finn?" I asked when Amy answered my video-call Sunday evening.

"I don't know what went wrong, Cass. He was having a great day, then all of a sudden…bam! He burst into tears at dinner and hasn't come out of his room since."

My heart threatened to crumble. "Did you follow the recipe I sent?"

"Yes! Every part…except we had to swap the bow-tie pasta for penne because Dad didn't have any."

I closed my eyes. Dom and Finn loved bow-tie pasta.

Her mouth parted. "I'm so sorry, Cass. If I'd known it was that important, I would've run out to the store."

"It's not your fault, Ames. It's mine. I knew this would be hard on him."

"What should I do?"

"Let me speak to him."

"I'll try…" She moved toward Finn's room. "Hey, squirt, your mom's on the phone."

"I don't care! I don't want to speak to her!"

"Come on, buddy."

"If she really wanted to be here, she would be here!"

I gasped at the pain in his voice. Perhaps he wasn't as mature as I thought. "Ames, put the phone on his desk and give us a moment."

Amy quietly opened the door, placed the phone on his desk with the camera pointed toward the bed, then bolted out of the room like she'd lit a fuse.

Finn lay on his bed with his head buried in his pillow.

"Finny…"

Finn's tears slowed as he glanced around the room, but when his eyes settled on the phone, he slammed his head back down with a wail.

"I'm sorry I'm not there with you." I could feel his pain through the screen.

"I just want things to go back to the way they were."

"That's why I'm here, baby. This job is going to make that happen for us."

"It won't bring Dad back."

A sharp pain sliced through my chest. "N…no…I know." I stumbled over my words. "But we're going to be okay."

With a sniffle, he turned his puffy eyes to the camera. "But what if you have to go away again?"

"This is a one-off, Finn. Once we're settled in our new place in LA, you're stuck with me."

He rubbed the tears from his flushed cheeks. "Promise?"

"I promise." The doubt clouding Finn's piercing green eyes broke my heart, so I endeavored to ease his worries with lighter conversation. We talked about how we were going to decorate his new room, how fun it would be living close to his cousin, and the West Coast swimming competition he was bound to dominate, until his smile returned.

"Happy Birthday, Finny," I rasped out. I could only mask my devastation with smiles and laughter for so long. "I love you so much."

He smiled. "I love you, too, Mom."

After ending the call, I could no longer contain my emotion. Tears streamed from my eyes until I was gasping for air. I hated seeing my baby in pain, and not being able to touch him and soothe his worries was torture. It wasn't natural for a mother to be away from her child this long, and for the next few hours, I wallowed in the misery it induced.

———

Once my tears had dried and the pain in my heart moved to a dull ache, I changed into my swimsuit and robe and crept down to the indoor pool. The room was too humid for my pounding head, so I opted for the outside pool. The cool air smacked my face as I stepped into the garden, but it was the shock I needed. Tension fell off my body as I maneuvered through the darkness toward the glowing pool in the center of the vast lawn. The steam floating above the warm water drew my gaze up to the star-filled sky, and it took my breath away.

As I approached the water's edge, I dropped my robe to the ground and didn't hesitate before diving in and swimming underwater to the other end of the pool. It was freezing out, and the warmth of the water instantly soothed my anxiety and cleansed my soul as it rushed over my body.

Once I'd swum a few laps, I let my body rise to the water's surface while gazing at the twinkling sky above, searching for the one that shined brighter than the rest. My Dominic.

As tears crept out of the corners of my eyes and fell into the pool below, a surge of water rocked me off balance. With a gasp, I waded to the side of the pool as a dark mass shot through the water toward me. Bracing myself for the wild animal to attack, I closed my eyes moments before it stopped short and broke the surface. Grimacing, I opened one eye to find Adam flicking his wet hair back.

"Fuck, Adam." I paddled away from him. I would've preferred a wild animal.

"What are you doing out here?" he asked, chuckling at my reaction.

"Isn't it obvious? What are *you* doing out here?"

His sly grin widened. "Isn't it obvious?"

"Not really, no."

"Well, I *was* reading," he said, lifting his head up to the mansion before us. "But the view from my window became entirely too distracting. So, I needed a swim to cool down."

"Oh…"

"I haven't had a night swim in years." He spun through the water to get closer to me. "Grayson and I used to sneak out all the time when we were kids."

I gazed back up at the night sky. "That must've been fun."

"Hey, are you okay?"

I blinked myself out of my daze. "Sorry. I've got a lot on my mind today."

His eyes searched mine. "Want to talk about it?"

"With you?" I almost laughed, but there was no humor in his face.

"I'm mean…there are other things we could do…" he said, sabotaging his own sincerity.

"Adam…" I looked away from his suggestive smirk. "You need to stop flirting with me."

"Why?"

I gnashed my teeth as beads of water sashayed down his stubbled jawline. "Because it's distracting…and I have a job to do here."

"You're not on the clock now," he said, circling like a hungry shark.

I turned for the ladder. My escape route. "Goodnight, Adam," I said, clutching the handrail.

"You regret it, don't you? That night in New York?"

My grip loosened as I sunk back into the pool, but I didn't face him. "Look at the situation we're in now."

"That wasn't an answer." He waded closer. "Do you regret sleeping with me?"

My heart pounded as I spun around. "Now? Yes."

His brow furrowed. "But you didn't before?"

"Why would I?" He was a fucking god in bed.

The lines on his forehead deepened. "Because you…cried after."

Fire scorched up my neck. "You remember that?"

"I can't forget it."

I sank into the water, drowning myself in mortification, but within moments, Adam grabbed my arms and pulled me to the surface. "You don't need to be embarrassed, Cass. I do." His penetrating gaze stole my breath. "If I hurt you—"

"You didn't hurt me!" I peered up into his azure eyes, mirroring the illuminated water around us. "If anything, you woke me up."

"From what?"

"I...I don't know exactly." I swallowed back the emotion rising up my throat. "I've never experienced anything like that before."

Adam gushed. "Tell me about it."

"No, you don't understand." I waded out of his reach. "I got married so young, I never got to explore that side of myself. So, what happened between us was...overwhelming."

"Wait..." His head recoiled. "Are you telling me...you've only been with two guys?"

"When I told you I wasn't that sort of girl, I meant it."

"Oh, fuck." Adam ran his hand over his mouth. "And you let me do all those things to you." He winced. "You should've told me."

My irritation piqued. "I didn't do anything I didn't want to, Adam."

"I made you cry!" He smacked the water. "Fuck!"

"You caught me off-guard, that's all. I probably went over my quota of orgasms for one night."

"Surely you've had multiple orgasms before."

"I'm starting to question whether I've had any at all...before you," I said, not recalling a single night similar. "Don't get me wrong, Dom was a beautiful husband, and I loved him with everything I had, but there was always something missing with us. I guess that was it."

Adam blew all the air from his lungs. "The way you were that night...I assumed..."

"I had one night in Manhattan to be anyone I wanted to

be…to *do* anything I wanted." I shook my head. "I'm sorry to disappoint you, but the girl you met was playing pretend."

"I don't know about that."

I lifted my gaze to meet his penetrating stare. "I'm not a risk tasker, Adam. Everything is reliant on this job, and I won't jeopardise that."

"What about after?"

"After what?"

"Your job here is done."

I frowned. "Then I'll go back to a very different life."

"What if I don't want you to?"

"Don't be ridiculous." My stomach somersaulted. "This is purely a case of wanting what you can't have. This may be the first time it's happened to you, but I assure you, once you know who I really am, you'll run a mile."

"You really don't think much of me, do you?"

"That's not true. I think there's a lot going on in that head of yours…you just filter the important stuff." My tired gaze met his. "There's more to life than work and sex, you know?"

He ran his hand over the water, watching the ripple trail his fingers. "I don't have time for much else."

"And *that* is one of the *thousand* reasons why I can't do this with you."

"Even if I can make you forget those reasons?" he asked, angling his gaze with a playful smirk.

"Look," I uttered with a sigh. "My life is super complicated right now, and when—*or if*—I decide to let another man in, it will be because he wants to wade through the mess with me, not because he can fuck me into oblivion."

"But we could have fun while you're waiting." He ran his tongue across his bottom lip. "It may be a while."

I grasped the ladder before climbing it. "It's not like I don't have options, Adam," I grumbled as I marched over to the pile of towels nearby.

"Oh yeah, like who?"

"Marc, for one," I shot back, wrapping the towel around my body.

"The *fucking doctor?*"

My gaze whipped to his onyx eyes, seething at his jealousy. "Yes. *The doctor.*"

"Don't you fucking dare."

His anger only amplified mine, but I endeavored to keep my composure as I turned to leave. "Enjoy your swim, Adam. I'll see you next week."

Chapter 19

Before dawn the next morning, I shuffled down the hall in my socks and peeked into Liam's room.

"Good morning, Cassidy," Adam said without lifting his gaze from the chessboard.

My heart raced as I casually strode across the room to Liam's alternate side. "What are you still doing here? Don't you have to get back for work?"

Liam tapped the top of his chess piece with pursed lips, saying nothing. He was too focused on his next move.

"I promised Gramps I'd finish our game before I left."

"And *then* you're leaving?"

Adam clasped his hands as he leaned back in his chair. "Are you trying to get rid of me?"

"We…have a routine, that's all."

"Don't fret, Cassidy." Liam moved his queen. "Adam will be gone in approximately three moves. Then you'll have me all to yourself."

I turned to Liam, ignoring his grandson's adorable chuckle. "Did you still want to watch the sunrise today?"

Adam checked his watch, then carefully maneuvered the chessboard to the side table. "I'll take him today…since I'm here and all."

Liam's chortled. "Stalling the inevitable, as usual."

"Well, since I'll be gone in *two* moves, why not spend a little extra time together?"

"In that case…can we watch it from the drawing room? I always feel closer to Betty there."

"Are you sure you're feeling up to it?"

"After this weekend, I feel like I could run a marathon."

I smiled at his confidence, but I knew he was exhausted. "Fine, but no overdoing it. You have your check-up this morning."

Liam grinned mischievously at his grandson. "We'll behave, wont we, Adam?"

"Don't I always?" Adam's playful tone clashed with the twitch of his jaw.

I stepped back to give Adam space to assist his grandfather. "I'll check in with Mrs. Fredrich while Adam takes you to watch the show. Should I tell Max to bring you both breakfast in the dining room?"

"Won't you be joining us?" Liam asked, gaining another line between his eyes.

"Of course she will." Adam tilted his head my way. "Unless you have a better option?"

I threw daggers into his piercing blue eyes. "Of course. I just have to do a few things first."

"Superb!" Liam panned his gaze between us and smiled. "Breakfast with two of my favorite people."

Not wanting to ruin Liam's good mood with my disdain for his grandson, I offered a curt nod before scurrying out of the room, seething with rage.

"Good morning, Cassidy," a happy voice greeted from the bedroom across the hall.

My anger dissipated immediately. "Nora! You're back early!"

Mrs. Fredrich brushed past, barely taking a moment to say goodbye as she zoomed down the corridor.

"I figured since Mrs Fredrich missed Thanksgiving with her kids, I'd get back a little earlier."

My eyes bulged. "Mrs. Fredrich has kids?"

"Well, I think so. Or was it cats?" Nora shrugged. "Who knows?"

"She definitely keeps to herself." *No matter how many times I'd attempted conversation.* "So, how was your Thanksgiving?"

"Amazing. I think I topped my sister's pumpkin pie this year." Her joy filtered through me, giving me the boost I needed. "How was everything here?"

"Liam had a wonderful weekend."

"And you?"

I lifted my shoulders and dropped them, like my eleven-year-old. "It was okay."

Nora pressed her lips together. "You need to get out of here on the weekends, girl. You're going to go crazy."

"I get out."

"And not to the beach." She placed her hand on her hip. "I'm talking clubs and bars. You're young and beautiful. I'm sure you'll find several men who'd love to keep you well and truly occupied on your weekends off."

I scoffed. "I don't think so. The last guy I picked up at a bar turned into a nightmare."

"Then agree to that date with Marc. I bet he could show you a good time."

I closed my eyes with a grimace. "I knew I shouldn't have told you about that."

"Come on, what's stopping you?"

"I don't want things to be weird around here." I wandered over to Liam's medicine cart and ran my finger over the bottles. "Plus, I've already said no."

"Then tell him you've changed you mind," Nora shot back. "You're a woman. You have every right to do so."

"It's really not a good time for me to get involved with anyone."

"Nonsense. When I met my husband, I was unemployed, studying, and caring for my dying mother. You *want* the right person to come along at the wrong time, because then you'll know if they're the real deal."

"I suppose..."

"And how wrong can you go with a doctor?"

"I guess..." But my heart wasn't in it.

"Unless you're waiting for someone else to get their act together and ask you out?"

My head spun to hers. "What? No."

"Okay." She lifted her hands with a laugh. "Then, get out of those sweat pants and put on a pretty dress. Marc will be here in a few hours."

I dropped my gaze to my casual attire. "But I like my sweats."

"Darling, if you're not wearing something nice by the time he arrives, I'll be forced to enlist Liam to convince Marc to ask you out again."

"Fine," I grumbled on my way out of the room. "But if this goes badly, it's on you."

"If it goes badly, he was never the right man to begin with."

———

While the sun rose, I showered, then rummaged through my closet. I didn't have an array of options, so I settled on the knit dress I wore for Thanksgiving. Apart from the glamorous number Adam bought me for Melanie's wedding and the green dress I wore for my interview *(that Adam promptly tore off)*, I decided this was the safest option.

"Oh, Cassidy, you look beautiful." Liam's eyes lit up as I walked into the dining room. "Isn't she a vision, Adam?"

He cleared his throat after a moment's pause. "Yes."

"Thank you." The heat in my cheeks deepened as I approached the only available table setting, right next to Adam.

With a stern look from his grandfather, Adam flustered out of his chair and pulled out mine. "Here."

"Oh, thanks." I was amused by his chivalry, which was clearly for his grandfather's benefit.

While Liam looked on approvingly, Max brought out various platters of breakfast options, and my stomach rumbled on sight.

"How was the sunrise?" I asked, trying to disguise the growl.

"Glorious as always." Liam's eyes glazed over. "The perfect way to start the day."

"I can think of better ways." Adam reached for the eggs as I added a pile of bacon to my plate, purposely grazing my arm in the process.

"Adam's not a morning person." Liam picked at his scrambled eggs, completely oblivious to the sexual innuendo, while Max hovered close by. Liam was a proud man, and Max would only help him with his food if asked.

"I prefer sunsets." Adam sipped his juice before licking the residue off his lip. "I'm more about finales than beginnings. I find them much more...satisfying."

"That's why Harlow Corp. is so successful," Liam continued as if having an entirely different conversation. "Adam takes struggling businesses and builds them up."

"At what cost, though?" I narrowed my gaze at Adam. "I don't remember my sister being too excited when Harlow Corp. took over *Maude* magazine."

"Well, it worked out in her favor."

"Not everyone's," I mumbled under my breath. Amy called me every night in tears over their ruthless layoffs. I could only imagine Adam being the instigator.

"You can't save them all, Cassidy."

I half chuckled. "Don't I know it." As much as I wanted to get through to Adam, he'd built an impenetrable fortress around his heart, and it made me feel like a failure.

Liam's laughter drew our attention.

"What?" Adam asked, glaring at his grandfather.

"Oh, nothing," he replied, but his eyes sparkled. "Just old memories of Betty slipping through. I've been having many lately...especially when you two are around."

My eyes struck Adam's, then quickly diverted to my breakfast. "This is really delicious."

Liam chortled again. "Yes. Yes, it is."

———

After we finished our meals, I wheeled Liam toward the elevator, eager to get him back to bed.

"I can do that," Adam said, appearing behind me.

"It's fine. Really." I made every effort not to groan as I turned Liam's chair into the elevator.

"Here." Adam moved my hands out of the way as his grasped the handles, then pushed Liam into the elevator with ease.

I stood there, frozen, suddenly out of place. "I'll take the stairs..."

Adam reached out and pulled me through the doors seconds before they shut. "There's room for one more." He ran his thumb over my hand as he stared down at me.

His sensual touch and intoxicating aroma flooded my senses, arousing every fiber.

"It's hot in here today," Liam announced with his back to us.

With Adam's soft chuckle, I tugged my hand from his to loosen the high neck of my dress.

"Lucky it's a short trip," I said, ignoring Adam's darkening eyes.

As the doors slid open, I stumbled out, gasping for air as I continued down the hallway. "Enjoy the rest of your game!" I called out, needing a little time to gather my senses and settle my awakened libido before returning to Liam's room.

______

"So…who won?" I asked as I stepped into Liam's bedroom a half hour later. To my relief, Adam had gone, and I could finally convince my heart to slow.

"Victory was mine today, but I think he went easy on me."

"I can't imagine Adam going easy on anyone." I puffed up Liam's pillow before easing him back down.

"My grandson doesn't let many people into his heart, but when he does, he's a big softy."

"Well, he must love you very much."

"I have no doubt who he loves," he murmured as his eyelids began to droop. His meds were clearly kicking in.

"Rest up, Liam," I said, packing up the discarded chess game. "I'll clean up a little before the doc gets here."

"Leave that, Cassidy." Liam's sleepy voice was barely audible. "Adam said he'll put it away."

"It's fine." I didn't fancy waiting an entire week for Adam to return from LA, so I continued placing the chess pieces into the antique wooden box.

Once Liam was sleeping soundly, I picked up the box and took it back to the library where it belonged.

Without thinking, I tucked the game under my arm and precariously climbed the ladder to find a gap amongst the crowded shelves.

"What the hell are you doing?!"

Adam's voice threw me off balance, but he launched forward to grab the ladder before I lost my footing.

"I thought you'd gone!" I cried out as my heart pounded against my chest.

"You're lucky I hadn't."

My temper spiked. "I was managing fine before you came roaring in here."

"The chessboard doesn't even go up there."

"Then where does it go?"

"Come down and I'll show you."

My eyes narrowed at his mischievous tone. "Step away from the ladder first."

"No way." He was now grasping both sides and running his gaze up my legs. "You're not breaking your neck on my watch. Gramps would kill me."

"Can you at least stop staring up my dress?"

"I'm not!" Adam diverted his eyes back to mine with a rascally smile. "Anymore…"

"Adam…"

"Come on, Cass. That dress is sexy as fuck, and you know it." He reached up. "Now give it to me."

My eyes bulged. "What?"

"The chessboard." He chuckled. "Pass it down."

"Oh." My cheeks heated as I handed him the wooden box.

As Adam placed the chess game onto a shelf close by, I took the opportunity to climb down the ladder.

"Thanks for tha—" was all I managed to say before his hard chest pressed up against my back.

My entire body stiffened as his breath caressed my neck. "So, tell me…why *are* you wearing that dress?"

I leaned into him, craving his scent. "I…I ran out of clean clothes."

"Bullshit," he whispered into my ear. "You dressed up for the doc, didn't you?"

"So what if I did?"

Adam toyed with the high neckline of my dress, exposing more skin. "He's not your type, Cass."

His smug tone irked me. "Of course he is. He's smart. He's handsome. He's…"

"Vanilla."

I spun around in his arms with a growl. "Marc isn't vanilla."

"He's Clark Kent without Superman."

"He's a doctor." I lifted my chin. "A good one too."

"He has Lego hair."

A burst of laughter shot out of my lips. "What?"

"I bet he's a pro at missionary," he continued, running his hand down my side while keeping the other firmly against the ladder.

"Well…I'm fine with that."

As I attempted to step out of Adam's grasp, his fingers tightened around my hip and pulled me closer. "You know *why* you'll be fine with that?"

I exhaled. "Enlighten me."

"Because while you're lying there…" His eyes grew dark. "Spread-eagle…" His hand moved down the curve of my body. "You'll be imaging all the things *we* did together." His hand slid under my dress, then in-between my thighs, cupping my mound. "The angles…" His thumb rubbed my nub. "The thrusts…" His fingers drew the thin material aside. "And the screams…" he uttered before sliding his finger through my seam.

"Oh God," I gasped as my knees buckled.

"But you know what the problem with that is?" he asked, delving in and out as he stared into my eyes.

I shook my head, unable to speak as the pressure built.

"Because when you're almost there…" His lips hovered over mine. "When you're about to feel how *I* made you feel…" He pulled out his finger. "He'll roll over and go to sleep."

Gasping at his abrupt departure, rage flowed through my veins as I peered up into the eyes of Satan. "You're a fucking jerk." Shoving him out of the way, I stormed toward the door, never *ever* wanting to see him again.

"You should really change before the doc gets here," he called out.

I whirled around, burning with fury. "Why? Because he might actually find me attractive?"

"No..." The corner of his mouth twitched. "Because your underwear is dripping."

<h1 style="text-align:center">Chapter 20</h1>

I did change. But into something much prettier.

After a long tear-infused shower, I blow-dried my hair, applied a little extra make-up to hide my puffy eyes and slipped into the green dress I wore the night I met Adam. If it worked on him, Marc was bound to appreciate it also—even better if Adam bore witness.

Before the doctor arrived, I walked into Liam's room where Adam was sitting beside him, reading a book. I refused to look his way as I approached his grandfather's bedside, but when Adam stumbled on his words, I knew he'd noticed my dress.

"My, oh my," Liam gushed. "Don't you look lovely."

"Thank you, Liam."

"But what happened to the other dress?"

I peeked at Adam to find his lips pursed and gaze tapered. "A silly accident that should never have happened. But this dress is much nicer, don't you think?"

"The doc won't be able to hear my heartbeat over his own."

"Oh stop." I giggled.

Adam slammed the book closed and leaned back in his chair, checking his watch. "He's late."

"Relax, Adam. You won't miss your flight."

I met his fiery gaze with a smirk. "We'll make sure of it."

"I think it's time I invested in my own plane." He rubbed his tense jaw. "Since Mom and Dad hijacked yours."

My brows rose.

"What?" he asked, seemingly impatient with me.

"Oh, nothing." I'd never even been on a plane, and he was talking about buying his own. How different our worlds were.

A knock on the door drew our attention. "Doctor Morrison has arrived," Max said, ushering Marc into the room.

"Finally," Adam mumbled under his breath.

With a quick scowl his way, I turned back to the handsome man strolling toward us. "Marc. Hi," I greeted with a warm smile.

His eyes brightened at the sight of my dress. "Cassidy. Looking beautiful as always."

"Inside and out," Liam added, raising his eyebrows at Adam.

Marc's smile faded when he followed his gaze. "Good to see you, Adam." He reached out to shake his hand.

Adam grasped his as he stood. "Let's see how the old man's doing, shall we?"

"Of course," Marc said, throwing another glimpse my way.

After the doctor completed his check-up and adjusted Liam's medication, he turned to me with a grin. "You're truly working wonders here, Cassidy."

"Well, it helps having a great doctor," I replied, curling my hair behind my ear.

Adam's groan only accelerated my game plan.

"Marc, would you mind having a private word with me in the hallway?"

"Not at all," he said, following me outside.

Adam glared at the doctor until I closed the door behind us.

"Is everything okay?" Marc asked, naturally concerned with the added level of privacy.

"Yes, everything is fine. I, um…" I cleared my throat. "I wanted to change my answer."

He frowned, completely lost in the conversation.

"To your dinner invitation."

"Really?" His smile broadened. "Are you sure?"

I nodded. "As long as Liam is stable, then I really can't see any reason why I can't have a little bit of fun."

"Would Friday night work for you? I have to get back to the city Saturday, and I'd rather not wait another week."

My heart fluttered at his urgency. "That sounds perfect, but I can't go too far from here."

"Of course. I know a place close by. You'll love it. I'll pick you up at seven."

I grinned. Mission accomplished. "Great."

As we walked back into the room, smiling like school children, Marc returned to Liam's bedside. "Well, I'll see you in a few days, Liam. I'm sure Cassidy and Nora will take good care of you until then."

Liam grinned my way. "That they will."

After their goodbyes, Marc offered me a bashful smile on his way out.

"What was that about?" Adam asked, trailing me into the hall.

"What was what about?"

My nonchalance infuriated him. "That look. What did you talk about before? In the hallway?"

"Marc asked me out last week, and I told him I had to think about it. Today I gave him an answer."

His eyes grew dark. "Which was?"

"I said yes."

"Predictable."

"At least he's man enough to ask me on a date."

His eyes froze over with his expression. "I never said I wanted to date you."

"Who's predicable now?" I uttered, ignoring the ache in my chest.

"Don't forget your purpose here, Cassidy."

"I'm here to support Liam." I scowled. "Not be your little play toy that you can pick up and discard anytime you feel like it. You may be used to treating women like that, but I've had the pleasure of knowing how a real man should behave...and you're nowhere near his league."

"And Marc is a fucking knight in shining armor, is he?"

"Maybe." I shrugged. "I guess I'll find out Friday night."

Adam's jaw pulsed as we stood in the hallway, staring at each other in a silent stand-off.

"Everything okay, here?" Nora asked, appearing behind us.

"Yes. Adam was just leaving." I broke my glare to find Nora eyeballing me.

"Well, have a safe flight, Adam. Cassidy, can you help me out with something?"

"Of course." I dropped my gaze as I moved toward her.

Moments later, Adam's door slammed closed, and Nora and I flinched.

"What is going on between you two? I can't tell if he wants to murder you or throw you over his shoulder and take you to bed."

"Who knows what's going on in that head of his?"

"Can't you feel what he's feeling?"

"That's the problem. He has so much bottled up, I can't decipher anything."

"I'm no empath, but it's pretty clear he has a thing for you."

I grumbled. "He has a thing for torturing me."

"From the way he was looking at you in that dress, I'd say you were torturing him."

"Hardly." I scoffed. "The man is made of stone."

"Oh, there must a heart in there somewhere. He wouldn't be so close to his grandfather if there wasn't."

"That's true…" I mused. "But how could you not love Liam?"

Nora smiled, but there was sadness behind it. "Liam has his flaws, too."

"Maybe so, but he has a good soul. I can feel it. Adam's is persistently on the edge of darkness and light, and I fear, once Liam's gone…he'll become the one thing he despises."

"And what's that?"

"His father."

———

After lunch on Friday, I snuck away to call Finn while Liam slept. He had another school swimming competition that morning, and I let him have the rest of the day off, provided he spent at least an hour of it on a video-call to me. It was bribery at its best, but I was in desperate need of staring at my boy's face.

"You won!" I squealed after he broke the news.

"Easily, too!" Finn's chest puffed out. "I can't believe I made it to the final!"

"I can. You're remarkable. When is it?"

"February." He paused. "We'll still be living here then, wont we?"

"I'll make sure of it, baby. I won't let you miss that race."

As I lay back on my bed, laughing at my son's antics, I caught sight of movement in the hallway. I'd left the door open, not expecting any of Liam's family to arrive for hours.

My heart lurched as Adam's eyes found mine, then fell to my laptop.

I quickly slammed it closed. "Adam...you're early."

"Did I interrupt something?" He folded his arms as he leaned against the door jamb. "A little phone sex with the doc?"

"What?! No."

"Then why arc you so flushed?"

"Because I was..." I ran my tongue over my dry lips as I tried to formulate an excuse that didn't incorporate my son. "Having a laugh with a friend."

Adam chortled. "Sure you were..."

"We're not all as perverted as you." I returned the laptop to my desk. "And it's really none of your business."

"You're right. It's not."

Surprised by Adam's lack of sleazy retort and the click of his door closing, I turned back to find an empty hallway and sighed. As much as he drove me crazy, I didn't want to fight. I wanted to be friends, and the date with Marc was another attempt at reinstating boundaries. Adam needed to know I wasn't an option.

———

My stomach had been tied up in knots all afternoon. I hadn't been on a date in so long I'd forgotten all the anxiety that went along with them. Perhaps that was why I'd avoided them for so long. Men would ask, but I'd politely decline. If I couldn't see them as a potential father to my son, I saw no point in pursuing a relationship that would inevitably lead to heartbreak. It wasn't fair to Finn, and I promised Dominic I'd never settle for anyone less than him, so the benchmark was high.

Before getting ready, I checked on Liam one last time. I was fishing for a reason to cancel the date, but when I peeked through the door and found him fast asleep, all hope faded.

"Cassidy!" Josie called out from the couch on the far side of the bedroom. Three faces greeted me...but only two were smiling.

"Join us for a drink." Grayson motioned me over. "We're ordering pizza later if you're hungry."

"Oh, thanks for the offer." I glanced at Adam. "But I'm heading out tonight."

Adam sipped his whiskey. "Cassidy has a hot date."

Josie's mouth dropped. "With whom?"

"The doc," Adam answered, expressionless.

I almost growled. I could speak for myself.

"Did you want to borrow an outfit?" Josie placed Harrison into Grayson's arms as she stood.

"I'd actually love that." Relief settled over me. All my dresses were entwined with memories I'd rather forget.

"It's no problem," she said as she passed. "I actually have these magical leather pan—"

"No!" the boys cried out in unison.

"Okay, okay!" Josie cried out. "I'm sure I have something else. Come on."

As I followed Josie out the door, I glanced back to witness Grayson throw a cushion at his brother.

"Idiot," he muttered.

Adam knocked it aside. "I know."

———

I twirled the ring on my finger as I stood in front of the mirror in the powder-blue dress Josie had bought on our shopping expedition before Melanie's wedding. She'd forgotten about practicality when it came to breastfeeding, so instead of it gathering dust in the closet for the next twelve months, she insisted I wear it before it went out of style.

The flowy knee-length dress fell flawlessly over my body. The sheer sleeves did nothing for warmth but were too pretty to hide away under a cardigan, so I opted to leave it behind.

As I built up the courage to make one final alteration, I drew a deep breath and slid off my wedding ring and placed it on the nightstand. A lone tear tracked down my face as I read the inscription.

My heart is yours. D.

Closing my eyes, I grasped the crystals around my wrist and pushed the pain away. This wasn't the night to wallow in my misery. This was my chance to enjoy dinner with a lovely man. A charming, smart, handsome doctor who cared about old people as much as I did. What could go wrong?

When my cell phone vibrated across the desk, I grabbed my shoes and handbag and headed for the door. I told Marc to meet me at the car to avoid gossip amongst the employees, but I wasn't sure if he'd taken me seriously, so I had to move fast.

With the aid of the door jamb, I slipped on one shoe and fumbled with the buckle, while dropping the other onto the floor. I hadn't worn heels this high since before Finn was born, and now I remembered why.

"Need some help?" Adam asked through the small opening of the room opposite.

"It's fine." I hopped around, trying to keep my balance while I attempted the second buckle. "I've got this."

He rubbed the back of his neck as he stepped into the hall. "Clearly."

"I forgot how hard these things are to put on," I said, resting against the wall.

"Here…" Adam bent down in front of me and wrapped his fingers behind my ankle.

My breath caught as tingles shot straight to my core. "Thanks," I muttered as he fastened the tiny buckles.

His eyes rolled over my body as he stood. "You look amazing." A touch of sadness floated through his eyes. "I hope he appreciates it."

Was he finally letting go? "I hope so, too."

"Cass…" Adam grasped my hand as I passed. "I'm sorr—" His lowered eyes locked onto the pale line around my ring finger. "Where's your ring?"

Guilt tore at my heart. "It's been four years, Adam. I think it's time I move on…don't you?"

His eyes bored into mine. "I do…but…"

"But what?" I asked, surprised by the tender stroke of his thumb.

Just when I captured a glimpse of real emotion, he dropped my hand and took a step back. "But nothing," he said, backing down the hall before whirling around. "Have a great night."

Chapter 21

"How did you find this place?" I asked as Marc pulled out my chair.

The inconspicuous little restaurant by the water was a hidden gem. A fireplace filled the dining room with warmth, while couples enjoyed quiet chatter over plates of glorious seafood. My mouth salivated on sight.

"I knew you would approve. When Nora told me you loved the ocean, I did my research."

"That's sweet. Thank you. It really is beautiful."

"And super discreet," he said in a whisper.

"Oh, it didn't need to be. Liam knows I'm on a date."

"I wasn't referring to Liam…" Marc said with a bashful smile.

Heat rose up my neck. "Adam?"

Marc frowned. "Liam's grandson? No. I'm talking about your husband."

"My husband?"

"Aren't you married?" He lowered his gaze to my hand resting on the table. "Oh, you took it off. I do that, too."

"What?"

"I don't wear my ring either. Too many questions."

All the blood drained from my face. "You're married?"

"I assumed you knew…that's why I can't visit Liam on weekends. I'm with my family in the city."

I struggled to fill my lungs. "You have kids?"

"Two girls."

"And a wife?" I could barely form the words.

"Yes, but we have an understanding." He placed his hand over mine. "As long as I'm discreet, I can…"

I pulled away as I stood. "I need to go to the restroom."

"Are you okay?"

"I just need a minute." I grabbed my handbag and maneuvered through the tables toward the back of the restaurant, searching for privacy.

Once I found the restroom, I stumbled into an empty stall and sunk onto the closed toilet seat, burying my face in my hands. How could I have been so stupid? How did I not know he was married?

As I took deep breaths and willed myself not to cry, my handbag vibrated in my lap. Expecting it to be Marc, wondering if I'd fallen in, I reached in and pulled out my cell. It was a video-call, and as soon as I saw my sister's face, tears filled my eyes.

I tried my hardest to keep it together. "Hey, Ames."

"Are you okay?" Her giant blue eyes examined my face. "I had a bad feeling…"

"I wish you'd called earlier. I could've avoided the humiliation."

Amy fell back onto her couch, next to Josie and Grayson's enormous dog. "What the hell happened?"

"I finally agreed to a date with the doctor, and I just found out he is married."

"You mean…separated?"

"I mean *married*…with two kids!"

Her mouth fell open. "Oh, Cass. That sucks. Where are you now?"

"Hiding in the restroom in a little restaurant called La Cabane—or however you pronounce it."

"I'll get Josie to come get you."

"No, it's fine. I'll get a cab."

"No way. It'll take too long. She'll be there soon."

Before I could protest, or even say goodbye, Amy ended the call.

Realizing I'd have to resurface eventually, I dabbed my burning eyes with cold water and returned to our table.

"I ordered us a bottle of red," Marc said, already through half a glass. "I hope you like Pinot Noir."

"I'm sorry, Marc." I straightened my back to assume confidence. "I don't think this is going to work out."

His mouth slackened. "But I thought we were on the same page."

"I thought so, too…but we're in completely different books."

"I don't understand."

"Tonight was the first night I've removed my ring since my husband passed away four years ago."

His face paled. "Oh, I…I didn't know."

"And I'm sorry about that, but you have a wife and kids at home waiting for you. Do you know how much of a gift that is? I would give *anything* to have that again, and you're treating it like it's nothing. You, of all people, should know how fleeting life can be."

Marc rubbed his jaw as he leaned back. "It's really not a big deal. My needs go beyond my wife's desires."

"If you love each other, it should be enough."

His brown eyes met mine. "Then maybe we don't."

As he downed the rest of his wine, I sensed his inner conflict. He loved his wife but needed more—a feeling I was familiar with. Dominic was a great husband and an amazing father, but I always felt like something was missing with us. He was my best friend, but the passion I thought only existed in books just wasn't there. However, I *never* would've risked my family to find it with someone else.

"I'm sorry you feel that way, Marc. I really am."

He turned his gaze out the window but said nothing.

"I've arranged for someone to pick me up, so I'm going to wait outside."

Marc nodded, but his thoughts were distant. "I hope you find what you're looking for."

"All I'm looking for at the moment is independence. I don't even know why I agreed to this date."

He looked up at me with a spark of hope. "It's okay to have a little fun from time to time."

"Yeah, but not with another woman's husband. I'm on this earth to relieve pain, not cause it."

"You're a pretty special woman, Cassidy." Marc poured another glass. "Adam is lucky to have you."

"You mean Liam…"

Marc made no attempt at hiding his smirk as he sipped his wine. "That's what I said, didn't I?"

My eyebrows drew together as I second-guessed my hearing. "Well, I'll see you next week."

"You will."

As he perused the menu, I made my way out of the restaurant and into the parking lot, hoping Josie was on her way. The breeze off the ocean was a refreshing contrast to the blazing heat inside, so I wandered over to the sand.

The waves glittering under the moonlight beckoned me. So, with the aid of a lamp post, I unbuckled my heels, slipped them into my discarded handbag, and approached the shoreline.

The freezing water rushed through my toes, relieving them of the pain caused by my ill-fitting heels. I hated wearing shoes, regardless of the style. I loved the feeling of the earth under my feet and its energy vibrating though my body, and tonight I needed grounding more than ever.

"Cassidy!" A distant voice drew my gaze from the water washing over my crystal bracelets.

I shook my hands as I stood, squinting through the darkness. "Adam?"

"Get out of that water. You'll get pneumonia." He tore off his hoodie as he stomped through the sand.

"What are *you* doing here?"

"Josie was feeding Harrison, so I offered to come get you. I've been trying to call, but you're not answering your phone."

I stared back at my handbag, half buried in the sand and winced. "Sorry…I wasn't thinking."

"Clearly." He handed me his sweatshirt. "Put this on."

I pulled it over my head until it swamped my body. I hadn't realized how cold I was until I was surrounded by Adam's body warmth. "Thanks," I said, hugging myself.

Adam stared at me for a moment. "Well, that was the shortest date in history."

"You could say that."

"Must've been bad if you're cleansing those crystals again."

I dropped my gaze as my grip tightened around my waist. "Yep."

"Hey, are you okay?" He edged closer. "Did he hurt you?"

"No…nothing like that." I exhaled my frustration as I peered up at him. "Can you just take me home?"

With a curt nod, he turned, picked up my handbag and stalked back to the parking lot.

"Nice ride," I said while brushing the sand off my feet.

Adam waited patiently by an old Rolls Royce before opening the door for me. "It's Gramps'."

Perhaps I didn't give Adam enough credit for his manners. His grandfather wasn't here to witness his chivalry now.

Once we were on the road, Adam took an unfamiliar turn. "I hope you don't mind, but I'm making a little detour. I'm starving."

"What about your pizza night?" I hugged my stomach to muffle its rumble.

"Amy called halfway into my first slice, and I prefer my pizza hot."

I winced. "I'm sorry."

"It's fine." Adam threw me a glance. "I'm sick of pizza anyway. Plus, I want to try out this new restaurant in town."

"Well, as long as they do takeout, I'm happy."

Adam kept his eyes on the road but said nothing.

"Adam…"

"Come on, Cass, you're all dressed up. I'm not taking you home until you've at least had a nice dinner."

"But I'm covered in sand."

Adam ran his gaze down my body. "I'll get a private room, then. You won't even have to put your shoes back on."

My head jerked back. "Really?"

A small smile crept over his face as he voice-dialed the restaurant. Within minutes, he secured a private room, a discreet entrance, and valet parking—the perks of being a Harlow.

"You really didn't have to do this," I said, once we were both siting in the most gorgeous restaurant I'd ever seen.

He signaled to the waiter. "I know."

The room was incredibly romantic with its velvet-draped walls and chandelier-clad ceilings. I could only imagine how many proposals had happened there.

"This place looks expensive," I whispered once the waiter left to fetch a bottle of champagne.

"It is."

"I would've been fine with a burger."

"I'm not a burger guy."

"What are you, then?"

His mischievous smirk returned. "A degustation."

"Oh my God, did you just make that sexual?"

"No. Your mind did."

My eyes bulged. "I beg your pardon?"

"I'm kidding." Adam laughed as he leaned back in his chair. "And you tell *me* I need to relax."

"Yeah, well, letting my guard down around you only gets me in trouble."

He folded his arms. "A little trouble is good for the soul."

"So is peace, love, and kindness."

Adam rubbed his stubbled chin. "Hmm…I'm not familiar with those."

"Why would you be? You actually need a soul for them."

He clutched his chest. "Ooh, burn."

I pressed my lips together, trying not to laugh, but when my eyes met his twinkling blues, it burst from my lips. "You led yourself straight into that one."

"Perhaps I'm the one who shouldn't be letting his guard down."

"I'm hardly dangerous," I said as the waiter filled our champagne flutes.

"On the contrary." Adam picked up his glass. "The prettiest things are often the *most* dangerous." He clinked his glass against mine. "Like the blue-ringed octopus, for instance. Beautiful… but it will kill you in minutes."

"Are you comparing me to an octopus?"

"No." Worry lines consumed his forehead. "I meant…"

I burst out laughing. "Wow, you were a lot smoother the night we met."

Relief washed over his gorgeous face. "Well, you didn't know me then."

"I don't know you now." I sipped my bubbles. "Not really."

"You know more than most." He picked up the menu. "You're the mysterious one."

I followed his move, taking in the spectacular array of dinner options. "I try not to talk about my personal life at work."

"What about on a date?" he asked, peeking up at me.

I met his gaze, challenging him. "You don't date."

"I could make an exception."

"What?" I snorted. "Like now?"

He shrugged. "Why not?"

"I'm sitting here, barefoot, covered in sand, and drowning in an old Lakers hoodie. This is not a date. This is charity."

"I wouldn't be here if I didn't want to be." Adam tapped his finger on the table as he took in my appearance. "And you look fucking adorable in my hoodie."

I looked away, trying to hide my smile. "Well, I don't think I'm ready to attempt another date just yet."

"What about dinner with a friend?"

"Wait…" I gushed dramatically as I turned back to him. "Are you referring to me as your…*friend*?"

Laughter erupted from his lips. "Jesus, Cass, there aren't many people on this earth who can make me laugh the way you do."

"That's a shame," I said, enjoying his unusually light mood. "It's a lovely sight."

His grin widened. "You like it, huh?"

"It's like seeing an endangered animal in the wild."

Adam shook his head with a chuckle.

"There you go lighting up the room again!" I couldn't help but tease.

He ran his hand over his reddening cheeks, assessing the room for witnesses.

"Blushing is rarer than laughing." I dipped behind the

oversized menu, and I peeked back when he didn't move. "Come on, we better order before you pull a facial muscle."

While Adam pressed his twitching lips together and read the menu, I narrowed down my choices.

"Order anything you want," he said as the waiter approached.

"But there are no prices."

"Cassidy…" He waited until I lifted my gaze. "I'm a billionaire. I think I can cover it."

I reviewed my options once more. "Fine." I looked up at the waiter. "I'll have the seafood platter for two."

Adam's brows raised. "I guess that's it, then," he said, handing back his menu.

"Oh, I'm not sharing."

He stared at me, clearly trying to work out if I was joking. "Fine. I'll have the eye fillet. Rare."

From that point on, our conversation revolved around Liam and Harlow Manor. They were safe topics with no chance of any sexual innuendo, and I could finally relax in Adam's company.

"I think I ordered too much," I groaned halfway through my meal.

"You think?"

I rubbed my stomach. "It's your fault. You said order anything."

"Well, I better get you home before you fall into a food coma."

After Adam paid the bill, he drove us back to Harlow Manor.

"Thanks for rescuing me tonight." I peeked his way as he concentrated on the road. "And for dinner. You really didn't have to do that."

"So, your night wasn't a complete disaster, then?"

"No." Disappointment surged through my veins as I gazed out the windshield. "Not in the slightest."

He glanced my way before returning his focus to the tree-lined road. "So, are you ever going to tell me what happened with the doc?"

My head fell back on the headrest. "Only if you promise not to laugh."

"Absolutely not," he said, grinning.

I crossed my arms. "Then no."

Adam wiggled his head from side to side. "Fine. I'll *try* not to laugh, but I don't promise anything I can't commit to."

"Alright…" I emitted a defeated sigh. "Turns out, Marc is…"

"Gay?"

"Married."

"He's what?!" His shock outweighed his amusement.

"You heard me." I closed my eyes in a wince. "And no, the irony is not lost on me."

"Holy shit, that dirty dog." He slammed his hand on the steering wheel. "I knew something had to be wrong with that guy. He's too clean cut."

"Everyone is flawed. Some of us are just better at hiding it."

He ran his gaze over my hoodie-consumed body. "So…what are you hiding?"

My thoughts shot to Finn. "Oh." I lowered my gaze to my twiddling fingers. "I have plenty of flaws."

"Unlikely."

I furrowed my gaze, rummaging up the safest admissions. "I chew too loudly."

Adam pretended to yawn. "You're going to have to do better than that, Cass."

"Well, sometimes…when I'm all alone…"

Adam's eyes widened, waiting for me to continue.

"I fold in the page corners of my books instead of using a bookmark."

He gasped dramatically. "That's outrageous!"

"It is!" I cried, smacking his arm.

"Well, it doesn't bother me. Go on."

"Fine." I grumbled. "I'm…highly sensitive."

A rascally smile covered his face. "*That* I know from experience."

I rolled my eyes. "No, not in a sexual way…in a *I-can't-even-watch-the-news-without-bawling* way."

"That's a flaw?" he asked as we approached the grand gates of Harlow Manor.

"To some it is."

Adam entered the passcode into the keypad. "I think I know a better one."

"Okay. Hit me. I can handle it."

He turned to me while the gates opened. "You rarely do anything for yourself."

"That's not true. I…I read."

"You read to relax." He accelerated down the winding driveway toward the huge garage behind the mansion.

"And relaxing is fun."

"Fun is jumping out of a plane, or going scuba diving, or spending a wild weekend in Vegas."

"I wouldn't know about that."

He sighed. "I guess not."

"But reading is fun and therapy rolled into one. With the work I do and the trauma I've been through, reading romance is the only thing that settles my soul. Knowing there's going to be a happy ending guarantees no heartbreaking surprises or disturbing twists…just love conquering all. It's what my heart needs, and it brings me peace, if only for a moment."

Adam maneuvered through the impressive collection of classic cars before parking in the only empty space.

"I know it's silly," I continued, unbuckling my seatbelt.

He took my hand. "It's not." He waited until I lifted my eyes to his. "Why do you think I work so much?"

"Because you like money."

"Because it's the only aspect of my life I can control."

My heart ached as his thumb ran over my knuckles. It was the first time Adam had opened up, and the glimpse of his gentle soul was blinding.

"But I'm fucking that up now, too." He released my hand to take the keys out of the ignition.

"How?" I asked, barely recovering from the loss of his touch. "You're the most successful man in America."

"Not in my father's eyes." He grabbed the door handle with more force than necessary and climbed out of the car.

I watched in a daze as he ambled around the car to open my door. "Maybe Harlow Corp. was his crutch, too," I said, stepping into an icy showroom of priceless automobiles.

"I guess." Adam closed the door behind me and tucked his hands into his pockets. "I've never really wondered why he is the way he is. I assumed he was born like that."

I wandered out of the garage beside him. "Maybe there are things from his past you don't know." *His little brother, for one.*

"He grew up with my grandparents. His childhood couldn't have been that bad." Adam closed the garage door and met me on the pebbled path to the house.

"But their dynamic is different to yours," I said, admiring the fairy-lit hedges as we walked side by side. "Do you think Harrison will feel the same angst against your parents that you and Grayson have?"

"Well, no. They adore him…" He lowered his head as he exhaled. "I see your point."

"My Grams was my best friend, but my mother hated her. She had her reasons, but they were *her* reasons. Not mine."

Adam stopped walking. "Did you just tell me something personal?"

I grinned back at him. "That's what friends do, right?"

"Friends…" He repeated the word in a chuckle before catching up.

I bumped his shoulder. "*Without* benefits."

His laughter was intoxicating. "I never asked."

"You were thinking it."

He wiped the smile from his face before detouring off the path.

"Where are we going?" I asked, following him onto the lawn.

"Your feet are covered in sand. Max will get an earful from Mrs. Fredrich if she finds contaminants in the hallways."

"Oh…okay," I uttered, moving closer to the luminescent outdoor pool.

Adam took off his shoes and rolled up his pants before dropping to the side of the steaming pool. "So, you and your grandmother were close, then?"

"Like you and Liam." I lowered myself beside him and dipped my feet into the glorious warm water. "I lived with her for ten years after my mom died."

"Where was your father?"

"He wasn't really fit to parent my sister and me back then, so the state moved us. It was for the best, though. Grams had an awesome little beach shack in Venice Beach, so I basically lived in the water throughout my teens." I stared down at my swirling feet. "She died when I was seventeen, so we had to move back to New York."

His brow lifted. "With your dad?"

I nodded. "Thankfully, he'd cleaned up his act by then and was desperately trying to redeem himself. Amy revelled in his attention, but as soon as I turned eighteen, I moved back to LA."

Adam grasped the sides of the pool. "Is that where you met your husband?"

"Yeah." My heart twinged. "I was working as a waitress in a shitty café in Santa Monica, and he kept showing up. We married less than a year later and moved to Encino."

"Encino? That's a big change from Venice Beach."

"I guess I had to alter my dreams to survive."

Adam leaned forward to pick a leaf out of the pool. "So, you were only eighteen when you got married?"

"We definitely rushed into things." I gazed up at the stars with a melancholy smile. "But I'm glad we did. We had three great years together before he got sick."

"That must've been hard."

"Incredibly, but the nightmare didn't end there. I had to sell our house to pay for part of Dom's medical fees and move back to my dad's."

"Jesus, Cass." Adam ran his fingers through his tousled hair. "That's a lot to deal with."

I smiled, appreciating Adam's sympathy. It was a rare sight from him. "So, what about you?" I nudged his shoulder. "Where have you resided all these years?"

Adam leaned back on his elbows. "I grew up in Bel Air, have a place in Malibu, but I mostly live in an apartment in the city to be near the office."

"What high school did you go to?"

"Summerhill Prep."

"Ooh," I cooed. "We hated you guys."

He puffed out his chest. "Everyone hated us because we were the best at everything."

I sniggered. "Except swimming."

"That's a load of shit," he cried, straightening up.

"It's true. And I must say, the Summerhill brats were very sore losers."

Adam tapered his gaze. "I never lost a race."

"Well, neither did I."

"Maybe we need to sort this out," he said, attempting to pull off his t-shirt.

I tugged it down with a laugh. "No way! I haven't swum competitively since high school."

"You didn't swim in college?"

"I couldn't afford college."

His stubbled cheeks grew pink. "Oh."

"Don't be embarrassed by the opportunities given to you." I placed my hand over his. "Just make them count."

Adam's jaw tightened as he stared at our hands. "Cass..."

"We should probably get back." I pushed myself onto my feet. "We need to be up at sunrise, remember?" I grabbed two towels from the bench nearby and threw one to Adam as he reluctantly followed.

"What are your plans after you finish up here?" he asked, seemingly unfazed by the cold.

"Pay off the rest of my debt and get back to Cali," I said, drying my legs. "All of my friends live on the West Coast, so Finn and I will most likely crash with them until I find a job and a place to live."

"Who's Finn?"

My gaze shot up to his. "Pardon?"

"You said, 'Finn and I.'" Hurt surged through his energy as he threw his towel into the hamper. "Are you seeing someone?"

My lips parted for air, but nothing could penetrate my closed throat. "No," I rasped. "It's not like that."

His eyes darkened as he stepped closer. "You're lying."

"I'm not." I fell back a step.

"Then, who...is...Finn?"

My chest rose and fell, once, twice, until I yielded under his burning stare. "He's my son."

"You have a son?!"

I kept my eyes lowered as I nodded, trying to block the anger and pain churning through his energy. "Josie overheard your mom say she wouldn't hire anyone with children, and I didn't want to ruin my chances of getting this job."

"So you lied?"

"I don't think you understand how desperately I needed this job."

"And Josie knew about this?" His face grew red. "And Grayson?!"

"Your brother has no idea, and please don't be angry at Josie. She was helping out a friend. No one else knows."

Adam's fingers tore through his hair as he paced. "You should've told me."

"Why? What does it change? My ability to do my job?" My heart dipped. "Or how you feel about me?"

He stopped and stared off into the distance, saying nothing.

"That's it, isn't it?" I almost laughed. "Well, I'm sorry I'm not your type anymore."

His hands curled into fists as his jaw turned to stone. "You were never my type."

I dropped my gaze as my chest threatened to cave in. "Well, that's a relief."

"That's not what I mea—" He pinched the bridge of his nose. "Fuck this. I'm going inside." Without a backward glance, he trudged back to the house, leaving me standing by the glistening pool, shivering uncontrollably.

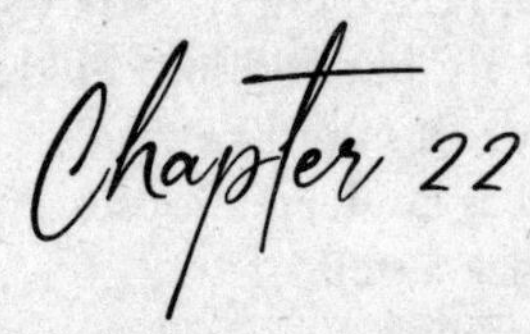

Chapter 22

"Where's Adam?" Liam asked when I wheeled him into the library Saturday morning to watch the sunrise.

My heart quickened. "Sleeping in, I guess."

"Good. That boy deserves some rest."

Guilt filtered through my body. He was missing the sunrise with his grandfather because of me. "How are you feeling this morning, Liam?" I needed to think of something other than the man who had plagued my dreams all night.

"It's the weekend, my family is here, and the sun is rising on a new day. I'm feeling marvelous."

"What about your pain?"

He placed his hand on mine. "It's no worse."

I could tell he was lying. "Just take it easy today. I know you love spending time with Harrison, but when he naps, so should you."

"Then Gramps will get no sleep at all." Josie walked into the library with her son. "His great-grandson refuses to sleep."

Grayson walked in behind her, holding a bottle. "Hey, Gramps. Hey, Cass," he said, approaching his grandfather. "Since we're all up, would you like to feed the little guy?"

Liam's face lit up. "Oh yes."

I smiled at the beautiful sight before me. "I'll leave you to it," I said, turning for the door.

"Wait." Josie placed Harrison into Liam's fragile arms. "Can we talk a sec?"

"Sure." I moved farther down the hallway as she followed.

Josie glanced back, making sure we were alone. "I know it's

none of my business, but did something happen between you and Adam last night?"

My breath caught. "Why do you ask?"

"Because he's not in his room, so he's either in your bed, or he's taken off."

"I can assure you he's not in my bed."

"Oh." Josie frowned, seemingly disappointed.

"But things did get a little tense...after he found out I have a son."

"Oh shit, you told him?" She pulled me farther down the hall.

"Not on purpose." I sighed. "But it's better he knows."

Her hazel gaze softened. "How did he take it?"

"Well, he's not here now, is he?" He was probably halfway back to LA by now.

Josie grumbled. "He'll come around...in time."

"Time isn't something we have in abundance here." I rubbed my tired eyes. I'd barely slept. "I've really fucked up."

"You can't blame yourself for his reaction, Cass."

My nostrils burned as I held back tears. "How can I not? Adam's supposed to be here, spending time with his grandfather, and *I'm* the reason he's not."

"No. His selfish, stubborn, infuriating nature is the reason he's not. It's about time he grew up and thought of someone other than himself for once."

"Do you think he'll tell Caroline and William?"

Josie thought for a moment before shaking her head. "He wouldn't do that to you."

"Wouldn't he? He's ruthless with everything else in his life."

"Not with you."

"I don't know why." I folded my arms. "He made it perfectly clear I wasn't his type."

"Because you're not stupid, plastic, or unavailable."

"But he said..."

"Forget what he said. There's more truth in his actions. And when Amy called to say you were in trouble last night, he was already halfway through the door before I could even find our car keys."

"Argh." I cried. "I've never met anyone so complicated. With Dominic, I always knew what he was thinking, but with Adam...he just stirs me up."

"In a good way or a bad way?"

"I...I don't know."

"I think you stir up some pretty conflicting feelings in him, too."

"The only feeling he has for me now is disdain. You should've seen his face when he found out I have a child."

"He'll come around."

"No, no... It's better this way."

"For whom?"

"For both of us. I need to concentrate on my job, and he needs to focus on his grandfather."

"I have to admit...the timing does suck," she said before a small smile settled upon her lips. "But love has a way of creeping up on us."

"Love?" I scoffed. "We barely know each other."

"But there's something growing, and if I can see it, you can definitely feel it."

I pushed away the absurd notion as I walked on. "All I feel right now is regret."

"Come on, Cass. He was going to find out about Finn sooner or later."

"*Never* was the plan."

"Well, he knows now."

I turned to her when we reached my door. "You should tell Grayson, if you haven't already. I'm sorry to put you in the middle of all this."

"I promised Amy I wouldn't tell a soul, and I keep my promises. Plus, it keeps Grayson out of Adam's firing line."

"What about you?"

"I can handle my brother-in-law," she said with a fearless smirk. "And don't worry, he can't be far away; the helicopter's still here. We'll call him again after breakfast."

"Thanks, Jos."

"It'll be okay." She reached out and squeezed my hand before disappearing down the hall.

If only I believed her.

———

On my way back from a swim later that afternoon, I heard an argument erupt in the drawing room. I hid in the shadows of the hallway with pricked ears and a desperate heart, needing to know what was going on with Adam.

"You knew?! All this time?!"

"I didn't think it would do any harm," Josie retorted. "Cassidy has been through so much, and I wanted to give her the break she deserved. She had to sell their home to pay for her husband's medical bills, for Christ's sake. It's not fair."

"That's not the point here," Grayson uttered angrily. "If Mom and Dad find out she lied on her application, they'll terminate her contract immediately."

"No, Gramps won't allow it."

"Gramps may not have a say," he snapped back.

"What are you talking about? Ultimately, he is her employer."

"Not if they convince the doc that he's not fit enough to make his own decisions."

Josie gasped. "There's no way Marc will agree to that."

"Well, as it turns out, the doc's a married man. My father could use his infidelity against him to manipulate the situation."

"What? Like blackmail?"

"He's done it before."

"No, Adam won't let him. He wouldn't stoop that low."

Grayson grew quiet. "You know how he gets when he's angry."

"He's only angry because Cassidy is making him feel something."

"She's got a kid, Jos. Adam isn't…he's never…*fuck*. He's going to tell Mom and Dad the first chance he gets."

"When are they due back?"

"Two weeks."

"Then we have two weeks to diffuse the situation. Give him a chance, Gray. Your brother may surprise you."

Grayson exhaled heavily. "For Cassidy's sake, I hope you're right."

———

There was no response. Not even disappearing dots.

It appeared my time at Harlow Manor was coming to an end. *Well done, Cassidy.*

———

"Hey, buddy," I said once my little boys face filled the screen of my phone.

"Hey, Mom. You don't normally call this early."

"I just wanted to see your beautiful face."

Finn scrunched up his nose. "Well, I'm playing online with Reed in, like, five minutes, and he's going to stream it."

"Okay. I won't hold you up."

"Is everything okay? You have puffy eyes."

I forced a smile. "Everything's great," I said with an unconvincing squeak to my voice. "But it looks like I may be coming home a little earlier than anticipated."

"Really?" Finn's eyes lit up. "Did the old guy die?"

"No!" I laughed. "Liam's doing great."

"But I thought you said…"

"Things change, bud. You know that."

"Trust the universe?"

"Exactly," I said, repeating our family mantra.

Finn bolted upright. "I've gotta go! Reed's online."

"Okay, baby. I'll speak to you tomorrow."

"Cool. Bye, Mom!"

Although my plans were coming to an abrupt and messy end, I had to look on the bright side, and that was Finn. If I got fired, at least I got to see my son. I'd already paid off our debt with my first two month's paychecks and was now saving for an apartment. It was going to take a little longer to get where we wanted, but at least we were moving forward.

I wouldn't let myself think of Liam and how he'd react when the news broke. We'd grown close in our time together, and I couldn't imagine leaving him now. Would he be disappointed in me as a mother, or would he understand my purpose and fight for me to stay? Either way, he didn't need the stress.

———

Once Josie and Grayson hit the road back to their apartment on Sunday evening, I wandered up the hallway to Liam's room. I wanted to spend as much time with him as I could before Caroline and William's return and my inevitable firing.

"Hey, Liam," I said as I approached his bedside. "Would you like me to read to you before dinner?"

"Oh, I would love that. Adam said he'd finish the book this weekend, but it appears he's MIA."

"I'm sure he'll be back next weekend," I said with little confidence.

"Well, he'll have to catch up when he returns."

With a shrug, I picked up the novel and lowered myself into the chair beside Liam's bed.

"I've missed your company over the last couple of days," he said as I searched for the bookmark. "Have dinner with me tonight."

I pushed past the dread that lingered in my stomach since Adam left and smiled. "I'd love to."

After Liam advised Max to prepare our meals, I read the remaining chapter of Betty's old romance novel while holding back tears. "Wow," I gushed, placing the book on my lap as I dabbed my eyes. If only real life could be that beautiful.

"I understand now why Betty read so many romance novels after Adam passed. They really push away the harshness of reality, don't they?"

I ran my fingertips over the frayed cover. "I've definitely read my fair share since losing Dom."

"I'm sure you have." He grew quiet as he pondered. "How long were you married for before he passed?"

"Six years."

"Oh, dear." Empathy rolled off him. "That isn't fair. I had decades with Betty, and even that didn't feel like enough."

"I would've loved to have met her," I said as Max walked in with two plates on a larger platter.

"And she would've loved you…and Josie, too." Liam peered up at Max as he positioned a plate in front of him. "Don't you agree, Max? These girls sure keep the Harlow men in line."

Max passed me my meal with a wink. "Indeed, they do—whether they like it or not."

Movement from the doorway caught my attention, and I almost dropped my cutlery.

"Adam," Liam announced happily. "I didn't think I'd see you again until next week."

"And miss spending time with you? Not a chance." He moved to his grandfather's side. "I organized a few days off to make up for my sudden departure."

"Oh, don't trouble yourself. I know how much work you have to do."

His eyes never wavered from his grandfather. "It's not as important as you, Gramps. Nothing is."

The comment stung, but it was well deserved.

"Well, join us for dinner. Max, can you please organize another meal for Adam?"

Max nodded. "Of course."

"It's fine. I'm not hungry," Adam cut in. "Plus, my seat is taken."

"Adam…" Liam rumbled in warning.

"It's okay." My knife and fork rattled as I stood. "I can eat in my room." I told him I'd stay out of his way, and I meant it.

"Nonsense. There is room for both of you. Adam, pull up another chair, and I'll have Max bring you some dessert. Perhaps your favorite ice cream will put you in a better mood."

"I doubt it." Adam retrieved another chair while I sank back into mine.

"So, you took my Rolls for a spin, I hear."

I peeked up at Adam as I picked at my meal.

"Yeah, I'm sorry about that. I should've asked first."

"It's fine. It'll be yours soon anyway."

Adam grumbled. "Gramps…"

"I know, I know," he uttered with a sigh. "So why the mad dash out of here? Is everything okay at Harlow Corp.?"

"The company is fine. Don't listen to Dad." He took the fork out of his grandfather's rickety hand to help him eat.

"Oh, I don't. I know it's in safe hands."

"Thanks."

"Then you must've been chasing a girl. Did you have a big date in the city?"

"What?" Adam fumbled with the fork. "No."

"There's no need to get so defensive." He took back the fork to feed himself.

"I'm not. I just… I had stuff to do, okay?"

"Was your husband like this?" Liam asked me as he placed his cutlery back on the plate.

"I…I don't know what you mean."

"Moody, defensive…secretive?"

Adam scowled in my peripheral vision.

"The opposite, actually." It was neither an insult, nor a compliment.

Adam crossed his arms as he shifted in the chair.

"And where did you meet?" Liam appeared to have forgotten his grandson was there.

"At the coffee shop where I worked…why?"

"See, Adam…" Liam turned to his grandson. "You're never going to find a nice girl in those bars you go to."

Adam huffed. "Who says I'm looking for a nice girl?"

"A boy, then? Because I'm okay with that."

I pressed my lips together, trying not to laugh. Liam had a cheeky sense of humor.

"Give me a break, Gramps. You're starting to sound like Mom."

"We just want you to be happy."

"Well, women have a tendency of getting in the way of that."

I pursed my lips. His comment was completely directed at me.

Liam's eyes twinkled like he was holding onto a secret. "Life wasn't meant to be easy, Adam, but the right woman will make it worth it."

"Alright." Adam slapped his hands on his thighs before standing. "If all you want to do is talk about my love life, I'm going back to my room."

"Oh. I'm just having some fun," Liam said as Max walked in with a bowl of ice cream.

My body heated on sight. *Is it mint chocolate chip?*

"I've got too much on my mind for fun, Gramps. I've barely slept in two days."

"Sounds like you need Cassidy's magic hands."

I cowered over my meal. *He did not say that.*

"No," Adam uttered sternly. "What I *need* is a break." He proceeded to walk out but paused beside Max. With a heated glare my way, he took the bowl of ice cream and scooped some into his mouth. "It's not the same."

Max frowned. "I assure you I've bought the same flavor and brand for the past seventeen years."

Adam licked his lips, sending my libido into overdrive. "It's never going to be the fucking same." He shoved the bowl back into Max's hands and stormed out of the room, muttering furiously to himself.

I took Liam's hand as worry seeped into the creases on his face. "I'll talk to him once he's cooled off."

"Thank you, Cassidy." His eyes glazed over. "He wouldn't behave this way if everything was okay. He needs someone... someone to..."

"I know," I replied when his voice trailed off.

"If anyone can get through to him, it's you."

"I don't know about that," I said, losing my appetite. "I think he'd prefer I wasn't here at all."

"If you weren't here, he wouldn't be either."

My mouth fell. "Of course he would be."

Liam yawned as he pushed his barely touched plate aside. "I'm tired, Max. Would you mind sending Mrs. Fredrich in with my pain relief?"

"Certainly," he replied, disappearing out the door.

I stood and moved my plate to the side table. "Would you like some Reiki?" I asked, sensing his heightened pain.

"Save it for Adam. He needs it more than me tonight."

With a tight smile, I moved away as Mrs. Fredrich entered to take his vitals. "I'll let you rest, Liam. Thank you for the lovely dinner."

"It's always a pleasure with you, Cassidy." His hazel eyes swirled with green. "I'll see you at first light."

———

Light poured out of Adam's room as I made my way down the hall. I hovered in the hallway, between our doors, not knowing which way to turn. Left, to the safety of my bedroom, or right, into the devil's lair, where Adam sat hunched over his desk, staring at his laptop.

His head rose but didn't turn. "What is it, Cassidy?"

I jumped. "Oh, um… I was hoping we could talk."

Adam's shoulders lowered as he picked up a freshly poured whiskey and tipped it into his mouth. "You can come in," he said, rotating his chair to face me. "I won't bite."

I stood motionless in the doorway. "Are you sure about that?"

"Probably not in the way you like." He sniggered into his glass before taking another sip.

Exhaling my annoyance and the memory of his teeth grazing my most sensitive parts, I stepped inside. "Look, I know you're angry with me…and rightfully so…but please don't leave like that again. Liam really looks forward to your visits."

"Just Liam?"

I swallowed the lump forming in my throat. "And the rest of your family."

His jaw twitched as his gaze challenged mine. "Was there anything else, Cassidy? I have work to do."

"No." I turned to leave before whirling back in a fluster. "I mean, yes. Would you like some Reiki?"

"Is that Gramps' idea or yours?"

"His," I said abruptly. "But you're clearly not sleeping very well, and I can help with that."

His brow lifted. "The same way you helped last time?"

"Argh, forget it." I turned for the door.

"Does Gramps know you left your son to look after him?"

Anger tore through me as I spun around. "You make it sound like I abandoned him!"

"Well, didn't you?" Adam folded his arms.

"He's with my dad!"

"Who you don't even like."

"I love my father…but our relationship is complicated. You of all people should understand that."

His eyes narrowed. "You know nothing about my relationship with my father."

"I know how you feel when you're around him."

Adam slammed his laptop closed and stood. "Can you fucking stop with that empath shit?!"

"Believe me, I'm trying!"

"Well, try harder! My parents are flying in next weekend, and I don't need you fucking around in my head."

Fear bubbled up inside. "Next weekend?" I thought I had two weeks.

"We're having a family meeting."

All the air left my lungs. "You told them about Finn?" I gasped. "Already?"

He stared at me, expressionless. "They deserve to know."

"You really are ruthless." My voice was barely a whisper.

"So they say."

As I blinked back tears, he turned away and sculled the rest of his whiskey.

"Goodnight, Adam."

He didn't look back. "Night."

Chapter 23

"The family has requested your presence in the drawing room," Max said shortly after Caroline and William returned from their trip.

My stomach dropped as I glanced back at my half-packed suitcase. "Sure." It was time.

I followed Max down the grand staircase and stepped forward once he announced me to the room. I lifted my eyes to the entire Harlow family, minus Liam, staring back at me. Adam was the first to look away.

Caroline offered a tight smile. "Cassidy, we've spoken to the doctor and it appears your presence has improved Liam's health and wellbeing immensely. Due to this unexpected prognosis, we'd like to extend your contract to a week-by-week basis after three months. We understand this is quite an ask, but we are willing to pay double for your time."

My jaw fell open. The wage was already incredible.

"This would require you to be here over the Christmas period," she added when I couldn't find my voice. "Will that be a problem?"

My chest constricted. "May I think about it?"

"We're offering you a lot of money here. Money that will be snapped up by someone else. Let me know your decision by tomorrow afternoon."

With a nod, I left, focusing extra hard to keep my legs from crumbling under me as I jogged up the stairs. Adam hadn't told them.

Sinking onto the edge of my bed, I stared at my open suitcase. If I stayed on, we'd have enough money to rent a house with a backyard and be financially stable for the first time in years. I could buy a new car, or put money aside for Finn's college fund, and maybe stop stressing about our future. Unfortunately, it came at a cost. I'd already endured over two and a half months without my son and was mentally prepared for two more weeks…but Christmas? *Finn wouldn't forgive me.*

"You going somewhere?" Adam's voice broke through my daze.

I followed his gaze from the doorway to the suitcase before me. "I thought I was getting fired."

He crossed his arms as he leaned on the door jamb. "I wasn't the one who called the family meeting, Cassidy."

"I realize that…now." I hated myself for assuming the worst. "But thank you for not telling your parents."

"It's not my place."

"You're right." I wiped the moisture from my eyes. "I should tell them."

"No."

"But I can't stay on, Adam. Liam will need a new doula anyway."

His brow knitted. "You're not accepting the offer?"

"I promised Finn I'd be home before Christmas, so…no."

Adam took one step into my room. "But Gramps needs you."

"Finn needs me, too." My chest threatened to collapse as my head hung low. "As much as I need that money, I need my son more. I haven't seen him in months, and I miss him terribly."

Adam took another step, then paused again.

"You can come in," I said, peering up at him. "I have nothing to hide anymore."

As his shoulders lowered, his gaze traveled around the room, pausing on the picture frame beside my bed. "How old is he?"

"He turned eleven the Sunday after Thanksgiving."

"You missed his birthday?" The lines on his forehead deepened.

"Don't…" Tears filled my eyes. "I'm a terrible mother, I know."

"I didn't say that." The bed sank as he lowered himself beside me.

"You don't have to."

"Well, you know very well I'm not feeling it."

The corner of my mouth twitched. "Is this you flying a white flag?"

He chuckled softly. "Something like that."

"So, you're not angry with me anymore?"

"I don't know what I am." He sighed. "But I don't want you to go."

Heat swirled between us until I doused it with reality. "I promised him, Adam. I won't break it."

"I understand." He returned to his feet. "But you should tell Gramps about him. He'll want to know."

"Do you think he'll be...disappointed?"

"With you?" His eyes twinkled like his grandfather's. "You're the highlight of his fucking day."

———

Come Sunday afternoon, after cleansing my crystals in the ocean, I stared aimlessly at the horizon. I wasn't ready to go back to Harlow Manor. Caroline and William were there, awaiting my decision, but something was holding me back.

My cell burst into song, and I rummaged through my bag, praying Liam hadn't taken a turn. To my relief, it was a number I didn't recognize.

"Hi, this is Sullivan Cody from Swimfit. I'm calling in regard to the letter we sent home with Finn a few weeks ago, regarding our annual elite swimming camp."

"Oh, I'm sorry. I must have missed it."

"We're very impressed with your son's results, and we'd like to offer him a place. It's by far the best training camp in America, and we feel it's what Finn needs to take his swimming to the next level."

My heart burst with pride. "That's amazing."

"We just need your deposit by next week to secure his place."

"Deposit?" I closed my eyes. "How much is it?"

"The fees are outlined in the letter, but it comes to approximately \$3,000."

My jaw dropped. "\$3,000?"

"Yes, but we can offer a payment plan under special circumstances."

I refused to take on any more debt, but I couldn't bear to say no. "Can I get back to you?"

"Yes, but make it soon. There are a lot of kids wanting this spot."

"I will. Thank you."

After I hung up, I frantically dialed my father's number.

"You didn't think to tell me about Finn's swimming camp?!"

Dad sighed. "He didn't want me to."

"I'm his mom. I need to know these things."

"I'm sorry, but I thought I was doing the right thing. Finn knows it's beyond your reach right now, and he didn't want you to feel any more guilt."

"Oh."

"Reed offered to pay, but Finn flat-out refused. He said you wouldn't accept any more charity."

"Well, he's right," I uttered proudly. "Everyone has already done enough for us. Will you let me talk to him?"

"Hang on a sec." There was some rustling before Finn answered.

"Hey, Mom." His voice sounded far away. Too far.

"Baby, why didn't you tell me you got offered a place at that camp you've been talking about?"

"Because we're saving for more important things."

My heart sank. Swimming was his world and the one aspect of his life he could control. "This is important, too…and there's a possibility I could make it happen."

"I'm not letting you sell a kidney, Mom."

Laughter settled my nerves. "No, baby, it's my job. They've asked me to stay on over Christmas, maybe a little longer, depending on Liam, and they've offered me a lot of money to do so."

"How much more?"

"Enough to rent a house with a backyard and get you to camp."

"Really?"

"Yes…but it's a sacrifice…and one I'll only make if you're on board."

Finn grew silent. "Do you think our new house could have a pool?"

I smiled. "We can definitely look for one."

"Then yes!" He clapped his hands. "As long as you video-call us like at Thanksgiving."

The tightness in my chest eased. "Of course. I wouldn't miss seeing your face on Christmas morning."

"And we'll be together for the next one," he added brightly. "And we'll have a pool!"

"I love that plan. Maybe you can start scouring the real estate websites for me."

"Oh my God! Yes!" he squealed. "I'll start now."

"I love you, Finn." I exhaled. "Your dad would be so proud of you."

"Thanks, Mom. I think he'd be proud of you, too. Love ya."

Once I ended the call, the spark Finn lit inside me dimmed. The reality of the situation was seeping in. I wouldn't see my son for the rest of the year. It was going to be brutal, but if it meant renting a bigger place, in a better area, and sending Finn to swimming camp, it would be worth it.

———

"What's wrong, Cassidy?" Liam asked as the sun shot daggers through the trees the next morning. "You don't seem like yourself."

"It's nothing for you to worry about."

"Nonsense. We're friends, and friends tell each other their worries. God knows you've heard a few of mine lately. What's going on in that pretty head of yours?"

"I'm just missing someone," I said with a sad smile.

"Back home?" Confusion clouded his eyes. "A man?"

I lowered my head. "A boy, actually. I…um…have a son."

"Oh, dear." Liam inhaled long and slow as he pondered my admission. "And you've been apart all this time… I'm so very sorry."

"It's not your fault." I grasped his hand. "It's mine. I didn't disclose that information in my interview because I didn't want to jeopardize my chances of getting the job."

"Oh, dear…had I known…I'd…"

"Liam, please. It's okay. We talk on the phone every night, and my time with you has been the best distraction."

His bushy brows pulled together. "But I'm living longer than you expected."

"That isn't a bad thing." I gently squeezed his frail fingers. "Seeing you with your family, with your great grandson, has been so heartwarming. You deserve this time, and I'm devoted to making it special for you."

"I'm not surprised to find out you're a mother. It's as clear as day how attuned you are to others' needs…and perhaps neglecting your own. Mothers tend to do that."

"So, you're not disappointed with me?"

"I'm disappointed that you didn't tell me the marvelous news, but no. I'm aware of your hardships, and I'm guessing you've had to make numerous sacrifices along the way."

I pressed my lips together, holding back tears of relief. "Thank you for understanding."

His hand rolled over mine, offering me comfort. "Please tell me about him."

"His name is Finn. He's eleven and incredibly smart and kind, like his father was. Oh, and he's an excellent swimmer."

"A swimmer?" Liam's eyebrows lifted. "My grandsons were both brilliant swimmers."

"I've heard."

Liam chortled. "Adam told you, I imagine."

"I'm sure he's brilliant at everything." *Particularly in bed.*

"Yes, but stubborn in his methods. The boy puts too much pressure on himself to be like his father instead of paving his own way."

"Has he always been like that?"

"Ever since puberty. The cheeky, playful boy I knew morphed into his father's right-hand man. At least Betty and I had him for the summers to soften him up."

"Ugh, I'm dreading those teenage years. It's a daunting time for a single mom with a son."

"You'll be fine." Liam emitted a husky laugh. "They come out good."

As if on cue, Adam walked in and perched himself on the window seat on the other side of Liam.

"Mostly," Liam continued, smiling at his grandson. "I'm still waiting to see how this one turns out."

"What turns out?" Adam's gaze zigzagged between us.

"Cassidy was just telling me about her son."

"Oh." His eyes softened when they met mine.

Liam watched us curiously. "I'd love to see a photo, if you have one."

"Um…yeah." I pulled my phone from my back pocket and swiped to a recent picture of him with a basketball tucked under his arm.

Liam squinted as I held it in front of him. "Oh, he's handsome."

Adam leaned forward to see the photo. "He has your eyes," he said, not even looking up to compare. "The girls are going to swarm on him in a few years."

"What?" My mouth dropped. "No."

Liam and Adam laughed.

"Girls aren't even on his radar."

"Oh, they will be." Adam continued to snicker.

"Argh, stop." I shoved my phone away. "I don't want to think about it."

"If he's anything like my grandsons…"

I blocked my ears. "I think it's time for breakfast," I yelled over their voices. "I'll go tell Max you're ready."

As their laughter followed me down the hall, I smiled in relief. Liam wasn't angry about Finn, and Adam didn't appear to be holding any grudges. With Finn ecstatic at the possibility of going to camp and moving into a house with a backyard, I

felt hopeful for the first time in years. I could make this work.
I could finally turn our dreams into reality. I just had to push
through my heartache to get there.

———

That afternoon, Max escorted me back to the drawing room
where Caroline and William stood with the rest of the family,
awaiting my decision. Their suitcases sat beside the front door,
awaiting their next adventure—Italy, apparently.

"So…" Caroline's brow arched as I entered the room. She
was holding Harrison, and for the first time since I met her, she
looked human.

Neither Adam, Grayson, nor Josie met my gaze as I peered
around the room. They'd already anticipated my answer. "I've
decided to accept your offer."

"Smart girl," Caroline uttered with a nod. "We'll adjust your
wages once your three months has lapsed."

"Thank you."

"And we'll see you at Christmas." She kissed the top of
Harrison's head before passing him over to her husband. "Max
will look after anything you need."

William welcomed Harrison into his arms before meeting my
gaze. "Thank you, Cassidy," he said with unexpected warmth.
"I'm at ease knowing my father is in good hands."

My jaw fell. "I'll do my absolute best to keep him comfortable."

With an almost smile, William turned to his wife. "Come on,
Caroline, the helicopter's waiting," he said, handing Harrison
back to Grayson.

After William and Caroline uttered their goodbyes to the
family, three sets of eyes whirled my way.

"You're staying?" Josie's dimpled grin lit up the room.

My smile was tight. "Yes."

"But Adam said…" Her voice trailed off as Grayson tugged
her out of the room. "Come on, Jos. Harry needs a bath."

As they disappeared up the stairs, Adam shifted closer. "You
changed your mind."

I cleared my throat as I stepped back, keeping a safe distance. "I had to."

"And you're okay with missing Christmas with your son?"

"No, I'm not okay with it," I snapped unexpectedly. "But my life is complicated. It's full of twists and turns, and just when I think it's going in the right direction…bam! I fall."

"Cass…"

"I'm sorry," I said breathlessly. "I just need some space."

He instinctively reached out. "I didn't mean to upset you."

My lower lip quivered as I stared at his hand. "There are worse things than missing Christmas with my son, Adam. I can deal with this."

As Adam's frown deepened, I pivoted on my heel and jogged back up the stairs where my heart caught up with my head and emerged in an onslaught of tears.

Chapter 24

Thankfully, the lead-up to the Christmas break was quiet, and without the family around, I was able to focus on Liam. Now that everything was finalized for his inevitable passing, I concentrated my efforts on reducing his pain and giving him the comfort he craved while his family was gone. I read to him, performed more Reiki, and exhausted myself to sleep every night to distract myself from the crushing reality of missing Finn.

Grayson, Josie, and Harrison were first to arrive on the Friday before Christmas. They left the city early to avoid the holiday traffic, along with their enormous dog, Luci.

"Want to go for a walk around the grounds?" Josie asked once Liam had fallen asleep that afternoon. "The light is spectacular outside, and I'm dying to capture it."

I smiled at the camera in her hands and her eager grin. "Sure. I'd love that."

While Luci bounded around the puddles of melted snow, Josie giggled. "He's such a goofball," she said, taking another photo of her dog. "He loves coming here."

"I don't blame him. I mean, these grounds, the house..." I gushed. "Everything is so beautiful."

Josie's smile faded as she gazed up at the house. "It'll be weird when Gramps is gone."

"What will happen to the property?"

"It'll stay in the family, but I can't imagine any of us living here full time. Grayson's parents live in Bel Air when they're not travelling. We love living in Manhattan. And Adam lives...well, at work mostly." She sighed. "I guess it will turn into one of the many Harlow vacation properties."

"At least you'll have a special place to spend Christmas every year."

"You're right. There are so many more memories to make here."

"And I bet you'll capture every one of them." I smiled as Josie took another photo of her dog rolling in the mud.

"Oh, I plan to. This family does *not* take enough photos."

"Well, I'm sure you'll fix that. Photos are important." If only I had taken more of Dom.

"I think so, too." Sadness flooded Josie's aura, undoubtedly thinking of her parents.

"Amy showed me some of your work in *Maude*," I said, wanting to lift her spirit. "You're an exceptional photographer. You really capture the essence of a person."

"Thank you." She lowered her blush-filled cheeks.

"Your parents would be proud of you, Josie. You've really made something of yourself out here."

Josie blinked back tears before quickly wiping them away. "Ah, you got me."

"I'm sorry." I grimaced. "I didn't mean to upset you."

"No, it's fine." She clutched my forearm as she turned to me. "I don't have many people in my life who understand my pain. They're supportive, yes, but they don't really know how it feels." Emotion flickered through her eyes. "And I never want them to."

I placed my hand over hers. "Well, if you ever need to talk, I'm here."

"That's very kind, but you're not here to tend to my wounds."

"Maybe so, but if you're important to my sister, you're important to me. You can call me anytime…even after I go home."

With a solemn yet grateful nod, Josie continued down the path. "I want to thank you again for staying on with Gramps. You've really changed our outlook for the holidays this year. Harrison may not remember his first Christmas, but we sure will. Having Gramps here to spend it with him is so precious, and I really think you've played a part in that."

"Liam's here because of Liam," I said while Luci barked at the trees. "Perhaps he loves Christmas as much as your husband." I snickered. "I saw Grayson piling all those presents under the tree when you arrived."

Josie covered her face. "Isn't he ridiculous?"

"I think it's lovely. It's clearly his way of showing his family how much he cares."

"I know." She smiled bashfully. "I think it's sweet, too."

The sound of an approaching helicopter cut through our conversation.

"I thought you said Adam was arriving tomorrow?" I asked, squinting up at the sky.

Josie's forehead wrinkled as she followed my gaze. "I did."

"Your in-laws?"

"No, they definitely aren't arriving until Christmas Eve. Grayson spoke to them this morning."

As we wandered closer to the helipad, icy air blasted across our faces as the blades grew closer. Once safely on the ground, the pilot jumped out and opened the passenger door. I strained my eyes to witness two long, skinny legs jump out….and I recognized them instantly.

"Finn?" I cried out as I ran toward his beaming face. "Finny!" Tears streamed from my eyes as I threw my arms around my boy.

"Hey, Mom," he tried to say while I smothered him with kisses.

"How did you…?" I puffed. "I mean…who brought you?"

Finn shrugged. "I don't know. Aunty Amy drove me to the helicopter and told me you'd be waiting on the other side. She said she'd pick me up New Year's Day."

I threw my gaze back to Josie who appeared as surprised as I was. "It wasn't me," she said, lowering her camera. "It must've been Gramps." She peered down at my son and smiled. "You must be Finn. I've heard a lot about you. My name is Josie."

"Hi," he spoke nervously.

"I'll leave you to it." Josie met my gaze with a wink. "Luci's harassing Tico again."

With a giggle, I watched her jog over to the helicopter before turning back to Finn.

He gaped up at the house. "This is where you work?"

"It sure is." I grabbed his hand. "And there's someone I want you to meet."

Consumed with happiness, I escorted Finn straight up to Liam's bedroom, promising a tour later on.

I peeked inside before walking through the door. "Liam," I whispered, careful not to give him a start.

His eyes lit up at the sight of my son.

"This is my son, Finn. Finn, this is the lovely man I've been caring for."

Finn moved toward Liam's bed and reached out his hand. "Pleased to meet you."

"What lovely manners you have." Liam grasped Finn's hand with a noticeable shake.

"Apparently, Finn is staying with us for the holidays." My eyebrows drew closer. "Are you sure that's okay?"

"It's my house, and I'm delighted to have another guest."

My heart filled with warmth. "Finn, why don't you go check out my room. It's back down the hallway, second door on the left."

With an excited nod, he raced out of the door.

"Oh, Liam." I held back another batch of tears. "Thank you so much for bringing him here. This means so much to me."

"It wasn't my idea," he said with a glint in his eye.

I frowned. "Then who?"

He patted my hand. "I think you know."

My lips parted as I drew in air. "Why... Why would he do that? He was so angry when he found out about him."

"Under all that bravado, Adam has a beautiful heart. He may have a very...*unique* way of showing it, but my grandson is very fond of you."

"Unique is a good word to describe Adam."

Liam smiled. "It's also a good word to describe you."

————

"I can't believe you work here!" Finn said after a quick tour of the mansion before dinner. "This place is enormous!"

"And that was only half of it," I said, unpacking a few of his things into my closet. "I'll show you the rest tomorrow. Just wait until you see the pool."

"I saw the pool."

"The *other* pool. It's indoor."

Finn's eyes rounded. "Oh…my…God."

"But remember, this is not our house. When William and Caroline get here, you aren't allowed to leave this room without permission. Until then, please try to stick to the rooms I've showed you so you don't get lost."

"So, I have until Christmas Eve to explore?"

"Yes, but then we'll have to stay out of their way. I'll set up our own Christmas tree in here, and I'm sure Max can arrange some yummy treats for us."

Finn flopped down onto my oversized bed. "This is going to be so much fun."

"I'm so happy you're here." My eyes glazed over again. "I've missed you so much."

"I've missed you, too, Mom."

After introducing Finn to Grayson, and Harrison, and the staff at Harlow Manor, we spent the rest of the evening catching up alone. I wanted to hear every detail of his life over the past three months and find out what my dad had been feeding him. He'd grown two inches!

Max brought up our dinner, and we ate on our laps while watching a new-release movie on the flat-screen. It was a quiet night, but it was just what we needed to reconnect. We cuddled on the couch, and I relished every moment until his eyes began to droop.

"Come on, buddy. Let's get you into bed. I'm not strong enough to carry you anymore."

With a tired chuckle, Finn dragged himself over to the bed and climbed under the sheets. "Goodnight, Mom."

"Goodnight, baby."

As I climbed in next to him, I picked up my phone and scrolled to Adam's number. I wanted to thank him for bringing my world to me, but no words could justify how I felt. I had to show him.

———

Before sunrise, I carefully climbed out of bed, threw on sweatpants and a tee, and kissed Finn's forehead. "I'll be back soon," I whispered when he began to stir.

He responded with a sleepy nod and rolled over as I crept out of the room.

"I didn't expect to see you this morning," Liam said, smiling on my approach.

"I'm too excited to sleep."

"I bet. You've been apart for some time."

"Did you want to go to the library?" I asked, not wanting him to feel an ounce of guilt.

"My window will do today. I'm saving my energy for my great-grandson."

"Big day planned?"

"Full of naps and pureed food. We're quite the pair, Harry and I."

With a belly full of laughter, I sat beside Liam's bed as brilliant reds and pinks filled the sky.

Liam gazed at the glowing clouds. "It's going to be a good day."

"I think so too."

Our long, blissful silence was gradually interrupted by the nearing sound of blades chopping the air.

"That must be Adam."

My head snapped to Liam's twinkling eyes. "He's early."

"Perhaps he was too excited to sleep also."

I bit my bottom lip as my leg started to bounce.

Liam motioned to the door. "Go."

"Are you sure?"

He chortled. "I'm always sure."

"I won't be long," I uttered before my heartbeat raced my feet through the mansion.

As I burst out the front door, the wintery air slapped me across the face, reminding me to get the hell back inside and put on a coat. Not wanting to waste time, I grabbed Adam's long winter jacket from the coat room and slipped it on before trying again.

The hammering in my chest matched the beat of the blades as I jogged around the mansion to the helipad. I had no idea what I was going to say, so I let my heart take charge.

Our eyes met through the window of the helicopter, but the strong winds forced me to lower my gaze as they touched down. I hugged my stomach and rubbed my arms as the blades slowed to a stop, and I slowly peered up once Tico stepped out of the cabin.

The pilot nodded my way before opening the door for Adam, and I smiled back nervously. *What am I going to say? How can I possibly thank him enough?*

While Adam retrieved his suitcase and thanked the pilot, my anticipation grew. When our eyes finally locked across the helipad, I was unable to wait another second before I flew toward him. My chest slammed into his as my arms snaked around his waist.

"Now, that's a welcome," he said, resting his suitcase on the ground.

I peered up at him with gleaming eyes. "Thank you so much."

Adam's gaze softened as he exhaled. "How's he settling in?"

"He couldn't be happier. *I* couldn't be happier." I squeezed him again, enjoying the beat of his heart against my cheek. "It's the most wonderful thing anyone has ever done for me."

He ran his hand down my waves with a soft chuckle. "I doubt that."

"Don't try to hide that beautiful soul from me." I poked his hard chest as I stared up into his piercing blue eyes. "I can feel it."

Adam's pupils dilated as I unintentionally ran my hand across his torso. "Cass..." He stared at my mouth while his Adam's apple bobbed up and down.

A wave of desire crashed over me, and I rose up on my tippy-toes only to be knocked off balance when a giant furry beast burst between us.

"Fucking dog!" Adam yelled as Luci continued to pounce on him and lick his face.

"I'm clearly not the only one happy to see you," I said with a giggle before eyeing the huge, wet paw prints on his cashmere sweater. "Oh, shit. You better give that to Max before it stains."

"If it does, Josie can buy me a new one." With a grumble, he picked up his suitcase and continued to the pathway.

I jogged up beside him. "Dogs can sense a good soul, too, you know?"

Adam paused before bursting into laughter. "Luci is the fucking devil. Perhaps he sees me as a kindred spirit."

My heart burst at the sight of his smile. "There's good and bad in everyone, Adam." I slipped my arm through his as we continued toward the house. "And your good is definitely outweighing your bad right now."

"Yeah, well, don't go telling everyone. I have a reputation to uphold."

I grinned up at him, relishing the relaxed state of his features. "Your secret is safe with me."

Once we reached the entrance of Harlow Manor, Adam held the door open while I walked inside. "You're wearing my coat."

Heat rose up my neck. "Oh, yeah. I'm sorry. I was in a rush and…"

"It's okay." Adam moved closer. "You can keep it. My Laker's hoodie, though…"

I pressed my lips together as I pretended to think. "Didn't I give that back?"

"No."

"I'm sure I did."

"You didn't."

"I must've given it to Max, then…to wash."

Adam's lips pursed. "Then I'll ask him."

We stood at the base of the staircase, staring at each other for some time before one of us spoke.

"You want to meet him?" I asked, breaking first.

Adam exhaled a shaky breath as he gazed up the staircase. "Of course, but let me change first." He winced down at his shirt. "I think Luci stepped in dog shit."

I screwed up my nose. "Fair enough. Finn isn't a morning person anyway."

"We have something in common already."

I tilted my head. "You seem okay this morning."

His twinkling eyes met mine. "There's a reason for that."

———

Finn and I were playing chess in the library when Adam finally resurfaced. Liam was asleep, and Grayson and Josie had taken Harrison into town, leaving us to enjoy some quiet time by the fire.

My gaze flickered up to Adam's stationary frame in the doorway, giving my heart a start. "Hey, Adam," I said with an unexpected rasp. He looked incredible in his casual attire with his freshly washed hair slicked back. I could only imagine how good he smelled.

"I thought I'd find you here." With hands tucked into well-worn designer jeans, Adam sheepishly edged into the room until he was standing before us. "This must be Finn."

"Finn, this is Liam's grandson, Adam."

Finn stood and reached out his hand. "Pleased to meet you."

Adam's eyebrows rose as he swamped my son's little fingers. "Likewise."

"Adam visits his grampa on weekends."

"I'll be here a little longer over Christmas, though," he said, glancing my way.

My heartbeat quickened. "But Adam is a very busy man, so we mustn't get in his way."

"Relax, Cass." Adam rolled his eyes. "It's the holidays."

I wrinkled my nose. "I didn't think you took off for the holidays."

"Well, I'm making an exception this Christmas."

I held his gaze as I absorbed the warmth of his smile. "Liam will love that."

Adam drew in a deep breath as he turned to Finn. "So…has your mom given you the grand tour yet?"

"I don't want him getting lost," I interjected. "So, I've only shown him a few rooms."

"Then you haven't seen the best parts."

Nora appeared in the doorway, drawing my attention. "Cassidy, would you mind seeing Liam? He has a little pain in his side. I'm hoping you can help ease it."

"Of course." I rose to my feet. "Finn, why don't you go back to our room and watch some TV."

As Finn's shoulders slumped, Adam spoke up. "I can finish the game with him, if you like?" His nonchalance confused me. *Didn't Adam hate kids?* "When you get back, we can show him the best parts of Harlow Manor."

"Are you sure?"

"Go," he said, nodding his head toward the door. He sounded like his grandfather.

My gaze panned between my beautiful boy and the man who stood confidently before me. "Thanks," I uttered through my bewilderment. "But don't go easy on him. You'll regret it."

Adam chortled as he sat. "How good can he be?"

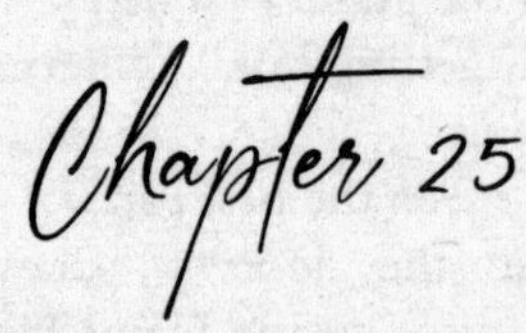

Chapter 25

After Liam drifted back to sleep, I walked up the hall toward Finn's distinctive laughter. When Adam's deep-chested chuckle followed, my heart liquified. I nudged open the library door to spy Adam rubbing his jaw as he contemplated his next move, while Finn grinned ear to ear—a look I knew all too well.

"Your son is about to beat me," Adam uttered, clearly sensing my presence.

I smiled. "He does that."

"It's really quite humiliating."

"He's been humiliating me since he was eight." I moved closer to assess the damage. "The only person who can beat him now is his grandfather."

Finn snickered. "Nah, I let him win."

My mouth fell open. "Don't let Pa know that. He prides himself on his chess skills."

"He taught you how to play?" Adam asked while succumbing to his loss.

Finn nodded. "He told me to always plan out your next three moves…in chess and in life…whatever that means."

Adam peered up at me. "You can't plan for everything."

My nerves emitted in a chuckle. "I never planned on being here, that's for sure."

"It's not all bad, is it?" he asked, packing up the chess board.

I gazed at my son who'd taken it upon himself to stoke the fire. "Not now. Not even in the slightest."

Adam stood with the chessboard and grazed my arm as he passed. "Good," he whispered before returning the game to the bookshelf.

"Can I see the rest of the house now?" Finn's bright eyes stole my attention.

"Um…only if that's okay with…" I turned to find Adam walking toward the door, and my heart plummeted. Perhaps we'd taken up too much of his time.

Adam stopped and turned back. "You guys coming?"

Finn leapt up and bounded out of the room while I followed at a slower pace.

Adam held the door open, waiting for me to walk through. "He's a great kid."

"He is." I beamed with pride.

He brushed his hand over mine. "I've missed your smile."

My lips parted, not for words, but for air.

"Which way?!" Finn called out from the top of the staircase, breaking our trance.

Adam ran his hand through his hair before pushing forward while I jogged to catch up with his strides.

"We'll do the west wing first." He pointed to the hallway ahead. "Then, we'll head downstairs."

Finn shot forward before freezing. "It's not haunted, is it?"

"Of course not," he uttered moments before his face dropped. He turned to me with a concerned whisper. "Is it?"

I winced. "Well…"

Adam groaned. "I don't want to know."

"You have nothing to worry about here." Ghosts weren't my forte, but I'd certainly picked up energies throughout the house that weren't attached to its living occupants. Fortunately, I felt no evil, only love. It surrounded Liam and the rooms he enjoyed the most. I could only assume his late wife was waiting for her love to cross over.

Finn peered up at the paintings in the hallway. "It's like Hogwarts."

"My grandmother was an artist, and she loved painting landscapes. They're all over the mansion."

"But what about this one?" He pointed to a beautiful portrait of a child holding a newborn baby. "It has the same signature as the others."

"You're right." Adam frowned at the scrawled initials in the corner. "Perhaps she dabbled in portraits, too."

Finn pointed to the older child. "He kinda looks like you."

Adam stepped closer. "Huh...I never noticed..."

"Perhaps we should head downstairs." I knew exactly who we were looking at. "Finn is dying to see the indoor pool."

With one last glance at the painting, Adam directed us back to the grand staircase and down to the ground floor. Ignoring all the rooms I'd shown Finn the day prior, Adam went straight to the good stuff; the indoor theater, the gym, the billiard room, and numerous other areas I'd never ventured to for fear of getting lost.

"Wait until you see the ballroom," Adam said as Finn gaped over the indoor pool.

"There's a ballroom?!" Finn and I said in unison.

Adam frowned at me. "You've been here three months and you've never wondered what's behind those doors?" He pointed to the lavish double doors at the end of the corridor.

"It's not in my best interest to snoop around."

Adam sighed as he grasped the door handles. "You are both welcome here."

My jaw dropped as he pulled open the doors to reveal an enormous room adorned with crystal chandeliers, velvet draped walls, and polished parquetry floors. Piles of chairs and tables were stacked in the corner, along with candelabras covered in white sheets.

Adam's steps echoed as he entered the vast space. "My grandparents had their wedding reception here."

"Liam and Betty? Oh, wow," I gushed. "What on earth do you use this room for now?"

"Well...one summer, when my brother and I were teenagers, we converted it into our own type of ballroom." Adam wandered over to the far wall and lifted a bundle of dusty sheets off two old basketballs. He picked one up and tossed it from hand to hand.

Finn's smile grew large. "Awesome!"

"That's not all." Adam pulled one of the drapes aside to uncover a basketball hoop attached to the wall behind it.

Finn bounced up and down on his toes. "That is so cool!" He held out his hands. "Pass!"

Adam tossed the ball his way and picked up the other while Finn proceeded to dribble twice and shoot.

As it swished through the hoop, Adam's eyes widened. "Your mom never mentioned you played."

"I don't." Finn ran to collect the ball, then did a layup.

"You should."

Finn's gaze flickered my way before shrugging. "It doesn't matter."

Guilt tore through me. "He had to pick. We couldn't afford to do both swimming *and* basketball. So, he chose swimming."

A small line materialized between Adam's eyebrows as he bounced his ball. "Well, you must be a kickass swimmer if basketball was your second preference."

"I'm alright." Blush filled his freckled cheeks.

"Alright?" I scoffed before turning to Adam. "Finn made the state finals."

A spark flickered through Adam's aura. "Are you kidding? That's amazing! When's the big race?"

"February 12th."

Adam crossed his arms, clearly impressed. "I'll have to come watch."

"Really?!" Finn's chest puffed out. "That would be great. You can keep Mom from embarrassing me."

Apprehension coursed through my veins. "Adam's a busy man, Finn, and he lives in LA. I doubt he'll have time to get to your race."

"No, it's fine." Adam turned to Finn. "I'll be there. It's an incredible achievement."

I swallowed the lump in my throat. My son didn't need any more heartache. "We'll see," I muttered, hoping Finn would forget come the day.

"You should practice your swimming while you're here." Adam passed Finn another basketball. "I won quite a few swimming comps back in my college days. I could give you some tips."

I shook my head with a laugh. "Forget it…he doesn't listen to anyone but his coac—"

"That would be awesome!" Finn blurted excitedly.

"Excuse me?!" The shock almost knocked me over. "I've been trying to give you pointers for years."

"But this is different, Mom. Adam swam in college."

I rolled my eyes. "So? I bet I could swim circles around him."

The corner of Adam's mouth lifted with his snicker. "Oh, really?"

I folded my arms. "Really."

A dangerous spark materialized in his eyes. "Then I propose a race."

"Yes!" Finn bounced on his feet again.

"Tomorrow? Unless you need more time to practice."

"Oh, I don't need practice." *Shit. Shit. Shit.*

Finn laughed. "Yeah, ya do, Mom."

"Fine," I grumbled. "Tomorrow, but Finn, Grayson, and Josie will be judging, so don't even think about cheating."

Adam's gaze tapered. "I may be some things, but I'm no cheater."

My knees weakened under his stare, and I quickly looked away. "Well, the more witnesses the better."

"So, what are you betting?" Finn's big green eyes zigzagged between us.

"Surely we can play for bragging rights."

Finn scrunched up his nose "That's a bit boring."

Adam sniggered. "Totally boring."

I placed my hands on my hips. "But I don't have anything you want."

Adam's eyebrow rose. "I'm sure I could think of something." He ran his hand over his smile. "What about a free session?"

My eyes bulged. "Pardon?"

"Of…Reiki?"

"Oh." I grasped my chest. "I guess I could do that."

"And if Mom wins, you could buy her a new crystal. She loves them."

"You don't have enough?"

I grinned. "Never."

"Then it looks like we have a deal." He held out his hand.

"That we do." Electricity surged through my body as my fingers wrapped around his. "May the best swimmer win."

Chapter 26

After a longer than normal Reiki session with Liam, I returned to my bedroom to find Finn missing. Assuming he'd made his way downstairs to explore the adventure playground below, I pivoted back to the hall to begin my search. I'd only taken one step before my son's voice floated out of the room opposite.

Peeking inside Adam's open door, I spied Finn sprawled out on a beanbag in front of the giant flat-screen, talking into a headset.

"Finn, what are you doing in here?" I asked from the door, not wanting to invade Adam's privacy.

Finn's eyes didn't budge from the screen, so I marched in front of him, blocking his view.

"Mom!" He darted his head from side to side.

"I said, what are you doing in here?"

"Adam said I could play his video games."

"Oh." My heart warmed at the gesture.

"Can you move?!"

Shifting aside, I turned my gaze to the game, and my body cooled on impact. "Turn that off immediately!" I yelled, glaring at the violent scene before me.

"What?! Why?!" His eyebrows pulled together as he met my horrified gape.

"You're too young to play a game like this."

Finn groaned. "But all my friends are pla—"

"I don't care!" My hands sat firmly on my waist, waiting for him to switch it off.

Adam walked into the room with a bowl of nachos. "Everything okay in here?"

"No, not really." Frustration rumbled under my skin. "He's not allowed to play this."

He glanced at the screen and winced. "I didn't think it was that bad."

"He's only eleven, Adam! It's too violent."

"Yeah, I guess it is." He rubbed his jaw. "How about we download some new ones?"

"Oh, you don't have to do that." Now I felt ungrateful.

"I'm bored with my games anyway." Adam fell into the chair beside Finn. "Any suggestions, buddy?"

Finn's eyes grew large. "You mean, I can get anything? Anything I want?"

Adam's eyes met mine. "Within reason. No blood and guts."

I mouthed the words thank you before retreating. "I'll leave you boys to it. I'm going to go read for a bit."

"Enjoy." Adam threw me a wink before switching his focus to the screen.

As my cheeks filled with heat, I wandered back to my room, content with the friendship they'd formed. Finn clearly loved his company.

Over the next few hours, I lay on my bed, reading, while listening to Adam and Finn laugh, shout, and cheer as they played their silly games. It wasn't until they grew silent that I crept closer to Adam's door.

"So, you like her, huh?" Adam asked while wrestling with his controller.

"Yeah...I guess...but so do Josh and Evan."

"Don't worry about those guys. Just walk straight up to her and ask her out."

Finn burst out laughing. "I can't do that."

"Of course you can. You're sporty, good looking, have great manners...what more could she want?"

I could sense my son's eyes rolling from across the hall.

"There's not much point now. We're moving back to LA soon."

"I heard."

"Mom says we might be able to afford a place with a backyard now! I can't wait. I'll miss my Pa, though, and Aunty Amy and Reed, but they said they'll visit for the holidays."

"Have you got family in LA?" Concern laced Adam's voice.

"My dad's sister, Tash, lives there with Uncle Bryce and my cousin, Tristan."

"You must miss them."

"Yeah. Not as much as my mom, though. Aunty Tash is her best friend."

"She doesn't have friends in New York?"

"Not really. She works too much."

"Well, she's lucky to have you."

Finn chortled. "That's what Mom always says. Mostly after Dad died."

My breath caught. Finn rarely spoke about his father.

"That must've been hard," Adam said after a moment of silence.

"I don't really remember him all too well, except for him being sick all the time. Do you think that's bad?"

My shoulders slumped against the wall at the despair in his voice.

"Dude, you were, what…four when he got sick?" Adam said without hesitation. "You know what I remember from when I was four?"

"What?"

"Absolutely nothing."

Finn's belly filled with laughter. "You're funny. I can see why my mom likes you."

I almost choked on air as I hid in the hallway.

"She does?"

"You should ask her out."

"Do you think she'll say yes?"

"You're sporty, good looking and have great manners…what more could she want?"

Adam chuckled. "Are you saying I should follow my own advice?"

"Hey, if it works for you, maybe it'll work for me."

I smiled at my son's cheeky antics.

"You're a smart kid, Finn."

"Mom tells me that all the time, too."

I tapped on the door, unable to handle their adorable conversation any longer. I hadn't heard Finn open up like that in years, and it had only taken Adam half a day. "Hey, Finn, would you mind if I drag Adam away for a few minutes?"

Adam grimaced as he placed the controller on the coffee table. "I think I'm in trouble again," he whispered as he stood.

"Ha-ha," I uttered as Finn giggled.

As Adam approached, I pivoted on my heel and strode back to my room, motioning for him to follow.

He paused in the doorway. "Are you sure? You made it very clear this room is off limits."

With a huff, I pulled him inside and closed the door. "I just wanted to say thank you," I said, swallowing back my apprehension.

"Ookay…" Adam's brow furrowed. "But couldn't you have thanked me over there? Finn and I are in the middle of a ga—"

I launched forward and slammed my mouth onto his. My yearning heart and body were no longer playing by the rules.

Adam jerked back, searching my eyes. "Fuck," he mumbled before grasping my nape and pulling me back. His lips devoured mine with fierce intensity while our tongues fought a never-ending war of forbidden lust. I wanted him. The heat between us was undeniable. The fire was out of control.

"Adam! I beat your score!" Finn called out as he crossed the hallway.

As the door opened, we flew apart.

"So, thank you," I managed to say to Adam, avoiding eye contact with both of them. "I really…appreciate it."

"Anytime," Adam uttered breathlessly before turning to Finn. "You beat my score?"

"Told you I would. Wanna play again?"

"Let's have a rematch tomorrow before the big race. I need a shower before dinner." Adam's electrified eyes panned back to me. "You guys are joining us, right?"

Finn peered up at me, pleading. "Please, Mom? They're having pizza."

I ruffled his hair. "I already told Josie we would."

"Good," Adam said with entirely too much heat in his stare. "I'll see you later."

———

"Hey, guys," Josie called out as we entered Liam's room. "Take a seat. The pizzas just arrived."

I smiled over at Liam, but he didn't stir. His medication must've taken effect.

Finn dragged me to the couch, where he dove onto the chair beside Adam, unknowingly creating the perfect buffer.

Adam peeked up at me, as if reading my thoughts, but I was unable to hold his gaze. Instead, my cheeks burned bright as I sank into the space beside Finn and fetched a slice a pizza from the open box before us.

"What is that?" Finn screwed up his nose at the glorious concoction.

"That's the Adam special." Josie laughed. "Gross, huh?"

Adam took a bite of his slice. "Your mom loves it," he mumbled through a full mouth.

I gaped at his choice of words.

"The pizza…I mean," he choked out. "She loves the pizza."

"We got it the first time, Adam," Grayson uttered while Josie held back her laughter.

Oh, my fucking God.

"Did Adam tell you about the race tomorrow?" Finn interrupted, unfazed by the awkward turn in conversation.

"Yes!" Josie's face lit up. "We're so excited to see someone beat Adam."

"Other than me," Grayson added.

Adam scoffed. "That was one time, dipshit."

"I told you I was the superior brother." Grayson nudged Josie's side. "That's why our parents skipped him and gave me the family name."

I peeked across at Adam as the energy in the room shifted.

Adam glared at his brother before throwing his pizza slice back in the box. "I need a drink."

"Hey, man. I didn't mean it," Grayson called out as his brother stood and marched toward the door.

As Adam disappeared into the hallway, Josie sighed. "Gray…"

"What? It was a joke."

"Is Adam okay, Mom?" Finn asked, peering up at me.

I ran my hand down his back, knowing he'd picked up on the energy, too. "He will be, sweetie."

Grayson rubbed the back of his neck with a grimace. "I didn't realize he was still sensitive about the name thing."

I frowned. "The name thing?"

"The previous generations of Harlows all named their eldest child William—except our parents. We have no idea why, and we know better than to ask. It's a sure way to get our dad in a foul mood." Grayson lowered his eyes. "I used to tease him when I was little that I must've been their favorite, but everyone knew that was far from the truth. My parents doted on Adam. Always have."

I gazed over at Liam, who was sleeping soundly beside Harrison's bassinet. "Perhaps there is another reason why he is called Adam."

"Or maybe my mom hated the name William…explains why she gave it to me."

"Wait." Curiosity got the better of me. "If your name is William, why does everyone call you Grayson?"

"Grayson is my middle name. I didn't want to be a carbon copy of my father, so I use it to avoid confusion. That's why Gramps goes by Liam. He had the same problem with his father."

"You're lucky William has a lot of nicknames," I said, taking another bite.

Josie mused. "There's still room for a Bill, Billy, Will, or Willy."

"Thinking of more baby names already?" Grayson shot his wife a wink.

"Don't ruin a perfectly good meal, Gray." Josie narrowed her gaze at her husband before biting into her pizza.

We all laughed at Josie's disgust before diverting our attention to dinner.

"So, Finn…" Josie said as Adam wandered back into the room, carrying two glasses. "Let's talk about this big race tomorrow."

"Mom is going to kick Adam's ass," he responded excitedly.

I gasped. "Finn!"

"Sorry…I mean butt."

Adam chuckled as he paused in front of me and lowered the drink into my hands. "You clearly don't know who you're up against, Finn," he said, returning to his seat.

Grayson's eyebrows rose as I took a sip of the gin and tonic. It tasted magnificent.

Josie cleared her throat, drawing her husband's gaze. "The Harlows used to have quite the reputation for swimming, you know?"

Finn shrugged. "But that was, like, a hundred years ago."

"Reputations change," I sang out before taking another glorious sip.

Grayson sniggered as he panned his gaze from my glass to his brother. "That they do."

"What?" Adam mouthed as his gaze tapered.

Grayson shook his head, trying not to smile.

"Did you still want to watch a movie tonight?" Adam asked Finn while reaching for a slice of pizza. "I mean, if it's okay with your mom."

"As long as it's age appropriate, it's fine by me. I'm hoping to do some Reiki on Liam when he wakes, so I'm sure Finn would love the company."

"Awesome! Thanks, Mom!"

As Adam and Finn delved into their favorite movies and quotes, there was no disguising the mystified faces of Grayson and Josie as they observed their easy conversation. While Finn was completely engaged, Adam had never looked so relaxed, and my heart warmed at their exchange.

"Adam?" Liam cried out from his bed. "Adam?!"

We all spun around at the panic in his voice.

"He's not breathing!" he yelled, peering over Harrison's bassinet.

Josie and Grayson grew pale as they rushed to their baby's side while Adam drew out his phone to call 911.

"Nora!" I yelled as I bolted to the door.

Within seconds, her door flew open, and she ran past me into Liam's bedroom. "What's happened?"

"He's fine," Grayson cried out as his shoulders slumped. "Jos, he's fine."

Josie held back tears as she scooped up her son. Harrison's cries were evidence to his breathing.

Liam flustered under his bed sheets until Nora took his hand. "Liam, honey…it's okay. Everything is okay." She checked his pulse before facing us. "He must've had a nightmare. We've had to increase his pain medication, and one of the side effects can be hallucinations."

"Adam wasn't moving," Liam whimpered. "I thought…"

Grayson moved to Liam's side. "Gramps, it's Harrison. My son. Not Adam. Adam's right here," he said, motioning to his approaching brother.

Liam's weary gaze panned to Adam. "Oh, yes…" He lowered his tear-filled eyes. "I'm sorry."

"It's okay, Gramps." Adam grasped his other hand. "He's a good-looking kid. Easy mistake to make."

"I thought it happened again, I…I…" Liam's chest rose up and down in quick succession. "I thought…"

"Liam, I want you to take three deep breaths," Nora ordered. "Cassidy, can you take over here while I call the doctor?"

"Of course." I wrapped my fingers around Liam's as Nora left the room.

"We'll take Harry back to our bedroom for a feed," Josie said, trying to settle her baby's cries. "We'll be back soon, Gramps."

With a nod, Liam closed his eyes to focus on his breathing.

Adam's eyes locked on our intertwined hands. "Is he okay?"

"He will be." I glanced back at the couch where my son stood, wide eyed and pale. "Would you mind taking Finn back to my room? Let him watch whatever movie he wants."

"Yeah, of course." Adam squeezed his grandfather's hand before placing it by his side. With a faint smile, he left with Finn, leaving me alone with Liam.

I ran my fingers over his sparse gray hair. "That must've given you quite the fright."

"My head is so…jumbled."

"I know," I said softly. "Let me do some Reiki while we wait for Nora."

"I don't know what I'd do without you."

As I stood with my hands hovered over his head, the room filled with the scent of freesias. "Can you smell that, Liam?"

He drew in a deep breath and every muscle in his body appeared to relax. "Betty…"

"Keep breathing." My hands warmed. "Focus on your love for her."

After a few minutes, Liam drifted back to sleep, completely at ease.

"I guess we won't be needing these," Nora said as she returned with a cup full of pills. She read his pulse and placed the back of her hand on his forehead. "You really are a miracle worker."

"I don't work miracles." I smiled solemnly. "If I could, my husband would still be alive."

Nora's sympathetic gaze met mine. "I bet he felt love until his last breath."

"He did."

"You deserve that, too, you know," she said, fixing Liam's sheets. "I hope that doctor hasn't deterred you from all men."

"No, but I think I'll wait until I have my old life back before I go down that path again."

"Your old life is gone, honey. It's time to create a new one." She nodded to the door. "Go enjoy some time with your son. I'll keep an eye on Liam."

"Thanks, Nora, but I think I'll sit with him for a bit. Just in case he has another nightmare."

"Suit yourself. I'll update the doc."

Chapter 27

Once Liam's breathing stabilized and I was confident he was in a deep sleep, I wandered back to my room, hoping to catch the end of the movie.

"Hey," I whispered, finding Finn sleeping soundly against Adam's shoulder while an old Disney movie played.

Adam pulled his gaze from the screen. "Hey…is Gramps okay now?"

"He's fine. Fast asleep…just like this guy." I smiled at the pool of drool on Adam's shirt.

"Yeah, I lost feeling in my arm about ten minutes ago."

I met his twinkling eyes with a smile. "I should get him into bed," I said, lifting Finn's heavy head off Adam's shoulder.

Adam rose to his feet and nudged me aside. "Don't wake him. I've got this."

"Thanks." I stepped aside. "He isn't as little as he used to be."

Adam scooped him up with a grunt. "Works for me. I missed my gym session this morning."

With a flutter of my heart, I watched Adam carry Finn to my bed and gently place him down.

He drew the covers up and scruffed his hair before turning back to me. "What?"

"Nothing," I murmured, turning my heated cheeks away.

Adam reached for the novel on my nightstand. "Is this your latest escape?"

I grimaced as he flipped through it. "Not a word."

His panty-dropping smirk grew. "Is it as good as the last one?"

"Adam…"

"Perhaps I'll read it next," he continued, encroaching my personal space until only the book separated us. "Underline your favorite scenes for me, will you?"

I snatched the book from his hands. "I think it's time for bed—for you to go to bed, I mean."

"I'm hardly going to make a move." He glanced over at my sleeping son. "I have some boundaries.

"Wonders never cease."

He stared into my eyes with a growing smirk. "Goodnight, Cassidy," he whispered as he floated past. "But don't think I've forgotten about that kiss earlier."

———

Sleep did not come. I couldn't even concentrate on my novel because I couldn't stop thinking about him. The man across the hallway. The kiss earlier. The yearning Adam induced by his mere proximity was driving me insane. I needed to clear my head, and I needed to cool the fuck down.

Throwing off my covers, I slipped out of bed and rummaged through the closet for the bathing suit I needed for the big race the next afternoon. The two-piece was hardly a competition number, but it would have to do. I didn't have the time or the money to buy a new one.

Deciding a little stealthy practice was in order, I stepped into my suit and concealed it under my robe. If anyone crossed my path, I would say I was merely fetching a drink.

Once I successfully opened the door, minus creaks, I peered down the dark passageway and crept out of my room. I tiptoed down the stairs and through the hallways until I was standing in front of the large glass doors leading into the indoor pool. I couldn't risk the outdoor pool, knowing Adam could see it from his bedroom window.

In lieu of turning on the lights, I used the moonlight to guide me toward the glistening water. I dipped my toes over the edge and sighed as the warm water enveloped my foot. I was going to miss this luxury.

While I stared into the still water, preparing to dive, I endeavored to remember my high-school training. I hadn't raced in thirteen years, and although I talked tough, I had no idea what I was doing. For some reason, I loved riling Adam up. The playful spark he kept hidden from his professional world was intoxicating. Every time I saw him, I wanted more, and it was leading me down a dangerous rabbit hole.

So now, for Finn's sake, I had to figure out how to walk the walk. I had to win the race or at least be deemed a worthy opponent. A Reiki session with Adam may have sounded innocent enough, but after our first attempt had led to an awkwardly arousing upside-down kiss, I wasn't sure if I had the strength to stop myself from going further.

I barely caused a ripple as I dove into the water, but I grumbled as I resurfaced barely meters from the edge. I needed a better swimsuit. My breasts were too big for professional swimming. All the boys in high school used to love watching me race—not for my skill, but for my *Baywatch* body. Even though I won almost every race, I could never get the respect I deserved. Even my swim coach loved to stare.

When my grandmother died and I had to move back to New York, I put my swimming dreams on hold. And when I fell pregnant months after my return to LA, I gave up on the dream entirely. The window of opportunity had closed.

As I flew through the water, I analyzed every movement. My muscles weren't as toned as they once were, but I was still fast. Maybe not fast enough to beat Adam, but at least I wouldn't embarrass myself.

Once my fingers grazed the wall, I pushed through the water's surface with a gasp.

"I thought you didn't need the practice?"

I lunged backward as Adam's shadow loomed overhead. "Adam!" I splashed water up at him. "You frightened me."

He crossed his arms over his crumpled t-shirt. "Well, now we're even."

"What are you talking about?"

"You set off the silent alarm."

My eyes widened. "Oh my God. Did I wake Liam?"

"Relax. The alerts are diverted to my phone when I'm staying here." His infuriating and arousing smirk returned. "I was pleasantly surprised when I checked the cameras."

I spun around in the water, squinting into the dark corners of the room. "There are cameras?!"

His grin widened. "Unfortunately, it was too dark to see anything of interest."

"I'll get out." I waded to the ladder.

"Why? You clearly need the practice."

My mouth fell open as I whirled back to meet his playful smile.

"You need to straighten your legs when you're kicking."

"They are straight!"

"Here, I'll show you." He tore off his t-shirt and shorts, then jumped into the water in his boxer briefs—his *white* boxer briefs.

Before I could protest, he shot through the pool, pushing me sideways with his wake. If it wasn't for his muscular arms pounding through the water, I would've scrambled for safety, but I was completely entranced.

His perfect strokes glided him to the end of the pool and back before resurfacing with a shake of his wet hair. My speeding heart was well ahead of my slow-motion vision. He was fucking Poseidon.

"Well, you need to rotate your body more," I uttered as I tried to repel all the dirty thoughts racing through my mind.

Adam's eyebrows drew together. "I do not."

I chortled. "And that's why Summerhill never made it all the way."

"Oh really?" His lips pursed as he waded toward me.

"Yep. Too damn cocky." I paddled back to keep him at the same distance.

"Cocky?" His eyebrow arched as he edged closer.

"You know the kind…rich…arrogant…"

"Your next words better be *incredibly good looking*."

I held back my smile. "I was going to go with…*mediocre*."

"Oh…" He snickered. "You're in trouble."

Adam's pupils dilated before he launched my way, sending me squealing through the water.

In my attempt to swim away, he grabbed hold of my ankle and pulled me backward until my back slammed against his chest.

"Okay! Good looking!" I cried out as Adam clutched my sides, intuitively knowing how ticklish I was.

"Just good?" His deep voice in the shell of my ear sent tingles through my body.

"Mmhmm."

When his fingers tightened at my futile attempt to wriggle out of his grasp, I burst out laughing. "Okay, okay! Great! The best! Fucking incredible!"

He spun me around, only loosening his grip a fraction. "That's better."

I pushed at his muscular chest. "You don't play fair."

His eyes fell to my breasts, bobbing up and down in the wake of our wrestling. "Neither do you."

With a huff, I attempted to cross my arms.

"Don't."

My chest filled with hot, humid air at his authoritative tone. I didn't know if I was irritated or aroused, but the pulse below suggested the latter.

"They're fucking beautiful." His hand ran up my side until it was cupping my right breast.

"Adam…"

His thumb rolled around my protruding nipple. "Cassidy…"

"Someone may walk in."

"It's 2 a.m." He pulled our bodies together. "Everyone is asleep."

"But there are cameras."

His mouth grazed my ear. "I'll erase it."

"But this is my workplace. I ca—" His tongue rolled over my ear lobe. "Oh, God." I swallowed back my desire. "Adam… please…"

"Just say the word." He pressed his forehead to mine while his finger traced the line of my bathing suit. "Tell me to stop."

I opened my mouth but emitted no words.

His eyes penetrated mine. "Say it."

"I...I..."

He let out a low growl as he grasped my face. "Say it now, or I won't be able to."

"No."

"No?" Uncertainty filtered through his face.

My body melted into his the moment I stopped resisting. "I don't want you to stop." I looped my arms around his neck until my pelvis pressed into his bulge. "But just this onc—"

His lips tore off the end of my sentence as he scooped up my legs and wrapped them around his body. With a growl, he spun us around and pressed me against the pool wall, grinding into me as he devoured my neck.

As my head fell head back in ecstasy, Adam tore down the straps of my bikini top while trailing his tongue along my collarbone.

"What a fucking sight," he murmured as my girls bobbed along the surface of the water. He brought his hand under my left breast and lifted it out of the water. "Just like I remember." He licked off the excess water before sucking on the nipple while his other hand cupped my ass.

My core throbbed as he switched sides, giving them equal attention.

"I remember, too..." I closed my eyes as he ravished me.

He pushed his hard length between my legs. "Do you remember this?"

With my speechless nod, Adam released my breasts and slid both hands under my swimsuit and over my ass, adding to the pressure.

His rhythmic strokes were making me dizzy with want. "Adam..."

"What do you want, baby?" His hot breath coated my cheek.

"You know what I want."

"Say it," he demanded, low and rough.

I almost orgasmed on the spot. "I want you to fuck me."

"Good girl," he whispered with a dark, devilish smirk. "Now, hold on tight."

As I tightened my grip on his shoulders, Adam released his length from his underwear while yanking mine aside. With one hard thrust, I cried out as I surrendered to the fullness I'd yearned for since our first meeting.

Adam slammed into me again and again until the water crashed over the edge, spilling onto the tiles above. Through an ecstasy-filled haze, I gazed up at the ceiling, full of dancing diamonds, and smiled. It was beautiful. *I felt beautiful.*

As my eyes rolled back, Adam's entire body tensed on release, giving me the warmth I hadn't felt inside since…my eyes widened.

"Fuck," he muttered as if reading my thoughts. "Please tell me you're on the pill."

"Yes," I cried. "But what about…" I pulled away and swam to the ladder, lifting my bikini straps as I climbed.

"Cass, I'm clean," he called after me. "I got tested a couple of weeks ago, and you're the only one I've ever done that with. Fuck, you're the only one I've been with since our first night together."

"And I'm supposed to believe that?" I grabbed a towel. "Oh my God, how could we be so irresponsible?"

"Cass, relax." He followed me out of the pool. "We got caught up in the moment."

I spun around to face him. "*Finn* is the result of one of those moments, Adam. It changed the entire course of my life."

"Calm down. It really isn't a big deal."

"Of course you would say that." I quickly dried myself off.

"What's that supposed to mean?"

"You have money and stability," I growled as I slipped on my robe. "And the one time I get close to having just one of those things, I jeopardize everything because I can't control my fucking libido around you."

Adam's frown deepened as he stepped closer. "You haven't jeopardized anything."

I moved aside, not able to meet his gaze. "That can't happen again. Not while I'm working here."

"Come on, Cass. We're both consenting adults."

"Yet we're acting like teenagers!" I attempted to leave, but he blocked my escape.

"That's because the tension between us is wound up so fucking tight." He grasped my arms. "Maybe if we relieve some of it, we'll be able to control ourselves."

I tried to push him off. "Then we'll have to relieve it the old-fashioned way."

"How can I possibly go back to my hand after that?"

"I'm sure there are a million women willing to help with that."

Hurt flared through his energy as he dropped his arms. "Is that what you want me to do? Fuck other women?"

I lowered my eyes as tears endeavored to burn their way to the surface.

"Tell me," he growled.

My quivering breath outed my truth. "No."

He lifted my chin to meet his dark gaze. "Then we have a problem, don't we, Tiger?"

Chapter 28

Tears of frustration ran down my face as I scrubbed off Adam's delicious scent in the shower. Who knew how many women he'd been sleeping with back in LA? Every image I found on the internet featured his arm around a different woman, and it made me feel physically ill. As if he hadn't fucked each and every one of them.

All the articles implied as much…notorious playboy, womanizer, lady killer…until one article took a new turn.

WHERE IN THE WORLD IS ADAM HARLOW?

Since Harlow Corp. acquired most of the Warren Media portfolio, Adam Harlow looks to have put aside his playboy ways to concentrate on the company, following his father's retirement.

Since becoming the wealthiest man under 35 and the most eligible bachelor in the country, Adam appears to have become a recluse, disappearing for days on end, leaving the who's who of women waiting for him to resurface.

After the recent marriage of his brother, William Harlow, to photographer Josie Spencer, high-society gossip suggests Adam may be tiring of his promiscuous ways and is finally ready to settle down with one lucky lady, rumored to be heiress Staci Warner.

As I settled back into bed beside Finn at almost 3a.m., the phone lit up on my bedside.

Adam: **I know you don't believe me. See attached.**

With a frown, I tapped on the file to download a recent copy of Adam's test results. A clean bill of sexual health.

Relief settled over me. It didn't make what we did okay, but it was something.

Finn poked his head into Liam's room while I read to him. "Come on, Mom! You have to get ready for the big race."

Liam chuckled. "Oh, I can't wait to hear about this."

"Are you sure you don't want me to stay and read some more? The silly race can wait."

"I'm feeling quite tired today, so I think I'll have a nap while everyone is downstairs."

"Come on, Mom," Finn cried out again. "Everyone's waiting for you."

With a sigh, I placed the book on Liam's bedside table. "Fine. I'll go get my swimsuit on."

"Wonderful." Liam grasped my hand with a tired smile. "You've brought new life into this house. Thank you."

I gazed into his drowsy eyes. "Make sure you're well rested for dinner tonight, or Mrs. Fredrich won't let you downstairs."

"Neither wild horses nor Mrs. Fredrich could stop me from sharing my last Christmas Eve dinner with my family."

Finn marched into the room and grabbed my hand. "Let's go!"

"Okay, I'm coming! Meet me downstairs."

As Finn bolted down the hall, I reluctantly followed. I hadn't seen Adam since our early-morning mishap, and I was dreading seeing him again—especially in the same place.

According to Josie, Adam had left early that morning to run some errands but said he'd be back before the race. I prayed for traffic or a work emergency, but it appeared nothing would hinder the embarrassment that was about to take place.

Loud cheers echoed off the tiles as I entered the pool room. The smiling faces of Finn, Grayson, Josie, Max. and some of the kitchen staff lined the walls.

"Oh my God." I glared at my son. "You invited *everyone?*"

Finn grinned. "Liam wanted to come, too, but the cranky nurse wouldn't let him."

I scuffed up his hair. "Just wait until your next race, Mister."

When I caught sight of Adam's broad shoulders at the end of the pool, my heartbeat accelerated. His back was turned, and my gaze followed the muscular lines of his body as he performed his warm-up stretches.

"Are you guys ready?" Finn asked, interrupting my wandering thoughts.

Adam turned, revealing dark goggles that obscured his beautiful eyes. His jaw was taut, his body stiff, and when he nodded to my son, I knew he meant business.

I made my way to the edge of the pool. "Let's do this."

Adam moved to my side, but I didn't dare peek up. He was huge in comparison, and I wouldn't let that deter me.

Grayson snorted. "I'm pretty sure there's a size advantage here. Maybe Adam should give Cassidy a head start."

Adam and I glared at him. "No," we shot back in unison.

"Alright." Grayson shrugged. "Four laps. Freestyle."

With a deep breath, I stared into the water, clearing my mind and conjuring focus, until Finn screamed, "Go!"

With a perfect take-off, I dove into the water, resurfacing a second behind Adam. As if I hadn't missed a day's training in my life, I pounded through the water, desperately wanting to stay in the game. To my surprise, I kept my pace. I performed each stroke with precision, but I needed an edge to keep up with Adam's sheer size.

On the final lap, I pushed aside my pride and took Adam's advice. I straightened my body and focused on my kicking technique. I regained the distance I'd lost and was now matching Adam's stroke to two strokes of mine.

The screaming grew louder in the final few meters, but when my palm slammed against the wall, everything silenced.

Adam tore off his goggles the moment we surfaced and met my stunned gaze.

"Looks like you've met your match, Adam!" Josie laughed. "I'd call that a tie."

His eyes flew to my smiling face. "Bullshit."

Grayson held his bouncing chest. "If you want proof, we can review the security footage."

"No!" Adam and I exclaimed together.

Josie watched us in amusement. "Wow, you guys are in sync today."

I gnashed my teeth, shooting Adam a "you-fucking-better-have-deleted-that-footage" look.

"I'm happy to call it a tie," Adam muttered with a grimace.

Finn jumped up and down. "Does that mean you both get prizes?"

"No, no." A nervous laugh left my mouth as I waded toward the ladder. An hour alone with Adam was bound to get me into more trouble. "It was just a bit of fun, Finn. Prizes aren't necessary."

"That sucks." Finn folded his arms. "I told Adam what your favorite crystal is."

I wrapped myself in a towel. "Aw, thanks, kiddo, but you didn't need to do that."

"I know. I just thought you could score something cool out of it."

I wrapped my arms around him and squeezed.

"Gross, Mom! You're all wet!"

"Hey, Finn," Josie called out as everyone was filing out of the room. "We're going to take Luci for a walk. Want to come with us while your mom and Adam dry off?"

His eyes brightened. "Can I hold the leash?" Finn always wanted a dog.

"Of course!" He glanced back as he raced toward the door. "I'll see you in a couple of hours, Adam!"

"What's happening in a couple of hours?" I asked once everyone was gone.

"We're playing basketball," Adam said, towel-drying his hair.

My gaze followed the beads of water traveling in every derisible direction. "Oh."

"Is that okay?"

My eyes shot up. "Yes...of course." I continued to dry my body. "But aren't your parents due to arrive soon?"

"So..." Adam wrapped the towel around his waist and crossed his arms.

"They don't exactly approve of my presence. I could only imagine what they'd think of Finn being here."

"I'll handle it."

My forehead furrowed as I gazed up at him. "Adam..."

"What?"

"Why are you doing this?"

"Doing what?"

"Being so...*nice*."

Adam rubbed his unshaven chin. "What would you prefer?"

I breathed out a heavy sigh as I wrapped myself in the towel. "I don't know..."

"You could be a little nicer," Adam murmured as he turned to leave.

My jaw dropped. "I'm nice."

"Not always. Not to me."

"Well, life isn't always sunshine and rainbows," I uttered as I followed him out of the room.

"Finn thinks it's because you like me."

My legs stopped working. "Well, Finn still believes in Santa Claus."

Adam slowed his pace. "Is he wrong?"

The silence between us grew heavy.

He spun around and marched back to me. "Cass...is he wrong?"

The desperation in his voice shook my core. "No. He's not."

His shoulders eased as he dropped his eyes. "Good," he stated before turning around. "Because I like you, too."

———

Caroline and William still hadn't arrived when a knock sounded at my bedroom door a couple of hours later. My son threw himself across the bed, destroying our card game as he bounded for the door.

Finn swung it open. "Hang on," he cried, running for my dressing room. "I've gotta find my jersey."

Adam leaned against the door jamb as his eyes locked on mine. "Whatcha playing?"

I bit my lower lip as I packed up the deck. "Um...Go Fish."

"Finn's a little old for that, don't you think?"

"Mom's terrible at cards." Finn slipped on his well-worn Lakers jersey. "It's the only game she'll play with me."

The corner of Adam's mouth twitched before he panned his gaze to my approaching son. "Whoa, Lakers fan!" He smiled in approval. "Sweet, bro." He held out his fist, and Finn bumped it with his. "If only I knew where my Lakers sweatshirt was…"

Warmth filled my cheeks as my eyes met his. "Well, you boys have fun!"

"You can come with, you know," Adam said, stepping back to let Finn pass.

"Yeah, Mom, come!"

"Maybe later. I think I'll read for a bit."

Finn rolled his eyes. "Mom *loves* reading."

"I've noticed." Adam's smile widened. "Hey, why don't you head down to the ballroom and warm up. I'll catch up in a sec."

"Okay! See ya later, Mom!"

Once Finn disappeared down the hall, Adam stepped into my bedroom, holding a box wrapped in brown paper that he'd kept hidden behind his back. "I know there was no clear winner today, but on the *freakish* chance you did win, I bought you this."

I waved him off. "Just leave it for Christmas."

"Then I'll have to buy everyone else something," he said before his smile turned mischievous. "Plus, I really don't think you should unwrap this in front of everyone."

My eyes grew large as I rose off the bed. "Why not?" I glared at the package.

Adam held it out. "You'll see."

"Adam…"

"Come on, it won't bite."

My gaze tapered as I apprehensively took the box from his hands.

"It may even be better than reading," he continued as he backed out of the room.

As his chuckle faded down the hallway, I stared at the mysterious gift. What the hell had he bought me?

Closing my door, I carried the box over to my bed and rested it on the nightstand. A small card laid tucked under the neatly tied string, and I slipped it out to read it.

Until next time. A x

Overwhelmed with curiosity, I perched on the side of the bed and unwrapped the brown paper to discover a black box hidden underneath. With a rush of exhilaration, I opened it to discover my favorite crystal nestled inside. It was long, smooth, and beautiful, carved into a—*oh my fucking God!* It was a crystal dildo.

I snapped the lid shut as my core ignited. *Well played, Adam Harlow. Well played.*

———

My body was still on fire when I snuck into the ballroom an hour later. After locking my door, I had drawn a bath and spent time getting to know my new friend with the aid of Adam's underlined passages. It wasn't as good as the real thing, but it was surprisingly cleansing.

Josie and Grayson were teaming up against Finn and Adam, while Harrison slept in his stroller.

I watched them, sight unseen, from the doorway, enjoying their smiles, their laughter, and brotherly banter. Adam was so natural with Finn it made my heart ache. They played in sync, like father and son, and I wondered how Dominic would feel.

Adam caught my gaze as he prepared to shoot. "Jesus," he murmured, eyeing his Lakers sweatshirt draped over my leggings.

"Cass!" Grayson cried out. "We need your help! Your kid is demolishing us." He squinted at my outfit. "Isn't that Adam's hoodie?"

"Wouldn't you believe it? I found it in my closet." I held back a smile. "There must've been a mix-up with the laundry, so I thought I'd get in the spirit."

Adam smirked. "Looks better on you anyway."

"Does that mean you're playing, Mom?" Finn asked while Grayson and Josie turned to each other with raised eyebrows.

"Of course she is," Grayson said. "Cass and Adam need a tie-breaker after that swim earlier."

Adam scoffed. "As if she could beat me at basketball. She's five-foot nothing."

"Size doesn't beat skill," I sang as my competitive nature kicked into gear.

Grayson hooted. "Then let's see what she's got, Adam. Pass her the ball."

With tapered eyes, Adam bounced the ball my way while everyone else stood closer to the hoop.

I confidently dribbled the ball, smiling as Adam hovered two feet in front. "You ready?"

"Bring it."

On my first attempt to pass, Adam lunged for the ball.

"Uh-uh," I sang out before changing direction.

He wasn't going to let me through, so I had to get clever—perhaps even dirty.

Whirling around, I kept my back to him, knowing if I hitched up his sweatshirt just a few inches and pushed out my ass, he'd be well and truly distracted.

I was wrong. The moment I attempted, he rushed forward and pressed his body up against mine. "That's a dirty play, Cass," he whispered, placing his hand lightly on my waist.

I swayed my hips from side to side as I dribbled. "So was that gift."

"Do you like it?"

"I do." I grinned, preparing my final play. "And it fits perfectly."

As his mouth dropped, I stepped around his long legs and charged straight for the hoop, scoring an easy two points.

"Adam!" Finn shook his head disapprovingly while Grayson and Josie cheered.

"Sorry, bud. Your mom…" He ran his fingers through his damp hair. "She took me by surprise."

I placed my hands on my hips. "I guess five-foot-nothing ain't that bad."

"Best out of three," Adam grumbled. "And no dirty tactics this time."

I grasped my chest. "Who me?"

"You're going down."

I winked. "Bring it."

For the rest of the afternoon, we played and laughed while Adam took advantage of every opportunity to touch my body. I didn't want to like it. I didn't want to crave it. But damn, his wanting hands felt good.

As I wrestled Adam to the ground, trying to steal the ball, a throat cleared from across the room, drawing our attention. Caroline's and William's surly faces glared back at us, and I instinctively jumped away from Adam and in front of my son.

"Mom, Dad! You're back." Grayson walked toward them with an obligatory smile.

Caroline's eyes didn't leave mine. "What's going on here?"

Adam tossed the ball from hand to hand. "Just a friendly game of basketball, that's all."

"And who gave you permission to install that?" Caroline pointed to the hoop on the wall.

"Gramps." Adam shook his head. "Twenty years ago."

His mother pursed her lips. "Well, why is that girl here and not upstairs with your grandfather?"

"*Cassidy* is on call." Adam's jaw tightened. "And if Gramps needs her, she'll be there."

William's eyes were fixed on Finn. "And the child?"

"He's mine." I lifted my chin as I stepped forward. "Finn, this is Mr. and Mrs. Harlow."

"I distinctly remember you stating you had no children on your application," Caroline said, ignoring Finn's attempt to greet them.

"Yes, well…"

"I told her to leave it off," Josie spoke up. "Her family really isn't any of our business."

"Our business?" Caroline glared at her. "The Harlow business has never been yours, Josie."

"Mom!" Grayson snapped, startling Harrison. "Don't start this shit again." With a growl, he marched over to the stroller and picked up his whimpering son while Josie gathered up their things.

"Come on, Finn," Josie called out as she wheeled the stroller toward the exit. "Let's take Luci for another walk."

Finn gazed up at me, full of worry. "Will you be okay?"

I grasped his face and kissed his forehead. "Of course, baby. Enjoy the walk."

With a small smile, he ran after Josie and Grayson as they vanished out the side door into the garden.

"Pack your things immediately, Cassidy," Caroline ordered. "I won't tolera—"

"No!" Adam roared. "You're not in charge here. Gramps is. Cassidy has been nothing but a godsend for him, and you will not send her away or make her or her son feel unwelcome."

"What has gotten into you?" his mother asked, flustered. "I'd expect this from Grayson, but not you."

"And why is that?" Adam asked while his fists grew whiter. "Because I've always done as you've asked? Because I've always lived by your fucked-up rules?"

William blew out a long sigh. "You're clearly not coping with the pressure of your new role."

"I'm dealing just fine, *Dad*. In fact, I've got a team of people looking after it for me these days...so I can take some well-deserved time off."

"Who?! Are they trustworthy?"

"Probably not by your standards, but I'm sick of working myself to the bone, trying to reach your level of perfection. What I've come to realize, since taking over the company, is that I'm never going to get your approval. I'm never going to do things the way you want them done. So, I'm not anymore."

William grew pale. "You're going to ruin everything I built."

"Hopefully," Adam chortled. "Then, I can do things my way."

As William and Caroline gaped, Adam grabbed my hand and pulled me out of the room.

I jogged to keep up with his strides. "Whoa, Adam...slow down."

With a backward glance, he dragged me into the media room and slammed the door shut. "Kiss me," he ordered with eyes full of anguish. "Before I break something."

Without taking a breath, I reached up and pulled his mouth down to mine. His body responded twofold, taking me into his arms until our bodies completely aligned. As our animalistic kiss deepened into something more sweet and sensual, Adam's energy shifted, taking us both by surprise.

"Wow," Adam gushed as we pulled apart. "Did you feel that?"

I rested my hand on his chest. "I feel everything with you. Anger...sadness...regret..."

He took my hand and moved it to his heart. "What about now?"

The overpowering wave of emotion stole my breath, rendering me speechless.

Adam lowered his gaze as I pulled away. "I'm complicated, aren't I?"

"Yes."

"Does that scare you?"

"Sometimes."

The corner of his mouth lifted. "Maybe I need to redeem my Reiki session."

"I think you just need to switch off for a while."

"I don't think I'm capable of relaxing."

I ran my hand over his silky basketball shorts. "Is that so?"

Adam's brow rose as a shaky breath left his mouth. "Jesus..." He slipped his hand around my nape as he pressed his forehead to mine. "That feels so fucking good." He pulled my lips to his and kissed me hard while I pushed down his shorts.

Once his length was free, I pushed him against the door and sank to my knees.

"Cass...you don't have t—oh my God."

As I took him inside, I peered up to see Adam's head fall back with a sigh. His jaw tightened while he ran his fingers through my hair, but he didn't guide or push. He let me take control. It was something he wasn't used to—but something he clearly needed.

"Oh, Cass," he rasped moments before spilling his warmth into my mouth. "That was...incredible."

With a newfound confidence, I lifted my gaze to his glassy
blue eyes. "I guess my books are good for something, after all."

"You learned that in a book?"

My smile grew as I rose. "I've learned lots of things."

"Like what?"

I opened the door to leave. "You'll have to wait and see."

Chapter 29

Adam chased me up the stairs. "I'll message Grayson and tell him to occupy Finn a little longer."

I spun around. "No. Whatever is happening between us doesn't go any further while Finn's at Harlow Manor. Plus, your entire family is here. You should be spending time with them."

Adam scowled as he slowed at my door. "Will I at least see you at dinner?"

"After what just happened with your parents, I think I'll get Max to send something to our room."

"No." His eyes snapped back to mine. "There's no way I'll… *Gramps* will allow that. You will be eating with us."

"Adam…"

"If you're not there, I'll hunt you down and caveman-carry you to the table."

"Fine," I grumbled before the visual took hold. "Although, that does sound appealing."

Adam's eyes flared with heat. "Cassidy…"

"I'm sorry." I backed into my room with a wince. "Just remember, you have to be on your best behavior. Liam has been looking forward to this for weeks."

"I'm not going to seduce you at the dinner table."

"I'm not just talking about that. I'm talking about you and your dad. No more fighting."

Adam sighed. "Fine. I'll make amends once he's had a few whiskeys."

"Good, then I look forward to dinner. But first…I need a shower."

He leaned in as I closed the door. "I could join you...save water...that sort of thing?"

"Ha-ha," I uttered before closing the door on his gorgeous smile.

———

Dinner wasn't a disaster, but it was uncomfortable. While Finn practiced his best manners, I focused on helping Liam with his food—anything to avoid the tapered stares of Adam's parents.

The conversation was polite, focusing on the family's new addition, Harrison. If I wasn't mistaken, I actually felt warmth exude from Caroline and William when they spoke of him. They were clearly smitten, as was everyone else.

Once dinner wrapped up, I excused myself, along with Finn, and made my way out of the dining room. They needed family time, and we...weren't. Once I reached the door, I turned to hurry my son along when I found him standing beside William.

"Thank you for dinner, Mr. and Mrs. Harlow, and Merry Christmas."

My eyes shot to Adam as the scene unfolded. His taut jaw mirrored mine.

William's eyelids fluttered in surprise. "Well..." He cleared his throat. "Merry Christmas to you, too, young man."

"Come on, Finn," I rasped out. "Let's get you ready for bed. Santa will be here soon."

"Can Adam tuck me in?"

My breath caught as everyone at the table froze.

"Of course he will," Liam finally spoke, breaking the tension. "Right after you hang your stocking on the fireplace."

With a grin, Josie pulled out a stocking from under Harrison's stroller and handed it to Finn. "You can pop it next to Harrison's, if you like."

Tears welled in my eyes as he brought it over. My son's name was professionally embroidered onto the side of the stocking, just like Harrison's. "Oh, Josie. It's beautiful."

"It's from all of us."

"Thank you so much!" Finn said, meeting everyone's eyes. "Sure beats an old pillowcase."

My cheeks heated. "It sure does." I directed him out of the room. "Let's go hang it up."

After Finn secured his place above the Harlow fireplace, I sent him upstairs while I helped Max get Liam into the elevator. As the elevator doors closed, I headed back to the staircase and flinched as I passed the dining room. An argument had broken out behind the closed doors.

"It's none of your business!" Adam snapped.

Caroline gasped. "This is our house. Our family. It is our business."

"This is Grampa's house, and this is *my* life. So no, it's not."

"You're playing a dangerous game, Adam," his father said. "This is her workplace. She could sue you for sexual harassment and sell her story to the tabloids."

"She wouldn't."

"You don't even know her!" William growled. "You didn't even know she had a child until a few weeks ago."

"Dad, come on," Grayson interjected.

"You encouraged this, no doubt?" William's tone darkened. "Don't you think this family has been subjected to enough gossip of late?"

"For fuck's sake, Dad," Adam cut in. "Leave Grayson and Josie out of this."

"Well, you never strayed off the path before."

"Whose path?!"

Caroline sighed. "Adam…don't be like this."

"Look…whatever is happening between us…it's new, and I don't even know if it exists beyond these walls."

"Well, that's something," William murmured. "I'll speak to our lawyer and make sure her NDA covers this. I can't imagine this going any further."

"And why's that?"

"Because of your track record with women."

My heart dipped. William Harlow was right. From what I'd read, Adam had never been in a long-term relationship. Not wanting to hear another word, I raced up the stairs and into my bedroom, where my reason for living was waiting.

After Finn's bath, he wandered to bed in his pajamas, where I lay reading. I lifted the blanket and he crawled under the covers as a soft knock sounded at the door.

Shuffling over in my slippers, I endeavored to slow my racing heart as I opened the door but failed miserably. Adam's handsome face never lost its effect on me.

"Someone requested a tucking-in service?" he asked, peeking over my shoulder.

I opened the door wider and stood to one side. "I thought you'd forgotten."

"No, I just got caught up with something."

With a small smile, I motioned for him to come inside. "I'll be in the bathroom."

"Hey, buddy," Adam said as I eased the bathroom door slightly ajar. "Did you enjoy dinner?"

"It was delicious. Not as good as my mom's lasagna though."

"I didn't know your mom could cook."

Finn laughed. "She can't...except for lasagna."

"Well, that's one more dish than I can cook."

"But you have your own chef."

"Well, I'm sure your mom's lasagna is better than theirs."

I peeked through the door to find Adam sitting beside Finn.

"Are you mad at your parents?" Finn asked, snuggling deeper under the covers.

Adam rubbed his stubbled jaw. "We don't exactly see eye to eye right now."

"But it's Christmas."

"You're right." He forced a small smile. "It's a time to be jolly."

"Mom gets sad at this time of year, too."

"She misses your dad?"

Finn shrugged. "I guess so."

"He must've been a great guy to win over a girl like your mom."

"I suppose so," Finn uttered with an awkward giggle.

"Did your dad ever get to see you swim?" Adam picked up the framed photo from my bedside. It was taken after Finn had won his first swimming race, a year after Dominic passed.

"Not competitively."

"Well, I think he'd be pretty damn proud of you. Only the best of the best make the finals."

"Are you really going to come watch?" Finn asked, peering up at Adam.

"Of course. I can't wait."

"Good. You can stop Mom from embarrassing me."

Adam's eyebrows pulled together. "How does she embarrass you?"

"Oh my God, she's the loudest screamer."

As blood burst into my cheeks, I stepped out of the bathroom as Adam erupted into a fit of laughter.

"What's so funny?" I asked, narrowing my gaze at Adam and his dirty mind.

"Oh, nothing." He caught his breath. "Just boy stuff."

I pursed my lips before approaching the bed. "Okay, Finn, say goodnight. You need to be asleep before Santa comes, or he won't leave any presents."

"Yeah, yeah, Mom." Finn rolled his eyes before rolling over. "Goodnight, Adam…and Merry Christmas."

"Merry Christmas, buddy," Adam said before turning to leave. His gaze followed the curve of my body under my silk pajamas. "And don't worry about Santa." His grin grew. "I'll make sure he stops by." His eyes burned into mine, saying so much more than words. "Goodnight, Cassidy."

"Goodnight, Adam," I forced out of my breathless state. "And Merry Christmas."

———

Once Finn's steady breaths confirmed he was in a deep sleep, I closed my novel and placed it on my nightstand. I tiptoed over to my hidden stash of gifts, bundled them into my arms, and made my way out of the room and down the staircase.

As I crept around the corner of the living room, I slammed straight into a hard mass and stumbled backwards. "What the fu—"

Adam pressed his finger to my lips. "Shhh."

My eyes widened. "What are you doing down here?"

"Playing Santa."

My shoulders sank. "You don't have to do that." I moved to the mantel. "I've got some things."

He eyed my hands. "Like?"

"Some candy for his stocking…and new swimming goggles."

Adam's brow shadowed his eyes, but he said nothing.

"I know it's lame, but I'm on a budget."

"They're not lame."

"Oh yeah?" I placed my hand on my hip. "What did you get him?"

His grimace was evident, even in the darkness.

"Adam…"

"Don't be angry. Everyone pitched in. Liam, too. We want it to be a surprise."

Dread infiltrated my body. "But I didn't get anyone anything."

Adam grasped my elbow. "We don't expect anything, Cass. It's really not a big deal."

"It is to me."

He pulled me closer. "You've already done so much for us. For Gramps. We didn't expect him to ever make it to Christmas. This is our way of thanking you."

I exhaled heavily. "He's not here because of me, Adam. He's here because of you, and Grayson, and Josie, and Harrison. Maybe even your dad. He doesn't want to let go until he knows you'll all be okay without him. I'm only easing his pain until that time comes."

Adam's back straightened as worry permeated through the lines on his forehead. "How much pain is he in?"

"Enough."

He lowered his eyes before lifting them to mine. "He's worried about me, isn't he?"

"He just wants you to be happy."

"I am happy." He grasped my other arm. "When I'm here... when you're here..."

A knot formed in my stomach. "And when I'm not?"

"Well...I thought...maybe we could..." Uncertainty rolled through his energy. "See where it goes..."

"I know where this goes from here."

"And where's that?"

"Outside these walls, things will be different between us. You're a wealthy, successful business man, and I'm a widowed, single mother who...reads romance novels. We couldn't be any more different. Too different to make it work."

He dropped his hands. "You don't know that."

"Your emotions are heightened when you're here, and you're confusing them with something more."

"I'm not confused, Cass. I'm... I'm... I don't know what I am. " His inner turmoil was evident in his pale-blue eyes. "Jesus, you're the only person who can turn me into a bumbling idiot."

"You're grieving. It's okay to feel confused."

"Gramps isn't dead yet."

"But the process...the emotions...it's already begun. Liam may have decided to stick around a little longer, but the time will come. Your feelings for me are merely a distraction until you accept it."

"A distraction?" He ran his fingers through his hair. "Cassidy...I've never felt like this before."

"Adam...please..." It took all my power to force out his energy.

"So, what am I to you, then?" His gaze darkened.

"I...I don't know."

"A distraction from *your* fucked-up life?"

"I have books for that," I murmured while fighting his penetrative aura.

"Your books can't do this." Grasping my face, Adam pulled me to his lips, kissing me with so much force it took my breath away. As his hands delved into my hair and around my nape, his tongue explored deeper territory, wanting…needing…

My body responded on instinct, answering his call with the same intensity, but just as I submitted, his lips were gone.

And when I opened my eyes, so was Adam.

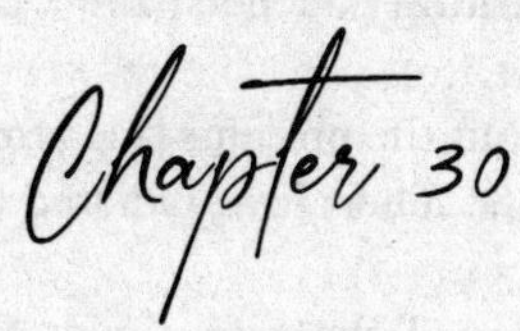

Finn's eyes glittered with excitement as he walked into the living room to discover the oversized Christmas tree swamped with gifts. His gaze shot to the mantel, then back to mine, silently asking for permission to pounce.

"Wait until everyone is here," I said in a hushed voice.

Josie was already cozied up with Grayson on the couch, while Harrison slept in his arms. Caroline was perched on the armchair opposite, while William stood, drinking what looked like eggnog. Both refused to meet my gaze.

Once Adam wheeled Liam into the room, Finn tugged my arm. "Can I?"

"Okay, go."

Adam caught my eye as Finn raced over to the fireplace. "Merry Christmas, Cassidy," he whispered as he wheeled Liam past.

His aftershave whisked me back to the kiss the night prior, and my cheeks warmed. "Merry Christmas, Adam."

With a knowing smile, he parked Liam in his preferred position, then moved to the empty couch beside the tree. He gazed up at me, then at the vacant seat beside him, and raised his brow. "Are you going to sit?"

"Oh, I'm sure Mr. Harlow would pref—"

"I'm fine where I am." William took another sip. "Please sit."

"Okay, thanks." As I sat beside Adam, Finn bounced over and squeezed himself between us.

He tipped his candy-filled stocking onto his lap. "Check this out, Mom!"

Since Dominic passed away, Finn rarely got more than a few candy canes and chocolate in his stocking, but today it was bulging with goodies. Giant candy canes, homemade rocky road, artisan chocolates, gaming vouchers, and a pair of goggles. Santa had my back this year.

"Adam can hand out the presents this year," Grayson said, not budging from his wife. Their love radiated through the room as they ogled their son.

As predicted, most of the gifts under the tree belonged to Harrison, but when Adam read out Finn's name, my son's mouth fell open.

He wasn't expecting anything, especially from the person whose name was on the card. Me. I'd promised him a proper gift in the new year, once we'd settled back home, so this was a surprise to me, too.

With wide eyes, he tore open the paper to reveal an official-branded basketball and a Lakers cap. "Oh, Mom! Thank you so much," he cried, wrapping his arms around me.

My eyes glazed over as they met Adam's. "Thank you," I mouthed, swallowing back emotion as Finn let go.

Adam offered a subtle nod before handing out the rest of the presents.

"There's just one more hidden in the tree." Liam threw me a wink. "Perhaps young Finn would like to fetch it out for me."

In a flash, Finn jumped off the couch and raced over. "Got it." He pulled an envelope from the pine and held it out to Liam.

"Read it out loud, would you? My eyes aren't what they used to be."

Finn smiled nervously before flipping the envelope over. "To Cassidy and Finn, thank you for everything. From the Harlows." He lifted his gaze to my slackened mouth. "I think you should open this," he said, returning to the space beside me.

"You really didn't have to." I gaped at the envelope in my lap. "But thank you." With a deep breath, I carefully opened it to discover two tickets.

"Oh my God!" Finn squealed, snatching them from my hand. "Lakers tickets?!"

"What?!" I took them back for a closer look. I'd always

wanted to take Finn to a game but could never afford it. "Oh, we can't accept this. It's too much."

"Of course you can," Liam said. "Finn tells me he loves basketball, and our family gets season tickets every year. Grayson isn't going, so I thought you and Finn could keep Adam out of trouble."

"Wait…" I stared at the tickets again, zeroing in on the date. "These are in a few days…in LA!"

Liam nodded. "Adam has to head back to LA for work, so you can share the private jet with him. He also has a house in Malibu where you both can stay while you enjoy a few days off."

"But…I can't." My stomach clenched with trepidation. "I have to stay here…with you…"

"Beautiful Cassidy, I'm surrounded by my family, and I'm happy." His smile radiated warmth. "But I'll be happier knowing you and Finn are having fun, too. You can visit all your friends while you're there."

Finn's emerald gaze pleaded with me to accept.

"Okay." I wiped the moisture from my eyes. "We'll go."

As Finn jumped around, Adam reached over. "You okay?"

"Mom always cries when she's happy," Finn interrupted with a laugh.

I wiped away a rogue tear. "I haven't been home in a very long time."

Adam's gaze softened. "If you're not comfortable staying at my place, I can organize a hotel for you. But like Gramps said, I have to work, so I won't be around much."

"No, it's fine. You've spent too much already. We'll be fine on your couch."

"Couch?" Grayson sniggered before Josie poked his ribs. "Just make sure there is food in the pantry for them. You almost starved my pregnant wife last time we stayed there."

Adam rolled his eyes. "Had I known she was pregnant, maybe I would've been more accommodating."

As the brothers continued their banter, Finn rested his head on my shoulder. "I can't believe we're actually going to a Lakers game!"

I kissed his dark mop. "Me, too, baby."

"And on a private plane! It's going to be so awesome!"

"It really is," I said, gazing over at Adam's striking profile. *And so much more complicated.*

———

"So, I can order anything?" Finn asked for the third time in five minutes.

Adam threw me a grin. "Well, anything your mom agrees to."

"We'll see, okay?" I fumbled with my seatbelt. "I don't want you getting air sick."

"Is that going to be a problem?" Adam asked, searching the compartments for something.

I finally clicked myself in and tightened the strap. "I have no idea."

"We've never been on a plane before," Finn uttered from the seat beside me.

"A private plane?"

"Any plane," Finn and I said in unison.

Adam's gaze snapped to mine. "How is that possible?"

"We've always driven everywhere." I flustered with Finn's seatbelt. It was entirely too loose for his little body. "I'm not sure if you're aware, but it's considerably cheaper."

"Let me." Adam reached over and adjusted Finn's seatbelt with ease.

"Maybe you should sit next to Mom." Finn scowled in my direction. "She's making me nervous."

My mouth fell open. "Finn…"

Finn undid his seatbelt, stood, and motioned with Adam to swap.

"But what if you need me?" I asked with a voice full of desperation. I was embarrassing myself.

"Mom, I'm eleven! I've got this."

I slumped back into my chair. "I don't," I grumbled, turning my gaze out the window.

Adam eased down beside me. "He's perfectly safe, Cass. The pilot will inform us if there's any turbulence."

"Turbulence?!" Fear bubbled up inside.

"You'll be okay, Mom." Finn giggled from his new seat. "Adam will look after you."

Adam's eyes tempered as they rolled over me. "You'll be fine, but I better get you both some chewing gum."

"Finn won't be able to sleep if you give him candy."

"Trust me, it will help your ears adjust to the cabin pressure. And don't worry, it's sugar free."

"Oh." I couldn't argue with that. "Okay, then."

Thankfully, the gum stopped my jaw from seizing as the plane rolled onto the runway.

"This is so cool!" Finn yelled as we picked up speed. "Way better than the helicopter ride!"

As we shot forward, I grasped the arm of the chair and closed my eyes. It wasn't until Adam's hand slid over mine that my shoulders eased, and my breathing regulated to a steady pace.

"Thank you," I whispered, lifting my gaze to find he'd been watching me the entire time. "That wasn't so bad." Unable to hold his stare or hand any longer, I turned my body toward the window where the twinkling lights below grew smaller and smaller.

"You should try and get to sleep," he said once the seatbelt lights turned off. "Or you'll be exhausted tomorrow."

The hostess gave us pillows and blankets while Adam demonstrated how to adjust our chairs into their reclined position. Once the lights dimmed, I tucked Finn in, then climbed into my bed.

"Night, buddy," Adam said as he passed Finn on the way back from the restroom.

"Night, Adam. Night, Mom."

As Adam settled into the chair-turned-bed beside me, I became acutely aware of how close we were.

"Goodnight, Cass," he whispered with a small smile playing on his lips.

I closed my eyes and focused on the rumble of the engine. "Goodnight, Adam."

Sleep came quicker than expected, but when the plane hit turbulence, my stomach dropped, and my eyes shot open. I searched the roof for fallen oxygen masks, but none had dropped. Instead, a warm hand slid over mine and stayed until my eyes grew heavy once more.

The morning light streaming through the windows pulled me out of my slumber. I was comfy, warm, and snuggling with… wait. My eyes popped open to find my arms wrapped around Adam's bicep. "Ugh, I'm sorry!"

"It's perfectly okay." Adam snickered as he stretched out his glorious arm muscles. "Sleep well?"

"I did, surprisingly." Better than I had in years.

Thankfully, Finn was too busy playing video games to witness me using Adam as a human teddy bear.

Once we returned the chairs to an upright position and had a lovely—albeit quiet—breakfast, I finally relaxed back into my seat and stared out the window. The ocean I loved dearly materialized in the distance, and I couldn't help but smile. *Home.*

Suddenly, a loud thud vibrated through the plane.

"What was that?" I spat, glaring outside, expecting to see the wing on fire.

"Relax, Cass. It's the landing gear."

"Oh." My heart rate slowed. "Planes are so much scarier than helicopters."

"Want me to hold your hand again?"

"No." I tightened my seatbelt until I could barely breathe. "I'm fine." And I was…until the wheels hit the tarmac.

With a gasp, I latched onto Adam's hand and didn't let go.

He grazed his thumb over my knuckles as the plane slowed. "You can breathe now."

I snatched my hand away. "I know that."

Adam chuckled to himself before turning to Finn. "So, what do you think? Prefer flying to driving?"

"Flying, definitely! We don't have to stay in dodgy hotels along the way."

"It's either that or sleep in the car, Finn." I was starting to wish he'd never gotten a taste of the Harlows' lavish lifestyle.

"Yeah, yeah, I know."

Adam grumbled. "You won't have to do that again."

"This kind of travel is hardly sustainable."

He raised an eyebrow in a silent challenge before unbuckling his seatbelt. "That's what you think."

I opened my mouth to protest but was interrupted by the pilot welcoming us to LA.

———

After Adam thanked the hostess, he ushered us out of the plane to a waiting limousine.

"This is too much," I mumbled under my breath as we approached the car.

Adam threw me a glance. "What is?"

"Come on…helicopter, private plane, limo! It's amazing, but it's too much."

Adam stopped abruptly while Finn kept moving. "Will you just let me do something nice for you? You're not the only one in unfamiliar territory here."

My mouth parted as I absorbed his uneasiness. "O…okay."

"Good. Then let's go."

———

"Oh. My. God." Finn squished his little face against the passenger window as we entered an incredible property in Malibu. "It's right on the beach!"

My stomach fluttered. "Is this really your house?"

Adam nodded quietly before climbing out of the car and he held the door open as we piled out. "Just wait until you see inside." After thanking the driver for collecting our bags, Adam motioned us through the front door.

The moment I stepped over the threshold, I was too stunned to speak. The wide entrance hall opened out into a huge open living space filled with an impressive kitchen and a massive living and dining area that overlooked the most spectacular view of the beach I'd ever seen. *This* was my dream house.

"You can't possibly live here." I took in the spotless, crisp, white interior and the notable fact that there wasn't a personal item in sight.

"I plan to...one day." He dropped his wallet and phone onto the kitchen counter. "Until then, I guess it's more of a vacation property."

"But you don't take vacations."

He mimicked my smile. "I'm on vacation now."

"But I thought you had to work."

"Not every day. So, for me, that's a vacation."

"Which room is mine?" Finn asked, gawking at the impressive horizon swimming pool outside.

"My room is at the end of the hallway." Adam nodded to the left corridor. "Take whichever bedroom you want along the way, or there's the guest bedroom to the right."

Finn and I turned in opposite directions.

I glanced back. "Finn...this way..."

"But I want to be near Adam's room."

"Finn, we're guests. We'll stay in the guest room."

Adam's brow furrowed. "I really don't mind."

"See..." Finn disappeared down the hall, completely disregarding me.

"Fine," I grumbled, trudging along behind him. "You choose, then."

Adam picked up our bags and followed.

"Definitely this one!" Finn announced as he stepped through the first door.

I gazed out at the ocean. "Good choice," I said, dropping my handbag on the bed.

Adam sidled up beside me. "There are plenty of other rooms if you're sick of sharing."

"Oh, I just thought Finn would like the company."

"Seriously, Mom? We've been sharing a bed for days."

"Fine." I swiped up my bag and marched to the next room.

"But it better have the same vie—Wow!" The view wasn't the same. It was better.

"You should see the view from my bedroom," Adam whispered over my shoulder.

"I can only imagine." I was still in a daze. The ocean was calling.

Adam dropped back as Finn ran past to check out my room.

"See, Mom! I told you! Can we go for a swim now?!"

"Definitely," I said, unable to control my smile.

"Are you coming, Adam?" Finn was already tearing off his top.

"I wish I could, but I really have to get into the office." He masked a grimace. "Please make yourselves at home, and if you need to go anywhere, my driver's number is on the fridge."

"Thank you. I haven't seen my sister-in-law since we left, and Finn is desperate to visit his cousin."

"Does he like basketball? We have a spare ticket if he's allowed to join us."

Finn almost choked. "Really?! I'll ask him now!" He grabbed my cell from my handbag and bolted out of the room.

I smiled up at Adam. "I can't imagine there being a problem."

"Good. I want Finn to have fun."

"He always has fun with you."

Adam's chuckle faded as he rubbed his jaw. "Listen, I'm going to have to meet you at the stadium tonight. I have a few things I need to do in the city, and I won't make it back in time. Is that okay? I'll have a car pick you up."

"That's completely fine. Just don't work too hard. We want this Adam…" I poked his chest. "Not the hardass Harlow who lives to work, okay?"

The corners of his mouth rose. "Okay."

"Then I'll see you later."

———

"Aunty Tash wants to talk to you, Mom," Finn called out as soon as Adam left.

I wandered back to his room and reached for my phone. "Hey."

"You're in LA?!"

"Just for a few days, and we'd really love to see you guys."

"Oh my God! I'm clearing my schedule. Come over now."

"We'll be there soon. There's just something we have to do first."

Once I ended the call, I raced back to my room, threw on my bikini, and chased Finn out into the waves. The water was cold, but warmer than the Hamptons, and it was glorious. As I gazed back at the shoreline, I became acutely aware of how quiet it was. The beaches I grew up with were heaving with locals and tourists, but there wasn't a soul on this beachfront. There was no noise from boats or jet skis, no rowdy volleyball matches or men comparing muscles, just crashing waves and squawking gulls, and I fucking loved it.

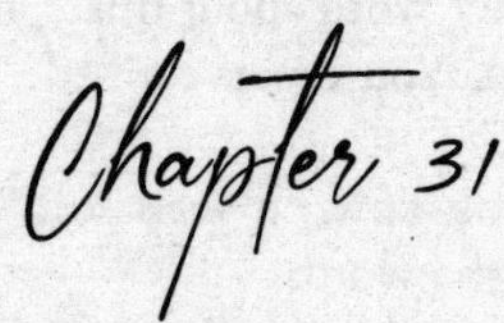

Chapter 31

"You still can't tell me who you work for?" Tash asked as she handed me my tea and sat on the couch opposite.

"I told you, I signed an NDA."

Her lips pursed before the coffee reached them. "They're clearly rich."

I laughed. "Very." Although *rich* didn't seem to fit the Harlows. They were beyond.

"And you flew in a private jet?"

I nodded.

"And this guy you flew over with…the grandson…"

"What about him?" I asked, wishing the heat in my cheeks was the result of the steam pouring out of my mug.

"What's he like?"

I took a sip as I endeavored to find a safe description. "He is…" I licked the residue from my lips. "Problematic."

"Asshole?"

I shrugged. "Sometimes…"

"But…"

"He's also generous, and sweet, and…"

She lifted one eyebrow. "Hot?"

My teeth gnashed as I covered my face with my hands. "You have no idea."

"Cassidy! Are you crushing on your boss?"

I slumped into the couch. "He's not my boss…*technically*."

Tash placed her cup on the coffee table and inched forward, glancing over at the closed door of her son's room. "So, has anything happened between you two?"

My stomach roiled as I stared at the sister of my late husband. "I'm not saying another word about this."

"Cassidy, come on. You deserve a little fun after everything you've been through."

"But talking to you now…it feels so…" I lowered my gaze when I couldn't find the words.

"It's been four years. My brother wouldn't want you to be alone for the rest of your life."

"I know." I blinked back tears. "But I'm not ready yet. Maybe once I'm back in LA, and Finn and I are settled, I'll put myself out there. I might even let you set me up with that guy you've been telling me about."

"And what about Mr. McFancypants?"

I scoffed. "Oh, it couldn't possibly work out."

"Why not?"

"He's…" I sighed. "Not the marrying kind. And his lifestyle doesn't leave much room for family."

Her gaze softened, knowing how important that was for me. "How is he with Finn?"

My entire body warmed. "He's great. Finn adores him."

"He seems to be making time for you tonight. A fucking Lakers game?! Tristan lost his mind when Finn asked him."

"Are you sure it's okay?"

"Are you kidding? Do you know how much those tickets are worth?"

"I'm aware."

Tristan and Finn burst out of the bedroom, already dressed in their Lakers gear.

"And Adam said we can get all the snacks we want," Finn said, following Tristan outside while tossing a basketball from one hand to the other.

Tash's gaze floated to mine. "Adam?"

I zipped my lips. "Not another word."

———

"So, when are you flying back to New York?" Tash asked as she applied a little makeup to my face while we waited for Adam's car to collect us.

"In a couple of days."

Her eyes expanded. "So, you'll be here for New Year's Eve?"

I shrugged. "I guess so." Everything happened so quick I hadn't noticed the date.

"We're throwing a party, and you have to come! Bryce is going to barbecue, and Tristan would love for Finn to stay over."

A sense of normalcy rolled over me. "That sounds great." Our families used to have so much fun together.

"You can bring *Adam* if you want…"

I emitted a nervous laugh. "Oh, I don't think backyard parties are his thing."

"Well, the invitation is there…and he's more than welcome."

I stared into her eyes—so much like Dominic's. "Thank you." I squeezed her hand. "I've missed you guys so much."

Her eyes glistened. "You have no idea."

As we hugged, my cell phone chimed, alerting us to the arrival of our private car.

"Time to go," I called out to the boys as we made our way to the front door.

I turned back to Tash as the boys ran outside. "Make sure Bryce takes you out for a romantic dinner tonight."

"Oh, I will…" she said, following us outside. "Holy cow!"

The boys applauded at the sight of the stretch limo in the driveway and proceeded to jump around like crazy as the driver ushered them inside.

Tash nudged my arm. "He's really pulling out the big guns with you."

"This is normal for him. Don't read too much into it."

"Well, you boys have fun," she called out as she blew her son a kiss. "And you…" She caught my hand. "Let yourself be happy. Whatever this is…just enjoy the time you have together."

I squeezed her fingers. "I'll try." With one last hug, I jumped into the car and gasped at the huge bowl of candy between the kids. "Slow down, boys. You have the whole night to fill your bellies. I don't want you sick before the first siren."

As their giggles filled the car, I glanced over at the bottle of champagne resting in the ice bucket and rehashed Tash's words. *Fuck it.* I reached over, poured a glass, and took a long sip as I relaxed into my seat. The bubbles on my tongue dissipated into a divine flavor that had me instantly pouring another once the glass was empty.

Half an hour later, the limo pulled up at the basketball stadium where Adam stood with his Lakers cap pulled low over his face.

"Adam!" Finn burst out of the car and wrapped his arms around his long legs. "Thank you so much."

Adam's jaw tensed as he surveyed our surroundings, then scuffed his hair. "Glad you could make it."

I moved closer with Tristan by my side. "Introduce your cousin, Finn," I said, meeting Adam's gaze with a sheepish smile.

"Adam, this is Tristan. Tristan, this is my mom's boyfriend, Adam."

My eyes bulged while Adam's eyebrows arched.

"Finn," I grumbled. "He's just a friend. You know that."

"Whatever," Finn said with a shrug. "Can we get a hot dog?"

Adam cleared his throat after a strained laugh. "Sure thing. We can visit the merchandise stand, too."

With matching squeals, Tristan and Finn ran ahead while Adam and I ambled behind.

Adam was the first to speak. "Did you have a good day?"

"The best," I said with a genuine smile. "Finn and I went for a swim, then spent the afternoon with my sister-in-law and nephew." I glanced over at him. "And you? How was work?"

He shrugged. "It was there."

"And they didn't crumble and die without you over Christmas?"

"Surprisingly, no."

"That must be a relief."

"In some ways."

His vulnerability took me by surprise. "Well, I think it's an incredible achievement to run a company as big as yours and be able to trust the people around you. It says a lot about your character."

"And what's that?"

"That you're not like your father. You're doing things your way, and it's clearly working."

"I wish he could see it that way." He pulled his cap lower as we passed a couple of photographers.

"He will. Just give him time to adjust."

Once the kids were covered head to toe in yellow and purple merch, we continued on to the food stand.

Adam watched the boys zig-zag through the crowd. "So, Tristan's mom is Dominic's sister?"

"Yeah, we've been best friends since the day we met."

Adam rubbed the back of his neck. "And she's okay with her son coming tonight?"

"Of course. Why wouldn't she be?"

"I…don't know." He grimaced. "I thought maybe she wouldn't be comfortable with you spending time with another man."

"Oh, it's fine. It's not like we're on a date."

Adam turned away before stopping. "But what if it was?"

"Oh." I froze. "Um…well…considering she keeps trying to set me up with a friend of her husband's, I don't think she's too concerned with my dating life."

With a curt nod, he kept walking. "I want to, you know?"

"What?" His energy was so jumbled I struggled to keep up.

"Take you on a date."

My eyelashes fluttered. "Oh."

"There's this charity ball on New Year's Eve that I have to attend, and I was wondering if you'd come with me—as my date, that is."

My footsteps slowed. "Oh…I…I can't…"

"Look…" He spun around to face me. "I know you think this complicates things, but we aren't at Harlow Manor, and I—"

"No, it's not that." I grimaced. "I already have plans. Tash invited us to her place for a barbecue."

"Oh." Adam's shoulders slumped. "Okay."

"I'm sorry."

"It's fine." He handed Finn and Tristan money to buy food. "You'd probably hate it anyway. You should spend time with your family."

Guilt tore through my body, but I forced myself to push it away. "Let's just have fun tonight. You've already done so much, and I haven't seen Finn smile like this in years."

Adam's tension eased as Finn goofed around with Tristan in the line, laughing and joking. "I want to make you smile like that."

My heart skipped as I sucked in my breath, but a blinding flash left me momentarily stunned.

"Hey!" Adam shoved a man with a camera backward. "Not cool."

A burly man stormed toward us. "Do we have a problem here?" He eyeballed the paling photographer while blocking his view of us.

"N...no," the man stammered before racing off into the crowd.

"What the hell was that?" Luckily, Finn and Tristan were too preoccupied at the counter to witness the altercation.

"Fucking paparazzi." Adam took off his cap to run his fingers through his hair. "They're everywhere."

"Paparazzi? But wh—"

"And this is Bruno, my bodyguard." Adam nodded to the huge man scanning the crowd.

"You have a bodyguard?" I gasped. "I didn't even notice him."

"That's how I prefer it."

"Sorry, Boss. He didn't look the type." Bruno shook his head with a scowl. "I suggest you make your way to your seats before more show up."

Adam placed his hand on the small of my back and directed me to the boys while they filled their arms with food from the counter. "Need some help with that?" he asked, like no altercation had just occurred.

"Nah, we got this!" Finn giggled with his cousin as they

precariously balanced hot dogs, hots chips, and sodas all the way to our seats.

"We're sitting here?!" Tristan's eyes grew large. "But this is where the celebrities sit." He glanced up at Adam before whispering in Finn's ear, "Is Adam famous?"

Finn shrugged. "I don't know. His family is super rich, though."

I smiled awkwardly, hoping Adam hadn't overheard their hushed conversation as he took the seat on the aisle.

"You boys ready?" he asked, leaning around me to see the kid's faces.

"Hell, yeah!" they both cried.

Our eyes met as he straightened, and his smile took my breath away.

"What?" Adam asked, watching me curiously.

His energy captivated me. I wanted to drown in his depth. "I..." The siren stole my words, and my face shot forward. I didn't even know what my heart was trying to say.

"Cass..."

"Let's go, Lakers!" I yelled, ignoring Adam's eyes searing my profile. "God, I hope we win."

Adam exhaled to the heavens before facing the game. "Yeah, me, too."

———

After the game, we all piled into the limo to take Tristan home. The boys chatted non-stop about the win until they passed out, while Adam and I threw each other heated glances from across the limo.

As we slowed at Tristan's house, I nudged him until he stirred. "Tristan, you're home," I whispered as the driver opened the door.

I helped his wobbly body out of the car while Tash emerged from the house.

"Hey, baby." She gave her son a kiss. "Did you have fun?"

"So much," he mumbled in a sugar-crash daze. "Thank you, Aunty Cass. Thank you, Adam. I'm going to bed."

I drew in a breath at the realization that Adam was standing behind me. "Night, Tris."

Once my nephew disappeared into the house, Adam stepped forward. "You must be Tash." He held out his hand. "I'm Adam."

Tash shot me an approving smirk before shaking his hand. "Lovely to meet you, Adam. I hope my boy behaved tonight."

"Both kids were great." He met my gaze as he smiled.

"Did Bryce take you out for dinner?"

"I took him out." She puffed out her chest. "He's been working so hard lately. He deserves a little TLC. He's already passed out on the couch."

I winced. "Still working twelve-hour days?"

"And some."

"He needs to find a new job. It's not healthy to work that much," I said, shooting Adam a glance.

Tash ran her hand down her belly. "It's not that easy."

I sighed. "I know."

Tash's gaze moved to Adam and narrowed. "You look familiar…"

"Well, we better get Finn to bed," I interrupted, making Adam snigger. "He's going to be exhausted tomorrow."

"Of course." Tash smirked. "And you need your rest, too. I don't want you sleeping through the fireworks tomorrow." She panned her mischievous grin back to Adam. "Did Cassidy tell you about the party? You're more than welcome to join us."

"Oh, he already has plans," I said before he could open his mouth.

Tash pouted. "Well, if they fall through, the offer stands. Bryce makes a mean burger." She gave me a hug before nodding at Adam. "Good night, guys!"

Adam was quiet the entire trip home. He kept his eyes glued to his phone, not once engaging in a mere glance or conversation. I wanted to believe it was because he didn't want to wake Finn, but this felt different.

"Is something wrong?" I asked once Adam carried Finn to his bed.

I leaned against the door jamb, waiting for his answer, as he tucked him in.

"I'm just tired," he said as he passed.

I followed him into the kitchen, where he rummaged through a cupboard.

"Do you have a headache?" I asked as he unscrewed a container of pills. "You should have said something. We could've gone home earlier."

"I don't have a headache." He popped a tablet in his mouth and swallowed without water. "It's a sleeping tablet."

My eyebrows drew together as I moved toward him. "You're having trouble sleeping? I can help with that."

"Yeah, I'm sure you could."

"With Reiki, I mean."

"I think it would be wise to keep your hands to yourself."

I recoiled at the harshness of his tone.

"I'm sorry." He dropped his gaze as he shook his head. "I'm… I'm going to bed. Goodnight, Cassidy."

Without a backward glance, he marched to his room, rendering me speechless.

Chapter 32

I couldn't sleep after that. Adam's personality flip shook me. He was so happy and relaxed before meeting Tash, and now he was cold and distant.

Moments before I finally drifted off, my phone chimed. I wanted it to be Adam. Even if it was full of sexual innuendos or an invitation to his room, I didn't care. I needed something to loosen the knot forming in my stomach.

Tash: **ADAM FREAKIN' HARLOW!**

Me: **Calm down.**

Tash: **I knew I recognized him!**

Me: **Please keep it quiet. I don't want the whole world knowing.**

Tash: **Too late for that, my dear.**

Tash sent a link to a social media post, published half an hour ago.

MYSTERY GIRL SIGHTED WITH ADAM HARLOW.

Adam Harlow was spotted at tonight's Lakers game with an attractive woman by his side. The blonde-haired beauty's identity remains unknown, but sources say she's just a friend, and his relationship with Staci Warner is still on track. So why does Adam Harlow look so smitten?

"Fuck." That must've been why Adam was so upset. He'd seen the post and was now forced to acknowledge the complications of our relationship. I was a nobody. He was a somebody. His world would eat me up and spit me out. He knew it. I knew it. Best this ended here, without casualties, for his sake and mine.

He belonged with a woman like Staci Warner. A rich, beautiful socialite. Everything I was not.

———

Early the next morning, I peeked out the sheer curtains toward the beautiful ocean. I needed a dip to clear my head, but to my dismay, the water was occupied. Adam's distinctive muscular arms chopped through the water, unfazed by the waves, until he'd had enough and returned to shore.

As Adam trudged up the sand, he turned to my window, and I jumped back. My heart raced as I launched back into bed, praying he hadn't caught me spying.

Unable to sleep in due to my regular sunrise dates with Liam, I lay under the blankets, succumbing to my reality. This whirlwind romance with Adam was never meant to last. He was a billionaire womanizer, and I was a widowed single mother. What chance did we ever have? Had our paths not crossed at such a vulnerable time, he never would've pursued me. I was a distraction—and one that was now trending on social media.

By the time I'd showered and dressed, I crept out of my room, past Finn's cute snores, to find the house empty. A note was left on the kitchen counter.

Cassidy,
I'll be at the office all day. If I don't see you, enjoy your night. Our flight leaves tomorrow at 10 p.m.
A.

So much for not working the entire trip.

"Where's Adam?" Finn asked, mid-yawn, as he dragged his feet down the hall. "He said he was going to take me for a drive in his Lambo today."

"Sorry, kiddo. He got called into work," I said, annoyed that he'd forgotten the plans he'd made with my son. "Any chance you want to come dress shopping with me today?"

"Please, no," he whined. "Can I go to Tristan's instead?"

I considered forcing him to keep me company, but if we only had a short time left, I wanted him to spend it with his best friend.

"I guess so." I sighed. "Call Aunty Tash and ask."

"She never says no to me."

I rolled my eyes. "I know."

"But can I swim in the pool first?" Finn peered out the enormous windows. "Adam said we could."

I gazed out at the luxuries that would one day be a fleeting memory. "Sure," I said, wanting them to be good ones. "I'll join you."

———

After dropping off Finn and evading Tash's questions about Adam, Adam's driver took me to the local mall. I hadn't been there in years, but it hadn't changed. Memories of Dominic holding my hand while we shopped for my wedding dress struck my heart and led me to the store where I'd found *the one*.

I stood out in front, staring at the gorgeous red dress in the window. It wasn't like anything I'd worn before, but I was instantly drawn to it.

"Would you like to try it on?" The shop assistant took me by surprise.

"Oh, I don't know. It's probably out of my price range."

"It's half-price."

I walked into the store. "Keep talking."

It was still a little out of my price range, but when I tried it on, I couldn't refuse. Its snug fit enhanced every curve and held my breasts firmly in place with optimal cleavage.

Happy to be on the opposing side of the spectrum to Adam's favorite color, I handed over the cash and left, determined to hunt down the perfect shoes.

Once back at Adam's beach house, I went for another swim in the ocean before jumping in the shower to wash my hair. I spent more time than usual drying and styling my hair, then copied the makeup Tash had applied the night before. Only this time I wore red lipstick.

Tash had alluded to all the single men attending their party, so I was making an extra effort to look nice. I wanted to have fun, and laugh, and flirt—but with a man who was attainable. I wanted an Average Joe, with a stable job and big heart. I wanted a man to be a father to my son. But most of all, I wanted not to want Adam.

Satisfied with my reflection, I grabbed my handbag and a cardigan and texted Adam's driver as I walked out into the living room.

"Hello there," a female voice stopped me in my tracks.

"Oh…hi."

A stunning brunette in an exquisite black gown stood by the kitchen counter, running her gaze over my outfit. "Cute dress. You must be Casey."

I didn't correct her. "Thanks…and you are?"

"I'm Staci," she said in annoyance. "Adam's getting his jacket."

My heart plummeted with my stomach. "Oh right, the charity ball."

"Our families are huge donators, so it makes sense for us to go together."

I forced a smile. "Well, I'm sure you'll look great together."

Staci lifted her nose with a smug smile. "Everyone says so."

Heavy footsteps came to a halt behind me. "I thought you'd left."

A shiver rolled over my body as I turned. "Finn's already there. I'm heading off now."

His chest expanded as his gaze rolled over my body. "You look really nice."

I glanced over at Staci's dress before straightening mine. "Yeah, thanks." I slipped on my cardigan. "You guys have fun."

"Oh, we always do, don't we, Adam?" Staci walked over to straighten his bowtie.

I cleared my throat as I stepped back, ignoring Adam's penetrating gaze "Right. Well, I better go." With a wobbly take-off, I walked out of the house with my head held high.

———

"So, how do you know Tash and Bryce?" the man who'd been eyeing me for the past hour asked.

"My late husband and Bryce used to work together."

His eyebrows rose. "Oh, shit. I'm sorry."

"Did you kill him?"

"What? No…"

Laughter burst from my lips. "Sorry, that was a joke—a bad one." But Josie would've appreciated it.

He laughed nervously. "Right. Well, I'm starved. I'm going to grab something to eat."

I groaned inwardly, but I really didn't care. I hadn't met a guy yet who induced an iota of the rush I got around Adam.

"What's wrong with you?" Tash asked as she sidled up beside me while I poured another drink. "You're scaring all the guys off."

I sighed. "I don't know."

"Is it Adam?"

"No!"

Her brow rose.

"Okay…maybe." I poured the punch into my mouth, enjoying the burn of the overpowering tequila.

"Look, I know he's hot—like ridiculously so—but from what I've read about the guy, you're better off steering clear."

"Trust me, I've been trying."

"If he was the real deal, don't you think he'd be here tonight, instead of at some fancy ball with that Insta-slut? He's a player, Cass. Just do your job, and move on with your life."

"I know…I get it. He's out of my league."

"Fuck that, you're out of his."

Tipsy laughter filled the air between us as we clicked our drinks together.

"Come on," she said, observing the new arrivals. "Let me introduce you to James. He's Bryce's team leader at Mac Digital."

I froze. "Did he know Dominic?"

"No, he's only been there a year. A little cocky for my liking, but your tastes seems to have changed recently." She motioned him over. "Just put that morbid sense of humor in your back pocket for a little while, will you?"

"No promises."

"James!" She threw her arms around him. "So glad you could make it."

"Sorry I'm a little late. There was another party I had to attend." His gaze panned to mine, then fell to my breasts. "Who's your friend?"

"This is my beautiful, *single* friend, Cassidy."

"Lovely to meet you, Cassidy."

I scanned the backyard for a rock to crawl under. "Hi."

"Oh, look, the punch bowl is empty," Tash said. "I'll be right back."

I poured the remainder of my drink into my mouth. "So…" I rasped. "You work with Bryce?"

James' arrogance filtered through his laugh. "I wouldn't really call it working *with*… I'm his boss."

An arm materialized between us. "And I'm pretty sure I'm yours."

James' eyes bulged as he grasped the waiting hand. "Mr. Harlow," he gushed, shaking it vigorously. "What an unexpected surprise."

My gaze snapped up to Adam's. "What are you doing here?"

James attempted to speak, but Adam paid him no attention. "I was invited."

Every molecule in my body ignited as James reluctantly disappeared into the crowd. "What about the ball?"

"We have one night left away from my family, and I didn't want to spend it with a bunch of conceited assholes."

"So, you just…left?"

"I snuck out as soon as we announced the award."

"But what about Staci? Won't she be looking for you?"

Adam grasped my elbows. "Cass, I never intended to go with her. She turned up at my house unannounced, and since we were going to the same function, I figured it would be okay. Plus, a small part of me hoped it would make you jealous."

I folded my arms as I focused on the patchy grass under my feet. "It did."

"And it felt worse than I imagined." He lifted my chin. "I'm sorry."

Entranced by his oceanic eyes, I drew closer. His lips beckoned mine, but a glass breaking in the house snapped me out of my trance. With a gasp, I stepped back, scanning for witnesses. "Not here." I panned my gaze around the small circles of rubbernecking guests. "You're drawing too much attention."

Adam scoffed. "Then, let's go."

My pulse quickened as my head and heart prepared for battle. "I was planning to stay here tonight…with Finn."

"Change your plans."

"But I'll miss the fireworks."

His dark eyes never left mine. "I assure you, you won't."

I bit my lower lip as I peeked over at Tash, who was whispering with Bryce while watching us from the punch bowl.

"Fine." I sighed, growing tired of the prying eyes. "I'll meet you out front in five. I have to check on Finn."

With a nod, Adam pulled out his cell and began texting as he sauntered away. Multiple sets of eyes followed him, then panned back to me with curiosity, including my sister-in-law.

"I'm going to head off," I said to Tash after finding my son fast asleep in Tristan's room.

"With *him*?"

I flinched. "Don't say it like that."

"Cass, I don't think it's a good idea. When Bryce found out who he was, he told me—"

"I don't want to hear anymore rumors, Tash. I want to have a little fun for once. Just like *you* told me to."

"But that was before."

"Before what?"

She closed her eyes and sighed. "Look, is it just a bit of fun, or is it something more serious? Because the way he looks at you…"

"You're reading too much into it," I said, cutting her off. "How could it be any more? It's Adam *Freakin'* Harlow, remember?"

Uncertainty plagued her chocolate eyes. "I want you to be careful, Cass."

"You make it sound like I'm getting into bed with the devil."

"Well...maybe you are."

My temper sparked. "Well...maybe I want to!"

"Okay, okay." She held up her hands. "I'm just trying to look out for you...for Dom."

"I know, and I love you for that, but it's time I stop playing it safe and live a little. Life's too short."

Tears crept into her eyes. "It sure is."

"I'll pick up Finn first thing in the morning." With a quick peck to her cheek, I ran out of the house before her warnings permeated my confidence.

———

There was no privacy screen in Adam's car, so we had no choice but to ride in silence. Our hands laid between us, interlaced, while we exchanged heated glances. The air grew thick with want, so much so that the driver wound down his window in the middle of winter.

Once we arrived at the beach house, Adam took his coat off my shoulders and hung it up in the hallway closet.

I immediately wrapped my arms around my waist as I wandered into the living room.

"Are you cold?" he asked, following closely. "Because I can turn up the heat."

I turned to find his eyes plastered to my ass and smiled. "I have no doubt."

His hands ran down my arms. "But you're shivering."

"I guess I'm a little nervous."

His forehead crumpled. "Why?"

"Because being here with you...like this. I feel...*exposed*."

"I don't understand."

"The night at the bar...that wasn't me. And the incident in the pool...I don't even know who that girl was." I grimaced. "I'm not experienced at this, and I have no idea what I'm doing." I closed my eyes and sighed. "I'm a goddamn nun compared to the girls you're used to."

"The girls I've been with have been shallow, self-centered socialites. There's no comparison when it comes to you." He tucked a wave behind my ear before tracing his finger down my neck. "Your soul is drenched with beauty, your heart is full of kindness, and when I'm around you, fuck, I get nervous about screwing the whole thing up."

A small smile played on my lips. "Adam Harlow doesn't get nervous."

He licked his bottom lip as he gazed around the house. "I've never brought a woman back here before."

"Really?"

"And I never planned to either."

"Then, why am I here?" I asked, through a conflicting mixture of insecurity and anticipation.

My body liquified as he grasped the sides of my face. "Because I didn't plan for you, Cassidy Ryan." He pressed his forehead to mine to seemingly catch his breath before angling my mouth to his. "And now I have to fuck you on every surface."

Chapter 33

He devoured my lips as he brought our bodies closer. The intensity of his kiss was incomparable to the others, and the others were incredible. His soul ignited with every caress and consumed me whole. My mind, my body, and my once safeguarded spirit.

A moan escaped my lips as he lifted me up and back-stepped to the kitchen. Holding me in his right arm with my legs wrapped around his torso, he opened the fridge and rummaged through it until he pulled out a bottle of champagne.

"Thirsty?" I giggled as he placed the cold bottle between us.

"You have no idea," he uttered, marching me up the dark hallway.

He kicked open his bedroom door before nuzzling his face into my neck.

My head fell back in elation, offering an upside-down view of his excessively large bedroom. "Wow, this is nice."

Adam's kisses trailed down to my collarbone as he placed the bottle on his desk. "*This* is fucking nice." He tore his mouth away to admire my cleavage. "You look so fucking hot in that dress."

"Even if it's not your favorite color?"

He lifted his gaze as he placed me on my feet. "Your irises give me that pleasure every day."

I bashfully looked away, endeavoring to hide my burning cheeks. "You have a beautiful view," I said, staring out at the glistening waves pounding into the shore.

"Just wait until midnight."

The sound of a popping cork had me spinning around.

"Want some?" He leaned back on his desk.

"Shouldn't we wait until midnight?"

His fingertip circled the opening of the bottle. "There are other ways to bring in the new year, Cass."

My brow lifted. "Oh."

He brought the bottle to his mouth and tipped some in. "Or we could do both."

"Both?" I rasped, completely clueless to the suggestion but entirely turned on.

As he took two steps toward me, his pupils blackened and seared my skin. "Take off your cardigan."

Without any resistance, I threaded my arms out of the sleeves and dropped it to the floor.

He took another sip before licking the excess moisture from his lips. "Now the dress."

Enjoying his dominance, I slipped the straps over my shoulders and shimmied out of the dress until it pooled at my feet.

"Fuck," he mumbled under his breath as his gaze soaked in the sexiest lingerie I'd ever owned, paired with my stilettos.

I stepped out of my dress and rested my hand on my hip. "Are you going to share that?" I asked as he took another swig.

His eyes never deviated from mine. "Come and get it."

My core pulsed as I stepped closer until the only space left between us was occupied by a $500 bottle of wine. I wrapped my hand around its neck and lifted it to my lips. The bubbles tickled my nose as the liquid filled my mouth, making me draw it away prematurely. A small dribble ran over my chin and dripped onto my chest.

"Leave it." Adam took the bottle and placed it on the desk.

As the bead of champagne traced the curve of my breast, Adam slipped his finger under my bra strap and pulled it down while unfastening the front clasp that held everything in place.

He threw the bra across the room as my breasts spilled out before him, allowing the cool liquid to continue its journey. Once it reached my panty line, Adam dropped to his knees and laid soft kisses across my stomach as his fingers looped into my underwear. He dragged my panties down over my legs while his hot breath lingered at my core, waiting to strike.

Aside from my heels, I was completely naked, while Adam wore an entire suit. As he waited for the last drop to fall, he trailed kisses up and down my thigh, and I felt absolutely worshipped.

How could a man so powerful be kneeling before me… pleasuring me? My head was foggy, and when his nose nuzzled between my legs, followed by his stubbled chin, I almost blacked out. The erotic sensation of his tongue colliding with the fizz of the champagne over my clit had me crying out.

"Easy, Tiger," he said with a wicked smile. "No coming till midnight."

"Oh God, Adam. I can't…" As he dove back in, I grasped his hair. My knees grew too weak to stand.

"Open your eyes, or you'll miss the fireworks." He replaced his tongue with his thumb, bringing me dangerously close to the edge.

His words couldn't penetrate the rolling orgasm.

With a growl, he tore his hand away, stood, and steered me to the window.

I rested my hands on the glass, attempting to catch my breath, when Adam pressed his body against my back and unbuckled his belt. "Keep…your…eyes…open."

Finally understanding his instruction, I opened my eyes to the scenic ocean, dancing under the moonlight, and whimpered when Adam slid his incredible length between my legs.

As he filled my center, explosions of color filled the sky outside, bathing us in light. His thrusts matched every burst and built with intensity until I feared the window may break under the pressure.

"Oh fuck," I screamed, unable to hold on any longer.

He slammed into me one last time before grasping my body as his pulsating length spilled into my core. "Happy fucking New Year, Cass."

I released an exhausted chuckle. "We sure ended the year with a blast."

He spun me around and pressed my body to the fogged glass. "Started, you mean."

I peered into his eyes, believing his energy but still hesitant to give him my heart. "I think we need to get you out of these clothes." I ran my finger over his collar, then through his damp hair. "You're a hot mess."

He kissed the perspiration off my shoulder. "Says you."

I eyed his Californian King and grinned with anticipation. "Let's take a shower before bed."

"I suppose we can do that." Adam pulled me toward the ensuite bathroom. "After I fuck you in it."

"Adam… You can't possibly be ready for another round."

He whirled around and cupped my hand over his growing bulge. "Every position. Every surface. Just like our first night together."

I swallowed. *Holy shit.*

———

This man was a beast. A sex god. I'd never been so thoroughly fucked in my entire life. At least this time I managed to evade the tears that had followed our first encounter.

"I thought you were mad at me," I said after a long silence.

Adam's fingers trailed up and down my arm as we stared out the window. "Why would you think that?"

"When we dropped Tristan off after the basketball game, your energy changed."

"I was pissed you didn't invite me to the barbecue." He kissed the sensitive area behind my ear. "I had to hear about it from Tash."

"But you had the ball…and I didn't think it was your scene."

"I wanted to spend the night with you, Cass. I didn't care where we were." He shifted my body so we were face to face. "I was starting to think this thing between us was all in my head… until I saw your reaction to Staci."

I poked his chest. "Dick move, by the way."

He grabbed my hand and kissed it. "What about you? Dressing like that."

"What was wrong with my dress?"

"Absolutely everything"—he lay back with his hands behind his head—"if I wasn't going to be there."

I wrapped the bed sheet around my torso and sat cross-legged beside him. "I wanted to find out if someone from *my world* could make me feel the way you do."

"And *James* was a candidate?" he asked, raising a brow.

"Maybe." I shrugged. "I didn't exactly get a chance to find out."

Adam shifted his body up against the headboard and crossed his muscular arms. "He's a pushy, self-centered, entitled little shit. But you would've known that within seconds with those empathic superpowers of yours."

"I try not to judge people…"—I lifted my chin— "for a few minutes, at least."

Uncertainty flickered through Adam's aura. "If I hadn't come, would you be with him right now?"

I dropped my gaze. "I think you know the answer to that."

He grabbed my hand, demanding attention. "I'm not like you, Cass. I can't read you like you read me. I need you to tell me how you feel." His eyes bored into mine. "I need to know I'm not the only one feeling this way."

"What do you want me to say?" I pulled my hand away as I blinked back tears. "That I'm in love with you?"

"Not if you don't mean it."

"And if I do, what then?" Unexpected anger lurked under my skin.

"Then, show me."

I gazed at him, wanting desperately to tell him how I felt, but how could I? I didn't even know myself. Instead, I climbed over his legs and cradled his handsome face as I pressed my lips to his. He didn't respond at first, but his arousal was as clear as his intention. He wanted me to take control.

Grasping his shoulders, I rocked my body over his as I deepened the kiss. Our tongues entwined, but his hands remained at his sides. My body yearned for his touch, and when he didn't answer, I drew his bottom lip between my teeth. Adam was playing dirty.

With a smirk, I released his lip and trailed kisses up his jawline to his ear. "You like me taking charge?" I ground harder against the sheet between us.

"I like everything you do."

I snaked my finger down his chest. "What about tantric sex?"

"You mean that slow, hippy shit?" His eyes tapered. "Is that your kink?"

"No." I laughed. "I mean…I don't know. I've only read about it."

"Oh, yeah?" He lifted his back off the headboard. "Tell me what to do."

"Stay exactly where you are." I maneuvered my legs around his body while his tucked around mine, creating the erotic lotus position.

Adam smirked as his eyes leveled with mine. "This is pretty fucking sexy."

"Now we breathe," I said, smothering my innate desire to jump him. "Deep and slow."

"I can do deep and slow."

I held back my smile. "It's about being in the moment and paying attention to everything you're feeling…" I ran my hands over his thighs. "Physically, emotionally, and spiritually." I massaged his legs, then arms, then chest, encouraging him to do the same.

His gaze intensified under my touch, and my yearning amplified under his. As we stared into each other's eyes, my hands gradually lowered onto his shaft.

His breath hitched. "Fuck…"

"Keep breathing," I said as I began to stroke.

With Adam's gaze still locked on mine, his hands slid between my legs and settled over my core. I held my breath as he slid in one finger, then two, and held them there. My head grew fuzzy as his smallest movements drove me closer to the edge.

"Keep breathing," he whispered.

For some time, we sat completely immersed in each other, drinking in each other's energies until the world around us ceased to exist.

The air between us sizzled with electricity, drawing our lips closer and closer until they finally collided. Like magnets succumbing to the pull, our yearning bodies interlocked in a passionate embrace. Needing more, I used Adam's shoulders to lift my weight while he guided me over his length. He slid in with ease, completing our circle of flowing energy.

With our heart and eyes aligned, and our spirit connected, I let myself go, opening myself to Adam completely. Elation flooded my body and mind as our hips maneuvered in slow, rhythmic circles, until I could take no more.

My body exploded with ecstasy, crying out in unison with the deep rumble of Adam's chest as he released a staggering, animalistic growl.

"Holy fucking Christ, Cass…" Adam panted in my arms once we'd finally returned to earth.

I savored the salty flavor of his shoulder. "I know," I whispered, moving my lips back to his.

"That was…"

I offered him a weary smile. "Incredible?"

"That was the best fucking sex I've ever had." He flipped me over. "Let's do it again."

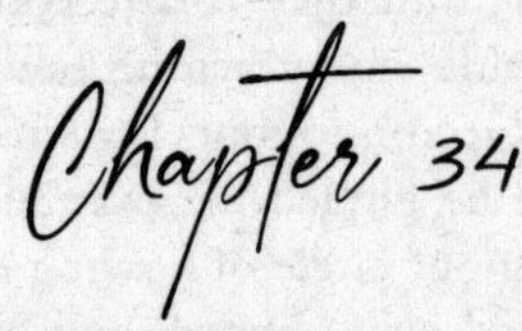

Chapter 34

A loud ringing infiltrated my blissful slumber. "Can you tell your phone to be quiet?" I prodded Adam's side. "I'm trying to recover here."

"It's yours," he grumbled, prodding me back. "I turned mine off last night."

My face whipped to Adam. "You turned your phone off?" I couldn't believe it.

His sleepy smile turned my insides to goo as he rolled onto his side. "I didn't want any disruptions."

"Oh."

"But you really should get that." He motioned to the persistent ringing. "It might be Finn."

"Shit, you're right." I scanned the floor, zeroing in on our cast-off clothes. "Where's my cell?"

"It must be in the living room." Adam pushed himself out of bed. "I'll get it. Do not fucking leave my bed."

With a giggle, I fell back into the pillows. "I won't argue with that," I said, tilting my head for a better view of his tight ass parading down the hall.

Adam returned to the bedroom moments later. "Why is Marc calling you?"

"Marc? Like Doctor Marc?" I shot out of bed and threw on Adam's old Stanford t-shirt.

Adam reluctantly held out the phone. "If he asks you out again, I'll fucking…"

I hushed his voice as I answered. "Marc? Is everything okay?"

"Liam's taken a turn, Cassidy," he said in a tone I knew too well. "You need to get back here as soon as possible."

I peered up at Adam, knowing my next words would break his heart. "How much time does he have?"

Adam's blue eyes turned to ice as his shoulders sank.

"A couple of days, maybe less. It's hard to tell at this point."

My lower lip trembled as I stared at the beautiful man crumbling before me.

"Listen, the family is desperately trying to reach Adam. Josie seems to think you'd know where to find him."

"Yes, I know where he is." Although, his far-off gaze told me otherwise. "We'll come back straight away."

I lowered my eyes as I ended the call, trying to rein in my emotion. I was entirely too close to this. "Adam…your grandfather has deteriorated. We need to get back."

"I'm staying."

"What?" I moved toward him, not understanding.

"I'm not going to watch him die, Cassidy." He stood and proceeded to pull on his swimming trunks.

"Adam, .please. He wants you there. You're his family."

His lips pursed as he looked away. "I'm going for a swim," he said, reaching for a towel.

"Why are you being so selfish?"

"Because that is who I am." He yanked open the sliding door. "You should know that by now."

I closed my eyes, smothering the burn. "I never should've agreed to come here." I shook my head as rage surged through my body. "I should've been with your grandfather, doing my job, not here in Malibu, sleeping in your bed. God knows how scared Liam's feeling right now."

His hard gaze sliced through my heart. "Then go."

As I sucked in my breath, Adam spun around and sauntered across the sand before diving into the churning ocean.

———

After shoving everything into our bags, I caught a cab to Tash and Bryce's to collect my son.

"Hey, are you okay?" Tash asked the second she saw my face.

"Liam's unwell, and I need to get back."

She peered over my shoulder at the waiting taxi. "Where's Adam?"

"He's…um…" I pressed my lips together. "He's not the man I thought he was, okay? Please don't say I told you so."

Her eyes softened. "Oh, Cass, I'm so sorry."

"It's fine." I forced a smile. "I'm fine. I just have to get back."

As soon as I told Finn that Liam was unwell, he understood instantly. His emotional maturity was tenfold Adam's, and he held my hand the entire flight back to New York. Amy picked him up from JFK and drove him home while Liam's helicopter flew me back to Harlow Manor.

When I finally arrived, Josie was waiting by the helipad and rushed to greet me.

"Where's Adam?" she asked, glancing back into the helicopter.

"I'm sorry." I couldn't meet her eyes. "He refused to come."

"Fuck, I knew he'd do this." She stormed back to the house. "I'll get Grayson to call him."

I jogged to keep up. "How's Liam?"

"He's still coherent, but he's drifting in and out." She wiped away a tear as her voice wobbled. "He's bedridden now, and his eyes…they aren't like they used to be."

I rested my hand on her back, feeling her pain. "And the rest of the family? How are they managing?"

She wiped away her sniffles. "Grayson's a mess, and Caroline and William are quiet…like, too quiet. And poor Max." We arrived at the front door. "He hasn't said anything, but he must be devastated. They've been friends for so long."

"I shouldn't have left," I uttered as I entered the foyer.

Josie took my hand and pulled me into the drawing room. "That trip was Gramps' idea. He wanted to give you and Adam time together, away from this place, to explore your feelings. Knowing there is something growing between you two has made him so happy."

I gnashed my teeth to dull the ache in my chest. "There's not."

"Really…" Josie scrunched up her nose. "Well, don't tell Gramps that. He told Betty you're the one."

"He told *Betty*?"

"Did I mention he's hallucinating, too?"

I closed my eyes as I exhaled. "I have to see him."

"Of course. Everyone's upstairs."

As I walked into Liam's room, tired eyes peered up at me from every corner.

"Where's Adam?" Grayson asked, panning his gaze between me and Josie.

"He's, um…running late." Josie motioned Grayson to the hallway. "Can we chat?"

As Grayson left, I approached Liam's bedside.

"He's asleep," William said from the chair beside his father. "Mrs. Fredrich has increased his pain relief under the instruction of the doctor, but it doesn't seem to be enough. We're hoping you can help."

"I'll do whatever I can to make him feel at peace, but I assure you, hearing your voices is all he needs right now."

William's eyes met mine for the first time and softened. "I know we haven't been very accepting of your position here, and I want to apologize. You have given us more time, and we're very grateful."

I gazed over at Caroline, who was nodding in agreement while dabbing the corner of her eyes with a tissue.

"I wasn't here when my mother passed," he continued, staring down at his sleeping father. "I was too busy building an empire then to take my father's calls." His voice broke. "I don't want that for Dad."

"Oh, darling." Caroline wrapped her arm around William's shoulders "You never told me."

"I hated myself for it," he muttered angrily. "I threw myself deeper into work, then expected my sons to follow. It wasn't fair to them. I see that now, and after the long talk I had with Dad yesterday, I know I have a lot of work to do to repair things."

I was surprised by his genuine remorse. "Relationships are complicated. *Love* is complicated. We are all entitled to make mistakes. It's how we choose to fix them that matters."

"Do you love our son?"

My breath caught. "I…um…it's…well…" *Fuck.*

William's brow rose. "Complicated?"

"Very." I ignored the enduring ache in my chest. I had to remain professional here. "Why don't you two go for a walk outside and get some fresh air? I'll sit with Liam in case he wakes."

William nodded. "That's a good idea." He took Caroline's hand as he rose. "We'll be back shortly."

Once they'd gone, I wrapped my fingers around Liam's hand and closed my eyes. William was right, the pain medication wasn't nearly enough.

"Betty?" His hollowing eyes barely opened.

"No, Liam. It's Cassidy."

"Oh, Cassidy." His hand twitched. "You're back."

"I could never stay away from you for long." The Harlow men clearly had that effect on me.

"My grandson didn't come back, did he?"

I swallowed the growing lump in my throat. "He needed to wrap up a few things first, but I'm sure he'll be here soon."

His raspy laughter turned into a cough. "You don't need to cover for him, dear."

"I pleaded for him to come back," I said as fresh tears arose, "but he just…"

"Closed himself off?"

I nodded. "Completely."

"I'm not surprised." He sighed. "Adam grew up in a home where emotion was treated as a flaw. Harlow Manor is where he has always felt unconditional love, and I dare say, he's terrified of losing that."

"But he has Grayson…and Josie…"

"And they have their own family now."

My eyebrows pulled together. "And Adam wants that?"

"I don't think Adam had a clue what he wanted…until you came along."

Frustration simmered under my skin. "Then, why is he so hot and cold?"

"Be patient with him. Adam's in very unfamiliar territory right now."

"He's never lost someone he loves before?"

"He's never *been* in love before."

Tears welled in my eyes. "But we're so different. How could we possibly make it work?"

"Did you know Betty was the daughter of one of my parents' gardeners? I was the sole heir to the Harlow fortune, and we fell in love instantly. There was no stopping us and we defied everyone. Betty and I lived a beautiful life together."

"Sounds like a romance novel."

"The best kind…full of love, heartache, and tragedy." His weak smile overpowered his weariness. "And it's almost time for my happy ending."

I quickly wiped away the falling tears. "I'm so blessed to have known you, Liam."

"No." He squeezed my hand as he closed his eyes. "I am the one who is blessed. You came into our lives when we needed you most, and I truly hope you stay. Your love story is only beginning."

———

Endeavoring to level out my emotions, I'd been swimming each morning since my return to Harlow Manor. Liam was too unwell to watch the sunrise, so I used those idle hours to refresh my energy in the indoor pool.

"He's still not answering," Grayson growled from the drawing room as I passed its closed doors. "Apparently, he hasn't shown up for work in two days."

Josie sighed. "He's hasn't replied to any of my texts either."

"Maybe I should fly back and drag him back here myself."

"And risk both of you not being here when the time comes?" Josie cried. "Hell, no."

"The doc said we may have a few more days."

"This time last week, we thought we had weeks. You're not going. Adam needs to grow a pair and get back here himself."

As Harrison erupted into tears, I quickly jogged up the stairs and into my room, where I continued to pace. Adam wasn't okay, but he needed to be *not okay* here. With a taut jaw, I swiped my cell phone from my nightstand and dialed his number.

After multiple rings, I was about to end the call when it connected. There was no greeting, only a staggered breath and the distinct sound of crashing waves and blowing wind.

"Adam…I know you're there, and I know you're hurting, but we need you to come back." My voice broke as I tried to keep my shit together. "Your grandfather doesn't have much time left, and he wants you here. You don't have to hold his hand or even be in the same room…he just wants you close. He loves you so much, and I just know, with all of my being, that you'll regret not saying goodbye."

After a moment of silence, the phone went dead, and I was overcome with emotion. Even with 3,000 miles between us, I could feel his heart breaking.

———

Early the next morning, I awoke to voices in the hallway.

"So, you finally decided to show." Grayson sounded equally smug and relieved.

"Don't."

Adam's deep voice had me launching out of bed and scrambling for my robe.

"You look like shit," Grayson continued, slowing outside my door.

"I feel like shit." Adam's husky tone screamed cigarettes and whiskey. "Is Gramps awake?"

"Not yet. Why don't you unpack first? Shower, perhaps."

"I don't plan on staying long."

My heart dipped as I rested my head against my door.

"Adam…what's goi—"

"Is Cassidy awake?" he asked, as if sensing my presence.

"I seriously doubt it. She's been up through the night with Gramps."

The silence outside made me wonder if they'd moved on.

"Just knock, you idiot. I'm sure she'll want to see you."

I jumped back from the door.

"I doubt that."

"Did something happen in LA?"

"I don't want to talk about it," he mumbled before slamming his door.

Grayson exhaled heavily. "I'll take that as a yes."

———

After I'd showered and dressed, I wandered up the hallway to check on Liam but froze when I overheard Adam's voice coming from his room.

"I'm so sorry, Gramps. It was selfish of me to stay away."

"There is no need to apologize. We all deal with these things in different ways. I'm just glad you're here."

"Are you in pain?"

"Cassidy is helping with that," Liam said, deflecting from the awful truth. "She's a very special girl, that one…but I think you know that."

My chest caved at the silence that followed.

"You need to tell her, Adam," Liam said finally. "Don't deny your heart from love."

"I'm going to screw it up."

Liam sighed. "You're your own worst enemy."

"And you've always been my voice of reason. Who's going save me from myself after you're gone?"

"With her, I don't think you'll need saving."

As my heart crumbled, I rushed toward the library. I promised Liam I'd find one of Betty's favorite books and read to him that day, so I had the perfect excuse to hide out until the coast was clear.

———

"Hey," Adam said from the doorway, only moments later.

I jumped, more guilty than surprised. "Oh, you're back." He must've seen me rush past Liam's room.

"Yeah." Adam rubbed his jaw as he stepped into the room. "What are you doing?"

"I'm…um…" I fumbled over my words and turned back to the bookshelf. "I'm looking for a book. It was your grandmother's favorite, but nothing is alphabetized in here."

"I think I know the one." He sidled up beside me and slid a tattered book out of the shelf. "My grandmother had her own system."

"Thanks," I muttered as I fiddled with my obsidian bracelet. I wasn't ready to be close to him. His energy was too unstable, and I was already exhausted.

"Would you mind if I read to him today?"

"Of course not." An invisible weight lifted. "Liam would love that."

He stared at me for a moment before breaking out of his daze. "Then I better get to it before he falls asleep again."

"Even if he does, keep reading. Your voice will carry into his dreams."

With a curt nod, he proceeded to leave the room before pausing in the doorway and turning back. "Can we talk later?"

I wrapped my arms around my stomach and dropped my gaze. "You need to focus on your family right now."

"I'm trying."

My eyes lifted to find his pleading with mine. "Okay." I momentarily lost myself in his vulnerability. "But tomorrow. You need some sleep."

With a small, albeit sad smile, he tapped the book in his hand before continuing on to his grandfather's room, where he needed to be.

———

In the early hours of the morning, I crept into Liam's room, hoping to relieve some of his pain while he slept, but discovered Adam hunched over Liam's bed, using the book as a pillow.

"Adam," I whispered before moving closer. "Adam…"

He lifted his head with a grimace, clearly disorientated. "I must've fallen asleep."

"You should go to bed."

He rolled his head from side to side, stretching his neck. "I'm fine. I still have a few chapters left to read."

"That you can finish in the morning." I slipped the book out of his hands and rested it on the nightstand. "You need a good night's sleep."

"And you don't?" He checked his watch. "It's 3 a.m."

"He gets restless around now. I can help with that."

Adam rubbed his stubbled jaw as he stared at his sleeping grandfather. "How long does he have?"

"The doctor is coming today to convince him to increase his pain meds. Once that happens, he'll be asleep most of the time."

"Do you think he'll agree?"

"Now that you're here…yes, I think he will."

"So, he's been holding out for me?" His shoulders slumped. "Through all that pain?"

"Because he loves you, Adam." I instinctively ran my hand through his hair. "He wants to see you happy."

"He has." Adam slid his hand over my wrist before pulling me down onto his lap. "Every day I'm with you."

Desire flowed through my body as he nuzzled his face into my neck. I closed my eyes and tipped my neck back for more until a tap on the door had me launching out of his arms.

I swiftly moved around the bed to start my treatment as Grayson stepped into the room holding Harrison.

"Has he woken at all?" he asked, oozing nonchalance.

"No." Adam pulled his gaze away from me to focus on his brother. "Not yet."

"I can sit with him." Grayson rubbed circles on his son's back. "Harrison has no intention of sleeping tonight, so you may as well get some."

I smiled softly at his newborn. "He's probably picking up on everyone's stress. Nothing a few cuddles can't fix."

Grayson sniggered as he seesawed his gaze between us. "Is that what you two were doing?"

"Grayson…" Adam seethed.

His brother held up one hand in defeat. "None of my business. Noted."

"I'm getting a coffee." Adam stood abruptly and left the room.

Grayson winced. "I didn't mean to scare him off."

"He'll be back." The heat in my cheeks subsided. "He's determined to finish that book."

Grayson walked over to the nightstand and picked up the novel. "I remember this one. Gramps used to read it all the time after my Gran passed." He flipped it over and read the blurb.

"I think it makes him feel closer to her."

Using his free hand, he opened the book and flicked through, only to pause on the title page. "I think I know why. This book was a gift. 'To my daring, Betty. Happy 27th Birthday. Love, Liam, William, and Adam.' *Adam?*"

My stomach dropped.

Grayson's forehead furrowed. "That's weird."

"What's weird?" Adam asked, sauntering back in with a steaming mug.

"This inscription. Our names are written here, but we weren't even born yet."

"That's because it's not you." Liam's husky voice tore through their curiosity.

The boys grew matching lines between their eyebrows as they drew closer to their grandfather. They could almost pass for twins if it wasn't for Grayson's darker features.

"What are you saying, Gramps?" Grayson asked, rereading the words in his hands.

"Six years after your father was born, we were blessed with another son. We named him Adam."

Grayson sank into the chair, while Adam didn't move.

"To our devastation, he was taken from us way too soon."

"Oh, Gramps…" Grayson took his hand. "That's awful. How did we not know?"

"Your father really struggled with the loss. All he wanted was a baby brother, and he absolutely adored him." A melancholy smile fell over his cracked lips. "That's the reason why he went against our family tradition and named his first son Adam."

Adam's facade began to crumble as anger surged through his energy. "Why didn't anyone tell us this?"

"It was a very dark time in our lives. Your father doesn't want us talking about it."

Adam pinched the bridge of his nose as he took slow, deep breaths. "If I'd known, I'd…I…" With a scowl, he slammed his coffee on the side table and stormed out of the room.

My eyes struck Liam's, and he motioned me to follow.

"Hey!" I chased Adam down the hall.

He spun around, barely holding himself together. "For the past thirty-three years, I believed I wasn't worthy of the title… that something must've gone wrong at birth to see me not fit to carry on the family name. I've spent my entire life working my ass off to prove my father wrong. I did everything he ever asked because I…I…"

"Wanted him to love you?"

Adam growled. "It sounds so fucking stupid."

"It's not stupid." I gazed up into his tortured eyes. "It's human."

"But to find out he named me after the one person he loved most in the world…it changes everything! If I'd known, I wouldn't be so…so fucking complicated." He hung his head with a sigh. "I don't even know who I am without that resentment."

I blinked back tears. "I do."

"How? I've been a complete dick to you."

I stepped closer and rested my hand over his chest. "Because I can feel your soul." His sorrow was crushing. "They shouldn't have kept that from you."

"Wait." He jerked back. "Did you know?"

"Not all the details, but yes."

"And you didn't tell me?"

I dropped my hand, trying to sever the hurt flowing through our connection. "It wasn't my story to tell."

"How long have you known?"

I drew in a deep breath, bracing myself. "Since my first day."

"So, when I found that photo in the library…you knew that wasn't me? And the fucking painting?!"

"Liam asked me not to talk about it. He's my client, and it's my duty to respect his wishes."

"That's right…" Adam emitted an ominous chuckle. "This is all just a job for you."

"You know that's not true."

"Tell me," His gaze tapered. "Is it your duty to fuck your clients' grandsons, too?"

I wanted to slap him. I wanted to unleash hell on the man who continuously tore pieces off my heart, but I couldn't. His heart was as broken as mine. Only his was bleeding out in cruel words.

"Fuck, Cass." He tore his fingers through his hair. "I didn't mean that."

He reached out, but I maintained my distance. "Go be with your grandfather, Adam." I refused to meet his gaze. "I'll come back in a couple of hours, once you've had a chance to talk. It may be your last opportunity."

He ran his hand over his fear-stricken face as he stared down the hall.

"Go," I ordered again.

His jaw grew taut as he battled an inner war. "Fuck," he muttered angrily before whirling back to me. "I'm sorry, Cass," was all he said before racing up the hall to share Liam's final hours of coherence with his little brother.

Chapter 35

"It's time," Marc said, turning to the family as they stood stationary in every corner of Liam's room.

The staff, including Max, had already shared a private moment with Liam the day prior, and now it was time to endure the hardest part of my job: watching his closest loved ones say goodbye.

I stood back, knowing my place. I'd done everything I could to ease his discomfort. It was Liam's time, and we needed to respect that.

A strong smell of freesias filled the room as the family approached his bedside, surrounding him with the love he deserved.

William was the first to latch onto his father's hand. "Dad, I know we haven't always seen eye to eye, but please know…I've always loved you. I promise I'll work on the things we talked about." He drew in a shaky breath. "Tell Mom and Adam I miss them, okay?"

When he didn't respond, Caroline covered her husband's hand with her diamond-clad fingers. "Goodbye, Liam," she said, struggling to maintain her usual coolness. With a gentle tug, she led her distraught husband to the sitting area to give her sons some space.

Josie wept into Grayson's shoulder as he threaded his fingers through his grandfather's. "Gramps, thank you for everything you've ever done for us. Without you, I wouldn't have won back the heart of my beautiful wife and created a life so full of love." He leaned forward and pressed his lips to his forehead. "See you in the afterlife, old man."

Josie ran her hand down Liam's face. "Grayson is the man he is because of you. He carries your heart and your eyes, and I know Harrison will, too. We love you so much."

Grayson and Josie joined William and Caroline, leaving Adam standing alone, staring at his grandfather's stilling body.

His jaw pulsed as he finally approached. "Hey, Gramps," he said, as if waiting for an answer. "I wish you could stay... but I know Gran is waiting." He encased his hand between his. "Thank you for never giving up on me and for always being my sounding board. I've sure fucked up lately, but your love never faltered. I won't screw up anymore, I promise." He whispered something into Liam's ear, causing the subtle rise of Liam's lips and his body to relax. "Love you, Gramps. I'll make you proud."

With a kiss to his wrinkled brow, Adam moved to the wall while his family returned to Liam's bedside, waiting for the inevitable call.

"She's here," a raspy whisper floated from Liam's lips.

As the family searched for answers, I closed my eyes as the smell of freesias danced past my nose. Liam had crossed over.

Marc gently placed Liam's arm back on the bed after reading his pulse. "He's gone."

While the family broke down, Adam didn't flinch. He stood there, staring at his grandfather's lifeless body like he was caught in a trance. As much as I could prepare someone for the loss of a loved one, it still fucking hurt. I had three years to prepare for the inevitable loss of my husband, and the paralyzing grief still swallowed me up whole. My only saving grace was Finn. My light in the darkness. I needed to be that for Adam.

Sidling up beside him, I slipped my hand over his before his fingers turned and engulfed mine. He held on tightly as his head dipped and his lips trembled, but there were no tears. He wouldn't let them fall.

Soft, classical music filled the room in the absence of voices as the family absorbed the reality of the moment. William Harlow II was gone.

———

At Liam's request, I arranged a bottle of his favorite whiskey to be served in the drawing room after his death, and no one dared decline. It was there that I had left three photo albums, personalized to each son and grandson. They contained photographs from Liam's collection that we'd collated and arranged in chronological order of their lives together, each with a letter.

After assisting Marc and Nora with Liam's final arrangements, I wandered up to the library, in need of a quiet moment. I curled up on the window seat in time to watch the sky darken over Betty's picturesque garden. The hedges lit up with twinkling fairy lights, and I gasped at the beauty before me. There was always a spectacle at Harlow Manor, no matter what time of day.

"Gramps loved that view."

Adam's voice ripped me out of my spell. I wiped the moisture from my eyes before turning to find him leaning against the doorframe, holding a tulip-shaped glass. "Hey, how's that whiskey going down?"

He took a sip as he moseyed into the room. "Smooth," he said with a tipsy smile.

"Liam thought you'd enjoy it."

"We definitely are." Adam poured the last drop into his mouth, savoring the taste. "Along with those albums you made." He moved closer to the window. "I haven't heard my dad laugh like that in years."

Warmth filled my heart. "Did you like yours?" I asked, wondering how many drinks he'd had. "I have to admit, you *were* pretty cute in your younger years."

"In my younger years?" His eyebrow rose.

"Oh, come on." I rolled my eyes. "Cute doesn't come close to describing you now."

"Oh yeah?" He plonked himself opposite me on the window seat and swung his legs up between us. "Please...go on."

"And inflate your ego some more?" I chortled. "Your head will explode."

His glazed eyes sparkled. "Which head?"

"Adam!" Lava flooded my face.

"Fuck, you're sexy when you blush."

"Stop," I uttered sternly. "You need to go back downstairs and be with your family."

His head fell back against the wall as he turned his gaze out the window. "Do I have to? It's too real down there."

"Adam…"

He refused to meet my gaze.

"It's going to be tough for a while…for all of you," I continued. "But you need to let yourself grieve. It's not healthy to keep it all bottled up inside."

"Ugh, you're such a mom," he moaned, dragging himself off the seat.

"Funny that."

His grin grew as he backed out of the room. "A… M.I.L.F."

I pointed to the door. "Go." I held back a smile. This wasn't the time to encourage his drunken antics.

With a wink, he turned to the door, banging his shoulder as he walked through it.

———

My phone buzzed in my lap, jerking me awake. I'd fallen asleep with my head against the cool glass of the window.

Josie: **We're heading back to our room. Thanks for those beautiful albums. Grayson already treasures his. If you get a chance, can you please check on Adam? He never came back downstairs.**

I checked the time with a frown. Adam would've either sobered up or be in a drunken stupor by now. With a sigh, I climbed off the window seat and ventured down the hall to his room.

I was about to knock when my gaze diverted through my open door, where a large hunched-over figure sat at the end of my bed. It was too dark to see his face, but I knew it was Adam. No matter how much I tried to block it, I was drawn to his energy.

"Hey," I whispered, closing the door behind me.

He wiped his nose with the back of his hand but kept his head lowered. "I know I shouldn't be in here uninvited, but I, um..." his voice choked up.

"Adam..." I waded through the waves of grief to get close to him. I lifted his tear-streaked face to mine and almost buckled under his heartache. "It's okay to feel this way."

As his chest convulsed into sobs, I stepped between his legs and held him tight, absorbing his misery, along with his tears, into my oversized sweatshirt.

With his face buried in my stomach, I ran my fingers through his disheveled hair and pressed my lips to the top of his head, desperate to make his pain go away.

Adam peered up at me through a glaze of despair. "Can I stay with you tonight?"

As a torturous mixture of grief and love struck my heart, I brought my lips to his, answering his plea. Our kiss was gentle, our touch subtle, but the underlying current of desire grew too powerful to ignore.

I tugged off his sweatshirt while Adam tore off my mine, kissing my stomach as he unfastened my jeans and slid them, and my panties, to the floor. Once I'd stepped out of the pool of clothes, he pulled me onto his lap and kissed me deeper as I straddled his legs.

My skin grew clammy as I rocked my pulsing core over the bulge of Adam's sweatpants.

"Fuck," he uttered in a low growl while pressing his forehead to mine.

Relishing the building heat, I released his imposing length and stroked, fueling the fire that was sure to turn me to ash.

Without hesitation, Adam hitched me up and glided into me. His chest rumbled as I adjusted to his size and the deeply penetrating position, and I almost came at the beautiful sound.

Adam removed my t-shirt and bra and tossed them across the room. "Fuck, you're beautiful," he said, rolling his gaze and hands over my moonlit body.

I rotated my hips in circles, begging for more. "Since when are you so tender?"

With one skilled flip, my back hit the mattress with Adam hovering over me. "What do you prefer?"

I gazed up at him, feeling too much, wanting too much. "All of the above."

"Good answer," he murmured, kissing me softly on the lips as he slid inside once more. "But tonight, we're taking this slow."

For hours, we made love. Deep, tantric, unforgettable love. With our bodies unified, the intensity of our connection surged. Our souls entwined, morphing pain into pleasure, lust into love, until our broken pieces smoothed over like ocean glass. Still broken, now beautiful.

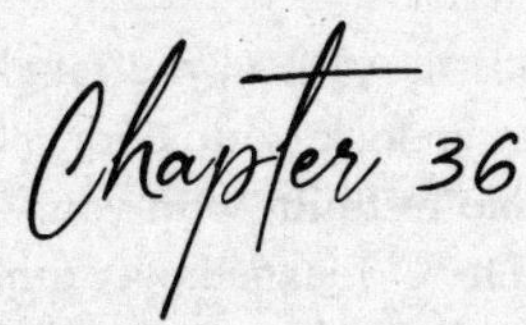

As much as I wanted to take away Adam's pain, he needed to face it. So, when he snuggled into the crook of my neck only minutes after yet another mind-blowing orgasm, I pressed my hand against his perspiring chest.

"Adam…you need to rest," I said, pushing past my everlasting desire to be ravished by him once again. "The next few days are going to be rough."

"But we can pretend…" He pulled my waist toward his.

"Not anymore." I ran my thumb down his cheek as I stared into his imploring eyes. "This is real, Adam. Liam is gone."

His chest deflated as he retracted his arm.

"Hey." I grasped his hand and pulled it to my lips. "I'll be here for you, but I can't be your distraction."

His jaw tightened as his eyes glazed over. "You're not a distraction, Cassidy. You're my fucking lifeline."

"You don't need me to get through this." I moved his hand to my heart. "But anytime you want to talk, I'll be here." My gaze lowered as I forced out the next words. "The other stuff will have to wait."

Adam rolled onto his back with a long sigh. "Do you want me to leave?"

"No." My heart ached at the thought. "Not tonight."

"But after?"

I exhaled heavily. "You know it's for the best."

"But I'm notorious for doing things that aren't good for me." I poked his side. "Exactly."

He stared at the ceiling, deep in thought. "How long?"

"Just until everything settles down. Then, we'll see where we are."

With a subtle nod, he yanked the tangled blanket over his body. "Then you better lock your door," he grumbled before rolling over. "I have no restraint with you."

My lips curved. "Deal." I leaned over him and pressed my lips to his cheek. "I'm going to take a shower."

"Cass…" His warning was evident and erotic. "Don't make this harder."

I sprang off the bed with a wince. "Sorry."

While Adam lay in my bed, I made my way to the shower. It wasn't until I was standing under the steady stream of hot water that I allowed my own grief to trickle through.

Losing Liam felt different than my other clients. In our short time together, he'd become my friend. My confidant. He understood how painfully beautiful love could be, and he made me feel like family when I was missing my own. Liam was an extraordinary man, and Adam was blessed to have known him his entire life…until now. Now, he was on his own.

Memories of my final days with Grams slammed into my chest. She meant everything to me, and I remembered the sorrow like it was yesterday. I had to learn to live without her, just like Adam had to learn to exist without Liam. It wasn't time for us to act on our feelings. It was time for him to grieve with his family.

The line I drew weeks ago was now a blurred mess. I was hired to support the family, not crumble along with them. Until my time at Harlow Manor was up, I had to remain professional. There had to be boundaries. But the moment I stepped back into my room and saw Adam fast asleep in my bed, I knew I was completely fucked.

I crawled in and tucked myself into the curve of his warm body. When his arm instinctively wrapped around my waist, I loosened my obsidian bracelet and slipped it onto his wrist, hoping it would ease even a miniscule of his heartache. He was going to need it.

The next morning, I awoke to the chime of my cell phone and an empty bed.

Josie: **Did you speak to Adam last night?**

Me: **Somewhat. Is everything okay?**

Josie: **Gramps' Rolls is gone again and he isn't answering his phone, so it's safe to assume he's taken off.**

My stomach churned. He had run away again.

Me: **I'm sorry.**

Josie: **You have nothing to be sorry for. He wouldn't have come back at all if it wasn't for you. I just hope he returns for the funeral.**

I closed my eyes as disappointment settled upon my shoulders.

Me: **I hope so, too.**

———

It was somewhat of a relief having Adam gone over the following few days. I was able to organize the funeral and wake and counsel the rest of the family through their grief without the added distraction of Adam's coercive energy and delectable body.

Solace was found in the eyes of Grayson and Josie's son. Over the days leading up to the funeral, the entire family and staff of Harlow Manor doted over him, and I could see why. He was a chubby little ball of new life, with eyes that swirled from hazel to green, just like his grandfather. His energy already reflected Liam's gentle and caring nature, and I wasn't the only one who could feel it.

Every night, I held my phone, desperately wanting to call Adam to see if he was okay, but I didn't. He needed to face his pain. He needed to face his family. And he needed to do it without me asking.

Adam hadn't responded to anyone's calls or messages, but we knew he was alive, because the papers told us so. After Grayson threw the latest article into the fire, I found the short piece on the internet.

Following the death of William Harlow II, his grandson, Adam Harlow, has thrown himself back into work. While the rest of his family grieves at a private residence, Adam has wasted no time resuming his lead role at Harlow Corp.

A private funeral will be held tomorrow in the Hamptons, but the question remains, will Adam be attending? Or is he really the cold-hearted business man we're led to believe?

———

The energy in the house changed the night before Liam's funeral. Anxiety over imminent goodbyes and resentment toward the man who hadn't returned had everyone on edge.

"Everything ready for tomorrow?" Josie asked, standing in my doorway.

I closed my laptop after going over my to-do list one last time. "Yes, I think it is."

"Good. Then, you can have dinner with us."

"Oh, it's okay. I'll grab something later."

"I'm not taking no for an answer. Max is preparing Gramps' favorite meal, and you don't want to upset Max, do you?"

"No, I don't want to do that. I'll see you down there."

Max had been an incredible help over the last week. He knew Liam better than most and assisted me with everything I needed. Although his loss was evident, he transferred his sorrow into action. He had the house immaculately cleaned, the beautiful gardens tended to, and the caterers well-versed on the requirements for the wake.

———

Silence fell over the dinner table when the distinct sound of the front door opening and closing traveled down the hallway. Wide-eyed gazes zigzagged around the table as footsteps approached then slowed outside the double doors.

Alerted to the new arrival, Max marched across the dining room and opened the doors to find Adam standing in the hall. "Mr. Harlow, just in time. I'll prepare a place for you at the table."

Adam moistened his dry lips. "Thank you, Max."

"So, you finally decided to show," Grayson grumbled as he shoved a large piece of steak into his mouth.

"There will be none of that, William." Caroline stood and kissed Adam's cheek. "We're all glad you're back."

Adam's eyes met mine over her shoulder, but I tore my gaze away. I was angry at his refusal to face his emotions and feared his impulse to run when life got hard. I couldn't have that in my life.

"Not everyone, it seems." He released his mother to shake his father's hand.

Grayson shook his head. "Well, it would've been nice if you'd stuck around to help me write the eulogy."

"I wrote my own."

Josie placed her hand on Grayson's arm as his fingers turned white around his cutlery. "Leave it," she whispered, dousing his flames.

Max seated Adam in the empty space beside me, but I couldn't bring myself to look at him. The room had filled with an unstable energy, and I was holding my breath, waiting for it to diffuse or erupt.

"I don't see the problem," Adam said, igniting the fire in his brother's eyes.

Grayson slammed his knife and fork down. "Are you kidding me? We talked about this. We agreed to write it together."

Josie rubbed her husband's back. "You should've told him, Adam."

"Well, I've been busy. Some of us have real businesses to run."

Grayson snarled. "Fuck you."

"Boys! That's enough!" Caroline yelled. "You both need to calm down. Your grandfather would be disgusted."

"Agreed." I was disappointed in both of them.

William sighed. "Now, tomorrow is a big day, with many family members and friends in attendance. You boys may not work together anymore, but you are still family. And, I dare say, that is more important."

Adam's and Grayson's mouths gaped as they turned to their father. "Are you drunk?" they asked in unison.

William chortled. "I've had a few, but it's about time I start making some changes around here." He rested his cutlery on his plate. "After my brother passed away, I tried to be everything for my parents. I thought my success would fill the void in our lives, but it was merely a distraction. I got so consumed I lost sight of the important things, and you boys suffered the consequences of that."

Caroline laid her hand on William's as he continued.

"It's taken me too long to realize my mistakes, but as my father said, 'It's never too late to make amends.' I know I've been hard on you, and it will take some repairing, but I want you to know that I support both of you and your choices…but I won't support you arguing the night before your grandfather's funeral."

Adam and Grayson grew quiet as they stared at their meals, clearly pondering their father's unbelievable words.

"Sorry, Dad," Grayson mumbled like a naughty schoolboy.

Adam cleared his throat. "Yeah, sorry."

"Now, let's enjoy this meal," William said with a melancholy smile. "Just as Dad intended."

———

"Will you all be joining us for a nightcap in the drawing room?" Caroline asked after we finished dessert.

"We'll come down once Harry's asleep," Josie said while Grayson nodded.

Adam turned my way, waiting for my answer.

"Thank you, Caroline, but I think I'll turn in early tonight."

Her eyes softened a fraction. "Of course. You must be exhausted. You've worked tirelessly all week." Her eyes flickered to Adam before frowning.

With a tight smile, I rose from the table. "I'll see you all in the morning." I thanked Max for the lovely meal and made my way out of the dining room and up the stairs.

"Wait," Adam called out once I reached the second floor.

I kept walking.

"Cassidy, wait."

"I'm tired, Adam." My shoulders sank as I turned around. "It's been a hard week."

"You don't think it's been hard for me?"

"I didn't say that."

"You're thinking it." He pursed his lips. "Just like everyone downstairs."

"You have no idea what I'm thinking."

He folded his arms. "Then tell me."

"Your family needed you this week," I hissed, releasing some of my pent-up fury.

Adam scoffed. "No, they didn't."

"Grayson especially."

"He has Josie. Dad has Mom."

I poked his chest. "And you had me."

He grabbed my hand and stepped closer, placing his arm on the wall behind me. "But you weren't going to let me through your goddamn door, and *that* is fucking torture."

"I said we could talk."

His blue eyes tore into my soul. "Touching you brings more peace than a million words."

"Sex isn't the answer to your grief," I rasped out as I melted under his stare.

"I know." He dropped his arm. "That's why I went home."

"What?" I gasped. "Because I refused to have sex with you?"

"I'm trying to uncomplicate things here, Cass." He rubbed his rigid jawline. "I know you want to be professional under this roof, and I respect that, but I also know myself. The thought of you across the hall, in that bed, alone...reading those fucking books..." His eyes grew dark. "I couldn't handle it."

"Adam..."

"And I've started seeing a grief counselor back home...so there are no blurred lines."

My head recoiled. "You have?"

"He even made me cry. Happy?"

My heart almost exploded. "Yes."

"Sadist."

"It's a good thing." Relief doused my distress. "Crying detoxifies the body, relieves stress, and lowers blood pressure. It's actually a highly evolved behavior."

"Are you saying I'm highly evolved?"

The corner of my mouth rose. "Maybe. But you're also a jerk. You need to apologize to Grayson."

Adam rubbed the back of his neck with a grimace. "Yeah, I know."

"He really needs his brother right now...and I think you do, too."

"I'll go have a drink with him," he uttered with a sigh. "We'll sort it out."

"Good." I stepped forward and pushed up on my tiptoes to kiss his cheek. "Goodnight, Adam."

He grasped my hand and ran his thumb over my knuckles. "Will you leave your door open tonight?"

"Adam..." I moaned, more annoyed at my work ethic than his impatience.

"Fine..."

A small smile crossed my face as I backed into my bedroom. "Thank you."

"But I'm fucking you senseless when this is all over."

My face burst into flames. "Oh my God, stop. Go see your brother." I pointed down the hallway. "Goodnight."

"Okay, okay." He shoved his hands into his pockets. "Night, Cass. I lo—" A blush crept up his neck as he cleared the frog in his throat. "I'll see you at sunrise."

His energy filled my heart. "You will."

———

I melted against the door as it closed behind me. How was I supposed to resist Adam now? He was actively helping himself and acknowledging his flaws, and damn, it was hot. The anger and resentment that burned inside him had settled to a simmer and had been replaced with passion and warmth. He was still heartbroken, but he was healing.

Although exhausted, I couldn't sleep. It was too late to call Finn, so I called Tash instead.

"Hey, hun, are you coping okay?"

"This one's hit me pretty hard, but I'll be fine. You know me."

"Just because you've been through a shitload of trauma, doesn't mean you're impervious to more. You need to look after yourself."

I sighed. "I know. I think I'll take a long break after this one."

"Good. I really don't know how you do it."

"It's exhausting, but worth it," I said, thinking about Liam's family reconnecting after years of conflict.

"That family doesn't deserve you."

I frowned. "Why would you say that?"

"Cass…" Her voice grew low. "Please tell me you're not sleeping with Adam again."

"You really don't like him, do you?" Tash had never been so quick to judge before. "He's really not as bad as the tabloids make him out to be."

Silence followed.

"Tash?"

"Look, I really didn't want to tell you this while you're still working there, but there's something about the Harlow family I think you should know."

"Go on…"

I could almost hear the grinding of her teeth. "Harlow Corp. was the company who bought the business Bryce and Dominic worked for. It was their decision to terminate Dom's job…and the reason you lost your health insurance."

"What?" I almost laughed. "No, they merged with Enviro-Tech."

"Which is a business owned by Harlow Corp. Bryce never thought to bring it up until he saw you with Adam at our party."

My blood ran cold. "Please tell me you're joking."

"I'm so sorry. I wish it wasn't true. You've been through enough."

Pain seared my heart. "So, they're responsible…"

"For leaving you dead broke and almost homeless. Yes."

"I…I can't believe it."

"They're a ruthless company, Cass. They make money by destroying livelihoods."

I covered my mouth as bile crept up my throat.

"But it's over now, isn't it? After the funeral, you can go home?"

"I said I'd stay on another two weeks."

"No, you need to get out of there before that man coaxes you into his bed again."

That man. Adam. *My Adam.* "I feel so…so…ashamed."

"Oh, baby. You didn't know."

"What would Dominic think?" A wave of nausea crashed over me. "And Finn?! Imagine if he found out."

"No one will blame you, Cass. Just get your ass back home where it belongs."

"I…I will." I barely recognized my trembling voice. "As soon as I can."

"Stay strong. I'm only a phone call away…and hopefully only a short drive once you move back here."

Once we ended the call, I crumbled onto the bed to stop the room from spinning. My heart pounded as my chest constricted until my churning stomach sent me running for the bathroom. The beautiful dinner Max had prepared spilled into the toilet as I surrendered to the irony of the situation. I'd helped the Harlow family through their turmoil, only to discover they were responsible for mine.

Chapter 37

Instead of watching the sunrise from the library, I arranged for the driver to take me to the beach. After the lost sleep and tears shed the night prior, I needed something to get me through the morning…and the ocean was calling.

Once I'd suffered a long swim in the bitterly cold water, I headed back to Harlow Manor to find it bustling with activity as the staff prepared for the wake.

"Hey," Adam called out as I passed the drawing room doors.

I slowed on the stairs and turned, using all my strength to block him out, but damn, he looked good in a suit. "Hey."

"You missed a pretty sunrise this morning."

"I, um…"—I could barely hold his gaze—"caught it at the beach."

"Did you go for a swim?" He touched the tips of my wet hair with a frown. "You must be freezing."

"Yeah." I rubbed my goosebump-covered arms. "And I really need to take a shower to warm up."

"Okay…" He clearly sensed something but pushed it aside. "We're leaving in an hour if you want to go to the service together."

"It's okay. I'll get a ride with Max."

"Are you sure?" he asked, searching my eyes.

"100%." I rose another step.

"Then, I guess I'll see you there."

With a quick nod, I rushed up the stairs and into my room, locking the door before entering the bathroom. As the warm water burned my ice-cold skin, I took refuge in the pain. I needed relief from the incessant ache in my heart that had persisted since my conversation with Tash. I'd betrayed Dominic and Finn, and I'd betrayed myself.

———

The funeral service was beautiful, just as Liam and I had planned. The eulogies were heartfelt, but Adam's was heartbreaking. It was obvious how much he loved and admired his grandfather, and his words were honest and unexpected.

Adam's gaze sought out mine in his closing sentence. "But most of all, I want to thank him for bringing happiness back into my life."

I closed my gleaming eyes and dropped my head, visualizing a wall between us. As long as he didn't touch me, I wouldn't crumble. I had to stay at a safe distance until I found the opportune moment to escape, then I could breathe.

Thankfully, the wake was full of distant family and old friends paying condolences, so Adam had no time to seek me out. I floated around the room, assisting Max, until the entire family became engrossed in a story from one of Liam's oldest friends, Alfie.

I took the opportunity to creep up the staircase and pack the rest of my things.

"What are you doing?"

My stomach plummeted. Adam wasn't supposed to notice I'd gone until well after the guests had left. "I'm packing."

The line deepened between his brows. "But you're supposed to stay another two weeks."

"I don't think that will be necessary anymore."

"But we need you here." He stepped into my room. "*I* need you here."

"You'll be fine." I zipped up my suitcase and placed it on the floor. "It's time for you to grieve as a family."

"You sound different...why do you sound different?" He tried to catch my gaze. "Did someone say something to you? Was it Staci? Because there's nothing going on between us, you know that."

"This has nothing to do with Staci." I tried to remain calm. "It's just time for me to go home."

"No."

His demanding tone irked me. "No?"

"No. You're not going." He lifted my suitcase and threw it back on the bed.

I yanked it off. "I have a life to get back to."

"A life?" he spat out. "You're not living. You're barely treading water. I can give you the life you deserve."

My lower lip trembled as I attempted to leave. "I don't want you to be my savior, Adam."

"I'm not trying to rescue you, Cassidy." He stepped in front of me until I almost collided with him. "I'm in love with you."

I fell back a step. "You don't mean that. You're grieving, and you're not thinking clearly."

His eyes never left mine. "My mind has never felt so clear."

"Well, mine isn't." The anger I was holding onto bubbled to the surface. "You've been clouding my judgment this whole time. With your looks and your charm…and your…your broody McBroodface. It was wrong of me to get involved with you. It was reckless and unprofessional…and it could never work."

Adam ran his hand through his hair. "Fuck, Cass, where's all this coming from?"

"Just let me go, Adam…"

"No." He followed me out into the hallway. "Not until you tell me what I've done."

I shook my head vigorously, fighting the burn of my tears. "It will only make it more true."

"What more true?"

"Excuse me, I have a car waiting."

"Cass!"

I glared into his wild blue eyes and aimed for his heart. "I can't love you, Adam. So, you have to let me go."

Before his pain could infiltrate my soul, I spun around and kept walking, only to flinch when the priceless vase that rested on the console between our rooms shattered all over the hallway wall.

<h1 style="text-align:center">Chapter 38</h1>

Three Weeks Later

"Come on, Mom," Finn cried out. "You can finish packing later. Coach said I need to be at the pool early."

"Alright, alright!" I placed down the tape dispenser and flattened my disheveled hair. "I'll go change."

The last three weeks had been chaotic. Between Finn's impending race and preparing for our move across the country, I had a lot on my plate. It was partially deliberate on my part. The busier I was, the better. I needed to keep Adam and his family far from my mind, so when Finn was offered a swimming scholarship on the West Coast after camp, I jumped into action. The only thing holding us back now was his swimming final.

Thankfully, Tash and Bryce had offered us a room at their house, which gave us time to look for a place instead of renting something, sight unseen. Since leaving Harlow Manor earlier than planned, we had less money to play with, so our rental price range had to be adjusted. We could still afford a small house with a backyard, but much to Finn's dismay, a pool was now out of the question.

———

As I handed Finn his backpack and towel and kissed his cheek in front of the swim center, a familiar sensation rolled over me.

Finn's eyes lit up when they diverted over my shoulder. "Adam!" he cried, bolting away.

I jerked upright and slowly turned to see my son squeezing Adam's waist.

He peered up at him in awe. "I knew you would come."

Adam's eyes flickered to mine before he crouched down. "I promised you, didn't I? Are you ready?"

"So ready! I learned so much at camp."

"Awesome. Did you practice that trick I showed you?"

Finn's grin grew as he nodded. "My coach was super impressed."

My anxiety grew as I watched the other families pile through the doors. "Finn, we've got to get in there. Your race is soon."

Finn's eyes rolled. "Now you're in a rush."

"Good luck, buddy." Adam gave him a fist-bump. "Not that you'll need it."

Once my son disappeared through the swim center doors, an uncomfortable silence fell between us.

"You didn't have to come," I said, finally meeting the eyes of the man I was supposed to hate.

"I told him I would."

I dropped my gaze to the ground. "Okay, well, we should get in there if we want to find a decent seat."

As Adam followed me inside and up into the stands, it was impossible to ignore the whispers around us. Moms ogled him from every direction, while others pulled out their camera phones. He was clearly more recognizable than I thought. If only I'd read more magazines before he had walked in that bar six months ago. I would've avoided a ton of heartache.

I hovered around a small gap in the bench, hoping Adam would find another seat, when he politely asked the lady beside us if she could make room. To my disappointment, she was more than happy to oblige and omitted a schoolgirl giggle when Adam smiled at her. I couldn't blame her, though. His grin was panty-dropping dynamite, and he knew it.

Squished together, I was forced to endure the smell of his aftershave while the pressure of his body against mine threw me back to a memory that was entirely inappropriate for a family event. I closed my eyes, drew a deep breath, and reminded myself why I was there. Finn. Watch Finn swim.

Finn waved from the warm-up area beside the pool, and I waved back, but his beaming smile was directed at the man beside me. He'd asked about Adam numerous times over the past three weeks, but I'd always changed the subject and pretended it was like any other job.

"He's happy you're here."

Adam kept his eyes on Finn as he prepared for his race. "Are you?"

"My feelings are irrelevant."

"Not to me," he uttered low enough to evade our neighbor's ears.

I clenched my jaw. "I'm here to watch my son race, Adam. Not talk."

He checked his watch. "We have a few minutes."

"Fine." My shoulders sank. He wasn't going to give up. "How's the family?"

"Managing."

"Did you spread Liam's ashes?"

"Yes, out to sea, as requested."

"In the ocean?!" My head whipped to his. "That's not what I instructed."

"I'm joking. He's under the elm with my grandmother and uncle."

"Fuck." I bumped his bicep. "That wasn't funny."

"It was a little."

I tried not to smile as I shook my head.

"Oh, he's getting up!" Adam grabbed my hand as he watched my son step up on the block.

"Do you have a bet on this race or something?" I asked when his anxiety surged through his touch.

"What? No." He scrunched up his nose. "I want him to do well. Even if he just beats his PB."

My eyebrows pulled together. "You know his PB?"

"Don't you?"

"Well, yes, but—"

"It's about to start," he interjected, refocusing on the race.

The blowing whistle stole my attention, and Finn was off. As he resurfaced meters into the pool, I sprang to my feet, screaming his name.

Adam tugged me down with a chuckle. "Stop embarrassing the poor kid."

"I'm sorry. I get so excited."

"Don't be sorry. I love hearing you scream."

I smacked his side as the ladies surrounding us gasped. "Come on, Finn," I whispered as my heart pounded against my rib cage. He was neck and neck with another boy.

"Come on, Finn!" Adam yelled, leaping out of his seat. "You've got this!"

I tried to tug him down, but when he wouldn't budge, I joined in to unleash all my competitive demons.

When Finn's hand grazed the end of the pool, Adam and I fist-pumped the air before throwing our arms around each other. Laughter escaped my mouth as he lifted me in the air, but when my lips hovered over his and his pounding chest vibrated through mine, my smile faded.

As if reading the caution in my eyes, Adam eased me back to the ground, and we both turned to find Finn beaming up at us, clearly witnessing our close encounter.

After Finn accepted his trophy and went off to change, Adam and I lingered outside the swim center.

"That was some race," Adam said, clearly feeling the need to fill the awkward silence with awkward conversation.

I searched my handbag for my car keys. "It sure was."

"Hey." He stepped closer. "Listen…"

"Finn!" I cried out as my son exited the building. He held up his trophy with pride, and my heart swelled. "Congratulations, baby." I hugged him tight.

"Congrats, bud." Adam patted his back. "I think we need to celebrate with some ice cream."

Finn's grin took on another level. "That sounds awesome! Can we, Mom?"

"We really need to get home and pack."

Adam's face fell. "Where are you going?"

"We're moving back home," Finn answered, blissfully unaware of the tension between us.

His gaze shifted to mine. "To LA?"

Finn nodded when I didn't respond. "We're going to live with Aunty Tash and Uncle Bryce until Mom finds a job, and then we'll buy our own house."

"Rent," I corrected.

Finn shrugged. "Whatever. As long as it's near my school."

"Which school?"

"Mom didn't tell you? I got a swimming scholarship to Summerhill."

Adam's eyebrows rose. "Summerhill, eh?"

"Mom says they have the best swim team on the entire West Coast."

"Did she?"

Heat crept up my neck. "Well, they must've upped their game in the last few years."

Adam let go of a deep, alluring chuckle. "Well, you'll fit in just fine, then."

"Okay, time to go." I took Finn's bag off his shoulder and placed it on mine.

"Mom, please!" Finn begged. "I want to go with Adam."

Adam rested his hand on my son's shoulder. "I can drop him home later."

"Please, Mom…"

"Fine." I grimaced. "You've got one hour."

"Thank you," Finn gushed out as he hugged me.

"I should probably get your new number." Adam pulled out his phone. "Just in case we get stuck in traffic or something."

"It's fine. Finn's got a phone now. He can call me if there's a problem."

Adam pressed his lips together as he shoved the phone back into his pocket. "Great. Okay, well…we'll see you later."

"One hour."

"One hour," the boys repeated.

As I attempted to open the car door with trembling hands, Adam and Finn sped out of the parking lot in Liam's Rolls. I should've been angry that Adam had shown up at my son's race, but there was something about his presence that lifted my spirit. My burning resentment for Harlow Corp. faded the second my son smiled up at Adam, and for a moment, I imagined how good our lives could've been together.

If only.

———

While I taped up another box in my bedroom, Finn's laughter burst through the front door.

"Mom, we're back!"

My eyes widened. Adam was supposed to drop him off, not come in.

Finn ran past me as I lugged the box up the hall. "Hey, where are you going so fast?"

"Bathroom!"

"Oh, okay." I continued to the front door where Adam stood talking to my father.

Dad motioned him inside. "Would you like to stay for a beer?"

I dumped the box on top of the others with a grunt. "I'm sure Adam has somewhere else to be, Dad."

Adam's eyes moved from mine, to the pile of boxes, then back to my father. "I don't, actually, so yes. I'd love one, Dean."

My eyebrows rose. They'd already introduced themselves. *Great.*

"Well, come on in. Cassidy hasn't had a friend over in years."

"That's because I grew up in LA, Dad." I didn't disguise the bitterness in my voice as I side-swiped Adam with my glare. "So I don't *have* any friends here."

"Yes, well, it's nice all the same," Dad muttered on his way to the kitchen.

"That was harsh," Adam whispered once my father was out of earshot.

"Since when do you care about other people's feelings?" I retorted before whirling around and storming back to my bedroom. I didn't have the time to argue with someone who knew nothing about my situation. Plus, the car wasn't going to pack itself.

"Finn hasn't stopped raving about that house in the Hamptons," I heard my father say after two beers fizzed open.

"It's definitely impressive. My grandparents cared for the property deeply."

"I'm very sorry to hear of your grandfather's passing. Cassidy was very fond of him."

My hands slowed as I taped up the last box.

"Thank you. She was very dear to him, too." His voice grew raspy. "It's been a tough time for everyone."

I gnashed my teeth, mentally trying to sever the connection between us. Even after three weeks apart, I could feel him. His energy sought me out and pulled me in, like that first night in the bar. I had to put distance between us—pronto.

"What sort of work do you do, Adam?"

Growing impatient listening to their casual conversation through the thin walls, I lifted the box and carried it down the hall.

"I manage a portfolio of media businesses," he said without too much thought, but it was a well-rehearsed lie.

"Actually…" I dumped the box next to the others. "Adam buys failing companies, callously strips them apart until they're making the most amount of money with the least amount of overheads, then either sells them or merges them, depending on what side of the bed he woke up on that morning."

Adam's mouth fell open. "That's not…completely true."

My brow rose as I stared him down.

"Sounds like you're a sharp shooter." Dad sipped his beer. "I like it."

With the roll of my eyes, I swiped my car keys off the kitchen counter.

"Where are you going?" Adam rested his beer on the coffee table as he stood.

"I'm packing the car," I grumbled before lifting the largest box into my arms.

He rushed to my side. "Here, let me help."

"It's okay. I've got it."

"You're really in a rush to get me out of here, aren't you?" He picked up another box and followed me outside.

I met his sparkling blue, make-me-forget-my-own-name eyes and popped the trunk. "You shouldn't be here," I said, sliding the box inside.

"Cass, I just want to tal—wait." He frowned at my car. "You're driving across the country in this?"

I pulled the box out of his hands and positioned it beside the other. "We don't all have private jets."

"This isn't safe."

I crossed my arms as my lips pursed. "It got us here. It will get us home."

"I'm not letting you drive this."

"You're not *letting* me?!" My eyes flared as I threw up my hands. "You're the reason I have to!"

Adam's brow furrowed. "I don't understand. How am I the rea—"

"When you takeover companies, do you *ever* give a second thought to the people you fire in the process? The people who lose everything just so you gain a few extra dollars in your pocket?"

"That's just business."

"It was our life!" I cried, fighting the rising tears. Adam reached out on impulse, but I recoiled. His touch would only make this harder. "My husband was one of those people."

"What?" Adam's face paled as his arm fell to his side. "Who did he work for?"

"Sunset Digital."

His shoulders plummeted as he pinched the bridge of his nose. "Fuck."

"He'd just started treatment, and instead of giving him the time off he needed, you laid him off. Your crappy health insurance policy ran out only a year later, and I've been drowning in debt ever since."

He ran both hands through his hair as he paced the gravel driveway. "That was one of the first companies I acquired. I was trying to prove myself to my father."

"You never even met with him. He was merely a figure on a chart to you."

"I'm so sorry, Cass." He gathered my hands into his. "You have to believe me."

I dropped my gaze. "The damage you caused my family is unforgivable. Had I known Harlow Corp. was responsible, I never would've worked for you. I never would've…"

"Then I'm glad we didn't know." He grasped my face to level our eyes. "Because you would've never given me a chance."

"There is no chance, Adam." Tears flooded my vision. "I betrayed Dominic. And Finn. I don't deserve any happiness with you."

"Tell me what I can do."

I shook my head as I stepped away. "There's nothing you can do to make this okay."

"Cass, please." Desperation radiated through his energy. "I need you in my life."

"And I need you to let me go." I turned back to the house, but his hand grabbed mine.

"I love you, Cassidy. Surely you know that by now." He moved my hand over his chest. "You must feel it."

I pulled my hand from his body to wipe away the cascading tears. "No matter how much my heart wants to believe that, I have to listen to my head right now. I need to focus on my future and Finn."

"I'll make this right," he said with fierce determination. "Whatever it takes. I promise you."

"Don't make promises you can't keep."

Anger flashed through his glistening gaze. "I don't."

"Adam?" Finn materialized out of nowhere, making us both flinch. "Are you going already?"

Adam knelt down in front of him as I cleaned up my tear-stricken face. "Yeah, buddy. I need to get back. There's a problem I need to fix at work."

"Will we see you in LA?"

Adam rested his hands on my son's shoulders. "I'm going to try my hardest to make that happen."

As Finn wrapped his arms around him, the sight tore my heart in two. Their bond was as natural as a father and son, and for a fleeting moment, I feared I was robbing him of a second chance. "Okay, Finn. Let Adam go. We've got a car to pack."

"Bye, Adam. Thanks for coming to watch my race today—even if you were more embarrassing than Mom."

"Yeah," he offered a sad chuckle. "I don't know where that came from."

I did. It came from love.

"It's okay." Finn's cheeks grew pink. He clearly adored the attention.

Adam's eyes floated to mine, but I redirected my gaze to my son. "Finn, can you get the last few boxes from your room while I see Adam to his car?"

"Sure thing, Mom," he said, as eager to get back to LA as I was. "Bye, Adam!" He threw up a wave before bouncing back into the house.

Adam drew a shaky breath as he stood. "Can you thank your dad for the beer for me?"

"I will."

With a gentle nod, he pivoted on the gravel and continued up the driveway, and my heart plummeted with each step.

"Oh." He came to a complete stop and patted down his pockets until he found what he was looking for. "Grampa wanted me to give you this. He had Max scribe us all letters in his final days." He held out an envelope as I drew closer. "Hopefully, yours offers some compensation for what my family has put you through."

I stared down at the envelope in his hand, but the dark glittering stones around his wrist stole my attention. "You're still wearing it," I said, unconsciously taking the envelope.

"Yeah." He tugged down his sleeve, blocking it from view. "I don't think it's working though."

"Oh." I lowered my gaze. "I'm sorry."

"Don't be." He continued to his car. "There isn't a crystal in existence that can protect my heart from you."

Chapter 39

Dear Cassidy,
When Josie told me about death doulas, I have to say, I thought she was joking. But as my time grew closer, and my anxiety got the better of me, I couldn't see any harm in it. The moment we met, I knew there was something special about you. You've helped me in ways a doctor never could. You gave me more time than I'd ever imagined possible after my diagnosis, and I've treasured every second of it. You have been a wonderful companion, a gifted healer and a savior for my family, and from the deepest part of my heart, I thank you.

I know you will refuse any bonus I offer, but I also know you want the best life for your son. I had my lawyer set up a trust for Finn, with enough money to attend any college of his choice. This amount will cover tuition, housing, materials and more than enough for return trips home for the both of you. Anything leftover, I'll leave to your discretion.

I only ask one thing in return. Give my grandson a chance. Just one. He needs you. You soften his edges and calm his soul. And I think you may need him, too.

All my love, Liam.

"Why are you crying, Mom?" Finn asked, stepping out the front door with another box. He immediately placed it on the patio and rushed over to the chair swing, like the beautiful, empathetic boy he was.

I wiped away my tears as I tucked Finn under my arm. "You know that nice man I worked for in that big house in the Hamptons?"

"Adam's grandfather?"

I nodded. "He left me a letter."

"What does it say?"

"Just that he thinks you're a special boy who deserves the world."

He scrunched up his nose. "Really?"

"Yep," I sobbed, unable to bottle my relief. "And I wholeheartedly agree."

———

After a restless night, the infuriating beep of a reversing truck had me storming through the house and out the front door in my pajamas. "What's going on?!" I asked my dad as he stood on the patio, watching the truck back down the driveway.

"Your friend arranged for a moving truck." He sipped his morning coffee. "And a tow."

My temper flared. "What?!" I attempted to march down the steps to demand they leave, but my father caught my arm.

"What are you doing, Cassidy? This is a generous offer. Your car won't make it to the state line."

"Then, how are we going to get there?"

"Adam arranged flights for you and Finn."

"What?" I spat out. "No. We can't accept it."

"Because of Dominic?"

"Yes!"

"Do you think he would want you driving across the country in that car? *With your son?*"

I swallowed back tears as I stared at my rusty old car with the tied down trunk. Dad was right. It was careless.

Dad's arm warmed my shoulders. "It's okay to accept help once in a while. It took me a long time to learn that after your mom passed."

I never thought I was anything like my father until that moment. When my mother died, he wouldn't accept any support, and I was left to pick up the pieces. I had to care for my sister because there was no one else. I made her meals, took her to school—everything my father was too drunk to do. His pride got in the way of our well-being, and perhaps mine was getting in the way of Finn's.

Dad squeezed my shoulder. "He's very remorseful."

My eyes bulged as I stepped back. "You spoke to him?"

"He called late last night to talk."

I squeezed my eyes shut. "Dad…"

"Look, I don't agree with what his family's company did, but it's clear as day that he cares deeply for you, Cass."

"He's the reason I'm in this mess, Dad."

"So, let him pull you out. He's desperate to fix things, and I know just how that feels."

"Fine," I grumbled. "I'll accept his help with the move, but once I'm back in LA, that's it. I need to move on with my life."

"Very well." My father peered down at me with welling eyes. "I'm so proud of you, Cass," he said, choking up as he wrapped his arms around me. "You have no idea how grateful I am that you've given me a second chance."

"Oh, Dad." I hugged him tight, pressing my ear to his beating heart. "We all have flaws. It's what we do once we recognize them that counts."

After a long overdue embrace, we silently observed the movers fill their truck with our belongings and hoist my little car onto a tow truck.

"So, when's our flight?"

"Adam said a car will collect you in a couple of days." Dad poured the remains of his coffee into his mouth. "Which is perfect because Amy and Reed are driving up tomorrow, and I know they'd love to see you before you go."

I winced. I was hoping to be gone before their next visit.

"Amy told me you've been avoiding her."

I sighed. "I didn't want to cause any problems between her and Josie. You know how close they are. I don't want her to feel like she has to take sides."

"Amy's got a good head on her shoulders, thanks to you. She can handle it."

"I suspect she already knows what's happened." She'd been calling every day since I returned. "Even if Josie hasn't told her."

"Well, we'll find out tomorrow. It will be lovely to have both my girls home again."

———

"Aunty Amy!" Finn cried out as he launched into her arms the moment she got out of Reed's Tesla.

My son loved Amy. Everyone did. People were drawn to her vitality, and for a long time, I'd resented her for it. She grew up a free spirit while I took on the responsibilities. I cared for her when our parents couldn't, but there was no one to care for me. It was no wonder I married the first boy who looked my way.

It's not that I regretted marrying Dominic, but I often wondered if we would still be together had he not been so cruelly taken away. We were so different in many ways yet bonded by the love of our child. Dom was content with the simple life, but I yearned for more. More love, more experiences, more everything.

"Cassidy!" Amy's smile lit up my heart as she ran over. "I'm so happy I got to see you before you left."

"Hey, sis." I hugged her while smiling at her boyfriend. "Hey, Reed."

"Hey, Cass." Reed gave Finn a high-five. "Hey, little man! Great game last night."

"I know! Did you post the vid?"

"Hell yeah, let's go inside, and I'll show you."

Amy grabbed my hand as we followed them into the house. "How are you, Cass?"

I forced a smile. "I'm fine."

She bumped my side. "It's me you're talking to, remember."

"I don't want to talk about the Harlows, okay?"

"Are you sure? Josie's been so worried about you."

"She shouldn't be."

"That's what I told her," Amy said proudly. "Everything will work out."

"You always say that, Ames."

"Well, that's because it's true."

"You always were the eternal optimist of the family."

"The future is so bright, Cass." She leaned into me with a dreamy smile. "I wish you could see what I can see."

"You could tell me…" I prayed for a life void of heartache and misfortune.

Amy giggled. "Now, where's the fun in that?"

———

Once we'd finishing devouring Dad's barbecue feast, we sat around the table, chatting about everything and nothing, until Amy's energy shifted.

She sheepishly glanced my way. "So, Reed and I have some news."

Reed placed his beer on the table and wrapped his arm around my sister. "I asked Ames to marry me."

"And I said yes!" Amy whipped out her hand, sporting a huge pink diamond. "Can you believe it?!"

The bittersweet memory of Dominic's proposal floated past, but I brushed it away. Amy deserved her moment. "Congratulations, guys!" I hugged them both. "Did you manage to surprise her?" I asked Reed while Amy showed her beautiful ring to Dad and Finn.

"Of course he did," Amy uttered with a familiar glint in her eye. I knew that look.

Dad launched out of his chair to find some champagne. "I'll have to buy a new suit."

"There's no rush." Amy squeezed Reed's hand. "We've decided not to set a date until we get back."

"Wait. Where are you going?" I asked, more confused than ever.

"My *fiancé* is going on tour through Europe, and I've decided to join him. We'll be gone for a year."

My jaw dropped. "That's awesome! It's about time one of us started seeing the world," I said, so proud of my little sister.

"Oh, you're not far off."

I made a face. "Yeah, right."

Reed turned to Amy. "Didn't you say we'd see Cass in—"

"Reed." Amy whacked his arm as she rose. "Can you help me with dessert?"

"Um…sure." He shot up and trailed after her before enduring an inaudible scolding in the kitchen.

I shook my head with a chuckle, not having a clue to what was going on. "Reed's going to have his hands full with your Aunty," I said to Finn, who'd grown unusually quiet. "Hey, you okay?"

He stared down at his plate. "Everything's changing."

I reached for his hand. "I know, but it's all for the better this time, I promise. Aunty Amy won't be gone forever, and I'm sure Uncle Reed will play with you online from wherever he is in the world. Just like before."

"And Adam?" He lifted his glistening eyes to mine. "When will I see him again?"

My stomach dropped. "We're going to be so busy when we get back to LA, it may take some time to see everyone."

Finn's bottom lip quivered.

"Is everything okay?" Amy asked as they all returned from the kitchen.

"I think I'll take Finn to bed." I motioned my son to follow. "Looks like the last few days have caught up with him."

He wiped away his tears as he stood. "Goodnight, everyone," he mumbled on his way out.

Once Finn brushed his teeth, I guided him into his bedroom where he threw off his clothes and climbed into bed. "Why do you hate Adam?" he asked with eyes swirling with emotion. "He's always been so nice to us."

My jaw slackened as I sat beside him. "I never said I hated him."

"You don't have to. I can feel it."

"Oh…" I closed my eyes, wishing he didn't have to bear the burden of my gift. "What you're feeling isn't hate, Finn. It's anger."

"What did he do?"

My mouth opened a few times before I could formulate the right words. "His company made a decision a long time ago that made our lives a lot harder than they needed to be."

"Is he sorry?"

The devastation in Adam's eyes when I told him about Dominic's health insurance was seared into my memory. "Yes, I believe so."

"So, you forgive him."

The knot in my stomach tightened. "It's not that simple."

"You always told me if someone is truly sorry for their actions, you should forgive them."

"I said that?"

"You meant it, too."

I lay down beside him. "I guess I need a little time and space to cool off."

"Like when I used the blender without permission and forgot to put the lid on?"

Laughter burst from my lips. "Oh, I remember that mess."

"I've never forgotten to put the lid on since, though, have I?"

"No, you haven't."

"Maybe Adam won't make the same mistake, either."

All the air released from my lungs as I stared at the ceiling. "How did you get so smart, Finn Ryan?"

"Dad's genes, I guess…"

"Oh, no, you didn't!" I flipped over to tickle his ribs.

"Okay, okay!" he cried out. "I got it from my momma!"

"That's better." I gazed down into his twinkling green eyes. "I love you, Finn."

"I love you, too, Mom."

I kissed his forehead and turned off his bedside light. "Sweet dreams, my boy. Our new life begins tomorrow."

"Mom," Finn's tiny voice floated through the darkness.

"Yeah?"

"Adam really likes you."

I froze in the doorway. "He told you that?"

"No." He yawned. "He didn't have to."

Chapter 40

Our overnight, first-class flight to Los Angeles was an unexpected turn of events. We would've been in Albuquerque by now, had my car made it, with approximately 800 miles left to drive. But instead, we were stretched out, drinking hot cocoa, and watching a movie, while our car and possessions were transported by road.

It was absurd, but necessary. Adam was right. My car wasn't safe. But what choice did I have? Two tickets on commercial flights would've blown my budget and set me back a month's rent. I had to make every cent count now.

Once we arrived, another car was waiting to take us to Tash and Bryce's house. Adam's driver greeted us with a smile before piling our suitcases into the trunk. "Mr. Harlow instructed me to give you this." He handed me a business card. "I will be your personal driver while your car is being repaired."

"Repaired?"

"Adam had your car assessed on arrival, and the mechanic found an issue."

"Oh."

Finn sniggered. "Just one?"

I narrowed my eyes at my son.

"It should only take a week or so," the driver continued. "Meanwhile, call or text my number and I'll take you wherever you need to go."

"I'm sure I can handle a week with no car."

"Mom! How are you going to get me to school?"

"Um…bus?"

"To Summerhill?!"

The driver chuckled. "You're going to want me to drive you there. That's a tough crowd."

"Please, Mom."

"Okay, fine. But school only."

With a gigantic smile, Finn jumped into the car while I cursed under my breath. This must've been how Cinderella felt as the clock approached midnight. These luxuries weren't going to last, and the impending slap of reality was going to hurt.

———

Tash, Bryce, and Tristan welcomed us into their home moments before our moving truck arrived with our belongings. Luckily, we didn't own much, so we were able to store everything in their garage. I promised them it was a temporary measure, and I meant it. I refused to be a burden, and my first step toward that goal was finding a job.

Once settled, I set to work immediately. All of the jobs I applied for didn't involve my unique skillset, but I wasn't in the position to be picky. Death doulas weren't the most advertised position, so I'd have to fall back into waitressing while I waited for the word to spread around.

While I stewed on my job prospects, I searched for houses close to Tash and Bryce. With my car in God knew what state, I didn't want to be too far from family or Finn's school in case we had to rely on buses. It wasn't ideal, but the thought of having to buy a new car made me nauseated.

"You look stressed," Tash said as she returned from the kitchen.

"Maybe we shouldn't have come back here." I closed my laptop with a sigh. I was hoping there'd be more rentals on the market in the new year, but I was wrong.

Tash handed me a coffee mug and curled up on the couch opposite. "It will be fine, Cass. You can stay here as long as you need."

"Are you sure about that? You're about to pop out another human, and Bryce doesn't seem all that happy we're here."

"Oh, sugar. That has nothing to do with you."

"Are you sure? He's giving off some cranky vibes."

"Things have been tense at work. They're making a big announcement today, and well, you know how they play out."

My stomach roiled. Those 'announcements' often led to job loss. "I'm sure Bryce will be fine," I said with little confidence. Anything was possible under the reign of Harlow Corp.

"We'll deal with whatever comes our way." She rested her hand over her ever-growing bump. "We always do."

"You're so lucky to have each other."

"Oh, Cass, I didn't mean to rub our relationship in your face."

"Oh, you're not." I never wanted her to feel that way. "You give me something to aspire to."

"Well, I have a long list of suitors." She grinned. "Once you're ready, that is."

"Tash…"

"You said once you get back, you're going to make a go of it."

"I know…but…" The ache in my heart deepened.

Tash grew quiet as she placed her coffee on the table between us. "You still have feelings for a certain drop-dead gorgeous billionaire?"

I stared at her, wanting to lie. "Is it terrible to say yes?"

"Oh, Cass…" Her brown eyes softened. "Of course not. He's a drop-dead gorgeous billionaire!"

"Adam's more than that, though…"

Tash exhaled as she turned away.

"I know, I know," I uttered, acknowledging her clear disappointment. "He's just done so much for us in the last few days, and it's messing with my head."

"That's because you're not used to someone looking after you. Don't let his guilt cloud your judgment."

I blew over my hot coffee as I pondered her words. "Do you think that's the only reason he's helping me? Guilt?"

Tash shrugged. "Your intuition is better than mine. What do you think?"

I reopened my laptop with a groan. "I have too much on my plate to think."

"Well, once everything settles down, I'll find someone to take you out and show you a good time without all that glitz and glamour."

"It was never abo—" I stopped myself. There was no point arguing. Tash's mind was made up about Adam. "Okay, that sounds nice."

"Good, because I promised Dom I'd help you find someone."

My brow furrowed. "You did?"

"He wanted you and Finn to lead a full life, and if it wasn't going to be with him, he wanted it to be with someone worthy. Someone willing to move mountains and love you both unconditionally." Her lips quirked upward. "And I take my promises very seriously."

My eyes flooded with tears as I chuckled. "If he gets your approval, I trust he's amazing." But it wouldn't be Adam, and I knew, deep down, no other man could compete. And it was a lonely thought.

While Tash washed our mugs and I proceeded to apply for another job, the lyrics of "Whatta Man" by Salt-N-Pepa blasted from Tash's cell. "Finally," she cried out as she launched for the phone and greeted her husband.

After a moment of silence, Tash's energy brightened the entire room. "Are you kidding? That's unbelievable." She rubbed her belly as it bounced around with her laughter. "I can't believe it."

"Did he get a promotion?" I whispered, desperate to know what was so exciting.

Tash smiled at me. "Can you send me the link? I need to show Cass."

Once she hung up the phone, I closed my laptop and walked into the kitchen. "What's going on? Bryce obviously didn't lose his job."

She lifted her hand over her gaped mouth as she read her phone. "Oh, Cass." Tears filled her eyes. "Whatever I said, I take it back."

I pried the cell phone out of her hand. "What are you talking about?"

Tash's screen displayed a news article, published only fifteen minutes ago.

Adam Harlow, owner of Harlow Corp., has issued a statement today to their companies, that all employees, regardless of job hierarchy, will have access to premium health care.

The insurance policy contains unique clauses that are so generous it has made Harlow Corp. America's most desirable place to work. Breaking their ruthless reputation—and surely the bank—this is the first time a company of this magnitude has modified their health care for the better, and it has other companies watching closely.

Has Adam Harlow made a costly mistake? Or has he singlehandledly changed the perception of one of America's most powerful families? Perhaps his legacy will be the return of the heart and soul of Harlow Corp., previously instilled by his grandfather, the late William Harlow II, who passed away peacefully last month.

The pounding of my heart amplified with every written word. "Oh, my God."

"He did this for you," Tash whispered over my shoulder.

I could barely breathe as I endeavored to reread the news that was going to change so many lives, including Tash and Bryce's. With another child on the way, they'd been worried about their finances, so it couldn't have come at a better time.

"This will cost Harlow Corp. billions," she gushed.

"I know." Tears filled my eyes. *He was moving mountains.*

"I'm so sorry, Cass." She placed her hand on my shoulder. "I think I was wrong about him."

"It's okay," I uttered breathlessly. "I think I was, too."

———

After the news broke, Bryce came home early to celebrate. Watching their relief play out side by side was beautiful, but I didn't know what this meant for Adam and me. His fight for redemption was evident, but could I really forgive him for the years of hardship I'd had to endure?

"I don't know what you said to Adam Harlow, but thank you, Cass." Bryce tucked his wife under his arm. "This is huge for us."

"I didn't say anything." I spun my ring around my finger, wondering how Dominic would feel about all this.

"Oh." Bryce's brow furrowed. "I assumed that's why they added the Dominic Ryan Clause."

My head shot up. "The Dominic Ryan Clause?"

Bryce opened the booklet he'd brought home and read it out loud.

"If your job is terminated while you're receiving treatment for any life-threatening disease or illness, your health insurance will remain in place for the duration of your care."

A sob burst from my mouth as I dropped onto the chair.

"Cass..." Tash's arms were around me in an instant. "Breathe, girl."

"Why would he do that?"

She wiped away the tear tracking down my cheek. "I think you know why. The question is, do you feel the same way?"

I closed my eyes as I nodded. "I do."

"Then, maybe it's time you tell him."

"But Finn's due home soon, and I..."

"I think we can handle Finn. Go call that driver and get your ass over to Harlow Corp."

I lunged for my handbag and kissed her cheek. "Thanks, Tash."

———

Once I arrived at Harlow Corp., I marched into the foyer, full of confidence, until a wave of power suits had me shifting to the outer walls. Their energy was intense. Determination, dedication, and stress were only a handful of emotions I picked up on my ninja-walk to the reception desk.

"May I help you?" the receptionist uttered without looking up.

I tilted my gaze to capture her attention and smiled when she impatiently lifted her eyes from the computer screen. "Hi, I was hoping to speak to Adam Harlow."

Her eyebrows rose in amusement. "Do you have an appointment?"

"Well...no."

She sniggered. "I didn't think so."

"Can I make one?"

"If he requests it."

I winced. "But I don't have his number."

"I've heard that before."

My confidence wavered. "Can you just let him know Cassidy Ryan is here? It's important."

The receptionist rolled her eyes as she adjusted her mouthpiece. "Leanne, I have a woman at the front desk wanting to speak to Mr. Harlow. Her name is Cassidy Ryan." There was a short pause. "Oh…really? She's on the list?" Her mouth fell open. "Oh, okay. I will." She ended the call and pushed the buzzer beside her desk. "Go right up," she said sheepishly. "Top floor."

The elevator ride was agonizingly long, but at least I had fifteen floors to think about what I was going to say.

Another receptionist narrowed her eyes as I stepped out. "You must be Ms. Ryan."

"Yes."

"Mr. Harlow is in a meeting right now, but you can wait in his office."

"Oh, ok." I scanned the foyer. "And where is that, exactly?"

"Through that door and straight down the hall. It's next to the meeting room. You can't miss it."

"Thanks." I offered her a small smile before attempting to follow her directions.

Once I stepped into the hallway, my footsteps slowed immediately. The walls were made entirely of glass. Beyond the open-plan lounge overlooking the city skyline laid two rooms. To one side, an enormous office, and to the other, a meeting room. One was empty, and one not—at all.

Adam stood in front of a large screen filled with figures and tables, addressing a room full of his colleagues. The entire boardroom table was engrossed in every word until he stopped mid-sentence.

His eyes struck mine as I fell back a step, followed by everyone else who'd turned to see what had stolen their boss's attention.

"Wait," he mouthed as if sensing my urge to flee.

Adam held up his hand as I edged closer to the exit, but my unplanned escape was futile. He was already pacing across the room. A shiver rolled over my body as he stepped into the hallway, and when our eyes met, my breath caught.

"Don't you dare run." Adam took cautious steps toward me.

"But you're in a meeting." I glanced at our curious onlookers. "I'll come back later."

"They can wait." He motioned to the room across the hall. "We can talk in my office. The glass is soundproof."

Adam's authoritative tone had my heart racing and body complying on impact. "Okay," I muttered, quickening my steps past his all-consuming presence and into his office.

As he shut the door behind him, I lowered my gaze, wanting to say what I needed to before losing myself in his aura. "I, um… just wanted to say thank you…in person."

"For what?"

I ran my hand over his immaculate desk, void of anything personal. "For your announcement today."

"Only five years too late."

My head snapped up. "It's never too late. You've changed so many lives today."

Emotion churned within his oceanic eyes. "Not yours."

"Had you done this five years ago, I may have been financially better off, but Dom would still be gone…and I…" My words faded as my emotions caught up.

"And what?"

I blinked back tears as I succumbed to my soul. "And I never would've fallen in love with you."

Adam stepped closer, never breaking eye contact. "You mean that?" He narrowed his gaze before a familiar twinkle emerged within his irises. "Or are you using me as some sort of distraction?"

I turned up my chin. "Look, if you don't want me, it's fi—"

"Are you fucking kidding me?" Adam's hand slid around my nape, pulling me toward him. "Of course I want you." He peered down at me with an insufferable hunger. "I haven't stopped since our first night together in New York."

I reached up and ran my hand down his jawline. "I haven't stopped wanting you either."

Adam pressed his forehead to mine. "You're a part of me, Cass. And as much as I've tried, I can't shake this feeling that we're meant to be together. That we're connected on some higher level…spiritual, even."

I blew out a shaky breath, knowing exactly how he felt. "I didn't think you believed in all that hippy shit."

"I don't." He cupped my face. "But I believe in us." My knees grew weak under his penetrating gaze. His energy aligned with every word.

"God, I want to kiss you right now."

He stepped back with a tapered gaze. "And why can't you?"

A giggle floated from my lips as I peered over his shoulder. "Because I feel like a zoo attraction in here."

"Oh." He shifted his body to block the view of his curious colleagues. "Well, that's because you're the most beautiful creature in the room—and also the most dangerous."

"Like a blue-ringed octopus?"

He chuckled. "Only when they're about to strike."

"And what's my poison?"

His eyes drank every curve of my body until he reached my face. "Your smile."

Said smile grew.

He grasped at his chest with a grimace. "Don't."

"Adam…" Fire surged into my cheeks as I peeked back at the swooning women and amused men sitting around the boardroom table, watching on. "You're making a scene."

His entire aura lit up with his smile. "A sappy, romantic scene? Or more of a rom-com scene?"

"Well, I guess that depends on what happens next."

Electricity filled the room as Adam's eyes locked onto my lips, but the moment he stepped forward, his foot collided with a wastepaper basket, scattering trash all over the office floor with a loud clash.

I covered my mouth as laughter spilled out. "Rom-com it is."

His sparkling eyes lifted to mine. "Fuck it." He slipped his hand around the small of my back and yanked my body against his. "I'll save the sappy stuff for later." As he encased my nape, he brought his lips to my smile and devoured what belonged to him.

The intensity of his kiss was like no other. With Adam's heart, body, and soul in sync, his energy radiated through my being, and it was fucking incredible. Every hair stood on end, every nerve tingled, and I forced myself to pull away before I moaned for more.

"That was some kiss," I puffed out, completely out of breath.

Adam curled my hair behind my ear. "I've been doing my research."

"Oh yeah?" I laughed. "What romance novel has your attention now?"

"The most romantic...*and erotic* one yet." He brushed his lips over mine. "And this is only page one."

Epilogue

Adam

"I thought I'd find you hiding out here."

Cassidy opened her gorgeous emerald eyes and turned my way with a sleepy smile. "You know how I get at weddings."

I sauntered over to the bench seat under the majestic elm and fell into the empty space beside her. "All this happiness must be exhausting," I said, wrapping my arm around her tiny frame swamped in silk and my old Lakers hoodie.

She nudged my side with a smirk. "It is. And it's worse because it's all directed at us."

My chest bounced up and down with my laugh. "I told you we should've eloped."

"I know, but I wanted Finn to be a part of this—and our families. And this place." She smiled up at Harlow Manor, then at the earth surrounding her bare feet. "This is where it all began."

"Not exactly." I nuzzled into the crook of her neck.

She giggled adorably as I nibbled. "Well, it's the story we're telling the kids, okay?"

A soft chuckle left my lips. *Kids.* I had never dreamed of having a family of my own. For years, I'd been content with living the bachelor life while my brother tackled the pressures of marriage. I never wanted more. I never needed more. My life was Harlow Corp., and damned if I was going to let anyone break my focus...until Cassidy. She shattered it to pieces.

With the intensity of my work, I didn't have time to nurture a relationship, nor deal with another person's expectations. Between my father, mother, brother, and a fuckload of employees...I was drowning. The only way I coped was to lose what mattered most—my compassion. Just like my dad.

It wasn't until Grayson met Josie that something shifted inside. I grew to envy the love they shared, and when they had that damn baby...fuck, I was a goner. I tried to fight it. I tried to ignore what my soul craved, but the universe had other plans. When I walked into that bar, hours after Harrison's birth, to succumb to whiskey and unavailable women, I saw her. The perfect distraction from my fucked-up life.

Green eyes, green dress, gorgeous legs...and the most impressive set of tits I'd ever seen. The best part? She was married...or so I thought. My dick was homing in on her before I'd finished my first drink.

What I didn't expect was how incredible the sex would be. Unforgettable, mind-blowing, life-changing sex. Our connection was more than physical, and I think our souls knew it before we did. Her body against mine was like fucking poetry, and when I found my bed empty the next morning, I was equally angry and relieved, because I wanted more. I never wanted more.

Cassidy's back straightened as she turned to me. "You *do* still want kids, don't you?"

"Of course. I know you and Finn are a package deal."

"No...I mean...*more*."

"Well, yeah..." I kissed her soft cheek. "You know I do."

The corners of Cassidy's mouth curved as she mused.

"Actually..." I curled my fingers around her hand and ran my thumb over the engagement ring that once belonged to my grandmother. "That's kind of what I wanted to talk to you about."

She peered up at me curiously.

"When Finn and I were getting ready this morning, he asked me a question." I swallowed back the nerves that had plagued me all day. "But I said I'd have to ask you first."

"Oh?"

"He wanted to know..."—I drew in a deep breath before clearing my throat—"if he could call me *Dad*."

Cassidy's body stiffened. "He did?"

"It's okay if you don't want him to. If you're not comfortable, or you think it's disrespectful, I totally understand."

"Do *you* want him to call you Dad?" she asked, raising her hand to my pounding chest.

"Yeah..." I blinked away the mist clouding my eyes. "I really do."

Cassidy's mouth parted while she drank in my aura. "Wow," she breathed out before rising to her feet. "I mean...you may as well start getting used to the name."

Just as relief and elation settled over me, I froze. Surely she didn't mean...

"I'm going for a dip in the pool," she said before wandering off into the darkness.

"Wait. What do you mean by that?" I called after her.

"A swim, silly." She pulled off my hoodie and threw it back to me.

"That's not what I'm talking abo—" The silk of her wedding gown dragging along the ground, drew my eyes up to the sexy sway of her hips, and I almost lost my train of thought. "Cassidy!"

A small smile played on her lips as she quickened her steps to the glowing swimming pool.

"What are you doing?"

I'd almost caught up when she pushed the straps of her wedding dress off her shoulders and let the material fall to the ground.

"Holy shit, Cass." I peered back at the house. "The guests are still here."

"And they're inside, having the time of their lives. And besides, it's not like I'm naked."

"Yet," I murmured with a familiar twinge below. She looked goddamn radiant in the moonlight. Her silk camisole traced every curve, and I knew, once she hit that water, it would stick to her like Cling Wrap. The mere thought had me readjusting my suit pants.

She was never this wild before me. She had too much responsibility, too many worries, and a lifetime of trauma to truly enjoy life. Knowing I was partially to blame for that, I'd made it my life's mission to take away the weight that smothered her soul. She deserved so much more, and I was going to give it to her.

With a light jog, I caught up, grasping her hand as she dangled her toes in the pool. "What are you not telling me right now?" I ran my hand down her waist, pausing above her hip as my heartbeat accelerated. "Are you…?"

She ran her tongue over her lip before biting it. "Yes."

My arms dropped to my sides, and Cassidy dove into the water, barely making a splash.

I slowly rotated to the pool, completely speechless. "You're pregnant?" I asked in a whisper once her head bobbed out of the water.

Her eyes twinkled under the moonlight. "I am."

As my heart threatened to burst and tears flooded my eyes, I tore off my shoes and shirt and dove into the water. I scooped her up and pressed my lips to hers as we broke the surface.

She cackled deliriously. "So, you're happy, then?"

"Are you kidding?" My head fell heavenward. "I'm ecstatic." I lowered my hands to her stomach, still stunned. "How far along are you?"

"The doc says eight weeks."

"Eight weeks?! And you're only telling me now?"

"I only took the test a few days ago," she retorted with a kiss to my lips. "I've been so busy volunteering at the nursing home and planning all of this that I didn't realize I'd missed my period until I was packing for our honeymoon. Up until yesterday, I was still convinced the initial pregnancy test was wrong."

"What happened yesterday?"

"The doc wanted me to have a sonogram before we left for the Maldives—to make sure everything was okay."

Fear trickled down my spine. There was so much I didn't know, so much I didn't have control over. "And is it? Are you okay? And the baby?"

Warmth radiated from her smile. "Everything is perfect."

"I would've come with you."

"I know." She sighed. "But with everything going on with

your work in preparation for your sabbatical, I didn't want you under any more pressure, especially if it was a false positive."

"Babe, if it has to do with you and our family, I want to know."

"I didn't want to freak you out."

"Freak out? I'm over the fucking moon, Cassidy. I've just become a husband and a dad…and now you're telling me we're having a baby?"

"See…" She poked my chest. "You're freaking out."

I grabbed her hand and pulled her close. "I promise you, I'm not. I may be a little overwhelmed, but I'm not freaking out. I want this, Cassidy. I want everything with you."

She ran the back of her fingers down my cheek. "I'm glad I'm not the only one dealing with all these emotions right now. Isn't it exhausting?"

"Is that why you jumped into the pool?" I pressed my hand into the small of her back so our bodies wouldn't drift apart. "To recharge?"

"These days…" She hooked her arms around my neck until her glorious breasts pressed up against my chest. "I only have to look into your eyes to regain my strength."

As I gazed down at her, I couldn't believe this girl existed. Never in a million years could I have dreamt her up. Beautiful inside and out, intelligent, empathetic, spiritual, and a fucking gift to mankind. I didn't deserve someone like her, but fuck, I'd never stop trying.

I barely let a month slip by before I popped the question on our private beach in Malibu, just like I promised Gramps. It was her 30th birthday, and with Finn's and her father's eager blessing, I dropped to one knee and bared my soul. She was hesitant at first, telling me it was too soon, but once she spied her son nodding encouragingly from his bedroom window, she burst into tears and threw her arms around me with a definite yes. It was the happiest day of my life…until now.

I pressed my forehead to hers. "I fucking love you, Cassidy Harlow-Ryan."

"I fucking love you, too."

As her wanting eyes begged for connection, I slammed my lips down to hers, fulfilling my desire to kiss her senseless on our wedding day. I agreed to keep it kid-friendly for the ceremony and reception, but now that I had her all to myself, she was in trouble.

"Are you sure no one can see us out here?" I murmured over her lips.

"You can't wait until tonight?"

"Oh, I can wait." I kissed the tip of her nose as my hand slid up her thigh. "But can you?"

"Adam," she gasped, glancing back to the house.

"I'll keep it all under the water." I grazed her wet panties. "Just in case." Her breath hitched as I rubbed in a circular motion. "Just concentrate on me."

"Adam…" she sighed out in submission. I fucking loved it when she did that.

I increased the pressure. "Let me take care of you."

Once Cassidy's resistance wavered, she closed her eyes and welcomed my hand into her underwear. As a seductive moan exited her mouth, I slipped in my tongue while my finger mirrored the action below. Her hips rocked over my hand as I deepened the kiss, and I grew hard imagining how good she was going to feel wrapped around my cock.

"Oh God." She clawed my shoulders as she shuddered all over my hand.

"Easy, Tiger." I rubbed her swollen lips before returning my hands to the safety of the surface. "We've still got the entire night."

"And the honeymoon," she uttered in a dreamy haze as she sank deeper into the water.

"You won't be leaving our bed on our honeymoon."

"But I can't ignore those turquoise waters." Her playful pout drove me wild.

"Fine…" I poked my tongue against the wall of my cheek. "But if you're not swimming in the ocean, I'll be fucking you in it."

"Oh!" She cackled with laughter. "I like the sound of that."

"You know what I like the sound of?" I dragged her back. "You coming all over my coc—Hey, buddy!" Thank fuck I spied Finn walking toward the pool before he overheard our dirty banter.

"What are you guys doing out here?" he asked, completely dumbfounded as to why we were in the pool.

"We decided to take the party outside," Cassidy said, wading in front of me while I readjusted my *situation*. We'd been caught in compromising positions numerous times over the past few months, so we were well-versed in restoring nonchalance.

"But it's freezing."

"Not in here." She splashed some water his way. "Care to join us?"

Finn's eyes lit up. "Would I ever!" he cried out before taking two large steps backward.

We held up our hands, yelling at Finn to shed some layers, but he was already bolting toward us. With a flying leap, he tucked up his legs and bombed into the pool.

Cass wrapped her arms around Finn as soon as he surfaced and spun him around while I sank back into the water, content with my family. I peered up at the stars, searching for the brightest, the one Cassidy spoke to often.

"Did you see that?!" Finn appeared by my side when a star sliced through the sky.

Its timing caught my breath. "Yeah," I blinked twice before finding my feet. "I hope you made a wish."

"I did." Finn took my hand and smiled up at me. "Did you?"

I wrapped my arms around him and scuffed up his hair. "I don't have to, buddy. I already have everything I need."

"You never said this was a pool party!" my brother's voice called out as he crossed the lawn.

Melanie marched to the edge of the pool and placed her hands on her hips. "I would've brought my bathing suit."

Scott chuckled. "Well, that's clearly optional," he said, rocking their stroller from side to side as he spied our drenched clothes.

Josie appeared with her camera. "Please tell me you're decent under there. I'm not photoshopping that shit out."

"And I thought I was the reckless sister," Amy called out from the comfort of Reed's back. She'd been dancing all night, and her feet had clearly had enough.

Tash sniggered. "I think Cass is giving you a run for your money, Ames."

"Speaking of races…" Grayson crossed his arms. "You two still need a tie-breaker."

My gaze snapped to Cassidy, then her stomach. "Definitely not."

Finn squealed. "Yes, you have to!"

"No." My eyes pleaded with my wife, but she gave me nothing. "I'm not racing you, not in your condition."

"What condition?" Tash narrowed her eyes.

Cassidy chewed her bottom lip as she peered up at her best friend. "I'm…um…"

"She's been drinking!" Amy interjected, climbing off Reed to dip her feet in the pool.

"Then, I'll go as tribute." Finn jumped out of the pool. "Come on, Dad!"

My breath caught while my heart almost burst with happiness. The eleven-year-old almost brought me to my knees with one word. "Fine." I pretended not to notice. "What do I get if I win?"

"Your balls back!" Josie shouted, and everyone laughed.

I narrowed my eyes at my sister-in-law as I climbed out of the pool. "Ha-ha."

"I'll return your Laker's sweatshirt," Cassidy said with a grin.

I pursed my lips as I panned my gaze from my wife to my son. "And what do you want?"

"Easy!" He smiled. "A baby brother or sister."

Everyone cackled again.

"I'd pay to see that," Grayson said, checking the baby monitor for the fifth time.

My gaze panned to Cassidy's twinkling eyes, and with her wink, the decision was made. "It's a deal." I moved to the edge of the pool.

Finn's eyes enlarged as he turned to the water. "Okay, then…"

As Grayson yelled go, Finn dove into the water flawlessly, while I hung back.

"What are you doing?" my brother hissed, motioning for me to go.

With a shrug, I dove in and pelted through the water. As Finn's arm reached out for the finish line, I pulled up next to Cassidy to watch our boy win.

I bumped her side. "Everyone's going to know."

She wrapped her arms around my waist. "I don't care."

Our family and friends grew silent as Finn's head bobbed out of the water.

"Did I win?" he asked, panning his gaze around the confused faces.

My face broke into a smile as Cassidy nodded. "You sure did."

He fist-pumped the air. "Yes!"

"But you'll have to wait about seven months for your payout," I said, running my hand up and down Cassidy's arm.

"Huh? What do you mean..." Finn's voice trailed off as the realisation hit home. "I'm going to be a brother?!"

Cassidy blinked back tears as she nodded. "You sure are, baby."

As our audience gasped, Finn burst into tears as he flung his arms around us. "This is the best day ever."

I kissed my wife's forehead as I squeezed them both. "It really is."

"You ready for the next chapter, Adam Harlow?" Cassidy asked, peering up at me with those eyes.

"With you by my side, I'm ready for anything."

She giggled adorably. "Are you sure about that?"

"Why?"

"Because apparently..." She pushed up on her tippy toes until her lips grazed the shell of my ear. "We're having twins."

Holy fuck.

Amy

4 years later

I always said everything would work out just how it should be.

For Josie and Grayson, Melanie and Scott, Cassidy and Adam, and now, it was my turn.

I rarely dared to peek into my future. My past made it difficult to trust that I had any happiness heading my way. I'd experienced so much lost and grief in my life, I'd come to expect it, but Reed had changed that. He'd given me something I'd only given to others. *Hope.*

"You look so much like Mom," Cassidy said while braiding my hair into crown of wild flowers I'd picked from the surrounding fields of our little farm. I wore my hair longer now. Reed and I had travelled so much before settling down, I'd let my hair grow from the peroxided pixie cut to shoulder length natural blonde waves, but he still called me Pix, which I loved.

"Thanks, Cass. It really feels like she's here with us." Warmth encased my heart as I twirled my engagement ring around my finger. It was something I used to do while curled up in my mother's lap with the ring my father had given her.

My sister's smile met my ear. "I think she is, Ames."

Although I barely held any memories of my mother, I knew she was beautiful. Not just from the photos that covered the walls of my father's house, but from the reoccurring flashbacks and feelings I 'd had since I was a child. Her smile. Her warmth. *Her love.*

Cassidy smirked at my reflection with her hands rested on my shoulders. "You're going to make dad cry, you know?"

I peered up at my older sister's welling green eyes and smiled. "And maybe you too?"

Cassidy swiftly brushed away the tear rolling down her cheek. "It's the hormones," she uttered, smoothing the dusty pink dress over her growing belly.

"I still can't believe you're having another baby." I turned and held my ear against the silk as if my future niece or nephew was telling me a secret. "But I'm so happy you are."

"At least its only one this time," Cassidy uttered with a chuckle.

I snickered. "Who would've thought the infamous Adam Harlow would've been so smitten with fatherhood."

She laughed loudly. "Oh, I know."

I peered up at her glowing face. "It suits him though. Softens those rough edges."

"Shh." Cassidy lifted her finger to her lips. "Don't say that too loudly. His reputation will be ruined."

"I won't tell a soul,' I said, zipping my lips.

"Won't tell a soul what?" Josie strolled into the room with a camera around her neck. It didn't match her dress, but it was an essential accessory. I refused to have anyone else taking photos of our special day, and she wouldn't have allowed it otherwise.

"Oh, you already know." Cassidy carefully slipped my wedding dress out of its protective sleeve. "That Adam's a big softy."

"Oh, god yeah." Josie laughed before taking a photo of my sister. "And clearly a baby making machine. You guys are crazy."

Cassidy grinned back at her. "Are you and Gray planning on having any more kids?"

"Hell no." Josie's eyes bulged. "I already have a mini Grayson and mini Adam on my hands. I'm not about to add another Harlow sibling into that equation."

"Well the more nieces and nephews I have, the better." Although I wasn't blood related to Josie or Grayson, their boys still called me Aunt and I adored them.

I was lucky enough to have Harrison and Spencer as my page boys, and Grace, Betty and Florence as my flower girls. With my father walking me down the aisle and Finn by Reed's side, along with his two brothers, I was surrounded by love and warmth.

Lanie waltzed into the room like the supermodel she could've been. "Okay, all the kids are dressed and ready and the Dads are on full supervising duty."

Cassidy and Josie's eyes collided as if simultaneously sensing the impending storm.

"I'm sure they'll be fine." Melanie's tight smile didn't match her confidence. "Between Grayson, Adam, Scott and Riley, what could go wrong?"

"Have you met my kids?" Josie laughed.

Cassidy cackled. "Or mine?"

"I'm sure Grace will have everything under control." Melanie's daughter was only four years old but she was already a force to be reckoned with, just like her mother.

Josie grimaced at the door. "Once I've taken a few photos of Amy getting ready, I'll get back out there before the kids ruin their outfits."

Melanie exhaled heavily before lifting her chin and resuming her event planning poise. "Okay, let's get you in this dress, before the Harlow children set something on fire."

As Melanie and my sister held open my dress, I stood up to stepped into it.

"Your 'Something Old'," Cassidy said, pulling the delicate lace of my mother's wedding dress over my shoulders.

As I stared at my reflection, the dress took form over my body as Melanie buttoned it up. "Why didn't you wear it, Cass?"

"I wanted you to have it."

"But why? You always told me how much you loved it."

"And I do, but I wanted it for you." She took my hands and gave them a gentle squeeze. "I have more memories of Mom than you, and you deserve more of that connection too."

"Thank you, Cass. For everything you've done, and given up for me."

Her love enveloped my heart. "I wouldn't have it any other way."

Snap.

We both jumped in surprise.

"Perfect," my best friend spoke, admiring the camera screen. "I think this one will be in my next exhibition."

Melanie nudged Josie before whispering. "She's missing something."

"Oh, shit." Her eyes widened. "I have something to add." Josie rummaged through her tote until a small box materialized in her hand. "Your 'Something New'," she said, handing me a small pink box.

"Oh, Josie."

"I'm just the messenger."

I pulled the ribbon and opened the box to find a small note with Reed's distinctive handwriting.

Pix, you'll always be my lucky charm. Love Echo x

Beaming at Reed's avatar signoff, I lifted the paper to uncover the most exquisite earrings I'd ever seen. Two intricate pixie wings, carved from crystal, swayed in my trembling hands.

Snap.

"They're perfect." I gushed, unfazed my Josie's camera.

"Reed had them commissioned by the same jeweller who made your engagement ring. Apparently, the pink diamonds are an exact match."

I held my engagement ring beside the earrings and gasped. The studs were the exact shade of pink that had adorned my hand for the last five years. "Oh, Reed."

Josie and Melanie proceeded to unhook each piece of art and position them into my ears. The pendants hung flawlessly beside my neckline, each crystal wing an ode to my avatar, PsyPixie. Where our story begun.

Once the girls were satisfied with my attire, Cassidy carried over my bouquet. The wildflowers complemented the blossoms in my hair and smelled like my new home.

Reed and I had bought a little farm upstate, not too far from my dad or his family, and have been slowly making it our own.

Not only did it offer a serene landscape to build our future, it gave us both space to be ourselves and embrace the quiet life we both craved.

Thanks to my bridesmaids coordinated effort and team of worker bees, our barn was now adorned with a million fairy lights and our garden ready for a ceremony.

"Check the bouquet for your "Something Borrowed." Cassidy handed me the flowers with a knowing smirk. "I know you gave it to my first, but I want it back."

To my surprise, the Garnierite crystal pendant I'd once given my sister, was tucked discreetly within the binding of the flowers. I'd given it to Cassidy before her interview to work at Harlow Manor. The rare crystal is known to heal and open your heart, and going by her radiant and carefree smile now, it evidently worked. Her life had completely changed since meeting Adam and she deserved all the happiness.

"Oh, Cass." I threw my arms around her. "Thank you."

Snap.

"Okay, okay," Melanie said, parting our tight hold. "You're going to crease your dresses."

"Don't care,' I stated, grinning at my sister who was already primping me.

"Plus, we have one more surprise for you." Josie picked a shoebox off the floor. "Here…" she said, passing it over. "Your 'Something Blue'. This one is from all of us."

I raised the lid and unfolded the tissue paper to reveal the same white wedding shoes I'd already purchased months before.

"Take them out," Melanie insisted.

Curiously, I lifted both heels out to study them. It wasn't until I flipped them over that my body filled with warmth. Each sole was covered in cobalt blue illustrations and tiny fingerprints. I grasped my chest as tears welled. "The kids painted these?"

Melanie nodded. "Some needed a little help."

"Okay, don't cry," she said, lifting my chin. "Your mascara will run."

"Then stop giving me beautiful gifts!" I cried at my bridesmaids, who were already laughing.

Melanie dabbed my eyes. "Press your tongue against the top of your mouth. That used to work for me."

The fact that Melanie knew techniques to stop tears hurt my heart. Although she'd been blessed with a perfectly symmetrical face and grew up in one of the wealthiest families in the country, she endured a torturous upbringing that had haunted her for years. Thankfully, breaking away from her family gave her the clarity to become more than an heiress. She now had a successful career, a booming business, and was thriving alongside the love of her life and their beautiful daughter.

What felt like a hundred photos later, Josie headed for the door. "I'm going to take some more snaps of the kids. Mel, can you help me wrangle them?"

"Of course." Melanie smiled back at us as she followed her out. "I'm sure these two would appreciate some alone time."

"So…" Cassidy sat beside me on the chaise lounge. "Are you ready"

"I'm more than ready." I leant my head on her shoulder. "He's shown me the entire world, Cass."

"Then he made my dreams for you come true too."

Our attention averted to the door that was creaking open.

"Is everyone decent in there?" My father deep voice filled the room.

"Yes, Dad," Cassidy replied as we both stood. "She's ready."

As he stepped inside, his mouth gaped at the both of us. "My girls," he uttered breathlessly.

I blushed. "Hey, Dad."

"Oh, Amy." His voice cracked as he approached. "You're a vision."

Cassidy attempted to step back from the moment, but I pulled her in for a group hug.

"I'm so proud of you both," he said, squeezing us tight. "Your mom… She would've wanted to be here."

The strong scent of lavender filled the room. "She is, Dad," Cassidy said and I believed her. Lavender was her favourite flower and I'd planted an entire garden dedicated to her memory on my farm.

"Um…" A newly-cracked voice softy interrupted. "Sorry to interrupt."

We all turned to Finn, who nervously hovered in the doorway.

"Hey buddy," his mom said, moving toward him, clearly sensing the same uneasiness. "Why aren't you outside with the others?"

"We…kind of have a problem."

My father tensed. "I swear, if Reed isn't out there, I'm going to—"

"Dad!" I laughed. "Chill out. Reed is here."

Finn grimaced at his mom. "We're just having a small issue with the kids."

"What have they done now?" My sister uttered in a groan.

"Harrison and Grace are missing."

Cassidy inhaled. "What!?"

"Everyone is looking for them."

"I swear, whenever those two are together, trouble follows." Cassidy grabbed her shoes. "I better go help."

A vision of Harrison and Grace running around our hedged maze floated through my mind. "It's okay, Cass. I know exactly where they are." I giggled at their cheekiness. "But you'll never find them without me."

"But you can't go…" Cassidy protested. "You're about to get married."

"And I'm in dire need of some fresh air." I was already headed for the door. "Grab my shoes and flowers, and meet me at the ceremony. I won't be long."

Cassidy, Finn and my father watched in shock as I threw on my trusty boots, hitched up my dress and ran out of the house. As I grew closer to the hedged labyrinth, I slowed my pace and listened. Through the clucking chickens, and goats shrieking, and all our other fostered animals on the farm, giggles erupted from deep within the maze. *Gotcha*.

As enticing as it was for the kids, no one was allowed to enter the maze without me. Not even the adults. I was the only person who knew the way, and it wasn't just because I'd memorised it. My lucky guesses were always my most trusty compass.

I ran my fingers along the shrubbery as I grew closer to the centre of the maze, where a dried-up little concrete fountain stood at its core. I peeked through the dense shrubbery, to discover Harrison and Grace mid argument.

"Why not?!" Harrison yelled, hands on hips. He looked ridiculously cute in his mini tux.

Grace stomped her foot. "Because I'm only four!"

"Then when?"

"When we're older," Grace uttered, exasperated. "Like Amy and Reed."

I held my hand over my mouth to keep from laughing.

Harrison frowned down at his suit. "So, I have to wear this again?"

"Of course." Grace spun around. "And I'll have a big princess dress covered in crystals."

"But you look like a princess today."

Grace dramatically rolled her eyes at her family friend. "But I don't have crystals, so it doesn't count."

"One day, I'll buy you a huge diamond. As big as the moon."

"Mumma said it doesn't matter how big the diamond is. It's the qwalaty that counts."

Harrison frowned. "What's qwalaty?"

"I don't know." Grace shrugged. "But I think it's something magical."

"Psst," I said, stepping out into the clearing.

Harrison's hazel-green eyes widened, while Grace's mouth dropped.

"Aunty Amy!" Harrison's back straightened. "Did we miss the wedding?"

Grace gasped. "Oh no!"

"No, no, no. It hasn't started yet. In fact, the wedding can't start at all without you two."

"We got lost in the maze." Grace pointed at Harrison. "He said he knew a shortcut."

I brushed dust from his shoulders. "You know there are no shortcuts in life, Harry."

"And *then…*" Grace plonked her hands of her hips. "He tried to marry me."

"Oh…Harry." I mocked surprise. "Did you ask Grace's parents' permission first?"

"No," he said, visibly confused. "Am I supposed to?"

"You probably should, but maybe wait a few years." I'd love to be a fly on that wall.

Harrison's shoulder's slumped. "I guess I can do that."

"Good." I squeezed his hand. "You never know, you may change your mind."

"I'll never change my mind." With that determination, he was definitely Grayson's son.

Holding on to my laughter, I held out my hands. "Let's get back. Everyone is waiting for us."

As each child took my hand, a vision flashed through my mind. *Holy shit*. Perhaps the Harlow's and Warren's will be related after all.

———

Waiting by my father's side, the most important people in my life walked down the aisle before me. First the children, then Melanie, then Josie, then my beautiful sister Cassidy.

"You ready?" Dad gently squeezed my arm. He was more nervous than I was.

With a deep breath, the relaxing scent of lavender filled my nose and I knew it was time. "Let's do this."

We left the house as the music grew louder and wandered slowly down to the lavender garden. Beside the aisle of flowering shrubs stood a small gathering of family and friends whom we both loved dearly, and their warmth guided the way to my future husband. This day would never have happened without their love and support.

As my gaze reached Reed, my breath caught. There he stood, smiling ear to ear, beside his two brothers, Asher and Rusty, and my nephew Finn, who was tending to my wedding gift to Reed.

An Irish Wolfhound puppy I'd adopted only days prior, just like our beloved Luci, who we'd all lost a few years ago.

Reed's eyes glistened, but kept his emotions in check as promised. If he cried, I would cry, and neither of us wanted to blubber through our wedding vows.

We'd waited a long time to get married. Not because we were unsure of our future together, but because there was so much I wanted to do and see before we settled down. Reed's love for me never wavered, nor did he have any doubts that we belonged together. He'd simply waited until I was ready, and now, after years of patience and understanding, we were finally doing it.

I'd loved Reed before knowing him. He may have started as a faceless avatar on a computer screen, but he'd become the most important person in my life. We'd fought many battles together, on and off screen, since we'd met, and I knew together, we could face any challenge thrown at us. *EchoWisp and PsyPixie had this in the bag.*

Once we'd reached the alter, Reed shook my father's hand before taking mine. Electricity surged through our fingers as they touched and continued to tingle as they held tight.

"Hey, Pix," he whispered before the celebrant began.

"Hey, Echo." I could already feel the heat rising between us.

As the celebrant introduced herself, my mind drifted into a place I'd only visited once before. *My future.* So many visions cascaded in, I could barely contain the rush of emotion and excitement that came with them.

Christmas' at Harlow Manor.

Thanksgivings with the Blackwood's.

Samhain bonfires at our family's farm.

Summers at Cassidy and Adam's beach house.

And a beautiful wedding that would, one day, unite all our families.

THE END

ACKNOWLEDGMENTS

To my husband and boys, thank you for your unwavering support of my dreams. The road is long and winding, but you are always by my side.

To my amazing editor, Jenn, my fabulous beta crew, Tanya, Mal, Sarah, Fleur & Jenn, and my incredible proofreaders, Kath and Shae, I truly appreciate every minute it took to make my work the best it can be.

To my readers, who have embraced my books and loved my characters as much as I do, thank you. There are many more to come!

Finally, to T.L. Swan and the Cygnets, thank you for creating a safe space for me to access all the help, encouragement and support I needed to keep chasing my romance writing dreams. And for leading me to Keeperton / Arndell. Life can change when you least expect it, and for me, it was when I needed it the most, and I'm so grateful.

A x

Ann Penny is a contemporary romance author from Melbourne, Australia, known for her emotionally rich storytelling that resonates with readers drawn to tales of passion, resilience, and hope. A two-time finalist for the prestigious Romance Writers of Australia (RWA) Romance Book of the Year Award, Ann Penny is quickly gaining recognition in the romance genre for the exceptional depth and heart in her stories.

Her journey into writing began in childhood, where she often found herself lost in daydreams instead of completing schoolwork—a trait that was later understood to be connected to undiagnosed neurodivergence. These early experiences, where she would immerse herself in imagined worlds and scenarios, ultimately became the foundation for her writing career. Her ability to weave intricate plots and create layered, interconnected stories is a direct result of her imaginative mind and her unique perspective on the world.

Her stories delve into themes of self-discovery, healing from past trauma, and the transformative power of love. Beyond romance, they offer readers tales of post-traumatic growth and personal empowerment, all delivered with a unique voice and a touch of quirky humour.

When Ann Penny isn't writing, she enjoys having a laugh with her husband and sons, cuddling her fur babies, and immersing herself in anything creative. Penny is always striving to craft something beautiful and unexpected while endeavouring to harness her hyperactive mind.

With deep emotional insight, and a huge backlog of untold stories in her head, Ann Penny will continue to embrace her storytelling skills to captivate readers with relatable characters and heartfelt stories—where love and personal growth go hand in hand.

Read on for more from
Ann Penny

Josie Spencer is determined to make the most of her fresh start in New York City. She lives for the simple things; pizza, good tunes, bad movies and watching the world go by through the lens of her camera. Love? That's not a priority.

Grayson Harlow is anything but simple. He's gorgeous, brilliant, and trapped under the iron grip of his family's legacy. When he meets Josie in a chance encounter in Las Vegas, he's left breathless—she's fiery, passionate, and completely off–limits.

Their chemistry is instant… and impossible to forget.

But months later, when Josie finds out Grayson is her new billionaire boss, the attraction between them becomes dangerous. His powerful family sees her as a threat and will stop at nothing to tear her down.

Now, Josie must decide: fight for the career she's built or risk it all for the one man she can't resist. Because falling for Grayson Harlow doesn't just risk her heart… it might cost her everything.

Sometimes, the greatest love stories begin with a second chance.

Starting over in New York City is **Melanie Warren**'s chance to prove she doesn't need her parents' wealth, high-society status, or her ex-fiancé, Grayson. Determined to stand on her own, she refuses to look back, until her new job brings her face-to-face with the one man she swore never to forgive.

Scott Blackwood is no longer the reckless boy with a troubled past. Now, he's wealthy, powerful, and everything he once dreamed of becoming. But to Melanie, he's still the man who shattered her seventeen year old heart and never looked back.

Their chemistry is undeniable, their past impossible to forget. As old wounds resurface and the lines between them blur, Melanie is faced with a choice: hold on to her heartbreak or risk everything for a second chance at love. Because the biggest secret of all? She never stopped loving him.

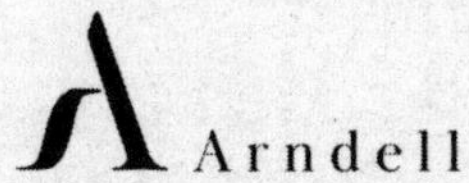

Connect with Arndell

Love this book? Discover your next romance book obsession and stay up to date with the latest releases, exclusive content, and behind-the-scenes news!

Explore More Books

Visit our homepage: keeperton.com/arndell

Follow Us on Social Media

Instagram: @arndellbooks
Facebook: Arndell
TikTok: @arndellbooks

Stay in the Loop

Join our newsletter: keeperton.com/subscribe

Join the Conversation

Use **#Arndell** or **#ArndellBooks** to share your thoughts and connect with fellow romance readers!

Thank you for being part of our book-loving community. We can't wait to share more unforgettable stories with you!